DOPPELGÄNGERS & DECEIT
THE DRAGON TASKER SERIES

Rachel D. Adams
&
Dawn McClellan

DOPPELGÄNGERS & DECEIT

Copyright © 2023 Rachel D Adams and Dawn McClellan.

All rights reserved. No part of this publication may be reproduced.

ISBN: 978-1-958442-00-5 (Digital)
ISBN: 978-1-958442-01-2 (Paperback)
ISBN: 978-1-958442-05-0 (Hardcover)

Any references to historical events

Front cover image by Donika Mishineva

Formatting design by Cherie Varian

Beta Readers: Leilani Austen

Printed in the United States of America.

First edition 2022. Second Edition 2023.

WTC Creatives

500 Westover Dr #16238

Sanford

www.racheldadams.com

Rachel dedicates this work to James, William, Tim, and Jack, who have put up with me and my creative and crazy mind.

Dawn dedicates this work to her family, Billey, Morgan, AB, Gavin, Laiynah, Ascension, Tisha, and Jody, who have stood by me and shown me I can do anything!

CONTENTS

1. Mad World — 1
2. A Day in the Life — 9
3. Pandora's Box — 17
4. Fascinating — 21
5. Tommy's Pub — 25
6. Derek's Ass — 31
7. Business — 39
8. Another Night, Another Victim — 43
9. On a Jet Plane — 49
10. The Taking — 59
11. Plan of Action — 63
12. In the Clinic — 69
13. The Good Doctor — 75
14. Excuses — 81
15. Figuring Things Out — 89
16. The Twins — 99
17. Truth and Realizations — 111
18. My Way or No Way — 117
19. Going on an Adventure — 121

20.	After the Explosion	135
21.	Back to Good?	141
22.	Angering the Director	153
23.	Prepping the Science	159
24.	The Failed Attempt	165
25.	The Pub	173
26.	Second Thoughts	183
27.	The Sanctuary	189
28.	A Needed Talk	197
29.	Waking Up	205
30.	Surprises	209
31.	Confrontation	215
32.	Opening Pandora's Box	223
33.	The Council	229
34.	Handling Business	239
35.	The Judgment	245
36.	What Has Happened	257
37.	Coming Together	264

Chapter 1
Mad World

What Director Ezekiel Skinner wanted, he got. And the director of Crimson rarely got his hands dirty. Hence, Jean-Michel, a Tasker of Crimson, was on yet another "undisclosed mission."

He passed face after face on the street of the mid-sized town outside of the Bay Area. This area was called the poor man's wine country. He made his way to the automated transit ticket station, gave up a ten spot, and took the ticket that the machine spat out. Off he went to catch a bus instead. He'd take a bus to the next station. Best to be a lost part of humanity than to make too direct a hit.

The sounds were harsh; car motors, bike bells, the fountain, the horns. He didn't want to be here. It was too loud and there were too many humans.

He got off the bus at the next stop and found the signs leading to the local rail station. His feet moved slower than normal over the pavement. He took in the way the breeze moved through the trees. Sometimes it was a good thing to slow down and take in the world, but then another car horn reminded him he was just delaying the inevitable.

The train that went underground near Oakland – that's where he needed to be. Yet, he couldn't force himself to pick up the pace. Blue-green eyes gazed into one window along the older building fronts downtown. His reflection. His eyes looked upward, trying desperately to form with his imagination what he once had been.

Instead, his eyes came back down to meet the gaze of his reflection. He had crow's feet at the edge of his human eyes; both frown and laugh lines. His dark, auburn-red hair had silver smudged at the ears and in the scruff of his beard.

He looked human and here he was, doing the bidding of a human. How did he allow himself to be brought so low?

He tried not to make eye contact with anyone. It wasn't something he enjoyed. Most humans could not see more than their own worries, anyway. No need to look into those hollow holes.

Down the stairs. To the right. Up the escalators.

Unless Director Skinner swept this mission under the rug, Jean-Michel would have to answer to a bunch of attorneys turned Councilors, all ready to judge him. They never got their hands dirty, either. Hypocrites.

Punch the ticket. Go to the platform.

Jean-Michel decided he'd go to a pub before the Council. He wanted to be drunk before even facing his own Councilor. He didn't want to be sober while looking into Gabriel's eyes after what he had to do.

This was what happened when you made a deal with the wrong human. The memory of the scowl on Director Ezekiel Skinner's face when he tried to refuse this task made him shiver.

If Jean-Michel knew what kind of magic he needed for killing Skinner, he would have done so a long time ago. Annoying that the human had many powerful contacts and access to magic. He was a keeper of secrets. And Jean-Michel did not want the man to know anymore.

Catch the train. Take a seat. Pretend.

Despite trying not to look, the impish grin of a little girl in front of him made him want to smile. Children could see things in their innocence that others could not. It pained him to think she would lose this.

He cocked his head to the side slightly; an instinctively curious movement. She smirked at him. He crossed his eyes. She did her best to hold back a little giggle. Her mother glanced his way. She got up to leave with her daughter.

He couldn't blame her. She was paranoid and protective. The little girl, missing her two front teeth, beamed at Jean-Michel. The mother sighed heavily as the Tasker got up and began moving in the opposite direction. He didn't want trouble.

"Mommy! Did you see his eyes? Mommy..."

"It's not nice to stare, Maria."

Jean made his way to the far end of the car and stood holding the pole. The click-clack of the train on the tracks slowed, heralding the approach to the next station. The train stopped for Oakland.

People got on, got off, shifted, and shuffled seats and places to stand.

Jean-Michel made his way off of the train and to the far end of the platform away from the other people. He sat on the bench and watched the girl and her mother walk toward the stairs. Little Maria waved and showed her snaggle-toothed smile again. This time, he couldn't help but return the expression. Innocence – wasn't the same as ignorance. She wanted to see more of what he truly was. She still had faith. But did he?

When would she lose her own faith? Were all humans destined to be this way? Was his own Councilor like the rest of them? Was Gabriel already lost? Even though the Councilor knew about supernatural beings, Gabriel Kennedy did not see what that little girl had seen. Or he did not want to see it.

The bell sounded, and the train lurched forward. The Tasker remained on the bench. Jean-Michel's eyes focused on the wall across from the platform. He took a drink from the flask hidden in the inside jacket pocket. Another drink and he closed his eyes. Opening them again, he stared straight ahead at the wall beyond the tracks.

He stared until his eyes watered and hurt. At the edge of his vision, on that far wall, there was light filtering around a double-door-sized expanse of beige-painted brick. The outline of light was a magical archway hidden from most eyes. Screwing the top back into the flask, Jean-Michel waited until the next train came through. He sat there, focusing on the outline of the door.

After two trains, as people transferred; getting on and off, he got up. When the bells sounded, he was making his way to one of the support poles and out of camera range. Just as the back of the train cleared the magical outline, the Tasker leaped from the platform and into that door. Taskers were masters of not being seen. They were the elite agents of the Crimson supernatural policing force. Most were supernatural for a reason.

Go inside. Find the leader. Do as tasked. Simple.

He paused, waiting for a rush. There was nothing. No sentry? No defense? The Tasker looked around for more magic but saw nothing.

Jean-Michel could smell them. He could smell the blood-not decay. That's what vampire lairs made by newly blooded creatures smelled like. They didn't let things decay or rot. Anything that smelled like true death was unwanted. But they liked the smell of blood and enjoyed having their prey in a gathering.

The corridor led out to an open area that used to be part of the rail line, or at the very least, had abandoned gear and equipment around a nice tile and cement floor. The place was more open than what he had been making his way through.

The Tasker pulled his gun quickly but only got one bullet off before the boot of an incoming vampire knocked it from his hand. Relaxing, Jean-Michel lowered himself to be prepared for the next incoming attack. His center of gravity stable, the Tasker dodged the incoming flurry and shoved the would-be attacker into the other.

He knew several kinds of martial arts, but the goal was to be captured, not to kill them out here. So he made some feints, rolled out of the way, and then moved to kick the one who had his gun. He caught the guy on the jaw and followed the hit by making sure that the gun was out of everyone's range for the moment.

Dodging three swings, he wound up backing into two others. He dropped into a crouch to let them hit one another, if possible. If the sounds were any indication, the maneuver had worked. He sprung forward and took the one in front of him out with a tackle, before rolling again and getting back into stance. But with the next attack, he purposely left himself open to the side.

The vampire available took the shot, and he felt the pain in his hip as he went down. They each got at least one hit in before he discouraged them. He might have some supernatural strength, but this was still a human body. He didn't need to be maimed.

"I have a message for Anthony!"

The vampires paused, looking over the man they had between them at one another.

"I come from Crimson. If I don't get to him, things could go very wrong for you," Jean-Michel warned.

"Yeah, well, Anthony's been waiting," one of them snarled. He walked further down the path and two others grabbed his arms, dragging him onward into the lair.

New-blooded amateurs.

The smell of cheap cologne, cigarette smoke, and fresh blood told him there were quite a few around him. His eyes adjusted to the darker area. They looked like they'd stepped out of a movie screen; either gothic or leather-clad punk-rock chic. It was so cliche that Jean-Michel choked on a laugh.

They made their way to what was obviously a throne. Did it get any better than this? He remembered what a vampire throne room looked like - a real vampire throne room. This was some cheap rendition and if a true pureblood had seen it? There would've been hell to pay.

They walked up a trail leading to a wooden dais of sorts. In a fancy upholstered chair, maybe a reproduction from the 80s sat their esteemed leader. Anthony appeared as if he weren't a day over twenty; a lie. He assessed his newly arrived guest.

"You successfully waltzed into a vampire lair. Your masters couldn't do this any other way?"

"I'm a Tasker. They tasked. I don't ask a lot of questions," Jean-Michel replied easily enough.

"On behalf of Crimson? Because that bunch lost something?" Anthony chuckled. It was the sound of a person who believed they had the upper hand. He gestured toward the opening of a cave to his left. From that tunnel, they led a young man out to the dais.

He had several bloodied marks on his arms and throat. His head was hanging down and he was hardly walking on his own. Anthony paid the entrance little heed. He kept his attention on the Tasker before him. He wanted to see the reaction.

For someone as experienced as the Tasker, the scene was amusing. However, he needed to force himself into the drama that was unfolding. He sighed loudly while watching them place the young man against the wall behind the raised platform.

"That bunch didn't actually send me." Jean-Michel studied the young man that was being brought forward. "I think perhaps we should be honest with one another, don't you?"

"By all means," Anthony replied, sitting with a flump on his throne.

It was another show of power. The vampire had a Crimson agent and was going to use his pitiful countenance to keep control of the situation. Jean-Michel knew exactly how this would go down. Anthony, on the other hand, did not know what was about to happen. The vampire actually thought he was in control.

"This isn't a normal mission. Since you took an agent, your importance has grown by leaps and bounds." Now the Tasker turned to the self-anointed coven lord. "This is an emergency mission assigned by the Director of Crimson himself." He knew this would only act to further boost Anthony's ego. "May I check him?"

The mention of the Director had Anthony preening and sneering in a wash of arrogance.

"Tender of heart for those less fortunate, are you?" His attention went from his guest to his captive and back again. "Inspect him all you like. Wouldn't want you to think we were animals, would I?" He scoffed.

Jean-Michel stood before the young Crimson technician. Johnny was someone that they called a specialist – because he had one duty in his calling. He specialized in hacking. Being part of a secret organization that kept its eyes on the wrongdoing of supernatural kind meant you had to bring something to the table. And most times, even something considered illegal to the rest of the world was an asset to Crimson.

"You're bitten." Jean-Michel touched the agent's shoulder, noting multiple puncture wounds. Wasn't much more than a kid, this one. He'd been missing for nearly five days. The vampires had not wasted their time, had they? "Have you taken blood from any of them?" he asked quietly.

"I… I don't know.." Johnny was weak; fevered. He leaned against the wall. His head was still down, and his breathing was shallow.

"Do you know who sent me? Do you understand that?" Jean-Michel asked, his fingers under the other man's chin to lift his head. He wanted to look into the boy's eyes.

As Johnny's head tipped back, his eyes partially opened to reveal dilated pupils and a reddish tinge to the outer edges of each.

"Skinner?" He groaned and one arm covered his stomach. "Can we get out now?"

The tone of his voice had been more demanding than hopeful. Jean remembered another set of eyes that were fading from the light. It saddened him.

~ What do you have on him that makes you so important, Johnny? ~ Jean-Michel asked, forcing his mind to address the boy's mind. In this addled state, the captive agent had no defense at all.

There were several images that went from pictures in a file marked simply #32. A flash of old languages and red ink. Then there was nothing. Sighing, Johnny swallowed and his eyes opened a little more for the Tasker.

"I... did good...?" he asked.

"Yes. Yes, you did, Agent." Jean-Michel placed a hand on the boy's shoulder. "Are you ready to be free?" he asked quietly, almost fatherly.

"Yes, please..."

Anthony's attention went from the doorway to the Tasker. "Well? What's it worth to you and your Director? Maybe official recognition as a true coven? The perks that the purebloods enjoy? It's only fair. We rescued him, right, guys?" The others sneered and chuckled.

Jean-Michel turned to face the self-appointed coven lord, and as he did, he snapped Johnny's neck.

"What!?" Anthony was moving further away from this agent, depending upon his other guards to protect him.

The Tasker slammed the vampire next to him into the cavern wall with such force that his head cracked like a watermelon. He was already on the next vampire before Johnny's body hit the ground.

"But the Director..." Anthony got behind some of the other vampires at his disposal. The Tasker was still coming.

"The Director didn't send me to bargain, you idiot." While he closed the gap between himself and Anthony, lights around the walls began flickering and losing power. Guns fired, but the Tasker rolled out of the way and to the sidewall.

The two that had stayed with their leader took defensive stances. Anthony took a step back. His vampires were shooting each other, bullets ricocheting off of the hewn stone walls.

"Stop shooting, idiots!" Tony was furious.

The lights flickered again and then went out one by one, leaving them all in darkness. Darkness made them more aggressive. Overconfident. These vampires thought they had the upper hand in the dark. Perfect. So long as he found a place out of their sight, they couldn't pinpoint his location with their infrared eyesight.

The two fledglings rushed their opponent while Anthony backed to the outer wall of the room.

For the Tasker, darkness was not a hindrance. He tripped a vampire, who was moving so quickly to get him that the bastard landed on his head – knocking himself out. They literally didn't understand their own strength. Anthony had turned them and not trained them. The next he took on, he met the thing's swinging fist with the palm of his hand. He turned the inertia of the hit against the vampire and had the creature off his feet and on his back. The crunch of a broken arm filled the air; then a gurgling scream.

"What...what are you?!" Anthony screamed. The only response he got was gunfire and the screams of other vampires. Jean-Michel made his way to the main door.

The light coming from the entrance was suddenly gone. The temperature rose in the area by fifteen; no... twenty degrees in a matter of seconds.

Anthony had made it back to the side of the throne and when he looked up into the face of his own death. Dark scales that moved like a living wall, teeth as long as swords, and those blue-green eyes the size of car doors mesmerized the vampire. The mouth of the creature opened and liquid fire dribbled out of it to the stone floor.

~ Do you know what I am now? ~ Jean-Michel asked.

He had needed this. He needed to remember who and what he was. They would know. And then they would all die.

Chapter 2
A Day in the Life

Gabriel Kennedy, the handsome owner of Kennedy Corporation and well-known philanthropist, stood on the grand staircase in his family's colonial mansion. He was ready to toast and give his opening speech before the eager crowd below.

"On behalf of my late grandmother, Amelia Kennedy, I'd like to thank each of you for attending this year. A lovely lady, my grandmother was very fond of both Whitley University and creativity while she was still alive. The University has been and will most likely be a grand institution of learning for centuries to come. All of that relies on gracious people such as yourselves. You are fostering the future of this institution, as well as the future of well-rounded student education. Reach into your pockets tonight and let go." He smiled with the current of soft laughter. "My grandmother had faith in the artists, the writers, the creative minds that had not yet been born when she set up this fund. She had faith that other people would keep this candle burning. Let's not extinguish it." Gabriel paused, taking a deep breath. "Welcome to the Annual Amelia Kennedy Gala."

The round of applause was deafening. The mix of socialites, business owners, CEOs, and politicians was a noisy lot. His anxiety was at an all-time high, and yet he took time to mingle, for that's what people expected. As he spoke to them, he mentioned the various fundraisers at the event, the private auction, and the drawings to be held later in the night. They were going to have fun, but they were going to spend their money. Of that, their host made certain.

Breathe. Breathe lightly. Don't cough. Smile. He stroked the side of his pants. Gabriel thanked and gave attention to every generous donor he recognized. His dark brown hair and chocolate eyes with a tanned complexion made most of the women here happy to be led around by the owner of the place.

"We want to supply three years of undergraduate courses in Fine Arts to five students this year. Not to mention, give the college incentives to keep funding more and more within the School of Arts and Drama. I hope you'll see to helping us fulfill those dreams." He wasn't sure how many times he'd said it while talking or dancing.

The atmosphere was subdued and no one really, truly knew him well enough to know who would catch the bachelor's eye. And that was part of the game, wasn't it? Many had tried. None of them knew he was practically untouchable. They saw the person he allowed them to see.

Gabriel let them enjoy his hospitality one night every year. They would cavort in their formal attire and eat meals from a locally chosen chef. That would be followed by a dance in the rear ballroom, which was already filled with the sweet melodies of the small orchestra put together by the University's Music Department. He paid everyone well during this event, for he saw it as giving back to the community.

As he spoke, his eyes moved over the dancers. He remembered learning to dance. He had enjoyed dancing at one time. Now, it was simply an obligation performed with donors.

It had been during one of his rounds through the crowded ballroom that his phone had vibrated. Slipping the slender device from his inner coat pocket, Gabriel excused himself and found a quiet place to answer the call. The name Derek told him what business he was about to attend.

"The good news is we think your witness is right. There may be a doppelgänger involved. The bad news is – it's the lack of a scent that's the clue. Which means we can't track this thing." The voice was bolder than his own and had a bit of a rough edge to it.

Gabriel took in this new bit of information. Closing his eyes, he pinched the bridge of his nose. He thought everything over. He must've taken too long because Derek was back on.

"I know you got the case because the witness was human and you're the human Councilor, but what do we do with this? We're doing this because we're your friends. But if Councilor Airsight finds out some of the lycan got involved without his permission, we're fucked. Jonas is a by-the-book sort. Have you figured anything out?"

"We still haven't received all the intel. The witness said he watched the victim die and then the assailant become the victim. But is it just one or more? How do we know which did what? I've not found a lot of genuine history on doppelgängers in the Chamber library. There was a petition to have given them a place on the Council and rights, with limitations on the European Council a year ago. But the European Council denied the petition. They supposedly sent those in this world back across to their own or Ordia. Gaia's apparently not ready for them. Have you tracked the so-called victim?"

"No. The guy paid with cash, and we don't have the authority to take security footage. That's what your Tasker's for. They carry the identification and have backup from Crimson. Devon's already nervous about this as it is. He just asked if you were sure this was legit because maybe your witness actually is the murderer?"

"I've been tracking odd and unexplained disappearances where the victim turns up later to claim their life. There've been 3 in the U.S. in the last month on the southeastern coast. I have no right to push forward and investigate these cases unless I can prove something about it is supernatural."

"So you need this one. If it's for real." There was a frustrated huff from the other end of the line.

"We need to interrogate them. Something is going on. I wanted Jean-Michel on this, but he's... on another task or some such. I've left messages. So it falls on you and Devon. I trust you and Devon. Do you understand? But whatever's going on will come to light faster if they are in our custody – not if they're dead."

"Got it." The call ended.

Plastering the smile back into place, Gabriel returned to the gala. His mind was scouring a thousand other subjects. He needed to be here a little longer. After all, keeping the appearance up for your cover was very important. And they wouldn't miss their money – considering donations were tax deductible.

Four hours later, Gabriel was with his trusted valet, Eva, in his office at Kennedy Corp. He was looking at his degree while holding a glass of flavored sparkling water. His eye moved to the picture of his grandfather and grandmother on the wall nearby.

"There were more people this year than last," Eva whispered.

"I feel like they take over. After a while, all I see is the mess they'll leave and not the people."

"Well, they can have at it. The staff will clean it all up before you get back. No troubles, ma boy. We can go to the Chambers, or maybe their library, for some peace if you don't want ta stay here." The lilting Caribbean accent had melded with the Weylyn pack accent when Eva spoke.

"I need someplace I can think. Devon and Derek are out there handling things Jean-Michel should deal with. His absences are becoming annoying." He left the wall to gaze out at the college town from his 6th-story window.

"So I see you're still researching de shifters," Eva said as she looked over the large table Gabriel had in the middle of his office. Her fingers slowly shifted the papers so she could read more. "I thought you'd never leave things like this in the office."

"I ran out of time before the gala. But you're right. I should clean it up. It's just..." He sighed before turning to make his way to the decanter nearby to pour drinks. "I'm mixing my human life with my Councilorship a lot lately. I used to think I could keep everything separate."

"Not as easy as you thought?"

"No," Gabriel handed her the highball. He took a deep breath before a drink. Then, he pointed at the far side of the table she stood at. "Our family's not as clean as I used to think it was. I tripped over some things when I was doing some research. Has me a little rattled, is all."

"I see..." Eva looked over the books he had strewn out and saw that they were about his ancestors across the drink and some were about dragons. She drank the entire liquor in one smooth gulp before settling the glass on the table.

"Well, you tell me what my mate and boy are up to and I'll begin gatherin' all of this. It needs ta go back to the Council Chamber Library, where it's safer."

"They've been following a doppelgänger. Not sure if we're on the right track." His hands massaged the back of his neck. His mind went back over everything. How could they handle such an elusive creature?

"Have you spoken to Director Skinner about this? You're a Councilor. It's your job to prosecute and defend, not send people to police things," Eva pointed out. "You're showing your grandfather's hero complex again, Gabe, taking on too much, and I'm not sure I like ya draggin' my pack into it. Truth be told."

"He's been slow to respond. Sometimes, I feel like they're not so worried about losing human lives. But we humans, we don't have the luxury of shifting or using magic or having unusual strengths and senses for defense." He hoped that Director Skinner had good reasons for his sluggish response. Maybe the man was too busy with other things?

Gabe always gave the benefit of the doubt. But for how long? He wondered this while he helped Eva with the last few books and then gathered his notebooks and pens and notepads into proper order.

"As soon as I can get Jean-Michel on task, Devon can be home dealing with your pups and Derek can go... do whatever Derek wants to do," He sighed.

"I'm gonna go use the bathroom before we leave. You stay here."

Gabriel had noticed the way her gaze had lingered over those books. He was almost positive she knew more than she let on. But, the important subject wasn't dragons anymore. Not since his client had reported seeing the doppelgänger.

The idea frightened Gabriel – being taken and someone replacing you?

How many doppelgängers had taken human lives already? Had this one not made a mistake, shining a light on other odd deaths or murders in recent months, no one would've thought about it. Gabriel placed the notebooks in his briefcase at the desk.

He stacked the other paperwork neatly and then placed them in a file. The Councilor thought back over the unusual amount of missing person reports in Whitley. For a college town, the possibilities were deadly. Students could go missing for weeks before they were reported.

The vibration of his phone knocked him out of those dark thoughts. Regarding the device, Gabriel sighed heavily. "JM Raudine" was on the screen.

"It's about time. What use is having a Tasker assigned to me if he never responds? I've been trying to get hold of you for two days." Gabriel was quick to admonish.

"This Tasker was on assignment for someone on a higher pay grade than you, Councilor Kennedy." Gabriel could hear ice and sloshing liquid. "Take my absence up with him."

"Apparently, the Director is too busy to be bothered. And you're my Tasker, not his." All Gabriel heard was a grunt and the sound of liquid being poured from the other end of the call. "Are you drinking, Jean-Michel?" Gabriel flattened the palm of his free hand on the desk while he waited.

"Yes. If you had a day like mine, you'd be drinking, too."

"No. I would do my duty," Gabriel heard a release of air from the other side of the call. "Sorry to be so boring, but there are things to do besides getting drunk. There may be lives on the line."

"There are always lives on the line with you lot. You should take that stick out your arse and pour your own drink," the Tasker chuckled.

Gabriel's eyes glared down at the phone he had just pulled from his face. Why did this man always get his goat? He took a deep breath, swallowed, and continued.

"In case you were blissfully unaware, there's an emergency happening here. I'm trying to save people from a horrible death."

"Let me guess, human lives?"

"Well, yes, but perhaps I'm trying to save supernatural lives as well. Who knows why doppelgängers are doing what they're doing? So," Gabriel took another pronounced breath. "I'm trying to find them. And for that, I need a Tasker who is available to me. And not drunk." If it were any other person…

"Oh, come on, Gabriel. Surely you don't think the Council and Crimson are here for supernatural benefit?" Jean-Michel took another drink.

"They state it in the vows and pledge of duty..."

"Fuck that! I want your opinion, not some fuckin' vow!" The Tasker growled from somewhere close to his soul. "Stop hiding behind someone else's words and empty promises!"

Gabriel's voice caught. Large brown eyes waited, trying to overcome the sudden catch in his throat and his chest. There was a flash of memory, a sleeker, younger version of his Tasker using that voice while arguing with his father. The Councilor could feel the anger and tension in the room that day - years ago - and he swore to himself he'd just felt it again. After all, Jean-Michel had been the Tasker assigned to several human Councilors over the years - all Kennedys. He was definitely not human, though Crimson listed him as such. Perhaps human magi? They had longer lives.

No. he knew better. His eyes moved to the cart where the books had been. He swallowed.

"Crimson just wants supernaturals cleaned up and out of sight," the Tasker scoffed. "Humans who know about supernaturals? They want to become them or wipe 'em from the face of the earth out of jealousy. So, which are you?"

"You... are...drunk..." Gabriel spoke with measured patience. "You know how I feel about drinking and being drunk."

"Why are the rules all made about you creatures? Humans don't even treat one another properly. Consider all these murders and wars. You use one another and us! Skinner's a fine example, using Crimson to herd supernaturals and keep 'em under control. We're not the ones out of control."

"That's news to me, considering I just got a report of a doppelgänger in Whitley taking the life of a human and becoming him. Supernaturals have the upper hand. We are here to keep a balance, Tasker. Crimson and the Council are about balance." This wasn't the time for a philosophical discussion. He cleared his throat and calmed his voice. "Jean-Michel, I need you to come back here. The supernaturals in question are killing humans, replacing them, and wreaking havoc on other people's lives." Gabriel's hand was popping his thumb against his thigh when Eva walked back in.

"Yeah, well, I'll get right on it."

"Raudine!" Gabriel shouted the Tasker's last name as if that would better get his attention, but the call had ended before he'd even finished the second syllable. He stared down at the phone. Where had that much venom come from? Why the sudden indignation? They had both taken vows, had they not?

"Not the best conversation, I take it?" Eva asked.

No matter how upset or annoyed he was with Jean-Michel Raudine, the Tasker had made a valid point. It was something to think about. Just...it hardly seemed the time.

"I just don't understand him, sometimes, Eva." He swallowed and put the phone back in his pocket before gathering the keys. He wished he could figure out Jean-Michel's scars. Maybe then he could help.

"That man has always been peculiar. But he has a semi-decent soul, I suppose. Otherwise, my mate wouldn't call him brother." She shrugged before taking the keys and indicating the bag to Gabriel. "Of course, Devon also calls him a jackass."

Gabriel smiled.

Chapter 3
Pandora's Box

The sounds of Richard Wagner's opera version of "Tristan and Isolde" drifted through the upstairs office of the antique store known as Pandora's Box. The owner, Miranda Garrett, studied the aged book before her. Most of her business happened earlier in the evening. So, she was free to make some calls. Or so she thought.

Reaching for the glass of red wine that sat at the edge of the massive desk, she brought it to her lips while regarding one last tattered page in the leather-bound book. Her eyes caught movement through the windows. Her assistant Yvette had come up the stairs and was now approaching her office door.

"There's a gentleman here to see you, Mrs. Garrett," Yvette announced from the door. That the woman had called her by her official name and not just her first name gave Mira pause. She had known Yvette since France – in the late 1700s.

"What's..."

"I think you should see this person." Yvette glanced back over her shoulder toward the stairs before returning to stare wide-eyed at Miranda.

"Alright," with a sigh of defeat, she capitulated. Miranda got up to place the book she had been reading over on top of an old podium and set her notes in her top drawer. When she looked up, it was to see an old friend, someone she hadn't had business with in quite some time. "Frenchie?"

"Mademoiselle, I was told you could be of some assistance to me." The words were soft and sensual as they floated from his lips.

His accent was the same as it had been years ago. And that was the tell. Sure, Jean-Michel Raudine still played the French accent card here and there, but not like this. And he knew better than to ever refer to her as a mademoiselle.

Miranda's features hardened; she frowned. "Yvette, go down and begin closing for the evening."

Yvette's eyes narrowed and her lower lip pouted, but she gave a small nod and departed, leaving the two alone.

"Tell me, shifter, why I should aid you when you walk in here, set on deceiving me? Why should I not rip...you....to shreds?" She made her way back to her seat.

The man sighed and turned to close the door to her office. He didn't answer until he sat in a chair right in front of her desk. Her eyes were glaring heat at him and her body was stiff.

"I did not intend to deceive you, Ms. Garrett. I only thought to take on an image that you would be more comfortable with and more inclined to help."

"Well, all you accomplished was annoying me. So rid yourself of the facade before saying anything else." What right did this jackal have to her beloved memories?! The nerve.

As she watched, his features slowly melted and reformed to that of an ash-grey-skinned individual with colorless eyes and no hair. He had slightly elongated ears, almost like that of an elf, and his fingers were twice the length of a human's fingers. He was very thin, almost fragile. When he spoke again, it was still soft and deep but held no accent.

"My chosen name is Malcolm. We are being hunted by Crimson. We have fallen on hard times because of this. We know you have connections to the Council and Crimson, but you also have connections to the Underground. We are taking a chance that we can offer you something worth your while to help us... and yourself... " Their voice had a gargling, watery sound to it as if it was filtered through the back of his throat with phlegm.

"Aren't you blacklisted? Like dragons?" Sure, they weren't capable of mass destruction, but Crimson couldn't easily control doppels. They could augment, perfect, and use their abilities as quite the commodity. "They could pass judgment on me for aiding you. I could lose everything."

"Not if you have the connections I believe you are able to use..." Malcolm pointed out.

"I assure you, I don't have that type of connection with the Council. And if they have seen fit to set Crimson on your trail, there is nothing I can do to help you. I'd prefer you leave."

"You have an attachment to the Tasker I had just taken the form of. Your... Frenchie?" Malcolm tilted his head while watching Miranda glare. "We believe you are mistaken or you are holding back." Emotionless black eyes watched her. It made her nervous.

"We?"

"I and my group of doppelgängers. We communicate," they pointed to their head.

"Just because I have a relationship with a Tasker doesn't mean that I can help you by using that relationship."

"You must. There is no other way. Accommodations need to be made..."

"Then seek accommodations legally, through Crimson and the Council – like all other supernaturals." Miranda didn't like where this was going. She knew what these creatures might be capable of. She doubted they could overcome her own abilities, but she wasn't sure.

"We will not submit to an agency that does not have our interests at heart, Ms. Garrett. To get to this world, we had to seek other than legal means. We cannot now reverse this and seek legal arbitration of our situation after the fact."

"What exactly is your situation?" Mira sat forward and really studied the impassive creature in front of her.

"That's none of your concern. We will work out payment both in advance and after you obtain the bodies. We will need 30 human lives to take on for long enough. We believe you can arrange this."

"Maybe if this were the Dark Ages!" she scoffed. "Or so I've heard...a lady doesn't give out her age so easily, especially when she can live for centuries." One hand went up to rub gently at her forehead. "It's taken me decades to keep Crimson off my doorstep. This is a legitimate business. If I do this, it could open my life up to them." She stood and leaned her hands on her desk in front of them. "I have no obligation or reason to help you." She saw not even a blink from the doppel. How many times did she have to tell them no?

"Your sense of self-preservation rivals that of our own kind. We respect this." The doppelgänger steepled his extremely long fingers. It made his appearance even more grotesque. "We didn't want to do it this way, but you leave us no choice." Reaching into the inside of their jacket, they pulled forth an envelope. "You owe a debt to someone. If you assist us, your debt the debt holder will clear it. If you do not, they will collect your debt. With interest." The doppelgänger handed the envelope over to the dark-haired woman. It was on folded card stock. The seal was in red wax, with a dragon with a spear through it.

"I see." Miranda licked her dark red lips and took the envelope. Her eyes moved over the details and her voice lowered. "I'll see what I can do, but I promise nothing." This was going to be a very dangerous tightrope to walk.

"We believe you have calls to make and scheming to commence, Ms. Garrett." The doppelgänger got up from their seat to leave. "Let me know when I can call my brethren."

"But I said I couldn't promise anything. Besides, I need to check on this..."

Malcolm made it only outside of the doorway before turning to look over their shoulder. "We believe that this place would suit us well as a place of respite before our transitions to new lives. And I shall endeavor to make all transitions as painless as possible." They turned slightly, taking on the look of some unnamed man in casual attire with warm hazel eyes and a gracious smile. Despite the warmth of their facade, what Malcolm said next chilled Mira to the bone. "Do you believe Crimson would make your brother's stay in their cells as painless ... as possible?"

She looked down at the stamped message and then back up at the doppelgänger.

"Correction. You need only find 28 viable lives for us, Ms. Garrett." The false man turned to leave.

The antiquities dealer wondered momentarily why the number had decreased. She decided she would rather not know.

Chapter 4
FASCINATING

He had been sleeping heavily when suddenly his eyes snapped open and his senses were telling him he was no longer alone.

Rising from his bed, the middle-aged male didn't bother with clothing while walking cautiously through his home. Prowling down the hall and checking each room, Jonas refused to stop his search until he had an explanation for that startle. He'd been alive for over three hundred years. Unlike the younger generation, he knew he should always listen to his instincts.

The lycan was thankful that his family was gone to enjoy a full moon celebration with a local pack. He didn't need to worry about them should this end up being worse than he expected. Maybe it was an intruder - a thief? Whoever had come into his home - they had been very unwise to do so. With each step, his nails lengthened just a little more. He was prepared for an attack. His eyes shifted to those of his wolf's side and he sniffed the air in each direction.

Not detecting anything on the second floor, he stepped down the stairs and completed the house check. Moving back to the den area, he caught the slight movement of the curtain and his brow lifted. There was a subtle snarl that curled the left side of his upper lip. Something had entered his home without his permission. It was about to be dead. He lunged quickly, swiping at the creature, catching flesh but not enough to find purchase. The thing was across the room, but Jonas lost it again. The lycan growled, his fists clenching tighter.

"What kind of fool enters the home of an Alpha? The Alpha who sits upon the Crimson Council...?" Jonas Airsight roared while he was trying to track the quick-moving creature. He took on a threatening stance.

"You have a lovely family, sir. And your culture is fascinating."

Jonas turned to find the thing again. He lunged forward, toward the sound of the gurgling voice. He swiped air. What was it? Some kind of chameleon? The scent of the blood was off-putting, but now it was in the room all around him. There was no other scent to follow.

"We had to know everything about you and your family. It took us a while, but obviously, it has worked. We have accomplished much in a short time." The creature seemed rather proud as it explained this.

"You what?" To the wolf's astonishment, it stepped forward, seemingly unafraid. "Why would you ... are there more? Where the fuck are they?!" The rumbling growl reverberated from the lycan's chest as he spun and turned to find anything else in the space.

"We just needed a few more situational modifiers that you had not provided on previous visits. We believe the time has come to get those modifiers." From the side table, the doppelgänger picked up a small hair bow belonging to Jonas' little girl. They then picked up a picture of Jonas and his mate from the same table. "You fit into this world very well, lycan – don't you?"

"Don't touch another thing," the growl became deeper. Slowly turning to face his intruder, the lycan's gaze narrowed even as his form began shifting to hybrid. Letting his wolf gain more control, the lycan seemed to double in size. His voice was more growl now as the feral soul within him was being let free.

The doppelgänger studied the way the muscles bunched and then loosened in the shifting. They'd been studying other lycan for at least two years and had a lycan shift down to a "T" as many mortals in this world might have stated. However, when one was studying to become a specific lycan, one had to have that lycan's body, habits, and accent in the mind for a perfect presentation.

"Perfection. Information. Knowledge. we need to know you. We've been able to gain a lot of knowledge over this past month. And now..." The gray-skinned creature slid to the side, still studying the lycan, his hands behind his back."Now, we see your motions while in this middle form. You take so much for granted. Absolutely fascinating."

"Threatening my family is a mistake."

"Oh, we're not threatening your family, Jonas. We rather like your family. We like them very much." The odd grey-skinned creature stepped to the side, out of shadow, so that Jonas could see him better. The doppelgänger was still out of range for an attack from the lycan's vicious claws. They needed to urge the lycan forward to be sure of how Jonas held those wicked claws; to see the scars, the old warrior still carried on his body, so they could better emulate it all.

"So it's me you're after, then?" Jonas pivoted to the left. He knew what it was. How could he not? But how had this one or... the thing talked like there were more, so - how had the Council not been aware?

"Why, yes, Jonas. You are the most fascinating of them all."

"Fascinating? Stop using that word!" He demanded in a roar. He was moving to attack again. This time, he didn't plan on missing. Jonas thought he was ready. Thought.

The doppel leapt upward in a surprising grasp of air. They were over the lycan and shifting. When Jonas turned, he was face to face with himself.

"What other things about this form do you take for granted? Shall we see?" The doppelgänger goaded the lycan. They wanted the Councilor to rush them, and after studying the creature, the doppelgänger was fairly certain it would happen.

The Councilor snarled at the shifter. His claws forward, he was swiftly charging in for the attack!

For this, the doppelgänger did not use lycan fighting to accomplish his goal. Why should they? There was no audience. There was no honor necessary. They ducked then lifted upward with all their strength, flipping Jonas. The mess made was of no consequence. They had time to clean up. But they preferred no blood. Therefore, when Jonas went for the next obvious move in his repertoire, the doppelgänger was prepared. They scurried around, bending backward at what seemed an impossible angle. By the time Jonas slid to a halt, his evil twin was on his back, hands on either side of his lupine head.

There was a grunt and a sickening crack of bone.

Jonas Airsight was dead, his neck broken. His replacement watched him die with the same cold detachment they had used in their study of the lycan Councilor all this time. The doppelgänger became the human form of Jonas and their head canted to the side while regarding the dead body.

"Fascinating."

Chapter 5
Tommy's Pub

It had been nearly 26 hours since Jean-Michel's last mission. 26 hours since he had taken yet another life. Perhaps he should have one of those little signs on the wall like workplaces had? The ones showing how long since the last accident? Maybe the levity would help.

He splashed water on his face, which landed on his neck and shoulders. His large hands pushed his messy auburn hair back and then his fingers moved to scratch through the rough beard.

Turning to reach for a towel, he glimpsed the brand just below his shoulder blade in the mirrors lined up in the hotel room. He held the towel and turned his head slowly, staring at the thing that marred his freckled skin. It was a reminder of why he never placed faith in anyone. Not anymore.

With a growl, he turned away, kicking several bottles and cans as he did. He looked inside the mini-fridge and found it bare.

"Welp...time to find a pub."

Jean-Michel got redressed and made his way out of his hotel room and down to the street. This time, he'd been sure not to bring his personal phone. That way, he wouldn't make the mistake of drunkenly calling his Councilor.

Only a few minutes into his walk to get more liquor, Jean had that feeling that he was being watched. Being a dragon added to the senses despite being in a human form. That instinctual fight-or-flight reaction was close to the surface.

He stopped to talk to the bums over near the bridges. They couldn't tell him anyone was following. He gave them some money all the same. He walked into the old Irish pub in the appropriately named Dublin, California, to find the bottom of another bottle and safety in numbers.

"Hey, Jean! How've you been? You need to make more excuses to get back here," the bartender called from behind the taps, happy to ignore the already tone-deaf, drunk nearby. "I got a whole case of Old Bushmill."

"You never let me down, eh, Tommy?"

"You got it! Where've you been hiding?" Tommy placed a glass next to the bottle he'd already picked up.

"East Coast, actually. Just here for business. Thanks for remembering. Keep it coming, will ya?" he tossed some bills on the counter.

"Sure thing. Just don't make me have to pour you into a taxi." The man chuckled before going back to his other customers.

Jean-Michel walked with his bottle and glass away from the bar to a table along the backside of the pub. He sat there along with a group of regulars – some of which actually recognized him.

Jean caught up on other people's lives as if they were old friends. He shared several bottles with them. They sang to the music when the band came in. He told stories more fantastic than any self-respecting man would denounce. Jean-Michel was definitely drunk. Of course, he'd describe it as "nicely warmed".

People enjoyed talking to him when he was like this. He would listen to their stories. Their lives were so very interesting to the old Tasker. He'd not lived a normal life. Sometimes, he envied them. Yes, he was angry at humans on a level most couldn't comprehend. But he wasn't angry with these particular humans. Not now.

Just like the little girl's mother on the train, they were just blissfully unaware of what they were drinking with. If the clock on the wall was correct, it was about time for Gabriel to be between his office and the Crimson Council meeting. Jean-Michel walked away from his table of friends and picked up the public phone near the front of the place. He dialed his Councilor's personal number from memory.

"Who is this?"

"Hello, Gabriel. How are you this fine evening?" The Tasker looked around the bar from his vantage point. He heard Gabriel scoff.

"So exactly where did you decide was more important to be this time?"

Jean-Michel could hear Gabriel return to typing on what sounded like a laptop. So either he was on speaker or in the man's ear. Considering how paranoid his Councilor could be, his bet was on wired earbuds.

"Are you going to apologize for hanging up?" Gabriel asked.

"Awww...now why'd you expect someone who has a real life to show up at your beck and call?" He held back a laugh and nearly dropped the receiver. As if it was the phone's fault, he frowned at the thing before placing it once again to his ear.

"Hmmm, yes, odd isn't it? I'd expect my Tasker at a Council meeting to help with witness testimony as an expert. How stupid of me..."

Jean-Michel heard Gabe sip his coffee. The Tasker was also observing the crowd. He saw a few colorful outlines around people now. The whiskey had worked. The auras of supernatural beings were unmistakable to his mind. However, his eyes looked almost feline when he did this. He blinked and tried to shield his eyes from any passersby.

There was a sigh over the line. "You still haven't told me where you are. Tell me, to what do I owe the pleasure of this call? And don't insult me by trying to say you were actually interested in knowing what the meeting pertains to."

"Oh, I don't really care." With a chuckle, Jean-Michel sighed and settled back against the wall to continue watching the crowd. Then he turned just enough that no one could see his mouth. "Did you send somebody to hunt me, Gabriel?"

"No, I didn't. If I had, they would have found you by now and dragged your drunken ass back here where it belongs."

"Mmm..." The Councilor had everything from lycan, to sorcerers, and even psychics at his disposal. So Jean-Michel believed him.

"You know, the only reason I haven't asked for a new Tasker is because you were my grandfather's Tasker and you have a history with Devon and Eva. You have a history with my family for some odd reason. So I was willing to give this a chance..."

"That the only reason, mon ami?" He played on the French for his Councilor, just to be a dick.

"Don't you insinuate..." Gabriel cleared his throat.

Jean-Michel chuckled because he could almost hear Gabriel's head explode.

"You obviously don't want the position, so maybe I should just request Skinner give me a new Tasker."

"One you can handle?"

"I can handle you, thank you very much. I've just been lenient. One of these days I'm going to tag you. You know that, don't you Jean?"

"Awwwwww….you don't need a tag when you've got a brand. But come now. You know you couldn't handle me. I have welcomed you to try."

"So you keep reminding me." The Tasker heard Gabriel snap the laptop closed. "If I were so inclined, how could I? I rarely see your face unless it's on a screen. Rarely hear your voice unless it's on the phone. When I've tried to complain to Director Skinner, he always has a convenient excuse at the ready. I'm very much done with this ritual."

"I like our ritual." He wanted to say more, but he shook his head to get himself together enough to continue, and he cleared his throat. He realized he really had dropped the receiver. It bounced from its metal cord against the wall.

"Jean-Michel?"

Thanks to the whiskey, his pupils were oval, much like a cat's eyes surrounded by the blue-green field. This is how he read auras, the radiation of the soul's energy.

It left him vulnerable and well – like any human his size, drunk. What startled him were the two people in the bar that had odd, fluctuating auras. What had Gabriel talked about on the previous call? Doppelgängers? A fluctuating aura made sense. He lifted the receiver back to his ear.

"Raudine, are you well? Do I … do I actually need to make arrangements?" Gabriel's voice sounded more concerned than Jean-Michel had ever heard. That question he had asked himself since Gabriel's 18th birthday came to mind… would Gabriel be like all the others? Would he care? He seemed to.

"I'm… not sure," Jean-Michel licked his lips. If these were doppels, the second one, in the guise of a lovely brunette at the bar, turned to look directly at him. Their eyes met. "Damn." He scolded himself and turned to the wall again. Laughing heartily, he blinked his eyes quickly.

"Jean… talk to me," Gabriel ordered.

Jean-Michel knew sometimes he was only alive because no one thought he was a threat. Right now, he hoped it would be his saving grace. He placed his hand on the wall, trying to keep himself from losing balance. His palm flattened and his fingers spread.

"Doppelgängers," he whispered.

"What?" Gabriel swallowed. "Did you just say doppelgänger?" Jean-Michel heard him typing again. "Where are you?"

"Tommy's Place. Dublin, California." Hearing the other patrons talking of toasts, he turned to hold up his own glass and nearly fumbled it. And that's when luck stepped in.

"Are you okay?" the young woman from his table asked.

"Shhhh," The hand that was still holding the liquor raised its index finger so he could put it over his lips. He did his best to keep his eyes lidded enough that she wouldn't see his draconic pupils.

"What?" she giggled at him. "Look, we're about to head out and thought we'd be sure you got home or to your hotel. It's the least we can do after you were so generous with your whiskey."

"Jean?" Gabriel's voice spoke into the phone.

"I have more friends than I thought I had," he whispered to her and Gabriel both. "That's what you should know. Least 3."

"Okay, but actually, it's just me and my friend Paula over there," she pointed over her shoulder to a redhead at the exit, impatiently holding keys. "You seem awful drunk. Just wanted to know if you needed a ride."

He saw her blush. Did she like him? Well then... Jean-Michel Raudine needed the exit, but he didn't like putting the ladies in danger. And the way she and her friend regarded him spoke of attraction and expectation. He had to play his cards right.

"Who is there with you?" Gabriel asked, his voice a bit more stressed than it had been before. "You've already said... Do you mean doppelgängers – is that what you mean by more friends?"

"Yep, and then... There's a nice human being here talking to me, love. What's your name?" Jean-Michel asked the woman with caring eyes. He could hear Gabriel typing, and then there was a pause.

"Libby." she grinned.

"I'm on the phone with my ... uhhh..." he halted and his hand made a rolling motion as he tried his damnedest to think of a...word...to describe Gabriel.

"Wife?" she asked, trying to help him.

"Raudine, don't you dare!" There was even a pissed groan from over the phone line that told the Tasker this was exactly where he'd go with the charade.

"You could call him that. He definitely nags enough," Jean chuckled. His eyes weren't wanting to cooperate and come back to regular sight. He saw another doppelgänger come inside. "Oh look! Another customer. So many beautiful ladies here." Jean hoped Gabriel hadn't completely lost track of what he was saying. Just because it came out like the ravings of a drunk didn't mean it was nonsense.

"I'm sending a message to Skinner. He needs to know you have multiple doppelgängers near you and where. Now... can you get to the airport?"

"Yeah, there are a lot of us, so, did you just want to stay here or..." Libby probably wasn't sure anymore if taking a drunken stranger out of a bar was the wisest idea.

"Could you... talk to my husband? If you can help me? Please?" Jean-Michel was only partially playing it up. He really needed coffee. He really needed their help. Making sure they thought he was gay might ease some of Libby's worries and close the deal.

"I mean, if he's on the phone, and he wasn't already mad, you are sooo in the doghouse." Libby giggled but took the glass from the man's hand. "I think maybe you've had enough of that." Putting that down, she took the offered phone.

"I need to get to the airport. San Francisco? I need to get a flight, but I've gotten drunk." Jean-Michel pointed to the phone and lifted his brows, "He's mad at me...." he fake-whispered, his eyes still squinted. While the woman and Gabriel made the arrangements, Jean-Michel was taking stock of all the doppelgängers' positions. He tried not to be obvious. Why were they after him?

As soon as the Libby gal had the flight information, they were ready. He put his arms over their shoulders and let them steer. The doppels couldn't do a damn thing to him so long as he stayed with a group of people. At least, he hoped that would be the case.

Chapter 6
DEREK'S ASS

Driving up to the front entrance of what looked like any other Urgent Care building, Devon Weylyn stopped the truck. The sign read Eastside Specialty Clinic. The big lycan stepped out of the driver's seat. He had plaited blonde hair on one side, beads woven in the mass. Blonde waves covered the other side of his head and down over his shoulder. His beard twitched as he sniffed the air. The man's nose wrinkled at the pungent aroma of multiple deterring scents that seemed to cling to the property and even the building.

"Should've stayed at the HQ and been working on other things. Jean-Michel even gave me a project..." Derek grumbled. He was the passenger, raised up on his side rump in an obviously uncomfortable position when Devon opened the door behind him.

Reaching inside to take hold of a muscled bicep, Devon rumbled. The sound wasn't one of annoyance so much as it was a sound he used to calm any of his pups. Derek definitely needed calming.

"Come on Dare, no more grumbling bullshit. Ya know we don't process copper that well, so let's get ya inside so they can get it out. Then yer healin' can kick in. That happens, I'll take ya back home, give ya a beer, and let ya kick yer feet up the rest of the evening."

"Really? That's your pampering?" The younger blonde glared. He was definitely younger, but nearly as broadly built as the alpha. Unlike the alpha, he cut his hair short. "It sucks. How do I kick my feet up if my ass is sore?" Derek was obviously less than pleased. "You know I hate anything medical Dev. It's gonna stink in there. We could just dig it out ourselves."

"I'm not goin' anywhere near yer ass." The bigger male stated. "Maybe luck'll be with ya and the doc'll be pretty and smart. You still looking for a mate, after all." He chuckled as he helped his limping beta from the car and into the clinic waiting room.

"Yeah, and this is how ya find one. Sure." Derek muttered.

As they made their way up to the main desk, Devon glanced around in his usual cautious fashion. The paint was dingy cream-colored and there were well-worn blue seats wrapping the outer walls. It was all dated, just like the brick outside. The scents of the cleaners stung his nose, and he huffed sharply before rubbing his eyes. There were a few people in there waiting. Human, from what he could tell.

"I can't believe I got hit like this. Dammit." Derek growled again, but the pain was severe enough that he wasn't fighting his Alpha anymore.

"How can I help you?" a woman wearing scrubs with a name tag that said, Holly, asked.

"Came in for the specialty part of the specialty clinic. Tell yer doc, I got her a patient." Dev flashed his canines and his golden eyes glittered to let the receptionist know they were more than an average human. "My eldest here needs copper pellets removed from his…uh… backside."

Derek rumbled his distaste from the side.

"Hang on, let me see where they want me to put him." The receptionist vanished to the back area, leaving the two men standing there before her desk.

"Say nothin', we'll talk about it all when there ain't a dozen or more ears listening. Stick with what we discussed on the ride here." Devon's expression never changed, and his tone was calm and pleasant. This was what the situation called for, after all. The last thing they needed was for word of this to get back to Councilor Jonas.

"Does Gabe know…" Derek tried to ask, but his Alpha cut him off with a growl.

Holly came back around the corner with Dr. Keene.

"Hello there," Samantha said as she came out into the lobby area from the back rooms. "I'm Dr. Keene." Sam introduced herself to the patient.

"Derek."

"Let's get you into a triage room so we can talk, Derek." She led them to the room as she spoke to them about the situation they were in. "A gunshot is usually something I have to report. I need to be sure about the details. The triage room I'm taking you to is soundproof." Once in the room, Samantha asked first, "Do you mind telling me how this happened? I'll treat you regardless, but I need to know what's going on."

The Alpha spoke first for them as he always did.. it came with the title.

"I'm head of security for Councilor Gabriel Kennedy, and his estate and businesses. This is my beta, Derek Weylyn. We were conducting training exercises this mornin' and needless ta say, a shot went off and Derek here weaved when he should have ducked. He got tagged in the... uh... backside with copper pellets. Didn't bring it to my attention 'til later."

"And lycan can't heal with copper in them." Sam finished. She at least knew that much.

"So here we are." The two lycan took up a sizeable chunk of the room with their size. Devon didn't like the tightness of this place. "Crimson already knows about it. I report all injuries from training to 'em."

"Good, because I hate paperwork. I have enough to do without the Crimson stuff. I'll just check on your report and add my initials as attending. But, quick question, if you don't heal well from copper, why in the world were you using it for training?"

"That's a damn good question." Derek glared over at Devon. The Alpha rumbled at him again and he lowered his head and his eyes. "Can he explain it while you take the things out? It really isn't much of a picnic here, lady."

"Oh! Yes, here," she patted the exam bed. "Lean over here, pull your clothes down enough that I can treat it. And right or left?" She went into the locked cabinet and the side and then pulled out a spray.

"Left."

Finding the wound where he mentioned it would be, Sam pumped the spray onto the site. "That should deaden it a little and begin cleaning. Anyway, why copper?"

"We use copper during training cause I know my Pack will actually put themselves into the training. If I used anything else, they'd act like it was a play day and not care. They heal pretty quick. I can promise ya next time Dare'll think twice before goin' the same way that got him hit this time. His backside will be out of the line of fire when I call clear."

There was a rumbling growl from the other lycan that was an irritated form of the affirmative to Devon's question.

"Let me know when it's not as painful." She turned on the light overhead and adjusted it so that the wound was easier to see. "I can always use stronger..."

"Topical will do. He's had worse and had nothing ta kill the pain. We don't do the heavy stuff." Devon cautioned.

"Speak for yerself, pops... damn..." Derek squeezed his eyes closed and his nails bit into the leathery cushion on the table, claws elongating as he fought the pain.

Devon rumbled deeply from his chest before walking around to stand before Derek so he could face the other lycan and be there to control him if the need arose to do so.

"We treat a lot of turned and what you call rogue lycan. And I'm glad you came in for this. Your shamanic physicians don't always have the best treatment for infections. You may fight off and heal most anything, but sometimes this world's infectious diseases can be quick to entangle lycan not born here." Sam began picking out the shot as quickly as possible.

Sam dug out the last piece of copper pellet and grimaced when she heard Derek make a low whine. Devon put his hands on the other lycan's shoulders and rumbled from his chest to the beta. The doctor irrigated the wound to be sure it was clean.

"Derek's body should soon heal itself. From what I understand, he'll just feel like he has a nasty bruise for a couple of days." Sam walked over to the cabinet and unlocked it to get the antibiotic.

"We developed an antibiotic specifically for lycan. The injection should be enough, no need to remember to take anything later. Your body will heal the rest." The doctor handed the liquid to Devon. The manufacturing label was from this very institution and a local pharmaceutical company. Meanwhile, she bandaged the wound and taped it.

"If it ain't for us, our bodies reject it. He'll be sick. So...we're trustin' you." Rolling the vial in his large hand, the Alpha decided. It was obvious this one did her research and possibly even gave a damn. She knew he was the one to make all decisions. Devon handed it back to the doctor. He watched her prepare the injection out of curiosity.

"I like to be an unstoppable force with promotions. Got us the deal without questions about any further purpose than what it could do for human medical science. It helps against MRSA –

which is ironic if you know the science. That's what they focused on."

Derek watched from over his shoulder. He squinted his eyes shut and turned the other way. He hated shots or carving or scarring or... well, anything like it. The pain was one thing, but the expectation was another. He prepared to be surprised by the needle.

When she handled it, Derek grimaced and grunted. "Ya had to do it above the deadened area?"

"Sorry." Sam put the needle in the sharps container and shrugged. Turning her attention again to Devon, "If some are rogue and I treat them, would you mind if I let them know about your pack? Give them a means of contact? I've only ever treated two, but they could've used help, even if it wasn't becoming part of a pack."

"My mate helps rogues and lone wolves when they need it from time to time. I'll ask her for the number she uses and get back to ya. She and some others have locations of shelters that are available." Devon helped Derek out of the awkward position. His head cocked to the side for a second, then nodded to Derek.

"Yeah, I heard it, too..."

Derek took a deep breath. "Jonas."

The Alpha of Pack Airsight walked past the front desk without a second thought. He could smell where the two lycan were and didn't need anyone to direct him.

"Sir! Sir! You can't be back here!" the front desk attendant was tiny compared to this man, and knew better than to even attempt to physically stop him. She was happy when Dr. Keene stepped out of the triage room.

"Whoa! Hey, uh...I'm Dr. Keene, and you are...?" Samantha stood between the big man and the doorway. Jonas stared down at her crossed arms and raised chin. He actually halted his forward progress.

"Councilor Jonas Airsight. I've been told that there was a lycan shot? I'm here because of that. Was on my way through town and knew they'd be here." He looked over the doctor's head and into the room. "Devon, you okay? I don't feel like telling that mate of yer's you'll be walking funny for the rest of yer life."

Devon and Derek came to the doorway, and the doctor turned to them slowly.

"Are you supposed to go with this Councilor?" she asked, not moving despite being human and quite capable of being lifted and moved by the lycan around her.

"Yeah. We have ta report any accidents, remember? Since it's a lycan incident, looks like our Councilor decided ta get involved." Devon nodded to the doctor.

"It's yer place to repair the injury, doctor. It's not yer place ta know all the details. Those two lycan have some explaining ta do for me. So, if you'll let them out? We'll all be on our way." He turned to make his way back down the hallway.

"Finish yer report, Dr. Keene. It'll be fine. Thank you." Devon and Derek stepped out once Dr. Keene moved.

She watched them leave and even walked to the front, as they had what looked to be an impromptu debate outside. She may have flipped on the intercom...accidentally.

"Live rounds in a human city?" Jonas asked.

"It was a doppelgänger. I swear by everything in me, Jonas. I've met one before. I started following it..." Derek didn't get to finish.

"Who told ya ta be investigating doppelgängers?"

"It was a favor," Devon explained quickly before Derek could continue. "Councilor Kennedy's Tasker is on a mission for the Director. Point bein' he couldn't do it. And the human that got killed the other night? He believes it was a doppelgänger. Says there's some other crooked cases that point in that direction."

"They have a certain smell for you to know and track? Did you see it shift?" Jonas asked.

"Well, no. That's the thing, they don't have a scent. They take on the scent of those they morph into when they use magical items. Here, he became the victim and so, we were trying to track that as much as possible. Then, someone shot at—"

"Hmmph..." Jonas looked between the two other lycan as if studying them. "I was born and raised here in Gaia's arms like most of my pack, so I wouldn't know. How dangerous you think they are?"

"Overall, I think they'd be weak creatures; pretty frail. But that ability? Ta become somebody? That's what's got 'em blacklisted from Gaia. Humans are vulnerable, so it stands ta reason, don'tcha think?" Devon pointed out.

"I don't think nothing when I don't know about it. Why is this the first I'm hearing about it?"

Derek and Devon looked at one another. Devon answered. "Not sure. I thought that was Gabriel Kennedy's responsibility, Councilor Airsight."

The Councilor growled and stepped closer to Devon, and there was a growl in return. Derek's eyes got enormous.

"Ya know, me gettin' shot in public ain't near as bad as a lycan fight in public. So, why don't we all just take a breath and talk this out?"

"I'm yer damn Councilor, not him. I say drop this investigation and I mean it. Yer chasing ghosts and nearly getting killed over it. I'll send my own Tasker ta investigate the shooting and I'll let Skinner know what you think about the doppelgängers." Jonas huffed and turned to walk toward the parking lot. "Go home and stay out of shit unless I call on ya to do somethin', Weylyn!"

Devon's golden amber glare didn't let up. He didn't back down. He watched the Councilor move off and get into a Jeep to leave.

"Well?" Derek asked. "He ain't wrong. And Gabe's what? 30? About ta be 30? He's human, got no experience with these things. Maybe he's wrong?"

"Then why did you end up with copper in yer ass? Doppels or not, somebody's aiming ta kill lycan." Devon took a deep breath, a rough, vibrated, sighing sound in his chest.

"Okay, fine," Derek muttered, "But I'm takin' a nap before I put my ass on the line again."

Chapter 7
Business

The sedan was driven smoothly, despite the traffic and the pedestrians walking hither and yon. Ezekiel Skinner had become accustomed to the ebb and flow of a college town. Right now, there were students beginning their classes by enjoying the many bars and pubs set up with them in mind.

When the college kids were gone for a holiday or even while the summer semester was happening, the crowds were not near so bad. He liked those times best. However, the crowds had advantages. People could easily get lost in crowds.

Tonight, he just wanted to go home and sleep. Unfortunately, he was being pestered by the petulant human Councilor and a reluctant accomplice.

He had already gotten five alerts from Kennedy – all while driving the distance of five miles. He knew this, not because of any supernatural hocus pocus, but because the ringtone set on his phone for Gabriel Kennedy was a barking dog. Be it a phone message, text, or email, the Kennedy Clan always barked.

A flit of a smile crossed his aged features as he made a left-hand turn down one of the side alleys to get to a difficult parking garage off of the main street. Finding a spot, he sat for a moment before perusing his email.

There was a report from the Eastside Medical Clinic that had him raising his brows. There were usually very few reports of violent happenings and so this caught his eye. A lycan...gunshot wounds and copper shot brought in another lycan male? No names given. He didn't need names. The Weylyn Pack had been a thorn in his side for years, and he could well imagine which two lycan had been in the clinic.

"Training exercise, my ass," Ezekiel muttered. He continued to peruse the inbox. Being the Director of the policing side of the agency meant the inbox stayed full.

The first email from Kennedy discussed the doppelgänger situation and demanded a closed-door meeting to discuss it all as soon as possible. The second email was simple and to the point:

Jean's found trouble. Unregistered Doppels at a pub Tommy's Place in Dublin, CA. Investigators need to be on the ground. Count 3/4.

It was obvious the Councilor expected the Director to do something about the situation that his Tasker found himself in. The question was, did Ezekiel feel this warranted help? He didn't make a habit of bailing others out. Got yourself in, get yourself out. And Jean-Michel was damn good at both.

He heard an alert hit his alternate phone, a simplistic flip phone still in his inner pocket. He took it out to see that Miranda Garrett wanted to talk. A pity. Malcolm must have failed to convince her without using the number. Ezekiel dialed the number, placing it on speaker so that he could construct a reply email for Kennedy on his official phone.

"Miranda?" Ezekiel's voice was quiet, almost tender.

"Why are you doing these things?" Miranda asked.

"You know me. You know control is necessary." He cleared his throat, as he considered what to type while also having this conversation. "People have gone astray. An opportunity presented itself. I'm not one to leave that door unanswered."

"What am I supposed to tell my brother? He'll get suspicious."

"The reason you're in this situation is to pay for a favor I did that benefited him years ago. If he gets involved, let him know that. Remind him we who trade in magic and power take our oaths and vows seriously. We also take seriously the consequences of failing in those oaths and vows." He reread the email while he talked.

I will not have a closed-door meeting about a doppelgänger situation. Crimson is handling the minor issue of a few unregistered beings causing trouble in the area as we speak. This is rather unimportant in the scheme of all things happening, Councilor Kennedy. You should not be worried about it. You should keep your business to the regulations and prosecutions upcoming. That is your duty. I will see to mine. As to your Tasker's situation, I will look into it with the local Crimson guard.

"You're both half-demons. Are you telling me you don't abide by your vows and deals? Because I didn't think that was possible." He hit SEND.

"What's the endgame? I might want to find some spare fortune in it?" Miranda's voice was that of a siren when she wanted something.

"My end game will be beneficial to you as it stands. There's no need for you to know any more about it, Ms. Garret. Or should I say, deSalucet... or was it Lady Val'Ashtar? I forget which pleases you most. Did you forget who you were talking to?" Ezekiel waited. The silence was telling. He had all the power when you knew a demon's secrets and its true list of names. He had known a lot about Miranda and her brother through the years, and that knowledge had helped tremendously.

"Fine. And my debt? After I handle 28 placements for doppelgängers, you agree it's paid?"

"You will no longer be in debt. At least, not to me." Ezekiel raised his head. Dark grey eyes framed by an older countenance and shoulder-length silvering hair stared back from the rearview mirror. "Just deal with Malcolm. Don't contact me again." He snapped the flip phone shut. In the rearview mirror, a nondescript man in slacks, a button-down, and a long coat walked from the shadows. Ezekiel got out of the car.

"Hello, Malcolm." Ezekiel buttoned his jacket. "I believe everything's going as planned. I've confirmed the deal with your new contact."

"We will have the portal for the next group? There will be no trouble?"

"So long as you and your doppelgängers replace the targets I've assigned them to, there will be no trouble. And my name is to stay out of it. You understand that, yes? Or any future you might have had here will be gone."

Malcolm's head bowed in acknowledgment.

"So far?"

"We took the lycan in Whitley, the human, and elf in Paris, along with the demon, human, and vampire in Japan. We will take the vampire here tonight," Malcolm updated. "This should give you a majority in each Council until we can take more."

Ezekiel couldn't help but grin.

Chapter 8
Another Night, Another Victim

Pushing through the glass double doors of the Eastside Specialty Clinic, a dark-haired man stumbled in and made his way to the front desk. His long coat was wet from the rain pouring outside, and until he got close to the desk, the nurse did not see the problem. He had his hand wrapped around the slender piece of metal that was in his side. He was so pale it looked like death had kissed him.

"Oh, damn!" the nurse pressed the buzzer that went off in the doctor's office at night. She came around the counter to help the man. "Come on. Let me help you to the room."

"I need… assistance of the.. special kind."

"Special kind? Oh… well… the doctor will be here in just a minute. What's your name?" She managed to get him moving toward the wheelchairs.

His ears were ringing, but once he made sense of what she was asking him, he could mutter, "Evansworth… Sebastian.. wallet's in the back pocket.. no police." The silver was like molten lava in his side and he would have pulled it out already, except for the damned barbs that kept it in place.

When Dr. Samantha Keene got to the room, the man was already on the exam table.

"Switch the lights, now. Call in the secondaries. Get the blood prepped," the doctor ordered.

"It's barbed, by the way," the vampire groaned as he held tight.

"The head of a war spear…" Dr. Keen was examining the weapon and the wound. "Holy shit, it's made of silver? Who did you piss off enough for this?" Sam asked as she moved her fingers around the wound, obviously trying to decide on an approach for removal.

Though it hurt, the vampire tried not to twitch while she inspected and worked on the wound.

"Shapeshifters. At first, I thought it was someone else." He was pausing for slow breaths. He watched the new nurse step in and get cleaned up. "No need to report."

"I'm kind of not worried about that right now." Samantha had successfully unlodged the barbed tip by an inch just in the pressing. She grabbed a swab package to hand to the newly arrived nurse for opening.

"I will find out. It may...mmmm... have been a misunderstanding." The way her fingers pressed through the material of his shirt to judge the damage reminded him why he usually took care of things on his own.

"A misunderstanding with a Councilor and Coven Lord? And they just happened to be carrying silver? Doubtful." Sam smiled. "Although, they may have chosen the wrong person to get into a so-called misunderstanding with." Samantha affixed the swabs on each side of the blade to keep it from going back inside as Sebastian watched.

"You know who I am?" He grunted as she moved the blade a bit more and continued.

"I make it a point to know the people I may deal with. I've treated some people from your Coven before, actually." She smiled as she stepped back. "I've placed swabs on each side to keep it from slipping back in. So you can relax your hold now." She looked at the nurse, who had been setting up the normal needs for a situation like this – something they had practiced but never had to deal with. "I'm ordering 5 pints. Do you know your blood type? And what type do you prefer to drink?"

"Doesn't matter, as long as it doesn't come from the dead. Blood type makes no difference." He'd felt worse, of course, but that didn't mean he didn't still feel the simple pains. "I enjoy a good glass of O+ when possible if you want me to be picky." He enjoyed making her smile. It was at least one bright spot in an otherwise very fucked up night.

Sebastian couldn't believe how stupid he'd been. He should have just ignored the man and gone straight from the park next to the Council Chambers Building. Instead, he allowed his curiosity to win over his common sense. This should not have happened!

Dr. Keene walked quickly to the side cabinet and came back to the table, sterile packet in hand. She began cleaning around the edge of the wound enough that she could see. The syringe entered his skin several times in quick succession. Sam was efficient with her procedures. She needed to get that out of him, and she didn't need him to experience the ripping.

Again he held still as she stuck him with the syringe.

"Anesthetics are unnecessary. I've suffered worse in battles. I can control myself…" Sebastian huffed as he watched her inject him. He didn't like to have chemicals running through his body.

"What is it with you supernatural types and your bravado? I swear I've heard that twice within a 24-hour period already. I don't care how many battles and wars you've been in Lord Evansworth, right now, you're my patient and I want you as comfortable as possible." Sam tossed the empty syringe into the sharps container. "Em, can you run and grab the blood and set up the appropriate lines? I'll also need plenty of gauze and sterile fluid. I'm about to make a mess and our sweet ray of sunshine here'll need that blood."

"Sure," Nurse Emily went about her duties.

"Trust me, madam, this really is me being polite. Also, the burning I have inside right now says you best double up on that order." His words slurred a little from the blood loss and his head eased back onto the exam table.

"Yeah, silver. Em…" Sam seemed to stare down at the spear for a long period.

"On it," Emily stopped one thing and added to the order before continuing. They wheeled in the first cart right after.

"What are you contemplating?" Sebastian asked. He was concerned.

"Déjà vu." Sam began moving her fingers along the wound and slowly untangled the layers of skin from the last barb. Once again, she retracted the spearhead out by an inch, then two, and with a turn of the piece of metal, she had it out without actually ripping more flesh than necessary.

It had taken long enough that Emily had the blood going into the vampire via IV. It was a quick replenishment.

"You said déjà vu," He prompted.

"Yeah, a lycan came in here earlier, injured by the very metal that could kill him. And now, you come in, stabbed by the metal that could kill you. So, whoever is trying really knows their enemy." Sam began cleaning and dressing the wound. "You knew how to turn, didn't you? Your attacker didn't get anything but flesh. My question is – what was an important person like you doing out alone and letting himself be so vulnerable?" Samantha paused and looked into his eyes. "You were alone, right? Tell me if I need to send somebody out after another victim."

"You ask a lot of questions for a clinic doctor." Sebastian just kept his breathing steady as he felt the blood moving into his veins.

"I'm a special doctor. I try to give a damn." Sam had no issue pointing that out to him before smiling at him.

That smile. He couldn't help but huff in humor, a smirk showing through the pain.

"One question at a time. First, yes, I knew how to turn. Someone has impaled me before, and I learn from my mistakes. Second, there is only a body out there. I think I snapped his neck before I broke the damn spear. The timeline is... fuzzy. You can inform Crimson of the location. It was in the park or arboretum off of Raleigh Street." The vampire grunted at the pinch of pain in his side. The numbing was helping, though.

As the pain got less and less, Sebastian could no longer keep from relaxing. His body would not continue without more blood and rest. He eased back on the exam table with a sigh while the doctor continued what she was doing to the wound.

"You can leave me in this room to recover. Just...no one in or out. And I'll need that spearhead bagged up for me." He could already feel himself drifting now that the spear was gone and the tear in his flesh was being cleaned.

"Yes, master," she did her best Renfield, and then rolled her eyes. Emily unsuccessfully stifled a giggle.

"Mmmmm...hilarious. You have a marvelous bedside manner, doctor," Sebastian chuckled. He could understand. He imagined supernaturals, vampires included, made entitled patients.

"Glad you like it, Lord Evansworth." The doctor continued to push the ripped flesh together, and using catgut, she sewed. "I imagine your supernatural healing process will finish within hours or days compared to the weeks that it would take for a human."

There was a growl of annoyance, but then his eyes closed. His heartbeat slowed so much that she could presume him dead, and he went cold with practically no breath. His mind was aware of everything that was going on around him. Normally, he did not go into this type of sleep in an unfamiliar, unsecured location. Unfortunately, he really had no choice.

"Remember, their vitals differ from ours; lower heart rate and barely any pulse when they do this." Emily nodded. Sam took a deep breath. "Finish with the blood. He needs it all." The doctor touched Sebastian's skin and then nodded. "Sleep stasis to recuperate. Good. When you're done, be sure this side of the ward has security in place."

"Will do," Emily replied.

Samantha paused and watched his face momentarily. Then she whispered, "This is good. I don't have to be ordered around while I finish cleaning and stitching you."

Oh, he'd remember that. Yes, he definitely would.

Chapter 9
ON A JET PLANE

At the private jet terminal, Jean-Michel waved goodbye to his ladies. It was rather sad that he hadn't enjoyed anything more than a conversation with them, because they thought he was gay and taken. His eyes rolled. Back in the day, they would've been on the jet with him, doing all sorts of naughty things.

"Raudine?" Gabriel's voice knocked him out of his revelry.

"You came with the plane?" There he was, Councilor Gabriel Kennedy, standing at the top of the staircase leading out of the private jet.

"It's my company's jet. Why wouldn't I?" His brows nearly touched in the front.

"Maybe so I could get a little shut-eye along the way without the nagging voice," Jean-Michel muttered under his breath.

"Yeah, well, you're the one that claimed we were married, so you get the nagging voice for free." Gabriel was happy to scold the man.

"You know you loved it." Jean-Michel's wicked grin did not diminish when Gabriel scoffed at the idea. He made his way to the grouping of seats around a table where Gabriel already had his work set up.

"How do you know for sure they were doppelgängers?"

"Right out the gate, huh?" Jean-Michel sighed as he took a load off. "They may list me as human, but we who have the gift can use it when a situation emerges."

Gabriel's eyes remained steadily boring into him while the pilot's voice came on the speaker above them. "We'll taxi as soon as our attendant is back with the food you ordered, sir."

Normally, the Tasker wouldn't mind the man's eyes looking him over. He'd noticed it more than once. But not like this. It was definitely not a lustful look. Jean-Michel was tired of being treated like he was some imbecilic servant of humans.

"Whether you like it or not, they assigned you to me as Tasker. When I need you, I mean it. In this case, you would have had a leg-up on the situation had you actually listened." Gabriel spoke as the flight attendant came on board, carrying the large brown bags from one of the high-end restaurants.

"Maybe. But if you want me so bad, you can have a chat with Director Skinner about his uncalled-for use of me. Tell him he has no right to place me on another mission." He sighed and let himself relax in the seat. "Gods know, I'd prefer to do anything other than what that man sends me to do."

"And what were you sent to do, Raudine?" Gabriel asked him suddenly.

Jean-Michel gazed into Gabriel's brown eyes and then looked down, shaking his head. "Not my place." He steepled his fingers in his lap and turned to look out the window.

"Not your place." Gabriel took a deep breath and asked, "Then what is your place, Raudine? Because you don't seem to act like you know." The human Councilor stared while the plane taxied.

He was afraid to look at Gabriel's eyes. Afraid of seeing the condemnation or worse, apathy and emptiness...what most other humans had in their eyes. The Tasker wasn't sure what was worse. He'd lost his right to tell them all to fuck off.

The take-off went smoothly and before they continued the conversation, the attendant was bringing out their meal.

"You know, you can also move around the cabin now if you like." She just paused. "Is there anything else I can get you?" The woman's bright green eyes washed over them expectantly as she brushed her dark hair back over her shoulder.

"I know, I was just checking the markets," Gabriel responded while he scrolled his finger over the face of his phone.

"I'm good," Jean-Michel finally stopped ignoring everything except what was outside and turned to look at the food he was about to enjoy. Something about the flight attendant watching him didn't sit right. It was the same uneasy feeling he had experienced back in Dublin. Had the doppelgänger really made it this far?

"We're fine, Roxanne, thank you." Gabriel was ready to dismiss her, and that made Jean-Michel second-guess his instincts. He studied the woman who was watching them. Apparently, his expression had given him away because the woman shifted her stance. It was a defensive move.

The Tasker was up out of the seat; the sandwich flying and the tray shoved in the woman's face.

"What?!" Gabriel's near squeak of an utterance told him just how startled the human Councilor was.

Instead of taking the woman down, Jean-Michel's foot got caught on Gabriel's leather bag, which the Council had apparently left on his side of the small table. Tripping had him being tossed aside.

The Councilor had gotten up and was making his way toward the back of the jet. The doppelgänger was right behind him. Jean-Michel wasted no time.

"Don't touch him!" The Tasker yelled as he hit the sidewall and then was pushing himself up to run. He grabbed the creature backward and put himself between it and Gabriel. He felt Gabriel's hands on his back and shoulder.

Both men stood, shocked, as the doppelgänger finished shifting. Gone was the form of the flight attendant, replaced by a humanoid with gray-mottled skin and large almond eyes black as coal. Its impossibly long fingers curled into fists.

"Move around the cabin? Why? So you can study how I move when you take my soul? Well, I'll tell you, there's not much left of it, so good luck with that!" Jean-Michel spat. He motioned for Gabriel to keep going with his left hand, his right glowing with magic, ready to use.

"I am not here to take your souls. Doppelgängers do not do that. I am here to request an audience."

"Where is Roxanne?! Have you killed her?" Gabriel's eyes were enormous and one of his hands was still on his Tasker's shoulder.

"Gabriel—" Jean-Michel wasn't sure if it was there to hold him back or to make the human feel better. Why was the Councilor not locking himself in the back of the damn plane? That was protocol!

"She is not dead. We do not need to kill in order to take a form. She is, however, incapacitated." The long fingers came together in an inverted steeple at the creature's waist. "I want an audience and you want your ward's safety. We have the making of a compromise. For I will do no harm at this point if it will save more of my people from slavery or death."

Jean-Michel couldn't help the low-toned growl in his throat. It was instinctual, draconic, and a definite warning to the doppelgänger in front of him.

"I believe her, Jean," Gabriel whispered.

"I am not *her*, sir. We do not have gender. We simply take on that which is convenient." The doppelgänger backed up and continued, "Apologies. I almost forgot my etiquette. Your Tasker surprised me. In accordance with your method of speaking and writing names, I am Vanishte. Van-ISH-tay. Our actual designations are more of a telepathic aura than a verbal construct."

"Now you're worried about etiquette?" Jean-Michel scoffed. He remained between Gabriel and the would-be attacker.

"Am I to understand that you are one of those in the bar that my Tasker saw?"

"Yes, Mr. Kennedy, I am one of those from the bar," Vanishte responded. "But let me say before anything else passes that those at the bar did not harm a human to take those forms, either. The Council denied access to you previously. We felt forced to take matters into our own hands this time." The doppelgänger swallowed, the movement of the skin over the throat very pronounced. "That being said, it is a pleasure to meet you."

"You may think differently before this is all finished." Gabriel's attention then shifted back to his Tasker, who seemed an immovable force between himself and this being. "We can talk."

"You should get back to your seat, Tasker Raudine. My politeness only extends to a certain point, so please do us both the favor of not pressing past it."

"You call this polite? Threatening me?" he tossed back. "Gabriel, you have no need…"

"It's a five-hour flight and I don't intend to stand here in defense of all of it. Tasker, stand down. They want to talk. I'm available to listen." Gabriel squeezed Jean-Michel's shoulder.

Taking a deep breath, the Tasker glanced momentarily at Gabriel. "You sure?"

"Yes." Gabriel motioned for his Tasker to take the seat right next to him. As Gabriel passed, he muttered, "For someone that always has to have every damned thing in place, you couldn't keep your bag out of my way?"

"My bag was in its place. You're the one who's out of place, remember? You're never here." Gabriel's expression matched that of his Tasker, eyes narrowed.

Taking the offered seat across from them, Vanishte watched and listened to them, their head tilting just slightly while studying them.

"So, you're tracking me. Here we are. To what purpose? What do you need from me?" Jean-Michel watched as they nodded their grayish-skinned head once. There was no emotion to read. Reacting to nothing was difficult.

"There is much that we need, Ancient."

"Ancient?" Gabriel looked aside at his Tasker.

Jean-Michel saw the expression. Great. A dog with a bone. He tried to just move past the moment.

"Sorry, but I've not heard that designation in quite some time. You could almost say it's out of date. Or out of style." Either Vanishte would happily play fast and loose with his life or they were up to something else.

"Is it not warranted?"

"No, it is not," Jean-Michel replied.

"Tasker..." Gabriel tried and failed to get control back.

"Why are you here? Why did you come to me?"

"I am here with you because my people are trying to survive. We are being slaughtered or forced into servitude. We need your help. Surely you can have empathy for our plight?"

Jean-Michel had to stifle a growl. "From what I hear, doppels make quite a profit for their services. If you didn't want to be used, couldn't you just say no?"

"Enough!" Gabriel's voice got loud, and he turned to actually face his Tasker instead of the doppelgänger. "You are my Tasker. You are not a Councilor and therefore do not get to ask all the questions or make judgments. And none of us make judgments before we've even heard the case!"

Jean-Michel had to bite his tongue. How many times he had pulled Gabriel's grandfather out of stupid situations? He felt like they were repeating history. He wanted to point out that the doppelgänger had followed him instead of engaging with him. They had made their way onto this jet through underhanded means. They were speaking to the very Councilor who had already been investigating their kind! Who knew what this doppel might do to Gabriel if they had the opportunity? The dragon paused in his thinking. Why was he afraid for Gabriel's safety? If Kennedy got himself killed, all the better, right?

The Tasker acquiesced. He didn't move, but his every muscle was tensed and ready. What bothered him most was that the doppelgänger was taking it all in - every move and every silent decision. It was nerve-racking.

"Now," Gabriel turned in his seat and faced Vanishte again. "Go on."

"I would like to answer your Ancient. We have not allowed ourselves to be anything. Doppelgängers have had no choice other than to die or watch others die. You have killed and worked for humans rather than die. Why should you look down on doppelgängers? We are the same."

He huffed air through his nose and shook his head just slightly, but Jean-Michel didn't actually speak. He could feel Gabriel looking at him.

"We wanted to contact Jean-Michel Raudine first and, if possible, alone. I felt that since we are both creatures disenfranchised in this world, perhaps he would listen and help us. I did not expect Councilor Kennedy to show up, but it is a positive outcome. He was the next contact on my list."

"There are accords in place…" Jean-Michel felt his Councilor's glare.

Gabriel watched him. His brown eyes searching. Jean-Michel looked at the floor, his hands meeting and fingers entwining to keep himself calm.

"We cannot take up our own case in a world where Crimson has deemed us dangerous. There must be someone willing or a reason to make a case. So far, we have had neither. I have tried in your European Council and their guards escorted me back to the portal for my trouble."

"Then how are you here with us?" Gabriel asked.

"I…" Vanishte paused.

"You're here illegally, not with a visa? Not with a sponsor that allows for the time?" Gabriel waited for her to answer his question.

"We were legal until recently." Vanishte got up, a hand going where a pocket normally would have been on the left. Their fingers moved over the gray skin, and it opened up. Elongated fingers pulled out a packet of papers. "Proof that I was once a legal, temporary resident of this world. I simply remained instead of going through the portal once again."

Gabriel tried not to cringe. He reluctantly took the small packet of papers from them.

"I swore to help my people by getting us out of indentured servitude and slavery in the other realms and setting up guilds or treaties. We have come far, even if we manage much of our income in less than savory duties. Alas, we have no rights here and no one will help us get them."

When you could virtually become anyone you wanted, that opened a lot of doors. Raudine couldn't imagine staying legal if he had that ability. Even with a moral code, there was pragmatism to think about. Luckily for his enemies, he couldn't shift into just anyone. Doppels could. It said a lot that this one wasn't just using her given abilities to get what she wanted.

"The Crimson Council in Europe refused our petition. There were cases of doppelgänger sightings while we were convening. There were alleged murders. The European Council did not legitimize us here. They are so short-sighted..."

"Why do you say, short-sighted?" Gabriel's brown eyes rose from the paperwork.

"As your Ancient knows from experience, a being's willingness to be governed is based upon the contract the creature has with those in charge. A being will abide by the rules of the state so long as the state protects them and those they care about. With no protection or withheld protection, the incentive to abide by the world's laws and ethics..."

"They have no reason other than their own morality to abide by the rules of the state." Gabriel easily finished the statement. The doppelgänger brought their long fingers together and bowed their head once.

"If they do not have that morality in place, or people have driven their morality from them by using and abusing them, they can be lead down a path that is precarious for us all." Vanishte waited.

"I've received reports of doppelgänger sightings, and there have been two murders. They shot one of my own investigators."

"What?" Jean-Michel really had been out of the loop. He didn't get to ask, because Gabriel held up his hand to stop him.

"Derek's fine." Gabriel waited for the doppelgänger's response.

"I will not deny this. However, these acts of violence come from those outside of our group of diplomats."

"How are we, or Crimson, supposed to know that?" Gabriel sat forward to take a pen and notepad from the side pocket of the leather case his Tasker had tripped over.

"I would not do this if I were part of that group."

"I have studied both of you. You seemed most likely to help me should things go awry. Councilor Kennedy is known both for his capable defense and dogged prosecution in the Chamber. He has a reputation for being unbiased." They turned their attention to Jean-Michel, "You, well, we chose you for what we recognized you to be. Also, because you are Councilor Kennedy's Tasker."

"Why the subterfuge?" Jean-Michel tried to ignore that Gabriel had paused in his writing when Vanishte had mentioned recognizing him for what he was.

"We have had far too many doors slammed in our faces. To speak to you both uninterrupted, we needed your undivided attention for at least enough time to make our case. Luck was on my side."

"Well, we're both still listening. And if it makes you feel better, I'm no longer trying to figure out how to overpower you. So, there's that."

"I will take it." The doppelgänger made a hideous face, but Raudine kept himself from reacting as best he could. He imagined it was a doppelgänger's attempt at a full-on smile. Vanishte morphed in front of them to be the flight attendant again. Then, they became a professional man that could have rivaled Gabriel for his good looks. Then, they did so one more time to become a professionally dressed woman in chunky heels and an A-Line skirt. They might have walked straight out of a 1940s office building with perfectly coiffed chestnut hair and bright red lips.

"Your flight attendant is sleeping in her seat near the cockpit. Unlike the stories humans tell, we do not need to kill, to become. With time and experience, we learn. Or, we can take on the name of someone's long-lost relative... someone with no family, who died alone, and no longer needs their identity? Someone like Jean-Michel Raudine?"

The Councilor's eyes narrowed. The way the doppelgänger mentioned his Tasker had him curious.

Jean-Michel's eyes remained cold as he watched the doppelgänger.

"No offense intended, only an example needed. If they granted us a Councilorship, those who applied to travel here for a new life would have a proper place and registration. We could teach them properly. There would be rules and protection from the Judicial Council and Crimson Guard. You would take the power from people who use our kind. Those desperate to come here would have a legal method and not rely on dealing with villains. We ask for the rights that every other supernatural has."

"You know this means you'll have to be the one that makes the example. You'll have to be taken into Crimson custody as an illegal migrant who knowingly let their visa expire." Gabriel was in business mode. He was writing his notes while speaking to them. "Then I can make the case in your defense. When I win the case, I can move to add doppelgängers as an official member race to the Council and laws will need to be drafted with doppelgängers in mind."

"If you win..." Jean-Michel whispered.

"When. I've never lost a case," Gabriel continued to write his notes.

"He's saying you will get locked up." The Tasker grinned.

"I do not care, so long as our voices are finally heard. So long as I have come to you in time."

"In time?" the Tasker asked. Both men looked at one another and then back at the doppelgänger. "What do you mean by that?"

"Some are very willing to keep the present state of affairs as-is. They make a profit and they enjoy their lifestyle. There are still villains who prefer to keep things as-is as well. They have access to rogue doppelgängers. I believe if I do not stand before the Council soon to stop this, there may be no Council left."

Chapter 10
THE TAKING

"Why are we taking the place of the Weylyn guards?" The question came from a lycan named Monty as he walked with his fellow packmate. "Shebal, don't you find this odd? I mean, normally Jonas doesn't get as involved in all the politics."

"Things are changing a lot and I suppose I just trust Jonas to lead us properly. He's been on the level as alpha for over two centuries and since he's become Councilor, he's not been as mindful of other packs. I think maybe he's seeing that Pack Weylyn is getting a little big for their britches, maybe."

"Because they're used for Crimson Guards more? Ever think it was because the pack owns a security company?" Monty asked.

"Owned by Gabriel Kennedy. He also just tells that pack what to do and they do it. I don't like it. Maybe Jonas sees that too. I don't think it's a bad thing. I want the chance to be more and bring in more for Pack Airsight." Shebal paused and turned to look at his friend. "I mean, they're not even from this world and they get all the special treatment. Their Alpha ain't the Councilor and yet, he's always getting treated like his opinion is worth more. If you ask me, I think it's about time Jonas put a paw down."

"I guess I really never thought of it that way. I'm pretty content, but if I made a bit more, I could add to the pack money and also maybe buy my gal that pretty ring she's always wanted." Monty nodded, imagining giving sweet Klisa the ring she had seen in the magazine from the newsstand in town. "She kept the page from the magazine and she's been putting back money. She thinks I don't know, but she wants it. I want to get it for her, maybe set things up like the humans do... to ask her to be my mate."

"That sounds nice, Monty." He clapped his friend on the shoulder as they continued walking.

"What'll you do with the extra money?"

"I don't know. Marissa always wanted to go on a trip to the beach. I don't think she's ever seen the ocean. Maybe we can get the pups watched and just take off for a few days so she can dip her toes in the sand. If we schedule it right, we could do it for a full moon and maybe find a place and spread out a blanket and ...well..."

"How long've you two been mates?" Monty could see the Alpha's big log cabin not far away.

"Goin for 12 years. Jade is 10 and Landis is 7. Marissa still wants a baby girl, though. And I definitely don't mind tryin' for one." He chuckled as they made their way up to the cabin, but then heard Jonas' deep voice from the backyard. Shrugging, Shebal made his way around the side of the big cabin to an enclosed space. Monty was right behind him. When they got to the gate, they saw their Alpha and his Beta training with one another in a rounded ring drawn on the ground. The sunken back of the cabin was surrounded by foliage, so unless you came into it, you didn't really see a lot. The two hybrid-shifted lycan traded stances and moved on one another using the fighting skills of their kind.

When Jonas saw the two come into the yard, he growled over to his sparring partner and both shifted back to their human forms. They were two large men with braids on one side of their heads holding beads woven in opposite directions. Neither wore shirts nor shoes but had on their long shorts.

"Monty and Shebal, how are you both?" Jonas asked as he held his arm out in greeting. The two lycan reached forward one at a time to grasp arms with their Alpha.

"I think we're healthy and happy, Alpha. We're both looking forward to bein' considered for your guardian positions up at the big house." Shebal put his hands on his hips. "I already wear the Crimson uniform 3 days a week and Monty's gone through the training. He's ready for something new."

"Well then, I've talked to your elders and your mentors. You impressed them and they impressed me with what I've seen and heard. So, if you're looking for something new, I'm willing to take you on. I believe in giving my pack opportunities beyond the normal roles around here. It'll mean traveling to Whitley and staying for a few weeks at a time sometimes, but if you're willing to take that on and your families can handle it, it'll be rewarding." Jonas let his gaze move to the dark-haired lycan he'd been training with while talking to these two.

"Then we're your wolves. I got lots of experience, as you know, and Monty's mentoring began five years ago. We've both passed our Crimson training and exams."

"Best scores I've seen and best fight moves, too. You've both earned the promotion you're getting." Jonas smiled. He turned as if he were going to walk to the side. Then, in a flash of movement enhanced by his lycan reflexes and musculature, he whirled back around. His claws moved across the field of view at the necks of the two lycan before him. Blood gushed outward in an arterial shower of crimson red. He watched their faces become confused, and then they both fell over.

Jonas' eyes shimmered silver for just a moment. He tilted his head while studying the way the bodies jerked as if they were still fighting to heal and react. Did they know that they were dead?

Two doppelgängers emerged from the forested area behind the Alpha's home. As they strode forward, their gray forms melted and reformed into the forms of Monty and Shebal.

"They were happy on their end. Blissful, almost," the false Monty commented.

"Such dutiful creatures," the false Shebal agreed.

Jonas looked over the dagger he had in his hand. "Hmmm...slaying weapons. No healing from that. Expedient. Fascinating."

Chapter 11
Plan of Action

The Council or The Council of Crimson or Crimson Council – handled laws and judgments dealing with supernatural beings. They presided over all trade agreements and disagreements, all civil and criminal cases, and many other matters of probate in this world. There were three Councils separated by thousands of miles. Their locations were Okinawa, Paris, and Whitley. If what Vanishte proposed was true, disaster could ensue. It had to be well-orchestrated to reach all Councils.

Control of a Council meant control of everything that came through it. Infiltration might lead to unfair advantages, people's rights stripped, and people placed in danger. Gabriel couldn't have that. He'd seen it through his research on dragons – what had happened to them, The Culling.

Once the plane was on the ground, Gabriel was on the phone, doing his best to set things in motion. He was trying to make Director Skinner aware that this was an emergency and that Crimson should look into the situation with the doppelgängers. He did so by voicemail, unfortunately.

He then made calls to the Council Chamber line. There, the administrators would type up his requests and send them immediately to all Councilors. He wanted an emergency meeting, and he wanted it yesterday! The things that the doppelgänger Vanishte had told them were eye-opening, no doubt. He looked up from his phone to see that Jean-Michel had gathered his things from the table.

"Paeter Aderas on the Draconis?" Jean-Michel smirked as he shut down the tablet before Gabriel snatched it out of his hand. "That's quite some Dark Ages reading you've got yourself into there. You know most of those clergymen were half-drunk or bombed out of their heads on opium while they wrote things, right?"

"And you would know, right? Ancient?" Gabriel's left brow rose. He got what he expected – a silent glare.

"So what did you accomplish while we were getting to the terminal?" The Tasker changed the subject while the copilot went to the door to wait for the stairs to be attached.

"Well, I didn't please the Director with my interest in this situation before and he's not answering now. That's why I am determined to have this meeting." The Councilor's suspicious gaze shifted from his Tasker to the fake woman nearby and back. "So, I'm still working on it."

"She's fine," Jean-Michel whispered with a smirk.

"It would not be in my best interest to harm you, Councilor Kennedy. Though, by helping me, you may incur the wrath of the rogue doppelgängers that have, until this moment, not bothered you." Vanishte shrugged.

"That makes me feel so much better," Gabriel replied, the sarcasm obvious. Once released, the trio made their way down the staircase to the tarmac next to his jet's hangar, where he had parked his car.

"You need enough of the Councilors to allow it. Not a majority, but at least two others besides yourself. Minlial Nedian will work. If she's available on this side of the portal, and not handling Elven business in the other realm. Sebastian is always curious about your endeavors. He'd allow the meeting just to vote against you later..." Jean-Michel smirked.

"That doesn't sound appropriate..." Vanishte began.

"It was a joke. Sort of." Jean closed the door once they were in. He went around the SUV to get in the driver's seat.

"I can reach out to Minlial and plan to meet with her. We can discuss the matter in-depth," Gabriel agreed before frowning and continuing, "But I'm going to be short the fanged Councilor, so that won't work." Not that it would have worked, anyway. The vampire was detestable for being finicky about a vote.

"The best time for me to pull my maneuvers is while you're safe and sound at the Chamber. Once I have you both there, I can be on my way to further invest... Wait..." Raudine's eyes narrowed before he asked, "What do you mean you'll be short Sebastian?" He placed his hands on the wheel.

"It would seem that Councilor Evansworth can't keep himself out of trouble. He's had a long history of getting into trouble and apparently last night he wound up at the clinic. Dr. Keene just sent out a report." Gabriel was furiously texting.

Raudine swallowed that piece of information before starting the car and getting them on their way. Gabriel noted the shift in tension, but he wanted to let Raudine know the rest of the situation. His friend, Samantha, was in charge of the Councilor's care. What she said was not good.

"Whoever attacked him knew how to take out a pure-blood vampire from Sebastian's standing. That's not the only thing. She just reported Derek getting hit with a copper bullet earlier."

"Copper?" The surprise in the Tasker's voice was understandable.

"Yes, copper." Gabriel was on his phone, texting, still trying to contact the other Councilors or anyone else that could help push this forward. "Whoever is doing this, they're trying to kill people."

"Did you get in touch with Bastian? Or was this a report?" Raudine asked Gabriel.

"Dr. Keene. She gave me the details as a matter of my investigation while Evansworth was resting and recovering. She's a friend of mine. Otherwise, I wouldn't know anything. Crimson hasn't even released a report that it happened."

"I'll see what I can do about Evansworth," Jean-Michel volunteered.

"If it were a doppelgänger that attacked him, it may not thrill the vampire that we want asylum and councilorship," Vanishte concluded from the back seat.

"Well, to be clear, you still need to convince me of everything. I've been investigating these things on my own for a month and I'm not sure where I stand on this. We have a lot to work on you and I." Gabriel pointed out. He noted the way Jean-Michel gripped the wheel and the stiffness in his upper body. He'd volunteered to deal with Sebastian Evansworth. How deep were those ties?

None of his business? Vanishte had called Jean-Michel an Ancient. They had mentioned his kind were like the doppelgängers – taking on the identity of another being. Deep down Gabriel knew and yet, he feared the idea. All this time he had wanted Jean-Michel Raudine to give a shit and now he wondered if that was unwise.

"You okay over there?" Jean-Michel spared some quick side glances.

"Yes, I..." Gabriel realized he had stopped typing on his phone and had zoned out for a while. They were already close to the Council Chambers. This was no longer a state highway coming off of the airport, but the cut-through they often took to the city of Whitley when they were in a hurry. The farmland was beautiful this summer season.

"Get Devon to talk to Jonas. Maybe the lycan Councilor will listen to our concerns if it comes from another Lycan Alpha," Jean-Michel suggested. "As for Skinner, I wouldn't worry about him. His opinion doesn't matter as much in a Council Meeting. We need to focus on swaying Councilors this time – not Crimson."

"I already had Devon speak to Councilor Jonas, and it was pointless." Gabriel was getting frustrated. "No help from him. He's forbidden any lycan from assisting, which is why Devon and Derek are out of sight." Gabriel had never actually worked with his own Tasker like this before. So getting drilled by questions was something he was trying to incorporate as needed. "They tell me that a lycan can track any scent. Maybe they can help."

"But we doppelgängers have no actual scent. Our bodies do not produce the things that other creatures do as waste." Vanishte added from the back seat.

Both men looked to the rearview at the unexpected addition to the conversation.

"There are magical items available for that, or if we have the clothing of the person's body who we are mimicking, that is what you smell. If a doppelgänger is masking their lack of scent, your lycan will be of no use."

"I need to talk to Sebastian about his encounter." Jean-Michel's eyes focused on the road again.

"Experience may win over in other ways if magic is being used. Your kind embodies all the elements, Ancient. You might be of use?" Vanishte supplied.

Jean-Michel pulled through the backside of a large fenced-in complex off of the main road for the Whitley Industrial Park. Pulling up to the gate, he typed in a number and then placed some fingers against the monitoring technology. The gate opened, and he continued through the field of summer growth of upland cotton and alfalfa.

"So, we need to find out where and how they're getting in. It's obviously not through a sanctioned portal." Jean's eyes once again looked into the mirror at Vanishte. "And you're sure you don't know who they are?"

"I do not, Ancient."

"Don't call me that. A man has his pride. I'm Tasker or Jean-Michel Raudine. Take your pick."

"Of course, Tasker." Vanishte bowed their head slightly.

"I guess the most important thing for you to worry about right now is getting at least two Councilors on your side and available." They pulled up to the front of a large castle-like red-brick structure. He reached into the glove box to pull out something.

Gabriel saw it and asked, "Is that really necessary?"

"Yes," was the only answer he'd get. The Tasker got out and went to Vanishte's door. "Be ready for the Elven Councilor. Lady Minlial Nedian is at least as old as me, if not older. So she will be a formidable ally, but she'll want her questions answered first." He opened the door for the doppelgänger. Then he turned and placed the anti-magic cuffs on the being.

Vanishte did not shift back to their gray-skinned self once the cuffs were on. Gabriel found his voice, finally. "Why don't you shift when he uses the cuffs?"

"Why, Councilor, our abilities are not limited by magic. Our abilities are physical and mental manipulation of energy, which differs from the standard." Vanishte walked where the Tasker directed them; toward the side entrance of the Council Chamber building.

"I'll hand them off, and you get to do your duty to represent not only Vanishte but their entire species' rights to be here, Gabriel. No pressure."

Gabriel silently absorbed what his Tasker had said. However, as they walked toward the entrance, he couldn't help but go back over something that was actually more important to him.

As old as an elf? No... that's not how Jean-Michel had phrased it. She's at least as old as me...

The Tasker made the comment without thinking; offhandedly. Gabriel's theory about Jean-Michel being a dragon was not getting any weaker, was it?

Chapter 12
In the Clinic

It took a while before Sebastian Evansworth was conscious enough to realize he was not alone in the room. He was still in the same room the doctor had left him in. He could still smell the disinfectant and hear the vents blowing the trash can liner around. But then, there was that scent, that breathing. Of course. His past had come back to not haunt him. Instead, it was harassing him.

"I already reported the attack, so why are you here?" Sebastian's sleep-graveled voice asked.

"It's my prerogative to check on you with my own senses." It was not as cold a tone as the vampire had used. Jean-Michel stepped closer, scanning the place where the wound was mending. "Silver? They prepared..."

Sebastian opened his eyes and faced the Tasker. "Almost sounds like you care." He couldn't help but spit the words at the other man.

"Mmm.. but you know better, right?" Jean-Michel chuckled. His blue-green eyes were piercing when surrounded by near darkness.

Sebastian pushed himself up from his position. He winced at the burn he felt where the wound was still seeping. It'd been so since being wounded in battle. Was he healing slower than he normally would?

"Don't do that. You'll hurt yourself." The Tasker almost reached out, but Sebastian's fierce glare made him rest his hand on the bar on the side of the bed.

"What do you want?" Painful or not, the shift was necessary to put space between them. The Tasker was no longer leaning over him, and that made the vampire more comfortable.

"You told Crimson you were attacked. You didn't tell Crimson what attacked you. Crimson hasn't even released details to the Councilors, yet. So, what actually happened?"

"It isn't every day you get to stare yourself in the eyes and then fight for your life. The term doppelgänger was literal." It had been disturbing, to say the least.

"That took balls. They thought they had you. What made them so confident, Bastian? Losing your menacing, intimidating swagger?" There was a curl to the side of his lips as he poked at the vampire's ego.

Sebastian finally let his gaze go to Jean-Michel. Damn, but he didn't like being this close to the man. The scent brought back a million memories, some of a heartache worse than death.

"Or perhaps he didn't have time to study your past?"

"Well now, unlike some people, I don't hide my past. So if he didn't know me, he was definitely lazy, eh?" He cleared his throat. This place was too dry. "He was also covered in magic."

"Covered in magic? That's what you just said. How so?" Jean tilted his head slightly, a brow raised and his attention wholly engaged.

"I could feel the disjointed energy. Several kinds. I imagine he had several items on him." The vampire's eyes closed as he leaned more onto his uninjured side. "But there was no scent. I take it that's a doppelgänger...thing?" He took another breath and cleared his throat before asking, "Anything else, or are we finished?"

"I need you to get better." The Tasker took a deep breath when the vampire's eyes narrowed. Sebastian knew that expression all too well. He watched as Jean-Michel took a deep breath. "I need you to be the voice that will sway the Council to an emergency meeting concerning the doppelgängers. Kennedy has been collecting information, evidence, and witnesses to prove that there is a genuine problem here. Skinner doesn't care. There may be people in Crimson using them, Bastian. They tried to take you. -They may try to take over the Council – all of it."

"Do you understand how ridiculous you sound?" Sebastian coughed and cleared his throat again. He felt the pain around his wound and shivered as he forced himself not to react.

"How close did this one get to finishing you? And this one was supposedly sloppy and lazy? So...what if the others aren't?

Magic. Covered in it? What if the others are, too? How long before more Councilors get taken, and a majority of those seats belong to doppelgängers or whoever brought them here? One person could be in charge of all the decisions governing supernaturals in this world. Who might end up on the blacklist next?"

"And the emergency meeting...is to handle this?" Sebastian felt the truth of the Tasker's words to his soul. Both of them knew what it felt like to be hunted. They'd both lost their families before. They'd both sought vengeance with one another's help. But Jean-Michel was correct. So far, the dragon was the only one that Crimson could kill on sight. Sebastian didn't like that, but at least it was just one group so far. "What does that Councilor of yours intend to do?"

"Gabriel has a doppel in voluntary custody. He's going to argue for their right to remain in this world despite their visa being expired. He's going to use the case to go further and have them released from the list of restricted species. That gives them the same rights and responsibilities to the laws as everyone else."

"What? For the doppelgängers?!" Wiping his forehead, the vampire turned to the opposite side of the bed so that his feet were on the floor. At least he still had his shoes on. And his pants.

"I know it sounds like you would do this for the sake of your attacker, but you're not." Raudine took a step back. "The one that came to us, they had a legal visa, came here legally, and want to make sure there is a process for them. That way, there's no need to go about hiding. There's no reason to replace public figures in important positions because someone offered them protection."

"What you're saying is ridiculous." He wanted to laugh – to scoff at the idea! He couldn't believe it! "In case you forgot, let me remind you I was just attacked by one. You just told me they may infiltrate the Council, and you want me to do what, exactly?"

"Oh, come on, Bastian. You know political strategy better than me. You can't see this?" Jean-Michel's eyes and voice were pleading.

"Apparently not. Why give them rights and what? A place on the Council, too? Why do all of that when they can change into any being they want to be? That's why they are too dangerous to be here, to begin with! Do you have scales for brains now?"

"I knew this was going to be difficult." Senias blew a breath through his nose.

"I'm not partial to being kind and helping any doppelgängers considering my circumstances, Jean." He put his hands on each side of him, flat on the bed. How could the man think he'd want to do anything that gave these creatures more power?

"What if it's him? Skinner? What if he's finally found a way to do what he's always wanted to do? Can you imagine what would happen if he were in charge of not only Crimson but the main Council as well? And what if he's using the doppelgängers for the other Councils, too? All he'd need is a majority in this Council, in the Paris Council, Okinawa? That's what? 4 in each...20?"

"He couldn't do it alone. You're being paranoid. Besides, he may already have that just off of shady deals. How do we know?" Sebastian couldn't believe this. He'd already have been gone if he felt like he could do it. As it was, he was fighting off nausea and dizziness.

"Statistically impossible. Most people despise him. If they seek freedom from their own places, where they're being hunted? If they're desperate enough? He'd just have to give them free passage to this side. Getting yourself or your family away from death would be worth a kill and time clocked pretending to be a powerful Councilor. The one we've got in custody told us they don't have to kill to emulate, by the way."

"Obviously, they don't mind doing it, though."

"The one who volunteered seems to not want any of them to kill. But because they have no reason to go by the laws..." Jean-Michel took a deep breath. "The point is, just because they can do these things, doesn't mean they will."

"Sen...Jean. They played you! Don't you get that?" Sebastian shoved his hand through his tangled hair, trying to get it out of his face.

"Being able to empathize with someone isn't being played by them..."

"Keep telling yourself that."

"If they have a reason not to be violent because they have a voice in a governing body that also protects them? If they can stay here using the same rules or a modification of the rules for everyone else? There is no reason for them to do underhanded things for underhanded people."

"Is that what you've been doing? Doing underhanded things for underhanded people? Will restoring your rights stop you?"

"I..." Jean-Michel hesitated.

"Mmmm..." Sebastian shook his head. He noted the Tasker moving around the foot of the bed toward him. The vampire looked at the monitor as his heart rate went up. He needed to get up. Jean-Michel's scent brought back memories that threatened to make this even more difficult.

"There's no incentive to break the law if they get all of their rights. So, yes, it's close to my circumstances. Maybe that's why I wanted to help."

"And you think Skinner's involved?"

"They have hope to come here and start new lives and it is absolutely Skinner's M.O. to use them in exchange for the opportunity. If he no longer has this to hold over their heads or his protection to offer..."

Sebastian realized the dragon was speaking about more than just doppels. But he was also getting too close. The vampire stood up quickly to get more space. He swayed on his feet, his hands went to the counter to help with balance.

"Didn't the doctor treat you?" Jean-Michel asked. He walked over to help steady the vampire, his voice growing warmer, almost pleading as he asked, "Bastian, you're weakened by the wound. Please let me donate or take blood from me..."

The vampire turned sharply to lean back against the counter to further distance himself from Jean-Michel. "Don't! Don't you dare act gentle and concerned! You left! You proved to me that I didn't need anything from you then, and I don't need anything from you now!" The burning sensation in his side was growing. He turned away from Raudine only out of desperation.

The Tasker's hands went up in surrender and he nodded. "Right," his voice was strained.

Sebastian's own magical glamor was wavering. Before the Tasker's eyes, the vampire's skin paled and swirling intricate markings ghosted the skin of his entire posterior body. His markings were natural. But the scars? Cutting scars and whipping scars – they were on his chest, his back, and even one down the front of his face that left his left lip disfigured.

Jean-Michel stepped back, his eyes filled with emotion at seeing those scars. And Sebastian saw it. Momentarily, the vampire felt vindicated.

"Yes. This is what you let Crimson do to me. You left. And I paid for our crimes. But you should know that...huh... Tasker? I didn't get to sleep it off as you did. Take a good look. And you think I give a damn about doppelgängers? Or you?"

"Those scars are all the more reason to give a damn, Bastian! Skinner allowed that to happen to you because he couldn't find me. What do you think he'll do if he has control of all the Councils?"

"You unbelievable, selfish bastard!" The vampire grimaced and held his side. "If you're done, you can leave!"

Chapter 13
The Good Doctor

Jean-Michel did what Sebastian wanted him to do. He continued to make his way to the door.

The vampire ripped the bandage from his wound to expose the neat stitches. They hid angry skin. He started pulling drawers open, looking for what he needed.

The Tasker turned from the opened door to call back the nurse and ask for help, only to find himself face-to-face with the short, blonde doctor.

"Get out!" The doctor ordered, before taking the Tasker's arm and yanking him the rest of the way out the doorway to the two security personnel. She ignored him after that to march herself into the room with her patient.

"What the hell are you doing?" Dr. Keene tried to figure out what to handle first.

Hearing the doctor's question, he immediately focused on his magic, his skin appearing more normalized to her.

"I'm going to open... the stitches." The vampire was snarling. "There's still silver inside... somewhere." His fangs were out despite his desire to control himself. "I can't wait any longer, Sunshine. It's going to kill me."

"There was no silver left in the actual wound when I finished." Sam came over to him and began pushing him back to the hospital bed. If he was still weak, she could handle him. "Get on the bed and I'll get an antihistamine ready. I'll order more blood."

"Leave off!" He stumbled and snarled at the same time he reached out to regain his balance. Sebastian tried to push off the irritating doctor. "I'll get it... taken care of."

"Get in the bed! You can't do this by yourself! Let someone who gives a damn try to help you." The metal table went crashing as he struggled, but she wouldn't back off. Not when it might cost him his life.

As the room spun, Sebastian kept his hand covering the stitches as the other reached to grab hold of the bed's edge. He felt like he was falling – and falling. Was this going to be it?

"I took the weapon to the lab while you had a sneaky visitor. I believe you're suffering nitrate or sulfate poisoning." Sam had apparently decided the bullying tactic wasn't working. She began using scientific facts. "Whoever attacked you knew to be ready for vampires and used something they knew all of you were allergic to – not just silver." There was recognition in the vampire's eyes.

"Let go so I can treat it." Her eyes went from being irritated to being truly concerned. "Please, Sebastian, let me help you. Don't make me stand here and watch you die."

Finally relenting, the vampire sat on the bed and leaned back on his elbows so that he could watch everything that the doctor did. As a scientist himself, Sebastian was interested in how she'd go about doing this. The old warrior side of him was on guard in case what she intended was to end his life instead of saving it.

Turning, Sam grabbed a power gun from the side cabinet and loaded it with a specialized substance that would help. They had combined the idea of an EpiPen with the needs of the supernatural. It was what her research had always been about.

"What are you intending with that?" Sebastian tensed when he saw the instrument in her hand.

"It's what I call an antidote to your poisoning, combined with an antihistamine, to calm your body's reaction. Be still. This'll hurt less."

The injections hadn't been horrid. He'd suffered worse in his long life. But what she'd put into him made the warmth in his body feel like acid. Every muscle in his body went rigid and his breathing became erratic as he fell back against the bed.

"What... did..." His body shook as he tried to hold still and breathe through it. "I need home." Sebastian tried to roll to his side to climb from the bed. If he was going to truly die, he wanted to do so in his own bed... not here.

"It's okay. You'll be okay. I know what I'm doing. This stuff works. You have my word. I won't let anything else happen to you. Just let the drug do its job." Her upper body held him in place.

The facade he kept over himself at all times wavered more. His body needed that energy to fight the poison running through his veins. Deep scarring was now visible on his upper arm and shoulder that ran to his back. The dark markings that swirled over his porcelain-hued skin returned as well. It was just a momentary glimpse before Sebastian realized she could see it.

"Don't stare at me!" He gave a low growl and with a quick swipe of his hand, the vampire caused the lights to go out. The entire room went dark and quiet. There was only their breathing. The doctor had grabbed his free wrist and had her hand pressed to his chest at his heart.

"Don't fight. I just want you to relax. Things will calm down inside of you soon." She felt him take a deep breath and then he relaxed more. Samantha found that her own breath had quickened. Pulling her hands back, Sebastian didn't move, so she grabbed the sheet back to help cover him up. "Here, it might make you feel better. I focused on treating you and forgot how old you might be. I apologize."

"Please, no lights." Easing back on the bed as the sheet settled over him, Sebastian drew in a steadying breath. "I won't fight, just…" His body was easing. Whatever she had shot him up with was working.

"It's just the medication moving through your bloodstream that hurts. I haven't figured out how to stop that, yet. But I will. Just a little more research." The doctor conducted herself cautiously to check his pulse despite the darkness.

Sebastian watched her with his reddish gaze, and his voice lost its commanding edge.

"Thank you, Dr. Keene. I appreciate your help." It wasn't often that the Coven Master found himself in another's debt, but this might be the case. He wondered if she realized it, as he let her check him over. She'd earned some respect.

"It's what I do. What I've always enjoyed doing." She grinned before walking over to the cabinets to turn on an under counter light. It kept Sebastian in partial shadow. Then she picked up everything that Sebastian had dumped on the floor.

"Keep us calm, and the beast will remain dormant. Remember that above all else when treating our kind, Dr. Keene."

"I've had human patients get more out of hand than you just did, Lord Evansworth," she pointed out. She picked up the last thing and placed the tray on the counter to be sent to sterilization. Turning to look at him, she added, "Your inner animal just seems a bit more frightening than a human's – at least to most people. Lucky for you, I'm not like most people."

"Oh, I was still in control, Dr. Keene. Trust me when I say that you do not have adequate enough staff to detain or contain me should I truly lose control." He sat up slowly on the side of the bed again.

"Not too fast. You don't need to go down from dizziness." She placed a hand on his thigh. "And I never said you lost control. I just said you didn't get out of hand."

"I pray the day never comes that you should have to handle such."

"Too late." Sam backed off, though she continued to smile. The brightness of the expression dulled. "I have a scar further down on my arm. It's not near as impressive as your scar, but it reminds me to never be disrespectful of the power a vampire has. That and I have a quirky bunch of aches that come from my leg sometimes. It's where the one that attacked me dislocated my hip. I wasn't going down without a fight. I'm pretty sure they would've ripped it off had that Tasker not been on alert." She backed up from him. "May I ask what your scars and other markings signify?"

His brows rose at the mention of his markings. Sebastian stared down in wonder at them, down the outer skin of his arms. They were definitely present, and Dr. Keene could see them. Clearing his throat, he did something he really didn't make a habit of doing; he gave in to her curiosity.

"My scars are mostly from battle. One or two were from fighting otherwise." His voice was much softer than it had been. "The markings are unique to every vampire. I know they look to humans like black or dark-colored reddish tattoos. Some swirls and designs in it show the family we belong to, but otherwise, they are unique to each, like a fingerprint in some ways. When we take a Chosen, we share our markings with them." Clearing his throat, he asked, to be sure, "You see, the scrolling black markings?"

"They're striking; beautiful – like ever-flowing henna but darker, almost tribal. I've never seen them before in other vampires. Maybe they weren't purebloods?" Samantha was honestly forcing herself not to touch them. Instead, she took the bag of blood from her smock to place it in his hand. "Type O? I believe it was your request?"

"Uh, no thank you." Sebastian handed the cold bag back to her. "Call me a snob, but I wholeheartedly dislike bagged blood. Thanks to you, I'm not dying anymore. So, since I have plenty of volunteers willing to feed me at my home, when can I get my clothes back?"

Chapter 14
EXCUSES

Ezekiel knew that Scott Proctor needed to have an update before someone else reported the mishap in the back alleys. So he called the man, but wound up leaving a short message. When he felt the vibration from his phone, the Director of Crimson wasted no time in answering. He stepped into an empty side hall.

"I just wrapped up the final case for the day, and saw the missed call. Things have become messy. Care to explain now or would you prefer to do so in person over a stiff drink?"

"I can't get a stiff drink until later. So, it depends on what you can wait on, Scott. I'm dealing with an AWOL Tasker and the situation you're probably talking about."

Ezekiel could hear the door shutting on a car and the whir of the motorized partition.

"I have things under control."

"Do you, Ezekiel?" There was a deep exhale that was slower than most likely expected from him given the situation. "All the recent occurrences say otherwise. If things continue as they are I'll have Emriess there to tie up loose ends for you."

Scott Proctor was a very powerful, very successful and very influential male. Ezekiel understood that it never bode well for those that got on the man's bad side. Emriess was his daughter and even more wicked. He and those connected to him had the power to either make or break people.

"The Paris Council got rid of the legal doppels. Pressure was put where it needed to be placed and that loose end will be handled. The others will be here in another day. They have their orders. One got seen, not caught. I've assured people that it's an anomaly, a coincidence. Nothing more. So long as you let this situation play out, we can get hold of who we need to get hold of. I just need to make sure my dog remembers his chains." Ezekiel's words spoke more to *Mr. Proctor* than anything else could. "Now, I have fronts and aliases to keep up before my next meeting rolls around. I just wanted to reassure you that the situation is being taken care of before my detractors tell you otherwise. So, if you'll excuse me, *sir*."

"Well, detractors can often reveal more than you think. I couldn't agree with your actions more. It is of great import that such reminders are made *Director Skinner*. After all, replacing your dog is absolutely impossible, but he shouldn't be allowed to think his actions have gone unnoticed. Just because one is irreplaceable doesn't mean he isn't expendable."

Ezekiel Skinner silenced his phone and took a moment. Scott Proctor had just reminded him of his place as well. The Director took some breaths to hold his temper and keep his control. He wasn't a pawn…more like a bishop. But how far would he go to protect the king? Some king… Proctor didn't understand his own precarious position. Far be it for a bishop to remind a king about the dangers around him.

Putting his phone away, he turned the corner into the next hallway in the old college building. Taking a deep breath, he walked into the next classroom. All of the students watched him and moved from their various social perches to take their seats. Skinner looked over the class, wondering what to expect. He hated this part of his job. But here he was – babysitting actual students for a Tasker whose identity was a college professor at Whitley University. One had to keep up appearances for the mundanes. And since their base was beneath the college itself, why not?

He had been here almost as long as the college and those that worked in the shadows alongside Crimson had been here just as long. So, this was his home. He had to make it work.

"So, we've got all of this due?" the cute blonde from the middle aisle asked. She then blew a loose strand of her hair from her face, as if that would get it out of the way. None of them seemed pleased. But they were a bunch of entitled children. He could readily pick the ones that were here on mommy's or daddy's dime from the ones that actually had skin in the game.

Skinner looked forward to being here the day these morons got the full-fledged joy of meeting their professor. Professeur Raudine, the competent teacher, had become a bit of a legend. Within the history and anthropology departments, he was a favorite.

Outside of this, most students were warned to avoid him. He turned dull subjects into exciting learning experiences.

One student had written in the rate-my-professor reviews, "... this guy blew me away. It was like he had been there! Only he was teaching it." Raudine's background within the annals of Crimson history took him back pretty damned far. He probably had been there.

"You have a small 2,000-word report due by Friday on any religious topic you choose that falls within the time of 300 BCE to 10 CE. You have the week ahead to read the assigned book, which is only what? 135 pages? Professeur Raudine will want you to have a good grasp of the reading material so that you can discuss it. My suggestion would be to write 10 questions you come up with while you read it, so when he gets back, you actually sound like you did something."

"But that's not on the online syllabus," the dude in the front row pointed out.

"No, that's just my suggestion. It couldn't hurt. Especially if you want a good grade." And again, he could definitely tell the entitled from those who were here for an education.

"So we don't have to do anything but turn in the essay by Friday?" the same guy in the front row, now scratching his head, asked.

Mr. Skinner stood up and looked out over the 30 students in this old college room. It was time for honesty.

"Look, you took this class for various reasons. You had no choice, saw it as an opportunity to get credits while learning, or you did not know what you were getting into. I would suggest you take this week to do the best you can to either put forth the effort it'll take for you to finish this class with good marks or beg your way out of it." Ezekiel let the stack of syllabi hit the table in front of him.

"As the Dean of the Anthropology Department, I can tell you that your professor in this class is worth your effort. If you show the least bit of interest in a topic, he'll be happy to explore it with you and your mind will be broadened by the time."

He then took out a pad of green paper with the title DROP/ADD at the top of it.

"Of course, if you plan on putting forth the minimal effort, you should probably rethink this one." He sat down at the desk and pulled out an expensive pen. "If you're still interested, the syllabus is there. Take one and leave. If you want out, come to the desk and I'll give you a Drop Form."

The lines began.

Twenty minutes later, Skinner was walking back to his office when he felt a familiar presence.

"Well?" Jean-Michel asked from behind him.

"You have 18 left. The syllabus always takes out at least a quarter. Then, I suppose after your first lecture…"

"Why did you want him dead?"

Ezekiel Skinner turned to look at the bedraggled Tasker. He cleared his throat before replying, "This is not the place. You know that. Or at least, somewhere in that brain of yours, you know this is not the place." The steel-haired man looked around, scanning the area for any passers-by. It was late and so perhaps there would be no witnesses.

"You heard me," Jean-Michel looked as though he were about to bolt forward when the other man's hand moved outward, his fingers spread, palm down. Symbols of ancient mages appeared on the ground in pale green-colored light. There was a flash emanating from those symbols as if a camera had just taken a picture.

When next their eyes could focus, they were in a contained training room, equipment against the walls and mats on the floor. People were around but at the periphery. It was the area set aside in the Crimson base beneath Whitley University, and Ezekiel knew the Tasker understood. He tossed the briefcase aside.

"If you insist." Ezekiel took off his jacket and tossed it aside, leaving him in his suit pants, shirt, and suspenders. He began rolling up his sleeves, looking a lot like a man from the '40s readying up for a street brawl. "You need to have a fight. Let's fight, shall we?"

"He was just a kid." Jean-Michel lunged. Equally quick counters met the flurry of hits and then Skinner shoved a burst of energy between them. The Tasker went flying backward. He rolled and was up in a crouched stance immediately.

"And that kid was a liability. You know that. Those wretches had turned him. He was weak, but he gave us a moral reason to eliminate the dregs in that nest. They were bound to be found out soon. Had you not cleaned the lair, a pureblood would have done it for us. Would you have preferred that?" Skinner moved forward and leaped to Raudine's side.

The Tasker grabbed the Director but failed in his plans. The Director wrapped his legs around his opponent's midsection and forced his weight backward to take the Tasker off balance.

Jean-Michel growled and used pressure points to send pain searing through Skinner's legs. The man released his hold so the Tasker could grab the front of his opponent's shirt to lift him.

"That kid was a human. Since when do you give two shits about humans?"

"I don't, it was just..." Jean-Michel clenched his teeth and turned to throw Skinner across the room.

Skinner chuckled as he slowly got up and wiped the blood from his mouth.

"Wasn't sporting enough for you? You and your vampire friend handled the deaths of thousands of humans, maybe even millions. Who knows - since it all happened hundreds of years ago and it'd take a very long time to compile all of those numbers from all of those wars you started and took part in. Hell, I know for a fact you were involved in keeping the Hundred Years War going. That's what, 2 million? Closer to 3 million? So yeah, millions. And how many of those deaths were just...kids? Did any of them wrong you?" Ezekiel brushed back some of his silver hair out of his face to join the rest of his stringy, shoulder-length mane.

"Shut it..."

"I didn't think so. You can't condemn me with a chalice of blood when you've bathed in a pool of it." The Director scoffed. "Anything else you want to bitch about or hit me for?"

"Evansworth." The two men circled one another, both looking ready to pop into offense at the drop of a hat. There were other Crimson agents gathering to watch outside the ring.

"What about the fang? Is he not alive and kicking, just like you wanted, Raudine? My part of the traded vows was easily enough fulfilled. Yours is… well…" Ezekiel watched the forward shift of the Tasker, but he over-prepared his defense. Instead of trying for a tackle, Jean-Michel's hands were on the ground, and his feet came in for a good slam into the Director's cheek. Skinner pivoted back with the first hit and dodged out of the way before he took the next shot from the Tasker's other foot.

As Jean let his body lead, he was up in almost a flip and turning already to land a swing. The movements were fluid, graceful, and almost dancer-like. When Skinner backed off, he went directly into a kick. The Director took the hit to the kidney, not making it to his next counter in time. He grunted and rolled forward with the hit. As he did so, he called forth arcane energy into his hands.

"Ye fockin' cheat!" the enraged Tasker yelled.

"ENOUGH!" The Director pushed the energy forward, and a greenish-gold light that exploded from his palms hit the Tasker in the chest. The energy staggered Jean-Michel, then wrapped around him, holding him like someone tied in a rope and hanging mid-air.

"Cheatin' bastard…" the Tasker struggled against the magical energy surrounding his body.

Director Skinner tucked his shirt and rubbed his lower back before turning to their audience. "Leave."

He didn't have to yell, and he didn't have to say it twice. Everyone vacated the training room and, with a twist of his hand and snap of his fingers, all the doors closed and locked.

"Why do you never fight me with magic, Raudine? We both know you're supposedly capable. Just like me. Perhaps not as powerful, but the question stands."

"I don't know Zeke, maybe I like to fight like a proper gentleman." He struggled against the magical bindings, the veins in his head bulging and his nostrils flaring as he did so.

"You? A gentleman? How much have you had to drink, monsieur? You are most assuredly not a gentleman." Skinner paced casually in front of the Tasker, his eyes studious. "What about the fang? Why are you upset about him? He was alive and full of piss and vinegar last I spoke to him."

"A doppelgänger attacked him – and I have it on good authority that you don't want to investigate the damned things. I've kept my vow for you...doing things for you. You should be keeping Sebastian safe. You're putting him in danger." Finally, Jean-Michel gave in. He closed his eyes and concentrated. A shimmering mist of magical energy soon enveloped him and the bindings holding him dissipated, allowing him to land on his feet before the Director.

"Better. I knew I could get you to use magic." Ezekiel grinned. "I didn't put him in danger, Raudine. He put himself there. I agreed to his freedom and his position for your services. I never said I would then protect the fool. If he wants to take strolls by himself in the dark, that's on him. He reported the incident. And I never said I wouldn't investigate the situation. I've just not gotten to it. I have aliases to keep up with, and I also have to cover for you. My assignment shouldn't have taken you so long. You should have been back here to your beginning class."

"Now? After an attack on a Councilor? Why not when Kennedy first contacted you?"

"I refuse to be ordered around by another Kennedy. You should understand how annoying they can be. You've been the Tasker of a Kennedy several times over." He walked up to Jean-Michel and straightened the man's shirt lapels before taking a solid step back.

"You have a face to keep up. You were supposed to report for your beginning classes today, and you did not. I covered for you – again. But it's not my job. We all have our parts to play, Professeur Raudine. Play yours. If you don't, I no longer have to play mine." He walked back to his jacket while the Tasker stewed on those words.

"As I was saying," he made his way slowly over to pick up his briefcase as well. He reached into the side of that case while moving over to Jean-Michel. "You have 18 students left in this one class you have to teach this summer semester. I've given you an excuse for a week. I expect you to be back on schedule and handling your alias to keep it in good standing after that. And when I task you to do something, you do it. You do it without question." Ezekiel handed over the green slips. "Otherwise, you'll build bad blood between us." He wore an expression of mock concern before smacking Jean-Michel lightly on the shoulder. "Bad blood isn't something either of us wants or needs. Is it?"

Jean-Michel didn't answer. Ezekiel noted the snarl on the man's face and he sneered right back.

"I get why you won't admit the truth, but remember, I know your truth. And just like I made you use your magic, I can make you reveal yourself. Then your scaly tail really will be on the line." Jean-Michel's eyes did not leave the Director.

"Get a shower, change, and for gods' sakes, brush your damn teeth," the Director of Crimson snapped his fingers. The doors unlocked and opened for him. "Oh, and don't challenge me again, Raudine."

Chapter 15
FIGURING THINGS OUT

Gabriel's mind urged him to stay in the Chamber library to research, listen, and review everything that had recently transpired. Therefore, after Devon and Vanishte had left, he'd ordered fresh coffee and closed himself off. Soon, he had a hot cup in his hand and Johann Pachelbel's "Canon in D major" playing low over the speakers on repeat. Gabriel Kennedy strolled around the large table, his hands usually clasped behind him. He was methodically studying the various files that were neatly laid out across its well-polished top. He scooted two of the files to match those beneath them perfectly. Everything had its place.

Down to his dress shirt and slacks, Gabriel paced, thought, read, made notes, and paced some more. He continued on even past the wall clock's chimes, announcing that they were moving into the later part of the night. His hand ran through his dark hair again and again in agitation as he scoured through the scrolls and books. Anything with information on doppelgängers or shapeshifters was open in one long column on the table. He made another column for creatures able to create portals. They were in order of relevance. He lifted a photograph of a doppelgänger, then placed it back down above the book he had last been reading.

It seemed as if he'd been at this for hours, but he couldn't get the pieces of this puzzle to fit together. Adding to his headache? The puzzle that was Raudine. He was an enigma that had been in Gabriel's life... all along? Jean-Michel had also been his grandfather's Tasker. According to Vanishte, Jean-Michel was a guide to his family for at least a century. So what did that make him? He had considered the man a sorcerer, much like one councilor known as Iscariot. He had magic in his blood, which prolonged his life. But the doppelgänger had added a piece to this puzzle by calling Jean-Michel an Ancient. Vanishte had called Jean his Ancient. What did that mean?

His knuckles popped against the top of the table while he looked over the pages open in front of him. He had turned to pages with sketches of what a doppelgänger looked like. The artist and author drew eerily accurate sketches in a book dating from 1799. And another, a book much older, was something his own ancestors had written. On the main page, the author painted his family coat of arms on the parchment. But surrounding the standard were two dragons made of Celtic knotwork. The book detailed the magical processes of finding and controlling dragons. He hadn't turned the pages.

Gabriel pinched the bridge of his nose.

Dragons. Yes. That's what he had landed on time and time again. And now, it was more important that he knew what he was dealing with. Especially considering the secretive relationship his Tasker had with Director Skinner. How much could he trust someone who lied about who he was?

And then he paused, back stiffened while gazing into a bureau case window. There was the mirror-like image of himself looking right back. Didn't he still lie about who he really was? Hadn't he been doing so since the 90s? AIDS was still on everyone's lips when he was going into the academy. It was still okay to be resentful and make jokes about gay people – even on national television. His father resented his illnesses. What would he have done had he realized his son was also gay? Things had changed, but...those memories still locked Gabriel's truth from seeing the light of day.

So how could he judge Jean-Michel? Perhaps his Tasker didn't really trust him.

He heard the Council Chamber door open, so he began putting away the books on dragons and trying to gather his notes.

"Put the fresh pot on the table and order up some breakfast," he called over his shoulder.

"Do I look like your servant, Councilor Kennedy?" Jean-Michel spoke, his voice deep and gruffer than normal. He was taking the stairs down into the table area two at a time. The man had freshly washed and wore nice clothes. "Though, I admit, coffee would be welcome at this point... along with whiskey."

"Coffee and breakfast are all you'll be getting." Gabriel returned to his work. He tried nonchalantly closing several of the books. He flipped his notes over.

"It's too early for breakfast. It's party time... club time... whatever it's called these days." Jean-Michel came to the table.

"Seeing as I don't party or catch the club scene much, I'll stick with breakfast." Gabriel lifted his cup and drank down the lukewarm dregs of his last coffee. The grimace on his face told his Tasker how much he enjoyed it. "You're here so... am I to presume that you were successful?"

"I, uh... wouldn't hold your breath. But it was a doppelgänger that attacked our lovely Vampiric Councilor. No doubts. And one that was prepared with a silver poisoned weapon."

Gabriel looked deflated. "Did you make things worse?" He couldn't believe it! "I need him."

"Don't worry about it. I'll talk to him later. Or you can talk to him. But the club scene? That wasn't a request." He shoved his hands into his pockets.

Regarding his tasker, Gabriel lifted a brow. "You're not kidding?"

"As I said before, it's club time. You need to get yourself refreshed because we have a place to be and people to see." Jean-Michel's eyes twinkled mischievously.

Gabriel both despised that expression and drank it all up at the same time. The idea intrigued him and how could he not get lost in the fantasy of dancing with Jean? But no. No, he'd not do that. He shook his head.

"More leads?" Gabriel asked as he plucked his jacket and tie up from the chair and walked to the side shelf. He grabbed the hanging crystal ornament there, and a hidden door opened. It led to a small room where one could rest and freshen up as needed. Gabriel used it often enough that he kept spare clothes and toiletries here.

"Councilor Evansworth said the doppelgänger covered itself in magical trinkets. Its scent was neutral, and the weapon was silver, coated in poison made for vampires."

"So, you did at least actually talk to him?" Stripping off the wrinkled button-up, Gabriel wiped down with a wet cloth, put on deodorant, and shaved the stubble away. Judging himself in the mirror while Jean-Michel spoke, Gabriel figured that was as good as the rushing would get.

"Yes. We talked." the voice sounded far away as if the Tasker was facing away from the door. That had Gabriel bothered. Was he looking over the books and notes? "Other than confirming it was a doppelgänger, what else did you get?" Gabriel rubbed aftershave on and ran a comb through his hair. Grabbing a clean shirt, he stepped to the door to hear the answer while pulling it on.

"They're able to grab hold of magical items and weapons made for purposeful intent. That's why we're going out. Not many places one can come by these kinds of things." Jean-Michel let his hand slide over an illustration of St. George and the Dragon in one of the old leather-bound tomes. A furious glare played across his face before his fingers grasped the cover of the book to slam it shut.

The act caught Gabriel off-guard. The subject had obviously annoyed his Tasker...his Ancient. And now, there was a moment of silence between the two of them. Gabriel felt like this was the first time he'd ever caught Jean-Michel being nervous. He could have dug in but decided against it.

"Careful not to damage the volumes. They are irreplaceable." Gabriel was looking and feeling like himself instead of the mess that his Tasker had come upon. He had just placed his cufflinks in properly and now was working on the tie. Sure, he'd have preferred a shower, but he apparently wasn't being given the time. He pulled on his jacket and then smoothed it all into place.

"Books aren't the only things that are irreplaceable, Councilor Kennedy," Jean-Michel replied. "But that's a fact, not a discussion. And we need to speak to people about the Underground. The people who know the underground best are Mira and Dante de Salucet."

"So you're taking me to see the infamous twins, then? I hear they can be cunning. No one's been able to get any charges to stick." Picking up his notes, Gabriel tucked them into his drawer. Then he stacked the books into two piles. The custodians would pick up one pile. The other he placed on his personal shelf above the drawer. "Do they give one such as you a challenge, Jean-Michel?" He couldn't believe he'd said it like that! Gabriel readjusted the stacks twice, to be sure they were perfect, before turning away.

"Mira's a fabulous tease and a better lay. I've never fucked Dante, but I've heard he's damned well sought after. Why? Are you interested in a challenge, Gabriel? Want to fuck around with two sex demons?"

The Councilor stifled a cough. Had Jean-Michel really taken it there? Of course, he had. His Tasker was always taking things to the limit. Swallowing, he turned to face the man.

"If I were in the mood for that sort of challenge, I'd not be here with you." Gabriel retorted as he started for the door.

"Somehow, I can't imagine you'd ever be up to the challenge. Not with that stick up your ass. Would make things very uncomfortable, no matter which twin you were interested in." Jean-Michel chuckled, "Worse if you went after both." He followed the Councilor to the door.

Gabriel's spine stiffened, and he took a deep breath while walking out. "Seems we know so little about one another; maybe we really shouldn't let our imaginations run too far?"

"Isn't that the truth?" Jean-Michel spoke quickly and sharply. He opened the passenger door for the Councilor and then walked on around to the driver's side of the truck.

Regarding the inside of the vehicle with disgust, Gabriel took a step back as if something was going to jump out and snatch him. He looked around and frowned. "Where's the SUV?"

"Oh, for the love of Pete, Gabriel, it's not gonna hurt you!" Jean-Michel yelled as he cranked the truck. Then, he bowed his head, both hands on the wheel, and just took a couple of deep breaths.

"Well?" Gabriel didn't move.

"If we're going to Dante's Inferno, we do not want to show up in official vehicles. I was on a bit of a stakeout last I used the truck. Those are just wrappers and receipts and newspapers. Nothing nasty." He turned his head to face the Councilor, "Please, just use the travel blanket in the glove compartment if you have to. No germs. But get in?"

It was more than he had expected from his tasker. Fighting everything in himself, Gabriel reached inside to unhook the compartment for the blanket. He unwrapped it and spread it over the seat. Once he was up on the side, with the toe of his shoe, he pushed the mess on the floorboard out of sight. Clasping his hands in his lap, Gabriel made sure nothing touched him outside of the blanket. He closed the door and buckling up took everything in him.

"So about the twins.." Gabriel took the hand sanitizer out of his pocket that he always kept around to use.

"I have a history with the twins. We've been associates for a long time. They should give us the information they have; just to steer clear of being compromised. After all, it's their job to compromise other people. Being on the flip side of that isn't fun."

"You have a history with a lot of people," Gabriel whispered. His Tasker once again ignored the words. Jean-Michel was good at that.

"Comes with the territory."

The more that Gabriel paid attention to his Tasker, the more he could see the truth. The way Jean-Michel twitched and shifted his body or his head when irritated and the small sounds he made when agitated were clues. Jean-Michel was not human. That had always been a lie.

"They're dangerous. They don't just sell illegal commerce, they sell information and know how to use it. The good news is, I can put on a show. It's part of what you have to do as a Tasker. I'll get the information we need. You? You just add an air of legitimacy. Go along with everything and trust me. Think you can do that?"

Gabriel gave a non-committal grunt. How was there supposed to be any trust?

The Tasker pulled into a three-story parking facility. "What do you know about them?" He continued to drive up to the top floor. It gave Gabriel time to answer the question.

"I've never had business with them personally, but I hear they deal with illegal goods. I'm guessing it's through an illegal portal. So they call it the Underground. Are you thinking they might bring the doppelgängers over?"

"They are an incubus and a succubus. Half-demons. They deal in not only magical items and components but the extravagant. However, I can tell you this for sure. Neither of them would ever handle slaves. I'm pretty certain they wouldn't handle indentured servants. From what Vanishte said, that's exactly what these rogue doppelgängers might be."

"You said that with a lot of confidence for someone that's just an associate," Gabriel pointed out. Again, there was no response. Gabriel watched his Tasker park the vehicle. Before he could get a hand on the door, Jean-Michel reached into the glove compartment, causing Gabriel to jump.

He brought out a black velvet pouch. He untied it and unfolded it on the seat between them. It was actually a plate-sized velvet piece with multiple small pouches sewn on it. Taking a finely decorated crystal from one of many pockets in the holder, he motioned for Gabriel to lean his head down.

"What is it?"

"You didn't want to touch anything else, and honestly, I'd prefer you not touch this with your hands." He motioned for Gabriel to hurry and just let him handle the necklace. With one hand, he pushed the silver chain over the Councilor's hair so that it fell to his neck. The crystal hung close to Gabriel's heart. Jean-Michel then reached over to unbutton the first two buttons of his shirt to be sure the crystal would be hidden beneath the cloth.

Gabriel sat there, his dark eyes on his Tasker. He sucked in a breath, which was another mistake. The smell of oak moss and almost woodsy vetiver, a splash of maybe sandalwood? Jean-Michel cleaned up well. Though Gabriel had to admit part of the allure was probably that he never cleaned up completely.

Gabriel looked from his Tasker to the hand near his chest. He swallowed. Jean buttoned everything back and withdrew to fold the materials back up into the pouch. What had probably only taken two minutes tops had felt like an eternity to Gabriel. His hand lifted as if to reach for the crystal he wore, but he let his hand fall back down to his lap.

"They have a very different set of ethics, but I've gotten along with them very well. Dante can be dangerous, though. Especially in protecting his sister. When either of them sees something they want, they go after it. Half of their souls come from a distant realm we can't portal to. So, I'm putting that crystal on you for protection."

"You think they'd take me? Crimson would be all over them." Gabriel's idealism was slipping daily. "The Council would prosecute them to the fullest extent."

"Well, if they aren't all doppels. And remember, the twins have gotten away with everything so far." Jean's blue-green eyes bore into Gabriel's soul with his words. "Take this to heart. Every one of them, including your family, has prospered from the portals and from those of us with magic in our veins. You should already know that. Not all of those profits came from trade that is pure." Raudine put the velvet pouch back into the glove box. "The Council and Crimson are here to keep order. People like Dante and Mira thrive in the background of that order, so they get away with a lot more than you seem to realize."

Gabriel swallowed. Lifting his hand back up, he put his palm over the cloth-covered crystal. "And this? What exactly does it protect me from?"

"It'll keep them from really wanting you so much. Think of it as mosquito spray that works on this demon. They may get close, but they'll smell something off about you and won't want to taste the goods." Jean-Michel had turned to get out of the truck but then thought of something else. "YOU... need to be very aware of yourself around Dante. Got it?"

"I need to be aware of myself? You just put a stone around my neck..." Wait, what was he saying? An old fear hit Gabriel's heart. Irrational or not, it bothered him.

"It can keep him at arm's length from you, Gabriel, but that crystal doesn't control you." The Tasker studied his ward closely. "And you've never experienced the power of attraction that an incubus can radiate."

"I think you're giving this man far too much credit, Jean-Michel. He can't be that mesmerizing." He watched the Tasker go for the door again, so he did the same. "Why are you so worried about him over the twin sister? What was her name again?"

"Her name is Mira and I'm not worried about her because Mira likes me. Her attention will most likely remain on me. She'd never think of charming you."

"I see." Gabriel felt like maybe everything was just a coincidence then, not a commentary on his secrets. Why did he care? Maybe it was because Jean-Michel had been around his father and his grandfather and neither would... well, they had specific ideas about gay men. Maybe his tasker was the same. Clearing his throat, Gabriel pulled at his jacket to get it proper as they walked toward the elevator. "Alright, will it please you if I said I'll be on my guard?"

Jean-Michel snorted. Strolling to the elevator, he punched the "out of order" button that was taped up.

Gabriel was confused but said nothing. When the doors opened, he actually went wide-eyed. It was golden plated, with red velvet on the side walls and a mirrored door beyond. It smelled so nice inside. He looked over his shoulder. Jean-Michel got in behind him.

"Welcome to Dante's Inferno."

Chapter 16

THE TWINS

Gabriel took in the place.. or what he could see of it. There was a dance floor, tables, booths, and a bar. The lighting was dim but perfect. This reminded him of an old-fashioned cabaret. The music was not so loud you couldn't carry on conversations, but it was at a level where those conversations remained private. He caught the scent of the alcohol being served, the sweet smoke in the air, and something else. The Councilor immediately felt lighter. Was something dulling his senses?

Dark stained wood furniture was all around; clean and classic. Same with the music. The dance floor was not full, but being used and the bar sat along the back wall and there were several patrons partaking there as well as at tables inside. The bouncers reminded him of his lycan friends and associates. Raudine motioned for him to keep moving. Gabriel heard that deepest, wickedest, most sensual voice a man could ever possess. It poured over his senses like warmed chocolate and he felt his breath catch.

"Well, well, look what the Tasker led in." Dante appeared from Gabriel's right and stepped in front of them. Obviously, this was Dante, the club's owner. He had dressed himself in black from the see-through material of his shirt to the hip-hugging pants and shoes he had on. Everyone got a lovely view of his well-defined upper body along with his piercings. Dante took good care of his dark, curly hair, which was cut to wave up top and fade to his neck. When he smiled, everyone could see a double set of fangs. This meant they didn't allow many mundanes here. The incubus wasn't trying to hide these parts of him. The incubus' dark ruby gaze roamed over the two men playfully. In one hand, Dante held a glass that was half full of an unknown liquid that shimmered even in the dim light of the club. In his right hand, he held a lit cigar.

"Councilor Kennedy, this is the demon known as Dante, the club owner, and the lovely belle of the ball coming our way is his sister, Mira."

"Miranda?" Gabriel didn't hide the shock. Mira de Salucet was the woman he knew as Miranda Garret? Owner of Pandora's Box?

"Gabriel. Well, this is awkward. I suppose the librarian look won't work any longer?" The succubus smiled at him before taking Raudine's opposite arm. "Frenchie, you didn't say you were bringing company," Mira scolded, clicking her tongue against her teeth.

They barely clad her in anything that Gabriel could describe as actual clothing. The mini dress was silver and slashed all over so that it clung to her curves. It was exactly as it was meant to be… an invitation.

"You know each other?" Jean-Michel was confused.

"Yes. She owns Pandora's Box. Remember? The shop I was telling you about?" Gabriel noted everything happening - especially the way the succubus welcomed Jean-Michel. Swallowing, he tried to calm his heartbeat. At least the conversation continued.

"Relax, Gabe. I can call you that, right? I know we just do business, but you're in my club with one of my guys…so…" Mira shrugged as she got cozy. "Frenchie, I've missed you."

"So I see…" The chuckle from Jean-Michel was warm for the succubus.

"I take it this is business and not pleasure, then?" The incubus turned to lead them all toward his table in the far corner. "Shall we drink first?" Dante asked, motioning for the staff to bring them a first round. "To old friends?"

"Not sure if business can wait, considering it found its way into our world illegally, and into the domain of the Council," Gabriel pointed out. He knew he wouldn't drink anything here.

"Why should I care?" The incubus tapped his cigar on the edge of the ashtray. His gaze left Gabriel for the Tasker before he asked, "Why do you care? Aren't you ready to see their world burn by now?"

"I'm wondering if you haven't already gained from the situation." Jean-Michel placed the statement out there to chew on. "Doppelgängers are being brought over through an unsanctioned portal. Humans are being attacked. We don't know how many people, supernatural or not, they've replaced."

Mira stiffened slightly and licked her full, red lips before taking the seat near the Tasker. She watched her brother.

"Shifters are entering this world illegally, and so you come to us? Are you making an accusation?" Dante eased back in a relaxed manner. However, his eyes drifted momentarily to his sister before returning his attention to the Tasker.

"It's a valid theory, built on years of experience," Raudine proposed. "They're getting here from somewhere and you know how to get things here without notice. They're using products I know you and your sister make or trade. So, you tell me, Dante. Why wouldn't I come to you?"

"You have a theory. That's not proof." Dante's grin was back. He took a good draw on his cigar. "Where are the Crimson guards and agents ready to raid us? Are they waiting for your phone call?"

"Do you think so little of our history? Think I'd come in guns blaring against people who have done me a solid in the past?" Jean-Michel scoffed.

"One would think you had forgotten our past, Jean-Michel." Dante finished another draw on the cigar before placing it on the tray nearby.

"If you know anything about them, I want you to give us information on these doppelgängers." For Raudine, it was cut and dry.

"Why are these creatures so special to you?" Mira asked. She twirled her hair. "Must be very important."

"Mira," Dante growled.

"Well, come on, the both of you," Mira scolded. She scooted her chair all the closer, and with but a wiggle she'd be in the Tasker's lap. "These games? I thought we were beyond that."

"I thought they were as well, Miranda. I thought we could simply put our cards on the table and get information from one another." Gabriel offered. He felt useless not speaking. His talent was in negotiation, whether it was at a conference room table in a company or in the Council of Crimson. The table remained quiet when their server brought drinks.

Gabriel felt he should continue. After all, no one else was speaking.

"These particular doppelgängers were taking healthy human victims, and one made the mistake of trying to take a Councilor. He had a lot of magic that got him close enough. Magic that's not readily available here, unless you know where to ask." Gabriel felt a slight nudge to his leg under the table. His Tasker was giving him a side-eye.

Mira was playfully stroking her nails along the Tasker's shoulder while drinking and listening. Licking her bottom lip, she leaned forward and got into Jean's field of vision.

"It went after your pretty little vampire, didn't it?" Her wickedness glimmered in her eyes. "How is dear Sebastian? He still hates you, Frenchie?"

That elicited a growl from the Tasker.

"I'll take that as a 'yes…'" she hissed the 's' before giggling. Then she found her hand being removed from its endeavors and placed on the table by his. "Ohhhh… have I been wicked?"

"Aren't you always?" Jean-Michel pointed out.

"Will you punish me?" Her eyes sparkled like rubies, and she bit her bottom lip.

"You want to know what you'll gain, don't you?" Gabriel had tried to remain quiet, but it wasn't in his nature. Besides, he needed to preoccupy his mind, considering what Mira had started. "Very well. Just so you understand, we're doing you a favor. If not us, you're right… Crimson would be here. I could have a team here right now, or worse, on your busiest night. They would question all of your contacts and pull your lives apart. But I've not done that. We're here for information, and if we get it, no Crimson."

"You've got balls threatening me in my club." Dante sat up straighter and gave the human another once-over as if re-evaluating him.

"Perhaps he's right, brother. Maybe we should just give them everything we know. He's sooooo powerful." She didn't hide her amusement. As a matter of fact, she giggled. "I thought we were going to be friends, Gabe?"

"You should brush up on your bargaining skills, hot stuff. They lack finesse." Dante's regard hardened a bit.

"He's used to business mergers and politics." Raudine's gaze rested on Gabriel's angry brown eyes for a second before he turned his attention back to the half-demon. "However, he has a point. This is about life and death. These doppelgängers are unregistered, unfettered by law, unmanaged. And for that, Gabriel's no-loss record as a prosecutor for the Council might come in handy. Anyone involved could go down."

"I will prosecute to the fullest extent of the law the doppelgängers and anyone implicated in being involved with their getting and being here. Unless those people help us in bringing them to justice." Gabriel doubled down.

"Do you realize how hypocritical you are?" The incubus rose and would have walked away if not for his sister's moving to place a hand on his shoulder.

"Don't leave yet, brother." She stood next to Dante, and her brother turned slightly toward her.

Gabriel enjoyed dealing with certainties. He'd never been in this position. He was at a loss. There was a cold, calculating way about the man and yet, how the half-demon now turned to his sister, showed something more. The silence was annoying, but just before he opened his mouth, he felt the shock of a firm hand on his thigh. Looking down with only his eyes, he saw Jean-Michel's hand there. He swallowed and wet his lips.

Dante settled back into his seat and motioned for Mira to do the same. This time, she sat closer to her brother, a pout on her lips.

"These doppelgängers you speak of, they threatened Mira." Dante clenched his teeth as if the ordeal still grated upon him. "My sister provided the products they needed only because of a threat. I don't want her name to be part of this any further, understand?"

"Go on," Raudine urged.

"They wanted the things that mask your supernatural aura and mimic the scent and even the aura of another being," Mira explained. She looked at Gabriel. "I'm worried about retribution, should they know I'm speaking to you?" Then, her attention moved to the Tasker. "They also wanted slayers."

That had Jean-Michel readjusting in his seat, and placing his forearms on the top of the table.

"Slayers?" Gabriel wasn't sure what they were talking about, but it must've been important. There could be so many meanings used for the one word – he needed to know precisely what it meant in this situation.

"Weapons that can kill specific creatures because of the magic within them," Dante explained. "The bane of all supernaturals,

Councilor. Some slaying weapons can destroy the living soul, no matter what path a soul traverses. No backup plans available."

"Not unless you experience a minor miracle," Mira agreed.

"So, there's your information, and we can provide more, but keep us out of it and don't make either of us testify. It'll ruin our reputation," Dante pointed out, taking another draw on his cigar before leaning forward to set it down again.

"I see no need to bring it up, so long as you can keep your eyes open for information about who's actually bringing these doppels over and who's manipulating them." Jean-Michel sat back in his seat. "Some examples of the things you've already provided to the doppels would go a long way."

"Wait, you can't guarantee that we won't need their testimony, Raudine." Gabriel couldn't help his demanding voice. "We do not know what we may face." Gabriel's jaw clenched after he spoke so tightly that his cheeks ached from the pressure. He itched the magical stone beneath his shirt.

Mira took her brother's hand and watched the Councilor with a glare.

"You are here to agree that the Council will not question Dante or Mira on this matter or ruffle their lives, so long as the information they provide benefits us. If everything pans out, why would you need to call them into the chamber?" Jean-Michel asked.

"The information will definitely pan out. Now, what you do about it is up to you." Dante watched the two with a keen eye. The incubus inhaled deeply and his eyes became heavy-lidded. He suddenly snarled. His gaze traveled to where the human was scratching his chest.

"I can't guarantee we won't be calling either of you to testify."

Dante stood up, letting his sister's hand go, and leaned over the table, moving his hands as if he were stalking across the top of it, a predatory move. He stopped when he was a few inches from the Councilor's face. He smiled, purposely showing off the double fangs at the sides. Gabriel hadn't budged. He refused to be intimidated.

Sitting up straight and stiff, Gabriel's chin lifted just a notch. The eyes of the incubus reminded him of a faceted gem in the lighting. The Councilor wondered if the incubus used them to mesmerize people. He would not let that happen. And then, the threat ended with Dante chuckling in his face. The incubus pulled himself back and actually laughed.

"I do not envy you in your duty to protect this one. He still has a lot to learn."

"Tell the man we agree to the terms and then he or his lovely sister can give us the rest of the information and samples they have. Like I told you before, I've worked with Dante and Mira. And I also know when they're telling the truth." He reached over to the drink provided to him and enjoyed some of it while waiting.

It was all back to trust. Gabriel thought about his grandmother and thought about his life. Maybe it wasn't just about trust. Maybe it was also about faith. His grandmother had taught him to have it. And he'd been without it for far too long, hadn't he? Licking his lips, Gabriel decided.

"Here's what I can agree to. I can do my utmost to keep your names out of it. I can definitely guarantee that Crimson will not be coming to your club or harassing either of you or your businesses. If you guarantee you will work with us both now and in the future."

"I enjoy looking at your face, Councilor, especially your mouth. Oh, the things I could do with that mouth." He smirked, but added, "I don't like dealing in vague timeframes. I guarantee I will work with you on this case, dealing with the doppelgängers both now and in the future."

Raudine made no response. He had a poker face. Mira, who had been oddly quiet, got up to walk away from the table. Gabriel nodded in agreement.

"Then we have an accord! A drink or smoke, Mr. Kennedy? I'll gladly provide either while you are here. You've ... well, you've earned some respect." Dante motioned for a server to come over and take orders.

"Not quite thirsty, and I don't smoke, so I think I'll have to pass." The usual chill was back in his voice after having to compromise on something he didn't want to compromise on. "So you helped get them here?" he asked.

"No. Neither of us knows how they got here. You can tell if I'm lying. Want me to step outside, in case you don't trust your magic here?" Dante poured more liquor from the decanter on his table. The server had brought over more glasses. "Nor can we help you with that. We aren't natural portal locators and they didn't come through the portals we know about."

"Natural portal locators?" Gabriel finally asked.

"Yes. I don't suppose Crimson has a dragon tucked away in one of those dusty old closets?" He winked at the Tasker before taking another draw and letting the smoke slither from the corners of his mouth and through his nose.

"Killed off," Jean-Michel replied quickly.

"Too bad," Mira whispered. She put a satchel on the table in front of the two men. Her bottom found Jean's knee, her fingers teased the back of his neck with her nails.

Gabriel took his handkerchief out of his inside pocket and began looking over what the succubus had placed in front of him.

"If you could find whatever portal they're using, you might figure out the responsible party. Or at least you might stop more from coming over." Dante continued, his eyes meeting Raudine's annoyed stare from across the table. "Too bad Crimson and the Council were so short-sighted. A dragon would have helped you tremendously." Dante's fanged smile was back while playfully poking his friend.

"I've done some research about it all. Crimson decision or not, I feel like it was a mistake. Witnesses to genocide rarely realize the loss until it's too late." Gabriel was careful to use the material of his handkerchief when he handled the magical crystals and the two necklaces Mira had provided.

"Your research hasn't turned any up?" Dante asked.

"Crimson's official stance is that they're all extinct in this world." Gabriel shook his head. He hadn't said everything. He might've had faith, but what was being said wasn't about him. "I'm afraid we'll need to find another way."

Raudine said nothing. He drank and watched Gabriel.

"All you can do is map the ley lines. Track anomalies on them until there's a triangulation of an area. That'll be where the unregistered portal is. See, I'm still happy to help, Councilor." The half-demon chuckled again.

Raudine took one crystal in hand to study while enjoying the physical pleasures given by Mira's fingers. He held her about the waist to keep her on his lap.

"What was the other information you had? What did you do when you made contact? They came to you...or...?" Gabriel didn't like what he thought of as a public display of... lust? He pretended not to care and continued to ask questions.

"I've only contacted one, a very talented one named Malcolm. He can switch to multiple forms. He took Frenchie's form the first time I ever met him. Thought it'd make me feel some kind of way. He almost got punted. I know my Raudine all too well to fall for that shit. But what he requested seemed little at first."

"You knew they were illegal, though," Gabriel pointed out. "Why not call Crimson?"

"Crimson will not help. Let's just say Director Skinner and I aren't on the best of terms. And I would prefer to just get rid of the bugger than risk having my other business be on that man's radar."

"What the Director thinks of you shouldn't matter." Gabriel shook his head. All three of the others at the table chuckled at his expense. "Really?" he didn't like Skinner. Never had. But had he overlooked something worse than a horrible personality?

"So, surely you want to dance?" Mira purred against Jean-Michel's ear.

"We don't have time," Gabriel began placing things back into the bag.

"I think he's jealous of the attention I'm giving you," Mira whispered, none too quietly in Jean-Michel's ear.

"Please," Gabriel scoffed, taking the crystal from his Tasker.

"We've kept our end of the bargain. Now, if we're done," Dante slowly rose to his feet and stood there eyeing his twin and the Tasker she was pouring herself all over. He was offering them an exit.

"Come dance with me. It has been a very long time and I've missed you. Just one and then I'll let you go." Mira was tugging him.

"My dear, your dancing may leave me wanting." Raudine tried to argue even as Mira pulled him up and into her arms.

"I believe we have other plans." Gabriel was trying to remind his Tasker of their duty over any kind of pleasure with that woman. He got up and put the satchel and the handkerchief back into his pocket before smoothing his hands over the fabric of his suit.

Dante was in front of him from out of nowhere...again. How did he do that? They were only inches apart. Gabriel's breath caught as he felt the incubus trace fingertips along his jawline.

"If Jean-Michel stays for my sister's attention, I would be more than happy to replace him as your companion for the evening." The voice was low, thick, and seductive. It made the Councilor swallow. He breathed in the spicy, potent scent of the male demon. The touch made his insides tighten and ripples went down his spine.

"I don't think..." He sputtered and shook his head, trying to clear it, "What I mean to say is—I think that's not a good idea." Why wasn't the crystal working? Why was the demon right here?

"Do you ever stop thinking, Councilor Kennedy?" Dante asked.

Gabriel's hand pressed against the chest of the demon. He had every intention of pushing the demon back to give himself space. The thin, see-through material was definitely not a barrier! They might as well have been skin-to-skin. Gabriel's heart raced. Unfortunately, the touch was his downfall.

Jean-Michel was walking with Mira to the dance floor already.

"Not a quick study when you lead with your ego." Dante pulled the Councilor close and nipped an earlobe with his teeth. Blood wouldn't have spilled if his prey hadn't jerked free. The half-demon licked the coppery liquid from his lower lip and his eyes widened with wonder. "Ooooh, you are a nice little surprise in a three-piece suit, aren't you?"

Still dazed, Gabriel lifted a hand to rub at his ear. He wanted to step back farther. However, he just couldn't. Dante stepped closer to him. Gabriel's breath was shaky as it left his chest. It didn't matter that seconds earlier he hated the creature. Gabe could feel Dante's warm breath on his lips.

"What's the matter, Frenchie? Is he like the others?" Mira asked, her eyes suddenly saddened as the Tasker turned away from her.

"Pleasurable sensation, isn't it?" Dante spoke, wrapping more of his spell around the human's wits, enthralling him further. "Want more? Take off that damned crystal and I'll show you everything you've always wanted..." Gabriel's hands were already on the chain.

"That's enough." Jean-Michel reached his arm out across Gabriel's chest and pushed him back. The Councilor had done a better job than most at keeping his own urges around the incubus at bay. "Entertainment's over." His eyes challenged the incubus to do more. The side of his lip lifted just slightly as if he were about to snarl.

Dante lifted his hands, palms forward. The half-demon backed off.

"Be sure to watch the Underground over the next week, Dante. Wouldn't want you to miss anything, or get blamed for anything." Jean-Michel said in a normal tone as he turned the Councilor around and steered them both to the elevator once again.

Gabriel stopped and turned in the opposite direction to glare at Dante.

"I'll remember this," he held his earlobe and continued. "And not in a good way. You'd better deliver on everything you've promised my Tasker, or I'll be happy to prosecute you in front of the Council."

"Oh, quite the fireball, aren't we?" Dante smiled, while Jean-Michel pulled Gabriel back to the elevator. Mira joined her twin, an arm going through his as the two left. "We need to talk more about your moonlighting, sister."

Chapter 17
Truth and Realizations

They had made it to the top of the building, where the Tasker directed Gabriel to put his back against the concrete wall. The man needed to clear his senses. His green-blue eyes watched the Councilor closely.

"Feel better? You got the last word."

"Son of a..." Gabriel leaned back and took a deep breath. "Don't say it. I know you want to – but don't." Finding the handkerchief in his pocket, Gabriel held it to his earlobe, which was still stinging from the assault.

"He had no right," the Tasker whispered, making his agitation obvious. He looked over the cut when Gabriel allowed him. Not that Gabriel couldn't handle something so small. It was the taking that bothered Raudine. It was a violation.

"Well, he's an incubus...you warned me."

"And you didn't want me to say that." Senias chuckled. "You did well for your first time. Though, letting him taste you might have been..." He shrugged, his eyes narrowing. Then, the Tasker took a breath and nodded, "Well, what's done is done."

"I just threatened a half-demon." Gabriel had just started digesting the situation.

"He meddled with you; tested your resolve. You didn't succumb and even put him on notice. I respect that. So does he, I'm sure." He wasn't sure if he would've handled it the same way. But then, he wasn't Gabriel Kennedy.

Gabriel shrugged his shoulders. He straightened his jacket for the fifth time. "What would he do? Drain my life away?"

"Oh, I doubt he would have done that immediately. Not quickly, anyway. You make it sound like he'd just zap you and take your energy in a kiss." It amused Jean-Michel the way Gabriel was so brave and had so much faith in his own future. He worked with beings much more powerful than himself on the daily, yet he was the holder of his own fortune.

"Not quickly?" Gabriel walked with Jean toward the truck. "What do you mean by that?" His eyes narrowed on the Tasker.

"He enjoys himself with the really handsome ones. You're gorgeous and useful. Dante probably would keep you around for a while. That way, he could drain you at his leisure. Building you back up again, draining you, a cycle." Jean-Michel wasn't sure if he was explaining it or teasing Gabriel with it. He enjoyed teasing the Councilor, after all. He opened the door. "And you'd probably love it. Well, for the most part, anyway."

"Thanks for that visual." An odd shiver went straight up his spine. Shaking his head to clear it, Gabriel climbed into the truck. "I doubt I would have enjoyed it, though. He's not what I'm into at all." Gabriel clicked the seatbelt and took a deep breath.

"Half-demons of their ilk can become your heart's desire. So who knows?" The Tasker closed the passenger door and walked around to get in the driver's seat before he added, "Did you not know that?"

"Thanks for the enlightenment," Gabriel muttered under his breath. He let his head bow forward and his hand began massaging his temple.

"What's the matter, Gabriel?"

"Just re-thinking that whole conversation again. It's hard for me to really pick apart details whilst it's happening. But now that I can, it has me wondering a few things." Gabriel let his gaze rise to stare straight ahead through the windshield.

"Take your time. I'm the only one waiting for you now." He started the truck and put it in gear. It was time to get the Councilor home. Or so he thought...

"I need to go to the Chamber."

"What you need is sleep. And I need to pick Devon up so we can get started on the other leads." Jean-Michel was ignoring the request for the moment.

"I don't need sleep." Gabriel snapped before taking a deep breath.

Raudine raised a brow. That had come out of nowhere.

"I need to go to the Chamber and sort all of this out while it's fresh in my head. And I need to get Derek out again." He rubbed the abused earlobe again, his breathing at a quicker pace. "And we have the meeting coming up. We need to have the meeting. So all of this needs to be in order before that happens." His hand shook as he placed it against the side of his neck. "Will the lycan be enough to find them? Should I come along? If it involves an unknown portal, a Councilor should be present, right?"

"You're no help if you're in such a state." Jean-Michel noted the tics that Gabriel was showing. The Tasker tried to lower his tone of voice, softening it. "I'll call them. Or you can. After you get some things written out of your head, once that is done, you... need... to... rest." The Tasker enunciated each part of the phrase. He turned the truck toward the Chamber.

"My god, Jean... they wanted slayers?" Gabriel loosened his tie and swallowed. He put his hands on his knees again and tried to stop the shaking. "They attacked Councilor Evansworth. Councilor Jonas won't approve any further investigations."

"Yeah, seems like Vanishte was right," Raudine shook his head.

Gabriel had closed his eyes and tried to regain his control. His chest was rattling, and a blush moved over his neck and cheeks.

Seeing that Gabriel was still fighting, seeing the man's hands shake, the Tasker reached over without permission and took the closest hand in his. He knew it was taking a chance. But he also knew Gabriel needed the help.

"Breathe. Listen to me. Breathe." The dragon's mind reached Gabriel, hoping he would feel a bit of calming power; just enough. A warm, calming flow of energy flowed to Gabriel's senses, and Jean-Michel hoped the man's tension would ease. Apparently, it was working, because Gabriel's breathing was slowing down. And then that look. Would it be fear or something else?

"What... How..?" Gabriel's eyes had quickly come open to look down at where Jean-Michel's hand grasped his own. He rubbed his forehead with his free hand. "How did you do that?"

"I thought you knew I was special?" Raudine tried to make light of it. Why was he doing this? He was so close to freedom. And yet, just feeling the warm hand in his caused an effervescence inside of him; a feeling that called to him. Gabriel...felt...good. Maybe he could back out of this. Maybe Gabriel wouldn't ask anything else. The Tasker almost laughed at the thought. It'd be against everything Gabriel Kennedy was to not ask questions. Jean continued to drive while holding Gabriel's hand in his. The calmness stayed between the two men, and it seemed neither was in a rush to let go.

"You are special. I've just been wondering what kind of special it is lately." Gabriel smoothed his free hand through his hair as he made the confession.

"You've been digging. You think people don't pay attention to the research you're doing? Could be dangerous for people in the Council and Crimson to look over the books you've checked out. They might assume things." Jean-Michel swallowed. "'They might assume things that would not be good for any of us."

"My research is simply a pastime, a hobby, maybe a diversion from my official cases. Why would that kind of thing be dangerous? Just because I'm curious…"

"Well, my life is on the line. Along with the lives of those I give a shit about." Jean-Michel let go of Gabriel's hand, considering the apathetic response he'd just gotten. "No time like the present to clear the air. We're moving along and no one's around to interrupt. So, tell me, Gabriel, what makes me special?" Jean-Michel wondered for just a few heartbeats if he wore a similar expression as Agent Hughes had worn right before he died.

"You're draconic. I don't understand how that is possible with no one in Crimson or Council being aware, but that is what you are." Gabriel swallowed, his eyes now on the driver. "Am I right?"

"Do you really believe what you said back there in the demon's lair? About dragons?" the Tasker asked. He needed to know.

"Yes, I do," Gabriel replied. "My grandfather taught me a lot growing up. He taught me that anything was possible and to keep an open mind at all times." He cleared his throat. "My grandmother taught me to have faith in what I feel is right, even if I couldn't see it. Grandfather often spoke of dragons as if they were real. Through him, I gained respect for the intellectual creatures they are instead of the mindless killers everyone made them out to be. "

"That's rather idealistic," he glanced over at Gabriel. "You know, the view that we're not mindless killers. But back a dragon into a corner and they'll become a mindless killer. The intellectual part is, mmm—" His eyes went to the ceiling, and he shrugged, "a compliment." Jean-Michel spared a few glances over at his passenger.

Gabriel stared straight ahead, brown eyes large.

"Your grandfather was a wise man – half the time. I'll give him that. One of my favorites." They were pulling onto the campus trails to go past the university and out to the Council Chamber. There was still some small bit of time before they would have to agree to silence. "You understand why I keep my secret, such as it is? Why I'll ask you to do so?"

This time there was a sound of exasperation from the Councilor.

"Of course I do. I'm not stupid. And...I have other reasons for looking into draconic history for the Council. I...what we're doing for the doppelgängers? I originally began outlining the same arguments for dragons."

Jean-Michel was speechless.

"I meant what I said back there. Dragons shouldn't be blacklisted. And as soon as we get this portal investigating and maybe find some witnesses, I can handle this case then move on to the dragon case."

"As it stands, at least you have what you need in order to find a rogue portal."

"You're not a tool," Gabe muttered.

"Oh, yes, I am." Jean-Michel chuckled. "I'm not stupid either, Councilor. I know my worth to people, including you."

"I haven't made the case yet, Jean-Michel. We can't let anyone know you helped find anything. They'll lock you up and ship you off or they could kill you on sight. I have to explain finding that portal without bringing you into it. I'd never be able to live with myself."

"Then you have a hired, unbiased mage study the ley lines and find out where there have been unexplained magical energy spikes. Just like the twins told you to do."

"The results may take too long," Gabriel whispered. "I'll shift gears and work on that tonight. I'll find a way."

Raudine tried to focus on the road. Gabriel's phone went off.

"Seems your visit to Sebastian and whatever you said did the trick. As did my call to Minlial. We have our meeting." Gabriel read the text message aloud. "Emergency Council Meeting Scheduled 48 hours hence, Whitley Chamber. Sponsored by Gabriel Kennedy, Minlial Nedian, and Sebastian Evansworth." He paused and smiled. "Once we get this case won, then the doppelgängers have no reason to be an issue. Not even the rogues.

I mean, they'll have to be prosecuted for their crimes, but...there'd be no reason to continue a coup." Gabriel tucked the phone back out of sight.

"Sebastian made the right decision, is all. He definitely didn't do it because of me, Gabriel." He had not hidden the heartache in the timbre of his voice.

Gabriel observed his Tasker.

"Don't get too full of yourself. If you get this case handled, that doesn't give any of the rogues an 'out' from continuing their crimes. They may still run. They may still fight. And we don't have proof of who's behind this. Nor do we have the portal found. So..."

"Yes, of course. I know..."

"I appreciate your silence. Unless, like others, you plan on using it against me. Then... well... things won't be so nice as they are right now, Councilor Kennedy." He stopped the vehicle in front of the Council Building.

"If you think I'm capable of using this against you, then you don't know me that well, Tasker Raudine." Once the truck stopped, Gabriel unbuckled and got out in silence.

"Perhaps I don't," Raudine whispered as Gabriel walked off. "Perhaps I don't know you at all."

Chapter 18
My Way or No Way

Minlial Nedian was very pleased to be back in this world. This had actually been the elves' original home, long before humans became the predominant species.

She adored the lushness of the forests that yet remained so much that she had purchased a home in the middle of one. Every sound was like a musical note, the wind whistling through the trees; the birds chirping and singing in chorus; the insects buzzing and droning like an orchestra. She had her large door-like windows open to those sounds while she prepared herself for meditation and then sleep.

Earlier, she had enjoyed her video conference with Councilor Kennedy. Speaking with both him and his doppelgänger witness had helped her to decide. She had already submitted her motion to call an emergency meeting.

After, she had simply enjoyed her time sipping her drink on the terraced back patio of a favorite shop, a little hidden gem known as Cafe Dryad. A small patch of forest surrounded it on a hillside along a trail that connected several parts of the city of Whitley. The shop and the surrounding tables and chairs were beneath a canopy of oaks and poplars. Since elves felt more secure in such settings, Minlial had dallied there for as long as she could.

She returned to her Gaian home by mid-afternoon. Her almond eyes were violet and the light in her room set them off well. Minlial was in front of a mirror as she let her long dark hair down to brush and prepare for bed. After all, she had to get back on schedule to be available for night meetings of the Council.

"M'Lady, there is a gentleman at the atrium. Director Skinner?" The housekeeper was at the door to her room with the news.

"Hmmm... tell him I'll be down momentarily." She settled on wrapping her long mane into a rope and getting it together and out of her way. Taking one more look in the mirror, she touched the tip of one pointed ear before shrugging and making her way to see what the director wanted.

"Councilor Nedian, I hope you didn't mind my insisting on speaking. This is very important. I couldn't wait on the official dossiers and appointments." Ezekial made his way to the Elven Councilor. However, he would quickly notice that the atrium was as far as he was going to get. The gate to the rest of the house was closed behind her.

Minlial's eyes narrowed. Her jaw set. Her face, normally a canvas of grace and beauty, became marred by a frowning brow.

"What is it that couldn't wait for Chamber, Director Skinner?" She secured the wrap a little more at her waist and closed the upper portion to prevent any mishaps. "I'd offer you a seat, but I was preparing for meditation. Please don't take long to get to the point."

"Some things have come to light concerning certain Councilors. I believe one that has been suspicious lately contacted you. Since I was told by the Secretary of Council that you desire an emergency meeting, I thought I would come by and personally discuss this with you."

"Isn't that against the rules? You are the Director of Crimson and may help in prosecution on the stage of judgment. Meeting like this is odd."

"Why did you agree to the meeting, Councilor Nedian?" Ezekial asked, his hands moving to clasp in front of him.

Arching one slender brow, Minlial crossed her arms over her chest.

"Not that I have to explain myself to you, Director Skinner. But I don't mind telling you that the matter was of some importance and from what I understand. It is better for all if resolved with Council rather than simply with Crimson. From what I can find, your agency has done nothing on the matter. Also, I believe the European Council might have been remiss in refusing the efforts of these people to find a footing in Gaia. We should check old biases at the door when acting as a Councilor. That is not what I have found in my assessment of the judgment against the doppelgängers in Paris."

"Are you sure it had nothing to do with the needs of your people to push forward into our world?" His eyes were penetrating.

Narrowing her own gaze, the Elven female drew in a very slow breath before even giving the ridiculous question a reply.

"Your world?" She scoffed. "My people understand how this world operates. We keep to ourselves with as little interaction with humans and their delusions of grandeur as possible. Our regions are plentiful in this world and we've no desire to seek any more than we already have. The natural world offers cover to our magical realms. Our people thrive no matter which world we're in. So why would you ever think to ask such of me?"

"Losing territory and pride in the Lycan Realm... that is what they're calling it now, correct? Your slaves have taken back what is their own. The increased magical energy here? You're saying that elves returning here have nothing to do with it? You forget how much data I can retrieve from our portal monitoring, Councilor Nedian." Skinner smiled.

"Then you'll find that no elf comes here that was not born here. All of us. This is our world, too, Director Skinner. Our laws within the Elven government are clear of who may come and go through the portals." Minlial took several paces away from Skinner before looking over her shoulder and then turning to face him again.

"Perhaps I should ask why you are so opposed to this meeting? Should the Council concern itself with your matters, Director Skinner?" She knew how to turn the tables on someone and knew Ezekiel Skinner didn't like anyone nosing about his business.

"No one has cared to ask me what I've been doing behind the scenes. I suppose that last time I heard such a question was—" He let his eyes drift upward in thought, before settling his gaze once again on the elf. "The last time someone asked that question of me was around World War II. I salvaged two of the four Crimson Councils and established them so that no other world war would affect them in the future. I suppose they may be so happy with me that they no longer indulge in suspicion against me."

"Then they are unwise. Crimson relies on checks and balances, as any governing body should. Power corrupts. Not a bias against any one species, but fact. Your extraordinarily long life is possibly the result of magic and possibly the result of deals made that could compromise you. So, I believe it may be past the time that someone checks on your actions or lack thereof. The doppelgänger case can be one such check."

"Only my enemies check up behind me, and I assure you, I leave very few of those alive." His eyes were warm, unfitting to his sentiment. "Are you volunteering to be my enemy, Minlial?"

"Are you threatening me, Director Skinner?" Her eyes grew larger when he grinned like he did. It was almost unnaturally large...that smile and those teeth. Minlial realized too late that she had no weapons. She was casting a spell that she could bring about with some thoughts when she felt pain rush white-hot through her chest. It radiated outward. She couldn't think. She couldn't breathe. Minlial's eyes remained on the Director, even as the gray-skinned creature that had gotten behind her gently placed her on the floor to finish bleeding out.

Chapter 19
Going on an Adventure

"I said, I'm going," Gabriel was not budging on this. "It's my case. Besides, I need to be the one that claims I found the portal, right?" He and the other two men were standing at the front atrium of his family home. The old style was actually more colonial in feel than antebellum, which suited Gabriel just fine. His ancestors had freed all slaves prior to the Civil War. The home had helped many over the years - not just African American slaves, but supernaturals with no place to go. He'd only just found out that Jean-Michel had probably been around for most of the thing's existence.

"Talk some sense into him," Jean-Michel's hand was pointing to the Councilor while his eyes were on Devon Weylyn.

"Me? What do ya want me ta do about it?" Now the Tasker had a pissed-off glare coming at him in stereo.

"You and Eva practically raised him. You should have some authority," the Tasker pointed out as if it were the gospel truth.

"Oh yeah, yer high and mightiness, I'll jump right on that." There was a low, annoyed rumble from the Alpha's chest. It wasn't his fault that Jean had waited too long to do this.

"Standing right here. Full-grown adult. I'm going." Gabriel continued for the door. "If we find this portal, you need me as an excuse. Besides, I did the homework. I think I may know where to look. Come on."

Jean-Michel's brows raised as he watched the Councilor ignore the both of them.

"Look, I ain't puttin' Derek back at risk. He's just fine on some wild hacker nonsense. So, we're down one stooge. If Shemp there wants ta tag along..."

"Gods, you date yourself with that shit," Jean-Michel pointed out before following Gabriel.

"Hmph, well, what can I say? I like good slapstick comedy." Devon shifted his attention to the businessman, who wanted to be an adventurer. They could see Gabriel through the glass door, already making his way to the vehicle. He sighed heavily. "You know, when he was a kid, he'd play with the lycan pups. They'd spar and hunt with him. Never told him he was any different. He was always eager for adventure and stories. But since his grandfather pushed him away, then he got put in charge of things so fast, he's pulled farther and farther away. This is the first time I've seen that spark back in Gabriel's eyes."

"And if we're out there and he gets killed? Is the spark worth it?" Jean-Michel asked his friend before he opened the door for Devon so they could both join their mutual pain in the ass.

"Gabe, maybe you don't belong out there in the grit of things. You need to be here researching and finding answers, don't ya think?" Devon tried half-heartedly to get the man to remain safe.

"All due respect, Devon – no." Gabriel removed his jacket to lay it over his arm in a very slow, deliberate motion.

"Fuck me," the Tasker muttered, shaking his head out of frustration. He stood still, his hands at his waist.

"Without my research…"

"I don't care if your research got us to within a block of the location! You are a Coun-ci-lor. That's what you do. You research and study and figure things out. I actually do the Tasking. Hence the title, Tas-ker. I do the dirty work. I actually go out and investigate. You stay safe. I don't. It's what we do!"

"And him?" Gabriel pointed to Devon.

"He and I have been through wars together. He's fine in a fight. You? Not so much."

"How do you know that? I've taken classes."

"Fuck it, Jean." Devon rubbed a calloused hand over his face and ended by tugging on his own beard. "If he wants to march in there and get his ass handed to him, let him do it. We'll see that he gets a nice funeral in normal human fashion." Devon stressed the human part.

"Et tu, Devon?" Jean-Michel cast a glance at the lycan. His shoulders were drooping.

"I ain't the one dabblin' his claws in uncharted waters now, am I?" Giving a very wolfish grin, Devon chuckled as he walked past them both.

"What do you…" Jean-Michel's expression was slack. Then his eyes widened. "No… I have *not*." He turned back to Gabriel and scoffed before moving on.

"What?" Gabriel's eyes glared. He double-timed it to catch up.

Raudine waited for Gabriel to follow him to the back of the SUV. Devon reached in and opened the back hatch. Gabriel walked up to see the gun cases. Jean-Michel took out a Glock and checked the chamber. "You remember how to handle one of these from military school?"

"Of course. I've just not shot one since. I don't have time for the range, not that I really care for it."

"Well, care or not, this is your best defense. This first. Only aim at what you intend to shoot. Don't aim if either of us or anyone else might get hit. Understand?"

"Yes." Gabriel took his jacket off and took the offered shoulder holster. With his Tasker's help, the thing was on quickly enough. Then he took the gun. Considering they had no clue what to expect, the Councilor didn't argue. Raudine and Devon always began with their guns. The lycan had a larger model thanks to meatier hands. He knew Jean-Michel always carried 9mm. He wasn't sure what kind, but it looked modified.

Closing the hatch, the Tasker got into the passenger seat, forcing Gabriel to take the back

"Eva's gonna love this when she finds out you gave her human pup a gun." Devon's laughter permeated both passengers' thoughts.

"You don't have to tell Eva, do you?" Gabriel asked, his eyes showing a bit of the same fearfulness all the boys had of Devon's mate. There was a growl from the passenger seat.

"Do not make me regret this," Jean-Michel warned, his blue-green eyes meeting Gabriel's gaze in the rearview.

"My mate intimidates everybody that meets her, little or not. I seem to recall you not getting along with her for decades." Devon's smirk spoke volumes.

"I'll try not to die if that's what you mean." Gabriel shot back.

"That's exactly what he means," Dev added. He cranked the engine and waited until his partner was scanning GPS and Gabriel had his notes out and ready. He needed to be told which direction to go. Jean was using the information Gabriel had written out and a map of the small city proper. He had turned around enough in the seat to have the materials in the center so Gabriel could help.

"You said you could get us within a block? You seemed pretty sure of your estimations. I just need to be close enough to feel it," Jean-Michel assured his Councilor.

"It's all dependent on the ley lines and the overlay I did. I'm relying on someone else's research for that part. But when or if it comes up during proceedings, I can use these as my reason for knowing where the portal is. I scoured over real estate and business information in public records. Unfortunately, two places fit the situation." Gabriel smoothed the map out and marked his calculations down. "It works at both locations. Here..." Gabriel marked an X in pink highlighter. "...and here." He marked again and then pointed at the spot he had tapped originally, "You need to be here." he pointed to a parking lot central distance between the two Xs. "It's bound to be around this area. And your...magic... should let you know something if you're there."

Within ten minutes, the scenery changed from country roads to city streets. Then it changed from busy streets and buildings to commercial area warehousing. There were large parking lots and equipment lots that edged a transportation center for buses and cabs. Owners had converted some buildings into clubs. This time of evening, it resembled a boneyard with all the scaffolding, cranes, and fencing that they drove past. The city was trying to revitalize this side of town and it showed.

"I don't think I've ever been to this area of the city. Strange, now that I think about it," Gabriel mentioned.

"Considering your company probably owns quite a few places like this and a lot of them most likely are right here in this area, odd." Jean-Michel glanced over at Devon. "Next left, toward the South Industrial, Dev."

"I saw the map. I know where I'm goin'." Devon turned down the next street.

"Well, I rarely have time to come out here to check on the warehouses. I have people who do that and make reports."

"You need to get out more. Especially for knowing the average employee. It'll make a vast difference to those employees." Jean-Michel offered his advice as they drive.

"Why? Do you think because I don't work for twenty dollars an hour, have four kids and a wife, and don't sit in a bar every evening tossing back a few while watching some sport on tv, I'm clueless about the world around me?" Gabriel had his hands on the top of each bucket seat, looking first at the lycan and then at the dragon.

"Well, you're clearly out of touch if you think the average worker makes $20 an hour. Maybe some of your specialized warehouse employees, sure. But not all of them." The Tasker turned enough to face his Councilor. "The point of view you're losing is that of the common man. You can see where your efforts go to keep them with a job. But they see you earning much more than they do and you are never available to them. You are aloof. You are untouchable. That is what they see." They pulled up into an empty lot and Devon turned to Jean-Michel. The Tasker nodded.

"They earn a living wage at our company, have good insurance, and I attend special events..."

"That's what your grandfather's generation was all about. Handle it without touching it. And times change, Gabriel. People see you're one of them and they trust you and support you more. That's all I'm saying. Show them you give a damn and be there with them. Take some breaks with them. Learn to live."

"I'm not that aloof or that unreachable." Gabriel could be cool and unemotional when he chose. Right now, that cool facade was well in place as he defended himself.

"Keep tellin' yerself that," Devon replied as he watched Jean-Michel step away from them.

The dragon took a deep breath of air. He walked in a circle in the part-paved and part-gravel parking lot. His arms went to his sides and then lifted slightly, palms up.

"I feel it." He could feel something drawing him.

"That was the idea. So we need ta get back in and..." Devon began.

"No. I mean...it's close." Jean-Michel's eyes widened as he realized just how close they were.

"Yer kidding," Devon watched.

"We're not even out of town!" Gabriel couldn't believe it. They had simply circled Whitley and come back in on the other side. Mundane, innocent people lived not very far away. They came and went to the local clubs. Lots of them! How had this gone on? And so close to the full arsenal of a hidden Crimson base?

The hair on the back of Gabriel's neck stood up. He turned to face the same building the dragon was now facing. It was a warehouse made of block and metal siding. There were doors chained shut, signs on them that said "For Lease" and "No Trespassing".

When the Councilor took a step toward the locked doors, the Tasker's hand went out to take hold of his shoulder.

"Wait." He handed Gabriel the flashlight. "Devon and I can see in darkness. You can't." Gabriel took the offered light. The Tasker nodded. "You definitely have delivered us to the correct place, Gabriel. You didn't really even need me. Good job."

Jean-Michel's eyes shimmered as he took in the feel of the portal magic that was pulsing from inside the building. He stepped in front of them both and took a deep breath, his head going back to the action. The energy and the scent were unmistakably draconic. That flew into his mind, followed by so very many questions!

Which dragon had done this? Where were they? Why would they do this? Were they working for the same person responsible for bringing the doppelgängers through? How long had this been here? Perhaps it was all a coincidence? But, then again, the dragon had learned a long time ago not to believe in coincidences.

He was both elated that there might be another of his kind near and fearful for the dragon. Who had used the dragon to do this? Or had the dragon done so willingly? And then he felt Devon's big hand on his shoulder.

"Why don't the two of you take a few steps from the magic and let me have a go first? Magic don't weigh on my shoulders so much." Devon took a position between the pair.

"You've got it." Of course, the lycan was correct. In this form, Jean-Michel was stronger than most humans, true, but he was not as strong as Devon. He turned to Gabriel and then looked past the human to all vantage points around this place. He just wanted to be sure they weren't being spied upon or followed.

There were other buildings surrounding this parking lot. A flight of stairs lead down from this parking area to what he assumed was another parking area, or perhaps just a delivery area. And then there was the graveled entry from the road.

Devon walked up to the door and felt the weight of the chains in his hands. He looked at the lock and then tugged it to the side. With a quick shove of his weight and strength downward, the chain snapped.

Gabriel glanced at his Tasker, who had turned back to the doors thanks to the sound.

"My heartbeat...is that what magic feels like?" Gabriel asked.

"Yes. Your first time?"

Devon motioned for them to join him. Inside, Devon took point and Raudine covered their rear. They cushioned Gabriel between them. The Tasker pulled the door too before moving onward. They were waiting for him.

"Can you feel it? The magic... the pulse?" Jean-Michel walked onward, now taking point and not really paying attention to the other two. His eyes were now draconic; fluctuating oval pupils in blue-green fields. They shimmered with reflected light, much like the eyes of a cat. The energy ebbing from the basement of this warehouse was something he hadn't felt in a very long time. It was exciting! Unfortunately, it was also familiar. He made his way through the old, closed-down club, using his supernatural senses until he found a doorway that opened to stairs.

"Hey! How about the plan, jackass? I go first?" Devon called as he tried to catch up. Seeing that not even Devon's words had any effect on his Tasker, Gabriel double-timed it to keep up.

Jean-Michel went down the stairs quickly and found himself in a room filled with a pale blue glow. He paused, his eyes closing so he could just feel the power. The room was big enough to be another floor of the club. There was an abandoned bar to one side, broken, moldy stools tossed here and there. He turned to face the right. By the time he had, the other two had joined him. All three were face to face with a swirling whirlpool of mist the size of a garage door. Its hues were various blues, whites, and sparkling silvers and it hung on the back wall like a supernatural tapestry. It was beckoning.

"Raudine..?" Gabriel called to his Tasker as the draconic man stepped forward, mesmerized. "Jean-Michel?"

Jean licked his lips and stepped forward, his hands palm up, facing the portal so that he could feel more of the energy that danced around it. This was part of why the Council deemed dragons dangerous; they could make portals. The energy for him was intoxicating, and it touched his soul. He'd not felt the energy of another dragon in decades. A tear slid down his face.

"It's ok," the lycan whispered to the Councilor. Clearing his throat, Devon turned from the portal to his friend. "We thinkin' dragon made?"

"Yes. But it took a lot of power to do this; a lot of energy shifting. Either more than one or they supplemented it with more energy." Jean turned to the others and added, "A dragon would not have left a portal just sitting in the middle of a human-occupied area. Either someone forced a dragon to make this and forced them to leave or they fell from exhaustion."

"Or did so willingly?" Devon added the other option.

There was a low growl from Jean.

"Would they?" Gabriel obviously didn't want to believe it. He looked from the magical whirlpool at the man next to him.

"As much as I hate admitting it, Devon's right. A dragon might have done this willingly. Actually, it's more likely, since it took a lot of concentration to make a portal so large. When I cast portals, they're simple magical constructs, from one point to another through which I and maybe one other can step. Nothing like this." To make something like this took a steady reserve of energy and a much better knowledge of magic.

"Dragons already have a permanent death warrant on their heads. If Crimson gets wind of this?" Devon didn't like it one bit.

"Either way, there's more than just a dragon at work here." Gabriel suddenly decided. The closer he was to the portal, the more he could feel the pulse get stronger; it was a pulse, wasn't it? "It's beautiful." He wanted badly to touch it and see where it led to.

"It's beautiful, yes. But get no closer. We don't know where it leads." The dragon had not seen the Councilor experience unbridled curiosity before. Sure, he liked to learn things, but the way Gabriel was moving toward that portal spoke of something more.

"We need a witness. If they're coming through this, couldn't we simply go through to find them? Be sure of where they're coming from?" Gabriel asked, looking back over his shoulder at them.

"The only one that knows the destination of that portal is the one that cast it. If we go through, there's a chance we won't be able to get back. We don't even know if the atmosphere contains enough oxygenated air. Doppelgängers are adaptable beings. There's no telling where that leads." Jean-Michel's attention went back to the swirling mist on the wall. Sounds. There were sounds of speaking. Motion. And then the portal flashed, and before them stood two doppelgängers. They were gangly with rubbery pale gray skin. They stood maybe five feet in height with bulbous black eyes and elongated fingers bearing sharp nails.

The Tasker grabbed Gabriel's shoulder and pulled him backward, so he could shield the other man from what was coming. He wouldn't let the doppelgängers touch Gabriel if he could help it. He was growling, his eyes glowed, and his body thrummed with power.

Seeing that they weren't alone, the two scouts took on a defensive stance and emitted a harsh high-pitched screech. Others were coming through the portal behind them.

Instead of abandoning their journey across, or spreading out to try for the door, each came through and took a stand beside the first until there were eight. They were forming a barrier. It was obvious the doppelgängers were going to protect the portal, and Jean-Michel needed to close it. This world needed no more unregistered doppelgängers.

That's when things got tricky. Several of the doppels reached into the skin on their sides and pulled out guns. Jean-Michel grabbed the bar stool closest to him and slung it into the ones closest to him and Gabriel. Then, he began pulling down tables and shoved the Councilor behind the bar for cover. Devon? Well, Devon didn't seem to give a shit. He just aimed and started firing.

"Take out the ones with guns first!" The Tasker rose from cover enough to get some shots off. "If they take us down—" Jean-Michel raised over the bar to fire a couple of shots, making them count. He ducked again and emerged from a different angle to keep firing.

"I'll be damned if they take me," Devon snarled and focused on his inner beast. "I've been through too much ta have what I got. Nobody's takin' my body and my life." He threw his empty gun back to the stairs and ran across the floor toward some boxes. His clothing was already stained with blood. Devon let some of his inner control go, and the wolf emerged. He was so old and experienced with this that the transition was quick. Those around him barely registered the snapping and rearrangement of his inner structure. He gained a foot in height and at least that in shoulder width. The muscle structure of his chest and arms became larger and his nails lengthened. Devon felt the bones in his jaw pop as they extended, ready to rip and shred his enemies.

Shots were ringing out. So much for keeping this quiet. The doppels came forward, rolled, dodged. Sen and Devon were killing some, but there were others coming through the mist. Gabriel got four shots off before one creature knocked the gun from his hand.

"Gabriel! You've got to get to the door!" All the dragon could think of was getting them out safely.

"Better said than done!" Gabriel yelled. His Tasker could see that several doppelgängers were now at the door, trying to keep them in and surrounded. The doppels didn't want witnesses, and they didn't want to give up their way into this world. The thought of being killed and replaced? It scared the dragon to his soul. And to think he might be responsible for the deaths of these other two men? A visceral cry and anger left his chest as he took on those that lunged for him.

Jean-Michel slammed one in the mouth with a fist and turned to send another flying backward into the swirling portal. He fired one gun into the head of a doppelgänger, blood, and brain matter flying while he drew his other weapon. Were they healing and coming back? A quick study told him there were at least 10 now against their 3!

"Devon! You and Gabe need to get out of here!" Jean-Michel found his hand sliced and his gun slung across the floor. "Fuck!" He was down on the floor, fighting for his life.

The lycan had one up in the air by the neck; its claws were rending his wrist. Blood was flowing, but he slammed the thing down before stomping on its head. A sickening pop told everyone this foe would no longer be an issue. The hybrid lycan continued to wade into the crowd of doppelgängers, taking swipes, ripping flesh, and slamming the things into whatever was around him.

"Witnesses!" Gabriel yelled as he watched some of the first go back in and vanish through the portal while fresh support came through to replace them. He punched another one that got through to him. Two of them lifted him into the air to throw him, but he grabbed hold of a thin leathery wrist. Using his weight and the force of the original throw, he went to his knees and pulled the doppelgänger over his shoulder so that it crashed into one of its own kind. Getting up, he ran to where his Tasker was being overwhelmed. He aimed and fired, sending one, then two away before he got snatched to the side.

"Yer kidding!" Devon growled ferociously and ripped the head off of one doppel before flinging all pieces back through the portal over its comrades. He grabbed the next two and bounced their heads together. They landed on each side of him. "Like this?" The wolfish grin on the lycan's face was short-lived. Three more of the things slammed into him. He pushed back while the two he'd just knocked out got pulled through the portal by their brethren.

"There are too many!" the Tasker yelled over the ruckus. He tried his remaining gun, but all he heard was a disappointing click. Dropping the gun, his hand was still out to slam the doppel's armed hand downward, the shot hitting the floor. He lunged forward to land a good knee to the thing's chest and finished breaking the bone to disarm them. Two more sent him flying backward.

The one with the broken arm was scrambling, but Gabriel clocked it with a barstool. "Perfect," Gabriel grabbed the thing and tried to pull it away from the rest of the battle.

Devon crouched and barrelled a bunch of the things over that had tried to cut them off from the stairs and the exit. Gabriel was dragging one of them over, stopping here and there to fight off more. They were slashing and fighting at least as good as the Councilor, some as good as he fought! He had to sling some off and barely shielded his eyes from a vicious hit.

Breathing heavily, the Tasker spared a glance at Gabriel. The giant wolf-hybrid was near the Councilor and that's what he needed. The Councilor was near the stairs.

"Get him out!" Jean moved as quickly as he could, grabbing a hold of one of the doppels, and literally spun with it around and around to get the others to back off. He let go, taking out several. How many were going to be here?

"It's dead..." Gabriel had gotten a moment's respite while Jean-Michel and Devon continued to fight off more of the doppelgängers. He scanned the room. The ones on the ground. Were they all dead or unconscious? He looked closer at the one he had thought was just knocked out. There was an odd-colored foam at the corner of their mouth. "Poison?"

"Let's go!" Devon didn't care. "We got lucky, let's not tempt it, boy!"

Jean-Michel was still fighting. There were more coming through, but worse – the edges of the portal fluctuated. The color went from blue to purple and indigo colors. The energy within it began crackling like the electrical currents made by static. "A portal would be helpful!" Devon had Gabriel defended nearby, waiting.

"Is it going to explode?" Gabriel watched as the magical energy pulsed and sizzled around the sides of the portal.

"Probably!" Devon yelled.

Getting a reprieve thanks to the portal fluctuating again, Jean-Michel ran back to them. He held his palm up to the back wall and pushed his magic outward to make a circular portal, much smaller than the one they were seeing in the back wall.

"We can't let that many innocent people die! There are people all around this thing!" Gabriel yelled over the din of the portal's reverberating sounds.

Jean-Michel looked into Gabriel's brown eyes. He remembered the eyes of the little girl on the train. Gabriel's eyes reminded him more of her eyes than of the empty eyes he usually saw when looking at a human. He remembered Ezekiel's words.

"...you were responsible for the deaths of thousands of humans, maybe even millions..."

"Get him out of here before he gets killed, Devon!" Jean-Michel ordered.

"Right." Maybe it was the odd scent of ozone that was suddenly in the air. Maybe it was the expression on the Tasker's face. But the lycan did as he was told. Forcing the shifted nails back, he grabbed the Councilor by the biceps. Devon turned and started out with Gabriel in tow.

"What are you...!" Gabriel blustered as he tried to jerk free of the iron-tight grip the lycan had on him.

"If it goes down wrong, you don't want to be here!"

"But... Jean!" Gabriel couldn't fight the grip the lycan had on him. They were out the other side of the portal and the Tasker closed it.

The once placid mist in the large portal was now a churning, menacing storm of electrical current and changing color. The doppelgängers even had trouble navigating it. When the doppels already on this side saw the Councilor and lycan exiting, they all pushed forward. Jean-Michel welcomed it. He swatted and swung and kicked and then felt them overwhelm him with bites and scratches and strength that belied their awkward looks.

It was too late. The dragon was pulling the magical energy from the portal. Several of the doppelgängers realized their fate and tried to scramble away. Again - it was too late. Draconic eyes glowed, and he felt the shift begin. This was going to hurt like fuck. But he couldn't stop. The basement of this place wasn't large enough to hold his bulk like this, so his scaley back broke through the floor into the empty warehouse above.

Doppelgängers screamed as the heat around the dragon's body escalated and rolled from him in waves to engulf them. Many pulled back and went running into the unstable portal to what would either be their safety or their death. Pushing his black and maroon snout outward to the portal, the dragon let himself pull energy from it. Getting to his haunches, the building's next two floors busted and fell in avalanches of brick, mortar, wood, and dust around him. The pain of the constriction and then the pelting of heavy objects had him groaning. His eyes closed on tears of pain.

His clawed hands moved palms out, and the blue energy coming from him flowed in the opposite direction of the portal energy. That chaotic energy beckoned his soul. After so many lonely years, it was that promise of nothingness that was so very tempting. He'd killed so many...maybe he deserved it. But what would happen if he left? Devon, Gabriel, and so many more would die.

His body felt the pull, but he couldn't. He fought the enticement and instead pushed that energy, along with some of his own more fiery energy, back into the center of the portal.

The swirling wild energy that had once flowed clockwise on the wall began churning counter-clockwise. There were screams from the other side as magic shot backward and into the other dimension. Thunder without a storm sounded from the implosion of the portal. The dark-scaled dragon felt pulled toward the center of the energy but then thrown backward by the concussive blast.

Outside, Devon shoved Gabriel into the car and placed his own body over the man, just as the shockwave hit. Alarms went off all over the city, radiating outward from this location. Transformers blew all around them, leaving the approaching twilight to the darkness of night to come.

"Stay put. Make a peep and I'll tie ya up so ya don't move again." Devon got up and spun to head back into the building for Jean-Michel.

"He's…he's alive?" Gabriel stared, gape-jawed, trying to catch his breath. He wiped at his mouth to catch some blood from dripping.

The big lycan growled, "He better be."

Chapter 20
After the Explosion

It was nearly midnight before he had gotten on the road from the airport. Ezekiel was going to the Crimson Base, located under the local college in the unassuming town of Whitley, NC. He already had a headache. Unfortunately, the reports had been coming in for the past half hour about a possible supernatural incident. He changed his direction. The headache got worse.

Police wrapped crime scene tape around the outside of a building. They even taped off the alleys and everything close to it. The warehouse and the lower floor had once been a nightclub. There had been a clear explosion that had temporarily taken out the power from the surrounding blocks. The investigation was underway by the local departments.

After talking to the mundane human officials, Ezekiel walked back to his sedan. He'd get more answers from his team of cyber investigators. But he'd had to at least try. People were being evacuated in case of a gas leak. No one could make heads or tails of how this had happened.

At least, no one without magical knowledge could understand this.

It only took seconds before his ringtone told him he had to answer some questions. He took in a cleansing breath before answering.

"Tell me why I'm standing here, watching you talk to police officers who are roping off the area around our portal." Malcolm's voice spoke of waning emotional control. "You were supposed to have kept the portal secure. I come here to welcome the last of my group to their new world, and I cannot get to the portal."

"The portal is destroyed," Ezekiel stated what he thought was obvious. But supernaturals were a pain in the ass for the dramatic. Skinner rubbed his temple while listening.

"What do you mean, it was destroyed? You told us... No, you assured us you had this under control." There was a pause. "Where are my people, Skinner? We felt some of them die."

"Meet me in the botanical garden a few blocks up." He ended the call so there would be no argument. It took a lot of power to destroy a portal so that it imploded. And one that large? Where he was going, there would be no cameras near. The rose garden pavilion would be empty.

As soon as he arrived at the student union building, Skinner got out and began strolling toward the quarter-block-sized sanctuary on campus. Sure, it wasn't a full botanical garden, but the students had created a beautiful arboretum through which you could walk and no cameras were around. It was nice, clean, safe, and public enough that it didn't cause questions. It was private enough that they wouldn't get overheard.

Soon enough, the doppelgänger entered and made their way to the clearing where Skinner stood.

Ezekiel was not facing Malcolm when the doppelgänger approached. He was busy piecing things together. Was it dangerous to keep your back to someone like Malcolm? Perhaps. But it would remind the doppelgänger who was in charge.

"It is becoming precarious, this situation. Many of us wonder, would it not be better to simply wait for the Council's decision? Perhaps the vote will allow us freedom of movement. Perhaps we were mistaken in trusting you, Ezekiel Skinner."

Skinner turned on the doppelgänger quickly.

"First things first. You work for me and not the other way around. If not for me, you wouldn't be here and your kind would still be in that cesspool of a slaver's camp. Would you prefer that?"

Instead of responding, Malcolm, skinned as a common business person, stood and listened.

"Second, you have no choice but to continue with the course plotted. Vote or not, you and yours have committed many crimes that you cannot back away from. If you had followed my instructions, there would be no danger. Everything goes back to that."

There was still no response from the doppelgänger.

"Third, your mouth could have gotten this found out. As far as I know, we could sling accusations all night long, but that wouldn't get us anywhere, would it?" His silver brow raised as he waited for a sincere acknowledgment from the creature.

Malcolm nodded once in agreement.

"So, here's what I know. You've got your first set of doppels here. We need to work with them. They need to get into place. I assigned you particular targets in a particular order. The obstacles that have popped into existence are here because someone didn't take that order seriously."

"You're referring to the human Councilor Gabriel Kennedy and his drunk Tasker," Malcolm stated with no emotion.

"Yes. Those are two of the six targets I refer to."

"The vampire was... impressive. We did not prepare appropriately. The other two—

"One of which I helped with?" Ezekiel crossed his arms over his chest.

"Considering this subsequent - obstacle - we will place greater importance on the taking of the other three. We will ensure the most experienced doppelgängers are prepared for taking..."

"Change of plan." Ezekiel put a hand in his pocket.

Malcolm placed his human hands together, fingertip to fingertip at his waist.

"Don't touch the Tasker. He's mine to deal with. Be ready to take the vampire. Once the Tasker is out of the way, only then do you target the vampire. Go after the human Councilor first. When the Tasker is not around. They most likely just tried to ruin our plans. They need to be out of the way before we bring any more of your kind over."

"Will you discuss this with Tal'Secus? They will not hold these things against us?" Malcolm waited.

"Tal'Secus will not hold it against you. No."

"If you are saying this human and his Tasker are responsible for killing those we felt die, we are very interested in taking them. We wish to expunge our mistake."

"You heard me," Ezekiel spoke bluntly. There was a long silence.

"We have done more than our share of ensuring your control, Director. We will continue our course for the benefit of all parties involved. Be sure another portal is available, and soon."

"I'm sure Tal'Secus will have it arranged."

"What kind of magic and physical protections might we expect when taking the Councilor?"

"Catch the Councilor alone. Should be simple enough. He's constantly pulling all-nighters at the Chamber or at his own office building. He's nothing. I'm fairly certain his family gifts have bypassed him. And if you have the tools, getting into either place should be simple. Especially considering the help you have." Ezekiel wore a pained smirk as his gaze drifted to the ground in thought, then raised to the doppelgänger again.

"We shall put the plans in motion immediately. We were unaware that things needed to move so rapidly."

"Some of you got caught in the middle of taking someone. That's where things went wrong. Our timeline needs to speed up considerably. Just make sure and get the rest of your picks into the Chamber. Make sure you do it now before they've figured out the entire puzzle. Otherwise, I cannot provide your other comrades with passage and placement. You're running out of time." Ezekiel turned to leave. He'd said what needed to be said. The doppel knew the plans. He didn't need to draw a diagram for him.

Malcolm watched the Director of Crimson walk away before stepping back into the shadows.

Once Skinner got to his car. His hands gripped the steering wheel as if he were choking someone. Taking a deep breath, he came out of the moment and pulled out his phone. A quick touch of a contact later and he had a ringtone in his ear.

"Yes?"

"Someone extinguished the portal. We'll need a new one if you want more doppelgängers to come through. If not, that's between you and Malcolm."

"Who could close a portal in such a fashion?" The deep male voice responded with a very direct question.

"Who do you think it was, Dezerian? Who hides that much power and can make or manipulate portals?" Skinner shook his head and rolled his eyes.

The man on the other side of the conversation growled, letting the Crimson director know he needed to lose the attitude. It also reminded the magus know he was treading on very thin ice with one of the rare few that could actually strip off everything that he was.

"It's Mr. Proctor, when we speak even like this. As for a new portal, I'll send my daughter to you. I'm fairly certain that I do not need to caution you where she is concerned."

"Of course you don't. Though, I'm not sure what you mean to do with Em, I mean... Amanda here. There have been too many close calls. It'd be best to open a new portal elsewhere. If you even want to continue with this scheme. You know, I swore my vows to Tal'Secus long ago. I'm only trying to carry out your orders."

"This entire scheme was not my plan to begin with, but Tal'Secus voted and I allowed it to grow to fruition. You simply had to direct the pieces, Ezekiel. Now that it is a problem, I'm left to clean it up. Or rather, you are with my instruction. If this fails, and things move to the Chamber for judgment, I expect you to see that no one gets the information the doppels are currently privy to."

"They know it's better to die than get caught. Their elders can take out the rest via mental manipulation. I've seen it happen. And I've ordered that the plans continue. I need to get Raudine on a tighter leash. I did not know he'd be an issue. Last I saw him, he was a shadow of himself. The only thing I can come up with is that this new Kennedy heir is pushing him."

"Is that so? Is this someone that needs to be taken care of?" This plan wasn't originally his to begin with, but he'd see it through.

"He'll be the next target. The problem is, he's now more cautious and the doppelgängers here are more nervous. It's the natural course of things. Unfortunately, once I get the actors on their way, I'll be on my way to another meeting. Everyone's going to want an explanation. You may give the orders and talk about cleaning it up, but remember, I'm the one left holding the broom and dustpan." Ezekiel paused. "If this wasn't your scheme, whose was it? I'd like to know who to avoid."

"Whose was it you ask? Tal'Secus is the one taking responsibility, but it isn't our fault entirely. Morfesa took it upon himself to come up with this little fiasco that we currently wade through. That old claw lets his emotions guide his actions. I figured out long ago that emotions only end missions and schemes badly. So far, you've been decently attending to it, aside from this current mess with the portal. As far as the rest know, all of Tal'Secus is behind this and it will remain as such until it no longer benefits us. The last thing we need right now is dissension amongst the members. That's a distraction when we least need it."

"Understood." Ezekiel knew Dezerian trusted him more than the others save his child. And Emriess or Amanda as humanity knew her, also trusted him. It might have been a loose trust, but it was at least more than nothing.

"Keep things going as they are for now with this scheme. When it takes a turn, handle your part and leave Morfesa out of it. I'll see to him and work this out in our own fashion." There was a momentary pause before Dezerian added, "As to the location for the new portal, I will leave that to you and my daughter's discretion." The call ended.

The Crimson Director had a great deal to think about. Being Dezerian's favored underling gave Ezekiel certain benefits. Now at least the magi knew who he was possibly dealing with. Finally, with a deep breath, Ezekiel got underway. It seemed someone needed to be reminded of his place.

Chapter 21
Back to Good?

"I thought you could heal..." Gabriel's voice penetrated his addled mind. Jean-Michel was sitting on the right side of the bench in the back seat of the truck. He was holding onto the passenger seat in front of him for dear life as Devon took the corners and curves.

"Not like lycan. I use potions. And that was a lot at once. I got sprayed with magic. Kind of does a number on my system, Councilor," Jean-Michel muttered.

Devon had dumped him into the back seat and hightailed it from the scene. The bulk of the injury had happened to his back. There were cuts and punctures down the left side. The Councilor had the first aid kit opened. He pulled out the normal saline and the antiseptic wash along with several packages of gauze that he tore open. Pouring the purified water over Jean's back, Gabriel worked and cleaned away some of the mess; pieces of wood and grit from the explosion. The rest he wiped down with the antiseptic wash and felt Jean tense from the action.

"This isn't exactly easy for me, either. Thank goodness for gloves and towels." Gabriel hated the idea of dealing with bodily fluids and blood. What kept him going was the fact that they wouldn't be alive if his Tasker hadn't done this.

Jean-Michel groaned when the wounds were being sterilized. His fingers gripped the cushion on the passenger seat from the back. He rested his head against it.

"Are you alright, Jean-Michel?" Gabriel's voice was softer than it had been in days.

"I'll live. I took some of the good stuff before we even left, so my body should heal a little faster than normal, and I can take more once we get to ...where are we going? Just hurts like hell right now." He swallowed. "We need to clean up, tell Vanishte what's going on, and see who we've rattled."

"I'm takin' ya to the estate first." Devon chimed in from the driver's seat. "You need to be cleaned up a bit before we go to the Chamber." He turned into the long looped drive that led to Gabriel Kennedy's estate.

As he pulled the remnants of the ripped shirt away from the wounds, something caught Gabriel's attention. There was a scarred tattoo that the draconic man sported beneath his shoulder blade. Wiping the dirt from it, he found he couldn't look away. The inked portion, now that he was quietly and gently washing away the blood and filth from it, matched the Irish version of the Kennedy Coat of Arms. Oak, helm, and shield. On the left side of this was a scar – definitely a slice or stab wound of some sort. The skin had not properly sewn, so the design and color of the tattoo were partially gone.

But on the other side, there was the puffed and partially blackened skin that spoke of a brand. The design of the brand was Celtic knotwork. At the top right was the stylized head of a dragon. The same as he had seen in the book about dragons; the book about spells used to capture the creatures. His mind went back over the times he'd seen something like this, from his grandfather's cane to the books and the rubbings from the old graveyard. Suddenly, Jean-Michel's voice cut through his haze of memories.

"I couldn't get one… you know…for a witness, Gabriel. There were too many. They all left or…" He huffed his frustration, "I'm sorry."

Jean-Michel's words pulled Gabriel back to the moment. It was the first apology that the man had ever given him. It was sincere. In a matter of five minutes, Gabriel got shocked more than once. He just continued to clean the fissures. He was watching the skin knit itself slowly before his very eyes.

"Don't worry about it. Here, use this on your face." He handed some of the wet gauze to the Tasker and scooted to the side a bit to be out of the way.

"Now, to figure out the plan. Since we can't trace the portal to its creator, I guess we'll have to figure things out another way." Devon pointed out as he parked the truck in the drive outside the side door instead of the main door.

"At least no more can get through. Not through that portal. That leaves granting legitimacy to Vanishte. Then, figure a way to set up rules for legalizing doppelgängers that haven't already committed a crime. You've got your meeting scheduled."

"Right," Gabriel whispered.

"Derek says Skinner went to the scene. I have a hunch we're gonna find out who has some stakes in this situation soon enough." Devon's gaze moved from his phone to the rear-view mirror.

Jean-Michel hadn't moved. He still had his head on the back of the passenger seat. Gabriel tried removing some of the filth-encrusted shirt again. But the expression on Jean-Michel's face concerned him.

The Tasker's eyes were closed tightly and out of nowhere he sucked in a gasping breath, which had Gabriel pulling back quickly.

"Did I hurt you?" Gabriel's brown eyes went large as he wound up facing those blue-green draconic eyes. They were beautiful and mesmerizing, and he hated the idea that he might've hurt the man who owned that gaze. Suddenly, the door behind him opened, and Devon was standing there.

"Hey Gabe, we'll meet ya inside. Head in and get things together for proper doctorin'. I'll help Jean-Michel in so ya have plenty of time to prep for him."

"Okay." He turned to get out of the truck and made his way to the door. He couldn't help but look back as Devon helped his Tasker from the vehicle. He wanted to help. But he knew to do as he was told. Considering Devon's expression, arguing would be a bad idea.

"I must've worried him. He didn't argue," the Tasker chuckled as he got out of the truck, holding onto Devon's shoulder for support. "They didn't rip a muscle at least. Just skin. Just blood and pain are all. Hand me my bag. Need a clean shirt."

Devon reached back in and grabbed the small duffel to hand to his friend.

"Sen.. brother, what the hell are ya doing? Have ya lost sight of what you're working towards?" There was a little touch of irritation to the rumble in his chest. The rumble was supposed to soothe, not aggravate, and he hoped it would.

"Don't call me that. I haven't gone by that name in centuries..."

Devon drew in a deep breath and huffed, "Yeah, seems ya forgot it altogether, Senias."

"Stop..." the Tasker held onto the doorframe and glared at Devon. "Stop calling me that." Jean slurred the words. Though he was trying to sound angry, he couldn't. He was once again looking at his reflection, this time in the door window. Soot, blood, and mortar dust were all in his raggedy ass beard. Who was he? What was he? What was he trying to do?

And that's when he found he was being taken by the shoulders and forcibly turned. Opening his blue-green eyes, he couldn't evade Devon's amber gaze.

"Ya have a real chance at freedom, brother. Ya just gotta keep yer mind on track and be awful damned careful with the road yer traveling down right now. I'm having this heart ta heart not just for yer sake, but for Gabe's. Well, and my peace of mind. My Eva wants to see that Gabriel Kennedy finds happiness and woe be unto the one that upsets that plan."

The lycan knew him too well. He was still recovering from the blast and the energy drain. He was taking breaths as he listened to Devon's words carefully.

"It's my place as yer friend, yer brother by blood, ta point it out, Sen. Ya made me vow ta help steer ya the right way. I'm trying."

"It's been so long..." He murmured. "My name..." He suddenly stiffened and touched his bare shoulders. "Shit, the mark—"

Devon's eyes went wide, and he turned the Tasker to see the bared mark. The boy had been treating those quickly healing wounds.

"Dammit, Sen. He's gonna slam ya with a million questions, and how are ya gonna answer those?" Devon watched his friend turn to get into his bag. He handed Devon a hand towel. "What am I doin' with this?"

"Make sure the bleeding stops and it's clean enough. I've got my workout shirt in here..."

"And the situation?"

"I'll... I'll think of something. You've said before I'm the king of bullshit, right?" He heard the text tone on his phone but ignored it. "Help me with this shirt. My head's splitting open." He tossed an old t-shirt to the lycan and, holding the side of the truck, waited for help.

"Yeah, but that one's like his grandfather and grandmother combined. And ya never could bullshit either of them." Devon began helping the Tasker with the shirt.

"I've tried to stay away from him ever since his grandfather introduced us. After Amelia died, I had my hands full cleaning up his grandfather's and father's messes. He doesn't remember me in most of it. Until now, he stayed out of trouble." Jean-Michel finished pulling the t-shirt into place. Picking up the bag in one hand, he closed the SUV with the other.

"Heh, yeah, perfect timing. He finds trouble right as it finds you." Devon made tsk-tsking sounds as they walked in.

Gabriel saw the blood in the mirror and touched the drop to take it from his cheek. Dragon's blood. Ancient's blood. *His Ancient?* He gripped the sink and closed his eyes tightly.

"No..." he whispered. His brown eyes looked into the mirror. He heard Devon and Jean-Michel in the sitting room. Moving the water over his face again, he turned off the tap and grabbed a towel for drying.

"What do you need from us? And do you have any painkillers?" Gabriel found some over-the-counter tablets in the medicine cabinet and refilled the water cup before making his way out to them.

Devon was watching the Tasker closely. Gabriel handed over pain medication along with water. "It's not much, but maybe it'll help."

"Thank you, Gabriel. Merci." Jean spoke quietly for now.

Gabriel was hovering. Devon cleared his throat to get their attention.

"I can take him home. He needs ta clean up. Maybe, he'll be able ta think clearer. What d'ya think, Gabe...?"

"Is that a Kennedy brand on your back? Were you a slave?"

There was a deep, irritated growl coming from Devon. The lycan looked from Gabriel to Jean-Michel, nostrils flaring.

"Your mess, you clean it up! I'm goin' home. You know how ta get me." And with that, he marched out of the room and, by the sound of the slamming door, out of the house.

Gabriel wasn't sure what to think. The expression on his Tasker's face said that Jean-Michel knew more about what was going on in the old lycan's head than he did.

"Maybe you should go with him."

"I know you too well. You'll want to go to the Chamber soon. After what we just went through, I feel like leaving you alone would be an idiot move." Before Gabriel could argue, the Tasker continued, "You just witnessed something no one wants to be known. You're also pushing for a case that has you dipping your fingers into someone's cookie bowl. You need protection." With a sigh, Jean-Michel made his request. "Just let me get cleaned up. Then we can talk or you can get some sleep. After all, it's been a while since you really had any, right? And you need to be sharp, not exhausted."

Gabriel let his eyes rest on the Tasker for an endless pause. Decision made, he opened the door to the bathroom and Jean tossed in the bag he'd been carrying. It was time to get cleaned up and change clothes.

While his Tasker showered, Gabriel stretched to ward off his own bout of weariness. He walked back out into the kitchen to get some coffee. Then he made it back into the sitting room with a small notebook and a pen and began writing out a list of things he needed to do. Once they got back to the Chamber, he needed to make sure everything was in perfect order. His other notes and star charts had to do with Jean-Michel. Perhaps he would put those reference books away. After all, Jean-Michel had made a good argument for not researching ...him.

Rubbing his temple, he finally stopped and nodded to himself. Gabriel tucked his notes back into his pocket. Out of sight, out of mind, right? No. Not that easy. Damn it, he wanted answers! Things unraveling like this? He didn't like it. It went past his boundaries and reached into the unknown to make him anxious.

"Now, what can I help you with?" Jean-Michel asked. He tried to be soft, but the natural, deep timbre made him sound more demanding.

"Oh, um, nothing really. We need to go to the chamber, obviously. I mean, I have my notes on the doppelgängers and will have Skinner's detailed report on the portal. Hopefully, we can find witnesses. Whoever's giving them a place..." The words fell off as his mind dove into the deep. Rubbing the bridge of his nose as he normally did when frustrated or beyond exhausted, he blurted, "This is about my family; my life. I should know."

"You never asked, Gabriel." Jean-Michel sighed before whispering something under his breath; something Gabriel recognized as arcane. A swirl of light, sparkling – swelled from his hand to cascade outward in a dome-like shape, disappearing as it came to the edge of the room. The sound of the doors locking followed. "I don't want anyone else hearing us."

"My family's crest. It's ... there was a brand on your back," the Councilor stated.

"Yes." Jean sat on the large table across the floor from Gabriel.

"Ignorance isn't bliss, Jean-Michel. It's a state of paranoia for me. I don't understand what's coming at me, because no one has ever told me anything about you, about the history of my family, or anything." He turned away, pacing. "All I've learned, I've learned from the Council and from my research. My grandmother died when I was a child and my grandfather was always jumping into my life when I needed him, but then fled from me instead of helping me learn."

"He was hurting. Don't hold it against him, Gabriel. He lost the love of his life when Amelia died and had to deal with your father and his wife – a chore I wouldn't wish on anyone."

"Try being their child!" Gabriel pointed out harshly, his jaw moving as he fought the emotions. "They shamed me for anything I did that wasn't perfect while I had to come home and clean up their mess."

"Touché," the Tasker took a deep breath. "Being the child of entitled drunks couldn't have been easy for you. I'm not arguing with you. I agree with you. But your life is not the only one affected by giving you the knowledge you seek."

"Is that why Devon's so angry?"

"A bit." Jean-Michel put his hands on the table to the sides of his legs. "Devon promised me he'd help me this time around in getting my life back...my freedom. He's like a brother to me and he's angry with me for giving you as much information as I already have."

"Why does your freedom depend upon my ignorance?" Gabriel was clenching and unclenching his fists.

"Your family has used their blessing in magic in the past to help them survive and to do so, they could also take dragons into their servitude." He watched Gabriel close his eyes, his shoulders droop. "We had no choice. Dragons were being wiped out, and we had no recourse with Crimson or the Council – such a young institution at the time." Jean-Michel took a deep breath before getting up and taking off the clean shirt.

Gabriel's eyes focused on the Tasker's shirt and then his chest as he pulled the cloth over his head. His face had flushed naturally. "Jean?"

"You wanted to know." He whispered and turned, revealing beneath his right shoulder blade the Kennedy family crest branded into his skin. Looking back over his shoulder, he continued. "I believe you saw it earlier. It's healed up again now, so you can really inspect it. In my true form, that was placed beneath a scale below my right wing. It hurt like a...like you wouldn't believe. Humans and their need to claim everything."

"Your other wounds, they're gone. Just bruising or streaks..."

"I took the potion I had in my bag and poured it directly over my back. It hurt like hell, but it worked. Unfortunately, I'm out of those..." He paused when he realized Gabriel wasn't interested in that. "Why not this? Why does this remain?"

"Yes." Gabriel got up from the chair to be closer to the presented back. No, the presented brand.

"I can change into a human body, not because of my magical blood, but because a Kennedy that was far superior to me in magical knowledge made this deal with me. I'd always be able to shift between two forms and their family would always have a protector. That is the seal of the deal and it cannot be removed. My body can heal quickly, but only if I use something to help it.

Like any human, I'd never survive a fatal wound. Or if I had too many injuries, of course. But this was also part of the bargain."

"So, was it worth it?"

"Perhaps." Jean-Michel felt Gabriel close to him and closed his eyes.

"Your ancestors wanted to remind me who I belong to. So long as there's an heir to the Kennedy line, I have a master or a mistress. There used to be a tattoo over it, which used enchanted ink. I had someone cut it with a blade at one point. But you can still see it. That's a testament to the magic they had command of back then."

Gabriel focused on the design that was forever imprinted on the man's skin. The Councilor had no tattoos of any kind or any other such markings to his own flesh, so he couldn't imagine what it had felt like for Jean. His head tilted just a little to the right to take in the somewhat faded details. It spread from just beneath Raudine's right shoulder blade to his spine.

"Devon and I theorized that if there was ever a generation of Kennedys who never even knew about it and so never called on me through the bond—"

"You'd be free." Mentally, his sleep-deprived mind pieced the information together, and it suddenly made sense. "Grandfather said I would always be watched and always be protected. I thought he meant in public, you know, a warning to keep up appearances and be prepared." Without even a second thought, Gabriel reached out with his fingertips to trace the design and whispered, "He meant you…"

The Tasker shivered at the faint electrical sensation that came from feeling Gabriel's touch. Gabriel's blood held sway upon him and made the sensation heighten when he touched it…or did his touch make it feel better?

"I won't hold you to some… some sick bargain they made. I don't work that way." Gabriel turned away. "I've prosecuted people for less than what my family has done to you. They've made me into a hypocrite."

"We have no choice in it. It doesn't work that way, Gabriel." Jean-Michel turned when the man stepped back.

"My Aunt Rose is still alive, and she has what? 5 kids? Wouldn't that mean, if I died…"

"Jonathan Kennedy chose you, not them. Don't you remember?"

"Yes." Gabriel well remembered the first time he'd set eyes upon Jean-Michel. "I was 17. He was showing me the Chamber. And you walked up. I remember you were taller than both of us. We shook hands and there was... a sensation."

"In the hand's palm. I remember it, too. Your grandfather told you that one day I would be yours."

"I thought he meant as a Tasker, not..." With a huff of breath, he made his way to the nearest seat and slumped down in it. "So if I can't break it, how can we work this so that you have choices?"

"I had choices and still do. I wanted to survive back then. And I did. I'm not sure what I want now."

"What do you mean?" Gabriel wasn't sure where this was going, but he wanted to know. He wanted to understand. What he got surprised him.

"I've tried getting myself killed, but I suppose fate doesn't take kindly to that. When you live a long life, find a reason to make it worth living. I'm trying to find that." He stood tall, pulled on his shirt, and continued, "What I know now is that I am needed. A dragon made that portal, Gabriel. And whoever brought those doppels through also used that dragon. I want to find whoever did this." He then grinned, adding, "Not to mention, you definitely entertain me."

"Good to know I can be entertaining. I thought you'd never let go of the phrase 'stick up your ass'. Entertaining is a much more acceptable description of me." He tried some sarcastic humor as well. The entire conversation had been so serious and much deeper than he had planned. A bit of levity was welcome.

"I'm not saying you don't..."

"Before you ruin this moment," Gabriel held up one finger to keep Jean-Michel from speaking. "Let me say I've come to enjoy your company. I never knew about the bargain, and even in knowing it, I'll never use it against you and I'll never reveal it. You have my word that once I die, the bargain ends. If I could end it sooner, I would. But I would like to live my life out at least."

"You should never make promises you're not sure you can keep."

"No. The promise stands. I guess what I'm trying to say is that if you walked away and never looked back, I wouldn't go seeking you out demanding the bargain. You could go, have a life or search for others. None would be the wiser and the bargain would die with me. There will be no more heirs."

"So I gathered. How is it you've hidden such an important thing from your family and associates for so long?"

"I simply gave them all what they wanted." Gabriel spread his arms wide, and he turned in a slow circle before the other man's eyes. "I try to be perfect at everything. So I'm not questioned. They see what they want to see. That's not the real me." His hands pulled in to smooth down the material of his shirt. "On the flip side, I'm selective about the men I associate with. They have more to lose by talking than I do."

"I imagine military school was quite the awakening." Raudine chuckled, and Gabe joined him in it. "Things are much more open and accepting in the world at large. Why not come out?"

"Being anything less than perfect was unacceptable. In my father's eyes and in the time frame, I was most impressionable – it was just not done. And for now, I have no reason to be out. Maybe if I had a reason." There was the start of an uncomfortable silence, and so, Gabriel broke it. "We need to get back to the Council Chamber."

Chapter 22
Angering the Director

The Tasker's phone went off again. This was the third text tone. Jean sighed before digging it from his pocket. "Great..."

"What?" Gabriel was a little frustrated that someone was interrupting them.

"Another man with an opinion wanting to tell me how I've fucked up." The dragon actually growled.

Gabriel's breath caught at the sound, but no sooner did that happen than he heard the yelling coming from outside. It had him turning toward the enormous doors at the entrance of the Chamber.

"RAUDINE!" Ezekiel's voice traveled from outside the door.

The Tasker grimaced, his shoulders actually hunching over a bit when he heard it.

Gabriel quickly stepped back to the table, placing some space between himself and his Tasker. Great. Now they'd all be in the same room for this party. Lovely. And they hadn't really had time to get their stories straight. Gabriel hoped he could get them through this.

"So here you are. And with your Councilor. Good." The Director turned and slammed the door closed behind him before glaring at the two of them. The normally cool and collected man seemed pretty damned perturbed.

"What?" Jean-Michel was happy to have at least had time to clean himself up before Skinner got there. And now he grew a perfectly crooked halo to go with the clean clothes and body.

"Director Skinner, what can we do for you?" Gabriel turned towards the Director with his very chilled business facade in place.

"Where's your third musketeer?"

"What are you talking about?" Jean asked innocently but with enough attitude to make the words seem natural.

"The lycan! Devon Weylyn. You're joined at the hip too much for me to have to explain this."

"He's home, I suppose. And considering you've included me in this, you will explain yourself, Director. This is not your place." Gabriel was already warning the man with his words. It also placed Skinner's attention mostly on him, which he hoped Jean-Michel appreciated.

"Tell me the three of you didn't just step on an undercover Crimson investigation a year in the making. Tell me you didn't ruin our chances of figuring out who's been experimenting with illegal portals in the middle of our territory?" He placed his hands on the railing and studied them. "Tell me. Just... tell me that eyewitnesses didn't just describe your vehicle to the LOCAL HUMAN police."

"A red king-cab truck or a black Suburban with tinted windows? I drive both." He kind of droned on for effect. "I use both and keep them here often or take them with me or let people borrow them. I wonder how many other people around this area own similar vehicles?"

"Oh, don't give me any of that shit. What were you doing there? Why?" Ezekiel wasn't backing down.

"Honestly, do I look like the type to go roaming the city streets managing daring deeds?" Gabriel asked. There was not a speck of dust on him. He was, as always, immaculate. After all, he'd cleaned up and changed before getting here. His Tasker had even had a shower.

Turning from Skinner to his Tasker, Gabriel sighed in irritation, "Where did you get off to this time? Was it drinking or fighting that you just washed up from? Are you about to go for a workout?" He lifted a dark brow as he watched Jean. "I thought you were following leads."

"You're going to use your drunken monkey play on this?" Skinner asked, crossing his arms over his chest. His eyes glared daggers at a man, who, ironically, had used the same ploy to get things out of people before – for Skinner's benefit. Oh, the director did not like being double-crossed.

Raudine reached up and scratched his head, then picked a piece of fuzz from it. He studied the fuzz and then flicked it off his fingers. After that, he eyed the director and shrugged.

"I know this game, you ass. It will not work." Skinner looked like he was ready to explode.

Watching Jean's antics made Gabriel want to smile. It was refreshing not being the recipient of that attitude. Right now, he could actually see the entertainment value in it.

"Now, what is this business of undercover investigations? I don't recall any mention of undocumented portals in the area being looked into. Were you overseeing a major investigation without Council approval, Director Skinner?"

"Why would we tell you? It was an executive decision." Ezekiel huffed a frustrated bunch of air from his chest. "The Council is on report for possibly being compromised – your own words. And that's also why we're having the meeting, remember? I took your word for it and continued the investigation. We know where the doppels were coming in, now. But it would've been better to have one of them as a witness. Unfortunately, the alleged portal is gone. So are the witnesses."

"Careful quoting policy and procedure to me, Director." Gabriel narrowed his glare. He had Ezekiel Skinner precisely where he wanted him. He'd turned the tables on the man. Known for his prosecutorial skills, Gabriel also had a penchant for understanding the rules and laws he worked with. "That could end up very messy for you. After all, my family helped write a lot of those procedures."

"Sounds bad," Jean-Michel spoke quietly from his place. And that's all it had taken to get Ezekiel's goat.

Skinner walked close to the Tasker, and he put a finger in the man's chest. Raudine's gaze followed the finger and then lifted to meet the Director's fierce glare.

"I'm onto you," he whispered through clenched teeth. "Let's not mince words. You've known that I've known for a very, very long time. Just because you won't admit it means nothing to me. Tuck that away deep into that alcohol-addled brain of yours."

"Excuse me!" Dr. Samantha Keene called from the doorway. She glanced at Gabriel with a brow raised before turning her attention to where Skinner was standing.

Taking a step back, Skinner turned to the doorway.

"They told me I could find you here, Director. I believe you have a body or more I need to autopsy?" Sam waited.

"I'll be right there, Doctor." Skinner's threatening eyes roved from the Tasker to the Councilor as the doctor stepped back outside. Finally, he turned to make his way to the door.

"Director Skinner!" Gabriel called, just as Ezekiel got to the door. He saw the stiff way the director halted. The man rocked on his feet, then turned around to wait for the rest of what Gabriel had to say.

"Being that I am Lead Councilor in this case, I will expect a full report on this investigation you've been working on without our permission. I need it before the start of the meeting." Gabriel turned from the Director and went back to casually moving papers around on the table.

After an exasperated sigh, the door opened and closed. Raudine's eyes closed. He let out a held breath.

"That was a dick move. Well done." Jean-Michel watched the Councilor, who hadn't actually stopped looking at the books and paperwork on the table. "Where were we?" Jean asked.

"Forget it.. you've explained and I've listened. I explained, and you listened. We're even." Gabe turned and had to put his hand on the table to steady himself. He was beyond the point of exhaustion.

"You barely made it through that confrontation. How long's it been without sleep this time?" The Tasker placed a muscular arm around his Councilor's waist to help him get to the secret room. "Come on. Let me help. You need to sleep."

"I don't know." Gabriel pushed his feet to work. He hated being coddled. He wanted to pull away from Raudine, but his body was just not cooperating. "I need to say something."

"No, you don't. You need to rest." The Tasker opened the wooden panel to the hide-away without a problem.

"I'm sorry Jean-Michel... if that's even your real name. I'm sorry that my family did those things to you. They had no right. They should've just helped you."

"You're about to fall over. You're so tired." He purposely said nothing about Gabriel's apology. Instead, he helped get Gabriel on the twin bed and stepped away. "Get some sleep. You have plenty of time to work on your studies for the meeting."

"I just need a couple of hours. I need to work. Besides, I've not told you..." he whispered even as his eyes were trying to close and he was yawning.

"You told me how you feel already," he whispered. "When we were talking to the twins. You told me what you think of dragons and what happened to us. I hope you're not like the others."

"Mmm..." Gabriel's mind was swimming, but he heard what was being said.

"It's... Senias."

"What?" The Councilor's eyes opened again.

"My real name. It's Senias. Senias of Clan Morias."

"Oh..." This meant something. This moment was important. But all Gabriel could get out of his mouth was, "Don't forget to close the door."

"As you wish," the draconic man replied.

Gabriel sighed when he heard the door shut. "No, it's not exactly as I wish, Senias," he whispered before going to sleep.

Chapter 23
Prepping the Science

Sebastian returned to the clinic with a bag of Italian takeout. The human at the front desk simply stared at him for a minute before actually speaking to him.

"Uh, what can I do for you?"

"Dr. Keene? Would you let her know that Sebastian Evansworth is here?" He watched her type something, her eyes never leaving him. With a smile, he turned to look back out at the empty waiting room.

"Lord Evansworth?" Samantha's voice was cautious.

"Sebastian, please." Sebastian took Samantha's hand and turned it up to place a kiss on the palm. "Dr. Keene, I hear you're rather fond of Italian. I thought perhaps I'd show my gratitude for your care. I also thought that we might have a conversation while you enjoy your meal. If you're able to break for it, that is." He gave a slow smile as he held the bag up for her to inspect.

"I'm in the middle of something, but you mentioned talking to me about research. So long as that's why you're here at my clinic, I don't see why I can't enjoy some food while we talk." She took the bag and motioned with her head for him to follow her. Her office was just further down the corridor and she didn't mind letting him in. The books she had been using for research were still spread out on the desk.

"Interesting reading, but I see nothing on vampires or lycan." He smiled and watched as she moved to take her seat to enjoy her food.

She pointed to a bookshelf that took up the entire wall on the other side of the office. "Lycan and vampire and parallel mythology, along with mage traits and differences in those with magical blood and mundane humans."

"I'm impressed, Dr. Keene. You seem very interested in my kind. The question is, what have these books truly taught you about the vampiric race?" Sebastian moved to the shelf and looked at the titles of a few of them.

"Oh, even from my experience, very little. I worked in Central Africa and Australia as a resident and a doctor practicing without borders. That's where most of my knowledge of vampires and lycan comes from. It's also where my respect for your ability to kill comes from. There are entire villages that are vampires in other cultures, just hidden. They try to keep in the darker places and only take what they need for survival." She began pulling out the cartons to mix the pasta and sauce.

"There are purebloods and turned vampires. Purebloods are less prone to afflictions, especially mental afflictions. I can withstand sunlight if I'm not injured or near dead, turned cannot. The turned are where most of the vampire myths come from. As you know, though, silver can and will kill us, but the rest... not so much. I mean, anyone can die from a stake to the heart or being beheaded, right?" Sebastian moved to take a seat in front of her desk and relaxed into it to answer her questions as he had promised he would.

"I believe, Mr. Know-it-all, the decapitations and stakes were more or less to ensure that vampires do not rise beyond death. Probably someone found a sacred place, where one was sleeping and ... the legends were born. Researchers have found human remains with those types of wounds and a silver coin left inside the mouth." She began eating her food.

"Tell me, Doctor, what is it you are needing from me?"

"I'm more interested in what I need to know to help vampires, not in fighting them. I'm a doctor, not a monster hunter." She continued to eat, not at all worried about Sebastian.

"That's a relief. I find monster hunters to be annoying and I find you everything but that." He attempted a small smile.

"Well, that's good." She giggled before reaching for her water bottle.

"I suppose, what I should have said is, sometimes to treat vampires, it becomes necessary to fight them. Your clinic needs help for fledgling and blood-lusting vampires. You don't have the proper equipment or staff. Do you have lycan on staff?"

"I have only two. I'm working on gaining some trust with the lycan packs in the area because I was hoping to pull a doctor or nurse from them. Crimson..." she looked down and huffed a sigh before trying to better explain. "Well, Crimson needs us. But they don't like to provide much. Their idea is to throw money at a situation and hope it fixes itself. If they need to clean up, that's where they exceed." She looked over her desk at him. "I don't want there to be anything to clean up, Lord Evansworth. My goal is to save as many as I can, human and supernatural. So, that leaves it to me for recruitment. And it's not like I can post a help wanted out there and add that I need someone with either augmented strength and durability or a werewolf or a vampire."

"Have you not sought such aid from your friend? Can he not provide you with further assistance?" Sebastian was enquiring out of genuine interest.

"My friend, Gabriel Kennedy? He's done as much as he can. That's how I got to meet with the Weylyn Pack Alphas. But I only got one nurse out of that situation, and only when she's not busy in her own packlands."

"I'll see what I can find to assist you further. You should also keep a room that is lined in copper from the doors to the floors and the same with silver. When one comes in suffering from blood lust or from the stirrings of the moon, you can place them in there and not fear for your or your staff's safety. Such conditions are best waited out and then treated. The rage will wear us down and then once we are exhausted, you can treat us."

"Unless the metal goes into their skin, it wouldn't harm them. But it would keep them contained. I'll have to ask Crimson about that kind of engineering." Samantha nodded to show that she was taking mental notes. When she swallowed, she asked, "Would you be willing to show my staff any maneuvers to help them? I also need a list of things NOT to do."

Sebastian paused, his brow furrowing.

"They should be prepared and not second-guess their decisions. I know from experience that vampires can pick up on that sort of thing. Lycan can as well. I want my staff to be confident. And so, I'll need them to get used to vampires and lycan. The best way to do that is to have them around and teach them. I can allocate funding for the room you're talking about. I apparently have plenty of room beneath this clinic for it. There's some sort of unfinished area that leads from the basement into the stone."

"I'll schedule with you to send others to teach them since I'm not always available to do so." Sebastian picked up a book from the desk. He flipped through it as he thought about the rest of what she had said. "I can also have one of my coven's engineers come by and look at the sublevel of this facility."

"Is it possible that they could leave a large space open? I can speak to them about designing and architecture of an emergency support framework to place around the clear area. I can't trust human workers with this. But I have several ideas about the use of the space." Sam had to give up on the rest of the food.

"I can arrange it." Sebastian was tracing some of the calligraphy with his fingertip. "You know if they catch you treating dragons it will not go well for you, Sunshine." He gave her a slow smile. "Not that I'd say a word. Just be wary of dragons. Their bite is just as deadly as their growl. Trust me on this." Sebastian closed the book with a soft snap. He studied her as she finished putting things away and got up to take the goodies to the mini-fridge.

"According to Crimson, dragons are all dead or on the other side of the portals. I simply want an area available in case of an emergency for multiple injuries." Samantha winked before she pumped some sanitizer into her hands and then motioned for him to follow.

He smiled and realized his fangs had popped. Sebastian kept his mouth closed as much as possible.

"But it's my oath that I'll do my best to treat anyone that needs it. It's not my job to place anyone in danger. It's my job to help. So, a large space ready for any kind of emergency would come in handy." Samantha opened the door and motioned for him to follow. "You're into research. I thought I might show you something."

The doctor led Sebastian to the third door from her office and opened a door and walked into a sealed area with observation windows lining the wall in front of them. There was a sanitation and sterilization area in there and a lab just beyond where two other people were working.

"We're close to finding a litmus for doppelgänger blood. Since there's been so much trouble with them recently, I thought that might be productive and necessary. I'm just missing, maybe one or two more ingredients. It's based on those I use for vampires, actually. I want to use the same method for as many species as possible. I just need one common reactive material."

"I'll send you my notes on things like that. Maybe it could push you in the right direction."

"As in, you'd do that now?" Sam asked. "Because you know how important this is."

"As soon as I get to my desk." He looked out at the lab. "It's a very nice set-up. Almost as nice as my own."

"You have your own lab? Of course, you have your own lab..." She rolled her eyes and Sebastian chuckled at the gesture.

"I'll let you come see it if you tell me about yourself and before you say it, yes, I really want to know even the minor details that you will probably say are boring." Sebastian smiled a little and the tips of his fangs became visible.

"You want to know more about me?" Samantha blushed. "Well foremost, I hate these titles and things when I'm talking to someone I hope to be friends with or, if you prefer, associate with. If you like them and need them, that's fine, but I will not keep calling you Lord Evansworth. And I'd prefer you just call me Samantha or Sam, though you seem to be fond of Sunshine. I don't mind that either."

"As you wish, Samantha, you may call me Bastian." He gave a small chuckle. "I wouldn't want you to keep referring to me by my title, Sunshine. I mostly use it in Council or with my Coven and, of course, with those that I'm not very fond of."

"Ah, a power play, then?" She couldn't help the continuing smile.

"Perhaps I can convince you to have dinner with me away from the clinic?" Sebastian asked.

"You mean a date? A date-date?"

"Yes. If you can forgive my rusty social graces." Taking the lovely doctor's hand, he turned it up and kissed the center of her palm and then her wrist at her pulse point. It was a show of respect that he doubted she understood since the old customs had been long forgotten. "Until later."

"I'm on call for this Council meeting. Then, I'm all yours." She smiled, looking down at her wrist where he had kissed it. Then, her eyes went to the shadowed markings she had seen before at his neck. Realizing that he had caught her, Sam cleared her throat. "Uh…so your tattoos? Are, how…how do they appear and disappear?"

"They appear when I'm attracted to another, when I'm feeling threatened, or when I'm hungry." His eyes gave off a soft, warm glow. That she could see his markings told him that perhaps he was being given another chance at happiness.

"Oh…" Samantha's cheeks reddened a bit more than they had been. "Well, that's not… unwelcome." She turned from him and began walking toward the elevator.

Watching her for a minute longer, Sebastian turned and made his way out of the exit. He was still smiling as he shadowed away.

Chapter 24
The Failed Attempt

Gabriel had been sleeping in the secret room for nearly four hours, and Jean-Michel had no reason to bother the man. Instead, he was continuing the work the young Councilor had been so kind as to share. With his shirt still untucked and wearing his jeans and boots, Jean-Michel seemed out of place amidst the classic design and luxury of dark wood and leather in the Council Chambers. The center stage reminded the dragon of large courtrooms, but as the space moved outward toward the door, it reminded him of a lecture hall.

The comparison to a lecture hall was appropriate at the moment, considering he was at Gabriel's assigned side desk, researching. Normally, he'd leave this part up to the Councilors, but he was more connected to this case than he had ever allowed himself to be connected to one before.

He had spread the maps haphazardly, or so it seemed. He knew exactly where Gabriel had placed everything and in what order. Using the same triangulation method Gabriel had used to pinpoint the portal, Raudine drew points on the central map that reflected doppelgänger sightings and alleged sightings. They were all in proximity to a specific neighborhood of Whitley.

He made a few more notes concerning street names and buildings in the area. He then looked up any businesses owned by supernaturals in the area. And damned if one stood out. Pandora's Box... owned by the lovely Miranda Garrett; better known as Mira de Salucet to him.

"Dammit, Mira." The sound of voices outside the large chamber door interrupted his thoughts. It wouldn't have bothered him except that there was a distinct familiarity to one voice.

The Tasker looked to the hidden door and then back to the maps. He tore out the page he had been writing on and, folding it, he shoved it into his back pocket. Closing his notepad and tucking it away in the desk drawer, he quickly rolled up maps he knew were important. He left out the ones that would prove to be of little use at all.

He was pouring himself a drink before anyone entered. He sat comfortably in one of the side chairs and watched as the person from outside backed into the Chamber room.

"I can be very quiet when I want to be. I just needed some air." The voice came from the top of the stairs near the door. Raudine listened and tried to hide his puzzlement. Before the door was closed, he heard the more familiar, sterner tone scolding someone. "From now on, you all need to pay closer attention to the comings and goings. Your job isn't to stare at the bottom of a coffee cup, gentlemen." Finally, clicking the heavy door closed, the man slid the bolt into place and turned to the interior, only to face Jean-Michel Raudine.

Of all the forms the doppelgänger could've chosen? Jean-Michel hid the amusement by taking a nice gulp of the liquor he had already poured for himself. It seemed Gabriel might get his wish for a witness after all! Because standing right there in front of him was an exact duplicate of his Councilor.

The doppelgänger pretending to be Gabriel walked towards the Tasker with a cool conveyance to his eyes. Oh, he was actually going to try to pull this off, was he? The doppel's testicular fortitude impressed Jean-Michel. Wait – did they even have balls?

"Raudine, what are you doing here?" Their attention went from the other man to the table with its mess of maps, books, and scrolls. "Don't you have a mission to complete or a bar to roll around in?"

Oh, they had the pompous attitude down cold, didn't they? Jean-Michel played along.

"I was batting around some ideas before the Council reconvened for the emergency meeting. Actually, I'm glad you're here. You can finally tell me what you thought of my ideas for the tracking of the rogue doppelgängers we discussed late last night." He got up and poured himself another glass and offered to pour Gabriel a glass of liquor as well.

"Come again? I was busy. What precisely were you wanting my thoughts on?" Taking the offered glass of liquor, they sipped from it while looking over the maps on the table. Human fingers

THE FAILED ATTEMPT

pushed them around; then similar to the books. They dallied but didn't really do anything in particular.

The way it distracted itself over the things left on the table was telling. That this being was in the form of his ward told Jean-Michel that his worry over the Councilor was warranted. He drank heavily of the next glass and contemplated his words. He hoped Gabriel would have sense enough to check on who was here before barreling out of that damned hidden door.

"We need to get this in check, and quickly. We need to take out the rogues. They're willing to kill for a place here, then they've already crossed a line. Where have you been? I must've missed you." He motioned to the door with his drink and then sipped it.

"I, uh... went out for some air," the false Gabriel turned to Jean-Michel.

"We need to find out who's responsible for all of this. You were right all along. They're bypassing the laws set in place for protection."

"Yes, well, I agree. We should find the one behind this. That's what we've been doing all along." The doppelgänger studied his glass; turning it this way and then that way. "But from what I understand, they sought aid from the Council on the other side and got turned away." Their jaw clenched slightly, and they set the glass down on top of the maps.

If the doppelgänger had paid attention to their mark, they would know putting a wet glass on the paperwork was something Gabriel would never do.

"Really? Then why weren't the Councilors of this world told? Why were you all caught unawares? Surely there are sanctions at play here, yes?" His accent was still pronounced even as he used his English rather than his actual French to speak. "I am but a...a Tasker, Gabriel. Enlighten me." Jean-Michel took another drink. As he took in more alcohol, he was beginning to see the outlines of various cover spells on the creature.

"I loathe the idea of bribery, but it happens. Especially in the other world. And we're facing more than that, remember?" The doppelgänger dressed in a Gabriel skin walked along the shelves of the wall, investigating the various decor and books. "Perhaps I should send you to the other side so you can question the Council in Iona?"

Raudine's eyes narrowed as the doppel came to a halt uncomfortably close to the hidden room. He nonchalantly walked closer, being sure there were very few items standing between him and his target.

"I suppose you can task me to it," Jean-Michel stated. He stepped closer, using the excuse of getting to the chair nearby, and snorted his disgust. "Oh, the notes you had out are over there in the desk drawer. I put them away." Raudine pointed to the desk that was directly across from where he was about to sit. It was conveniently away from the hidden door. "Shouldn't leave shit like that out for anyone to see it. You can thank me later with a good drink at a much more fun place than this." He acted as though he were about to sit.

The doppelgänger tapped their fingers on the shelf. Their gaze shifted from Jean-Michel to the other end of the table, then back to the man uncomfortably close to him. They arched one brow in a perfect Gabriel pose.

Really, if the thing had simply been better with timing and more appropriate with keeping things in order, they would have had Gabriel down cold.

"My notes? Yes, I suppose I owe you for that." They stepped away to withdraw the tablet with Gabriel's scribbles all over it. Even for odd bits of nonsense, it was nice penmanship. "Thank you again." They waved the tablet at the Tasker, then opened it further.

"De rein." The game played out. It was apparent he'd not get any new intelligence from this creature. However, the longer he waited, the more the creature could skim. The doppelgänger was at the appropriate angle, with nothing in the way. Raudine was ready to end this.

"I really have nothing for you to do, at the present, Jean-Michel. Perhaps you should follow up with the Director and I can task you to go to the other side?"

Obviously, the creature wanted to entice him to leave quietly.

"I'll get right on that. When my real Councilor actually tasks me with it."

The doppelgänger looked up. Seeing the smile on Raudine's face was enough.

"You know you can't protect him forever, Tasker." They dropped the book and made for the entry.

"I can protect him long enough." The Tasker was crossing to the door as he spoke.

The doppelgänger was faster, yes, but they had locked the door. As the doppel grabbed the old mechanism and fumbled with it, the Tasker slammed them against the heavy wood.

"Didn't think you'd need the door unlocked, did you?" Jean-Michel chuckled. The doppelgänger rolled and kicked, hitting a sensitive spot on the Tasker's upper thigh. He growled and hopped twice before taking off back down the stairs after the doppelgänger. He leapt halfway down and tackled the creature. Both of them rolled to the bottom of the pit.

"You're not very well trained, are you? Did you think because he was human, this would be easy? Oh, and if anyone else is listening through your brain, I want them to know – I can and will always protect my charge. So think twice about trying again."

The doppelgänger wrenched themselves away and then charged him, thinking to tackle and toss the larger man over his shoulder. But Jean saw the attack for what it was and leaned back, getting his center balanced and prepared. He rolled his competitor to the ground and got a kick to the face for his trouble.

The doppelgänger of Kennedy slammed into the door, their hand fumbling on the bolt when the Tasker hit him from behind again.

"Raudine, what are you doing?!" Gabriel demanded as he strode double-time across the chamber from the hidden room. Jean-Michel was holding someone pinned against the door by the throat. All the noise had brought him out, and apparently at the perfect moment.

"They... won't... quit. The reward... is too great." The doppel had a hand covering the Tasker's wrists. He was struggling for his breath. His hands changed colors, the fingers elongating.

"What the...?" When the Councilor recognized his own face was glaring back at him, his pace quickened. He halted a few steps behind Raudine. One hand lifted to settle on Jean-Michel's shoulder, "Wait... I want to know what's going on here. We won't find that out if he's dead."

"Like he'd tell us the truth in the situation he's in right now? Anything you need to know won't be told by this one unless you have some sort of truth serum on you. I know I don't."

Jean-Michel had snapped an innocent man's neck less than a week ago. He'd have no issue snapping a guilty being's neck.

There was a gleam in the creature's eye that kept Gabriel from getting any closer. It was as if the being had no care for his own life. But this didn't keep the Councilor from studying. Perfect brown hair, dark eyes, tanned complexion, and even the clothes were the same designer he used. No. He wouldn't just give up on this opportunity.

"There are things much worse than death, shifter. I need to know who's really behind this. I need to know where to find the rest of your group. Tell me these things."

"I know a lot about you," the doppelgänger growled; such an odd sound coming from the facade. "It was my job. I also know there are limits to your powers. You can't do anything…to me. Crimson will lock you up."

"Limits? Yes, but you forget – the Tasker does what the Councilor needs. So…" Gabriel's brows arched high while he swirled his finger around in a circle in the air, letting his Tasker know he needed to prove those words.

The Tasker's head tilted to the right side and his gaze bore into the creature. "You've successfully wasted ten more minutes." With that, he brought his free hand to the creature's arm and snapped the radius.

A loud hiss of pain and the thing morphed through several forms before finally becoming itself. The gray-skinned doppelgänger's breath was tumultuous as they fought for more air. One long-fingered hand swung out, trying to reach for Gabriel in its angered, wild state.

Raudine switched hands, pivoting the intruder and slamming them against the wall again. He had those arms pulled tight, the bones already broken were crunching and the other arm's ligaments felt pressure. The doppelgänger cried out in pain.

"Ahh… ahh… ahh… That's a no-no. You will not get to him."

"Then… kill… me.. and be done."

"Not yet. When I'm done asking my questions," Gabriel warned.

Still struggling against the hold the Tasker had, the doppelgänger groaned and snarled at the same time. Spittle flew as they asked, "What do you want from me?" They glared at their target.

"Who helped you get over here? Who are you working for? Are the other Councilors being targeted for replacement?" Gabriel stood out of reach and tried his best to look unimpressed. He knew the answer to the last question, but why let the doppel know that?

"You are...target. Others... perhaps. We...don't always know. ..each other's missions." The gray skin paled.

"That's a lie. You've probably got someone in your head right now. I'm not stupid," Gabriel glared.

"I... I can—" Suddenly, the doppelgänger went stiff as if he were having a seizure. And within seconds, it was limp in Jean-Michel's hands. The Tasker held the creature long enough to ensure it was really not breathing or alive before letting it fall to the ground like a bag of trash.

"Why did you..."

"I didn't kill it. I think maybe you're onto something. Someone was listening in and knew how close we were to getting answers." Shaking his head, he walked to the table where Gabriel was. Jean-Michel studied his Councilor. "Gabriel?" He watched the man start.

"I'm fine. It's just not every day that I face myself." He lifted his dark eyes to meet his companion's own steady gaze. "That was close. If you hadn't been here—" Gabriel took in a deep cleansing breath.

"It's what I do, remember? At least when I'm doing my job." It was the closest thing to an apology he had.

"I'll, uh, have the lycan take care of that. They let it in, they can take it out." Gabriel looked over at the thing lying on the floor. His brow furrowed. "The guards, the lycan that let them in? They aren't from Pack Weylyn."

"No, they're from Jonas' pack. Pack Airsight." Jean rolled his eyes and sighed deeply before finishing his statement. "Need more proof that they're in on it?"

"Vanishte?" Gabriel asked quickly.

"I had Derek take her to the Weylyn Pack lands, so she'd be safe. I didn't like how things seemed here. Now, I'm glad I did. She's safe, Gabriel. Unfortunately, you're not. We need to go." Jean-Michel grabbed the rolled-up maps he had been using earlier and placed them in a carrying case. "Get your things. Whatever you need."

"We need to warn everyone." Gabriel gathered all his notes and placed them in his briefcase.

"Yep." Raudine screwed the lid on the carrying case and tossed the strap over his shoulder and head.

"I need to get the guards replaced. We need to replace anyone the doppelgängers may have compromised," the Councilor pointed out.

"Well, let's go out, then you can call back about this. We need to leave. And if we're surrounded by the enemy, I think it's best not to talk about your plans." Raudine was already at the door to the chamber, unbolting it. He would not wait for an argument.

"I have to come up with proof of what they are. Sam texted about blood tests?"

"If you can get them all to allow for the blood testing. You know they'll see it as an infringement. But you said you can convince people of anything, right? Never lost a case? And… why are we still here?" Jean-Michel motioned toward the door.

"Okay, fine, I'll make calls on the way." Gabriel grabbed what he needed, his computer and briefcase. Soon enough, they were out the door.

Raudine placed a palm on the small of Gabriel's back to urge him onward.

As they left, Gabriel was still silent.

Jean-Michel opened the door to his truck once again. This time, the Councilor seemed to have no issue with climbing in. And then, the Tasker heard something unexpected come from the man's mouth.

"I need a drink."

CHAPTER 25
THE PUB

Jean-Michel opened the door to the large pub and waited for the Councilor to cross the threshold. It was a chain, so how "authentic" could this Irish Pub be? Well, they had some Irish memorabilia and part was a restaurant, part was a true pub, part in the very back was a sports bar, and in the middle was a stage where performers were lacking tonight. The part that drew Jean-Michel was the Guinness on-tap and served right. He needed a drink, too.

Running a dark assessing gaze over the interior of the place, Gabriel slowly followed his Tasker. At the cheers and rounds of noise going on in the back, one of his dark brows arched up. At the front bar, Jean-Michel beckoned him.

"A pint for me and whatever he'll be having." He motioned to Gabriel while pulling a card from his wallet. Since Gabriel had just been through the wringer, he wondered if he should even bring up all the business on his mind.

"Sauvignon Blanc or a Chardonnay." After giving his order, Gabriel seated himself at the bar next to the Tasker. "So, this is a working man's bar?"

"Ehh... sort of. Not sure you'd call it that. Too many college kids. But it'll do."

"I have a list of the wines we have." The bartender finished the pint to hand over to the larger man, and then he went to search for the list. Gabriel was already taking some napkins to wipe the bar in front of him.

"He'll have the local muscadine – red and kind of dry." The Tasker let his focus wander back to Gabriel. "They have a great local red..." Raudine tried to suggest. But seeing the glare, he shrugged and drank a nice long couple of swallows from his mug.

"What are we going to do about Skinner?" He scratched his reddish short whiskered beard and drank some more. "He's pissed." Jean-Michel thought to put Gabriel on a subject away from the attack.

The bartender set his glass of wine before him and Gabriel lifted it and swirled it a moment before actually tasting from the glass. A slight wince played over his handsome face at the taste, but he said nothing. Taking another sip, he rolled it across his palette and set the glass down before swallowing.

"There are procedures and protocols that we must follow. This evening's little fiasco bypassed it all. I believe Skinner may be a worry, but he's the least of them."

"He's never been the least of mine. And he shouldn't be the least of yours." Jean held Gabriel's gaze. "He won't wait on your piddly procedures and protocols for long. So far, he's apparently gotten around them. he always comes out smelling like a fuckin' rose. And..."

"And? I don't know why you bother asking me if you already have your own opinion." The Councilor stiffened before taking another drink. At least his expression wasn't as bad this time.

"Discussion and sharing information, so we come up with the best plans, Gabriel. I'm not..." he took a deep breath. "I'm not trying to argue with you." Jean-Michel knew the attack had already spun Gabriel up. Telling him more wouldn't help. So he changed the subject.

"We can get some drinks here, let ourselves calm down, and then I can take you somewhere safe and get hold of the Pack to help. You need to work with Vanishte and get ready for the meeting. I need to backtrack some information..."

"It isn't that I'm not taking Skinner seriously. I know he's involved in this mess somewhere. The way he reacted to the portal, his involvement just makes sense. But I also know that he's doing everything that he can to clean up and cover up before the upcoming meeting. So he doesn't have time to focus on us right now." There was a sigh before his brown eyes shifted from Raudine to the bottles lined up behind the bartender. "Out of all those bottles, I see no decent wine. And I don't like this one. Is there another you can suggest by any chance?" Gabriel watched Raudine motion for the bartender.

"We'd like the local pinot grigio. Iron Gate, maybe? Something not too sweet and not too dry. And I'll have another pint." Raudine got a nod, and the guy walked off to find the bottle.

He took the last drink of the pint and looked over at the Councilor with an amused grin. "What? It's on my tab and I say you should get off your habits and try something new. You'll like it. It's not two-hundred-dollar wine, but it's a local with just the right pop. It's the best I can do for a man who'll order wine in a pub."

"Oh, it's...it's not that. I'm thinking about it all. I never stop thinking," Gabriel admitted. "When Vanishte told us everything, I sent a warning to every Councilor I have contact information for, Jean. I reported the incident to everyone who needed to know. I turned off the ability to track my phone. I...I don't know who to trust. We could literally walk from one room to another and one of us could get replaced..."

Jean-Michel snapped his fingers in front of Gabriel's face, "Hey...sorry for the snap, but you were, uh...getting loud?" His gaze moved from Gabriel to the bartender, who was coming back with the drinks.

The dragon licked his lips and sipped some of the froth from the icy mug. He took his time to swallow and consider his own explanation. Turning on his bar seat to face Gabriel, he scooted closer and was very near the man now. He didn't want to be overheard, which is why he liked bars and pubs, anyway.

Jean-Michel noticed how Gabriel scooted back, his hands going to the counter as if he were ready to run.

"We agree. They want to replace the Councilors. They've failed with two. The odds are they've most likely succeeded with the others. Who knows? But they have to have a place to hide and bodies to use until they take over a Councilor." He sat back up properly and took another drink. "You were working on something in the Chamber. I saw it. Another try at finding their safe house?"

"Mmm..." After taking a drink of the new wine, he placed the glass on the bar. He kept his fingers clasped on the stem. "Ten times the better flavor. Thank you for the suggestion." He took another drink.

"You're welcome, mon ami," Jean replied with a warm smile. The booze made him comfortable. The low buzz of the surrounding people said much of it being a quiet, midweek night in the bar. He was thankful for that. "And my questions?"

"I don't know if it's true, and Miranda Garret claims she's not hearing anything about the doppelgängers on the streets. But Derek got shot and said the one he was tailing went down the alley near her shop, Pandora's Box. It's close to where Crimson found the body of the doppelgänger that attacked Sebastian. And the twins admitted to being contacted and doing business with them." Gabriel went quietly back to his wine.

"What makes you believe she would help doppelgängers?"

"I know you have a past with the twins; with her. But set that aside. Think about it. If she knows about the Councilors who are not actually Councilors, couldn't she and her brother use that information to their benefit? Perhaps there has been a deal made?"

"Mmmm..." there was a bit of a grimace on his face as he considered the suggestion. "It does and then doesn't add up. Mira would be into a scheme, but she and her brother have worked for centuries to keep themselves away from Crimson dealings. Why risk it?" This truly puzzled Jean-Michel.

"Blackmail?" Gabriel offered. "They've come close to getting into trouble before." He turned on the barstool this time to speak more closely to his Tasker.

"Really?" Jean-Michel went still as Gabriel moved closer. Every tiny hair on the dragon's human body stood up. That voice tickled over his senses. The Tasker fought any facial reaction. For once, it was a real challenge. Especially when he also took in the other man's scent. "Interesting..." Jean placed his fingers over the lip of the mug while gazing into the nothingness of the mirrored shelves on the back wall. No. Nope. No. He made it a mantra in the back of his mind. Back to business.

"Maybe you should give her a discreet call?" Jean-Michel suggested. "Make a script for not losing track of the proper questions? Or maybe we can test the waters a bit with more investigation there?" He took another drink of his stout.

"Or maybe you should. You seem to have a better relationship with her."

That earned the Councillor a long, uncomfortable stare. "Anything else you want to talk about?"

With the half-empty glass in hand, Gabriel once again turned his face towards the draconic man. "Not business?"

"Anything. Business can't be the only thing discussed, especially not in a pub." Jean took another drink.

"Oh, I have hundreds of questions – not that you'd answer." Finishing his wine off, Gabriel rose to his feet.

"Where are you going? Are you that much of a lightweight?"

"Wine has a stronger effect on me than other things. I don't want the rest of the night to be little more than a blur, Jean-Michel." Gabriel shrugged. "Not like you'd tell me much, anyway."

"I might surprise you. I've been told I have an inclination to talk about myself." The Tasker chuckled before imbibing the rest of his Guinness and motioning for the bartender to refill both of their poisons. This was Raudine's turf, not Gabriel's. And that was more apparent over the next few minutes as the young Kennedy did the unthinkable.

Gabriel watched as the bartender refilled his glass. The younger man had a choice to make. Soon, he was back on that barstool. With a stern set to his lips, he lifted the glass towards Jean-Michel in a silent toast. The Tasker obliged. Then Gabriel emptied his drink with three swallows.

"Thirsty are we?" Jean-Michel watched, amused at this. Could the younger man hold his liquor – or wine? He doubted it so much he made a mental bet with himself before drinking another large swallow of the dark draft in his own glass. He had thousands of years of practice. And some said he had a hollow leg. Now, had this been liquor, he would've been drunk quicker. He watched Gabriel push the glass over, almost lose it, and then settle back to loosen his tie. Bet already won.

"I've had enough." He looked at the Tasker, his cheeks reddened. "I shouldn't have come here."

"Why not? Come on, Gabriel. When you live a long life, you need to find reasons to keep living. Enjoying a pint seems insignificant, but it's just one small joy of many that help me and others who will not live as long as me."

"Well, enjoy it. It's time for me to go."

"Oh, is it now? Because I was apt to have another one or two. Perhaps spread them out more and relax in one of the side rooms to watch a game. I'm sure I can find some soccer fanatics." He sipped the head of the Guinness that was left in the glass and then took a swallow.

"Not allowed," Gabriel murmured under his breath. Jean-Michel watched as he stripped off his suit jacket and held it bunched up in one hand. That was a sure sign that the Councilor wasn't thinking straight. Reaching for his wallet, Gabriel tossed a hundred on the bar. "Head on straight, Kennedy, temptation only leads down roads best not traveled." Tucking the wallet back into place, Gabriel began toward the door.

The Tasker got the bartender's attention and pointed to the bill. If Gabriel was buying, he'd make sure his tab was on that as well. Gabriel's mutterings were something Jonathan, Gabriel's grandfather, had been fond of saying.

"Temptation is the changer of worlds, mon ami. Without temptation, and without several virtues that most men find evil, there would be no progress. We would all just be the same savage beasts living in the caves we were born in. It takes temptation and desire of something that is out of reach – to elicit change." He drank the rest of his draft and sighed.

"Stop calling me 'mon ami'. I'm not that. I don't think I am. Besides, it gets old. Damn, you and your twisted logic. And for bringing me to a pub. I should have gone home." Gabriel turned and started out...for the third time.

"Fine. Mr. Kennedy? Gabriel? Whatever." The draconic man shook his head. Sliding his glass over to the guy, he shrugged and got up from the bar to go join his ... responsibility.

"I have... I have a lot to do before stepping into Chamber and this will not help me accomplish one damn bit of it. So while I thank you for the drinks, I really must go."

"Yes, you've been pretty damned clear about that. And thank me? You just paid for it, you drunkard." The laugh that left him was genuine and hearty. It might have been the first time Gabriel had heard such a sound come from his Tasker.

"Not that funny, Jean. I'll get a taxi."

"Yes, well, it's ironically funny. At least give me that. And don't bother with a taxi or an Uber. Drivers aren't exactly happy to drag a drunk man of your size up to the front door." He walked ahead and opened the door for both of them. "You'll be bunking at my place and when you're sober, I'll drive you home or I'll get Eva and Devon to keep eyes on you. I'll not have the rogue doppels take another shot. You need to lie low or have the best security around you 'til the meeting. I have herbs at home that'll ward off a hangover. You'll actually be thanking me by this time tomorrow night – and at that point, I'll deserve it." He spoke the last few words in a sing-song voice.

"So.. how far are we going to walk, because if it's too much further, I'll drive." Gabriel was looking around for their car.

"You're not fit to drive." Jean was still trying not to chuckle too much. The smile he had shined even in his eyes. "Besides, I have the keys." He motioned for Gabriel to follow him down the sidewalk to where he had parked.

"I'm staying with you? Is that...proper?" Gabriel's cheeks reddened.

Jean-Michel noticed the blush but tried his best to ignore it. Then he felt the vibration of his phone.

"I think your pants are ringing. Want me to answer for you?" Gabriel asked, a wicked grin on his face.

"I'll get to it. It's probably Devon or Eva calling me back," Jean-Michel said as he placed the key into the manual lock on the door of his red pickup. Then, his blue-green eyes got enormous as he felt, then gazing downward, saw Gabriel reaching into the pocket of his jeans to grab the cell phone. "I said I... would... get to it." His voice had a bit of a higher pitch than normal.

"Oh, but I insist on helping you." Gabriel was all drunk grins as his hand slid along the warm insides of Jean-Michel's pocket. He felt the jut of the hip bone and then farther in was the crease where groin-met-thigh. His hand continued as he felt the hard muscle of the Tasker's thigh tighten up beneath his touch. He chuckled at the reaction but kept feeling his way along.

"Are you sure you're just grabbing my damned phone? Come on." They didn't need anyone he knew walking by or anyone that recognized Gabriel seeing this. What a lovely mess that'd make. Gabriel, a well-known businessman, enjoying a drunken homosexual PDA with a professor from the local university. Then there was the fact that Gabriel was his Councilor. There was no end to the problems that this situation could cause if seen by the wrong people.

"Gabriel, I'm not sure what kind of fantasy you're trying for here, but uh, maybe not the right place and time for it?" The Tasker gave in and put his arm around the other man, so they looked like maybe a couple walking away from the car to the little sitting spot next to the building made for bus riders. They needed cover.

"You said I should loosen up. You said have something worth living for. Why not a fantasy?" Gabriel whispered before he felt the stone wall on his shoulder and Jean-Michel's package against his hand. "You enjoyed teasing me all those nights. All those calls? Payback." Finally, he grabbed the phone to show the auburn-haired Tasker. He grinned as it rang again. "Told you I'd help and here you go."

Taking the phone from the Councilor, he put his arm around the man's shoulder to hold him steady, facing the building. Raudine maneuvered to speak with whoever was on the line. He'd created this monster, hadn't he? How the man was drunk on three glasses of wine - THREE!?

"Salut!" Jean said in greeting. Thanks to Gabriel, he didn't get the chance to see who was ringing him.

"Umm... yeah alright, so what are ya doin'?" Devon asked over the phone.

"Oh, nothing much, Dev! Me?" He chuckled nervously. "I'm just out on the town trying to relax after a long day. I take it you got my message?" The draconic man's eyes widened as he felt Gabriel's hand slide down from the pocket to the front of the pants to rub the bulge that was hidden beneath the material.

"Stop it...." Jean growled between clenched teeth.

"Stop what, Sen?" Devon asked with concern in his voice. The big lycan pushed his chair back from the table and rose to his feet, something Jean-Michel could hear happening. "Just what in the hell are ya doin', exactly?"

"Make me." Gabriel leaned to press his lips against Jean's other ear and purred the two words to him. Gabriel followed those words with a low, deep, and very secretive chuckle.

"Uh, not you, Devon. I have a pest here that needs proper training." Jean-Michel was simmering. Kennedy was getting a glare hot as flame. For someone who had been in the closet all his life, Gabe had this portion of the game down to an art!

Grabbing Gabriel's hand, he twirled him in place so that he had his arm pinned against his back. If he needed to apply pressure and make this painful, he would. Now he had control.

The change in position surprised Gabriel almost as much as the sharp twinge of pain that shot up his shoulder from the captured arm. There was a quick intake of breath and Gabriel stilled as his forehead rested against the wall in front of him.

"I didn't get a message," Devon pointed out.

"Oh... well..." He would have continued the conversation with the elder lycan while his captured Councilor tried to figure out the predicament he was in. However, Gabriel had turned his head so that he could watch Jean-Michel. The way Gabriel was licking his lips had taken the Tasker's attention. Provocative was the first word that came to mind. He cleared his throat. How many pints had he enjoyed? The sound of a rumble coming from the phone let Jean-Michel know that the old wolf was very suspicious now.

"I actually called because Eva says her Gabriel hasn't made it home yet. And seeing as the last one he was with was you, I thought it best to check with ya before she calls a hunt for him."

"He's here with me. He's perfectly safe. Unless he makes me kill him for misbehaving." Jean warned Gabriel with his words while speaking to Devon.

"Gabe misbehaving? When has that pup ever misbehaved? Unless he gets in over his head because of you."

"Is Vanishte safe?"

"Yes. She's staying here with us. Are things getting shady up at the Chamber?"

"Dev, I'll need him to have full-time security starting tomorrow. There was an incident at the Chamber. I don't trust anyone but you and yours now. A doppelgänger got in."

"For the love of the Goddess. Of course. Damn, I'm sorry I didn't listen to the message. Let me know when yer bringing him to the big house and I'll have the Pack on alert. We'll talk about things then."

"Of course. Thank you, Devon." What started out as a precarious position and a pinch of pain actually did quite the opposite of what Jean-Michel was expecting it to. The Councilor actually arched his back and pressed his ass against the Tasker's groin.

"JEEsus... H..." Jean closed his mouth before he got Devon and Eva riled and quickly ended the call.

Gabriel chuckled as he heard the last bit of the conversation and felt the effects he was having on the dragon. But his chuckle got cut short as Jean pushed him fully against the wall, then let him go. The air left Gabriel in a wine-scented rush.

"You really want some trouble, don't ya?" Jean asked, a bit of the old country coming through the accent he spoke this time.

"What?" With his other hand, Gabriel held himself steady on the wall. "If you're going to be that way, Jean-Michel, I'll thank you for making me enjoy the world and loosening up, but it definitely doesn't seem worth the trouble." Adjusting his rumpled clothing and stepping to the right, Gabriel placed his hand on the stone wall to keep balance before walking forward. "I'll find my way home. That way, I won't interrupt your phone calls or cause you further irritation." He had blushed again, and his eyes were downcast.

Jean moved to stand with his hands on his hips in front of Gabriel. The Councilor looked up at him with those warm, hurt brown eyes. Gabriel Kennedy never showed weakness. Or he hadn't until this. That vulnerability had the dragon's heart in a whirl.

"What?" Gabriel asked.

A Tasker was supposed to run investigations, handle specialized operations, and protect their Councilor, right? So many people thought of him as someone who improvised well. They knew his impetuous nature in Crimson. The truth was, they never realized how much he thought things through. Like now. He was weighing his options instead of running full steam ahead. And most times, when he thought things through, he did the proper thing.

Most times.

He turned Gabriel so the man's back was against that stone wall, his hands upon his waist, and he kissed him deeply. When he let go of the kiss, he placed his forehead on Gabriel's forehead and asked, "You still want to go to your home? Or want to go to mine?"

Gabriel actually stared at the dragon in awe of this fantasy becoming reality. He was nearly breathless.

"Yours. Absolutely yours."

Chapter 26
Second Thoughts

Malcolm paced in the basement of the antique shop known as Pandora's Box. The proprietor had found homes or bodies for many of his people. Malcolm had their best still in the area, whether Ms. Garrett was aware, they didn't care. They had targets that needed to be handled. One of their doppelgängers had definitely failed and come close to ruining things for the rest. This was what happened when one rushed a situation! Skinner had been wrong to do so. They were causing more and more attention.

Malcolm had to admit that they had sent the wrong doppelgänger for the job of taking Councilor Evansworth. When working with a species known to be psionically gifted, you couldn't afford to fuck up. They had. They wouldn't get a second chance. Not like that. The setback placed them all on very unsteady ground.

Had they not already made the deals they'd made and become enmeshed in the machinations of Ezekiel Skinner, they would have concluded that Vanishte's method was sound. As it stood, Malcolm had no choice but to continue. Or at least they would allow for the primary plans to continue.

This operation had been extensive, and they were reaching a critical point in the plan of action. They needed nothing else to go wrong, and that meant the focus needed to be on this Tasker and Councilor duo. Skinner had said not to touch the Tasker, but the latest loss said otherwise. It was absolutely necessary to take the Tasker out.

If Skinner would not back down, a backup plan needed to be ready. A backup plan was never a bad idea. The doppelgänger took on the human form they preferred, a non-descript brown-haired, middle-aged man. They made their way to Miranda Garrett.

Upstairs, Miranda was in the open area she referred to as her office. She set the desk in a corner with her credenza and files behind her. She was on the phone, trying to make the reluctant change their mind. Her contact said his piece and then hung up. Had she made the incorrect decision to help these creatures? Probably. Did she have a choice? Not really. And she had no one to tell.

On the flip side, her name would be mud in the Underground if she had reported this, and it got around that they couldn't trust her. She didn't want to do that until she absolutely had no choice.

However, things had shifted. Despite what it might do to her, Miranda felt driven to report this situation. If she did so, it would need to be in a rather devious manner. Pretending nothing was wrong, lying to her brother, convincing contacts to allow shifters into their homes or businesses, she sighed heavily from the strain that the past 48 hours had put upon her. Miranda had gathered as much information as she could – insurance for the unspeakable. Now, the succubus tapped her fingernails on her desk.

"To what end?" she whispered to herself. Miranda didn't like unanswered questions. And she especially didn't enjoy having to make blind plays. Rising to her feet, Miranda paced. Why this shifter chilled her to the bone, she did not know. She could not ignore this. She moved to the door, but when she opened it, the very being she was thinking of walked into the room. The half-demon pretended apathy over apprehension as she closed the door and turned to follow their movements.

"There was a delay. However, the others will eventually arrive. I will let you know as soon as they have. They will need shelter and bodies as the others have needed."

"I don't know who you think you are, but this is my place and I will say who enters and who doesn't." She was tired of this being's ways and exhausted by their bullying antics. Only once in her life had she taken such from any other being. She wouldn't tolerate it now, no matter how uncomfortable he made her feel. "We agreed on 28."

"You misunderstand us yet again, Ms. Garrett." Malcolm stepped towards her and Miranda took a step back, her chin rising. "We are not asking for permission. We are explaining to you they will be at your establishment in a matter of days, with or without your cooperation. Do not make us harm you prior to finishing our business. This can either be lucrative for you or destructive. We care not which you choose."

Fury and rage flashed across her features as she listened to them practically command her as if they owned her and then – threaten her. Oh, they did not know what was about to happen.

"You arrogant son of a bitch." Her eyes flared to ruby facets. "Don't you dare think to lay a finger on me. I may have set up your little meetings and found housing for your bunch, but you won't get two meters near anything without me."

For the second time, they stood facing off against each other.

There was an odd wash sound from deep within the faux-man in front of her. For a split second, his eyes shimmered silver instead of the hazel he used in his glamour.

It was Miranda that spoke next.

"I know what you are planning and can tell you without a doubt that it won't work."

"Really? I suppose you're going to tell me why I've come to this world?"

This time, the doppelgänger didn't use the terminology that pooled all of them together. They had used the singular. And this time, they didn't stop when they approached her. Closing the small distance between them until they pressed her against the closed door, Malcolm's eyes began shifting first from the colorless silver to sparkling ruby, matching her own.

Miranda's eyes widened as the shifter stood face-to-face with her. Dull gray skin took on a creamy pale to peach coloring. Their head became covered in long curled brunette locks, and within one minute Miranda was staring at herself.

"Tell me what it is you think I will do." Even the voice was perfect. The false Miranda smiled.

Regaining her focus, the succubus gave a snarky laugh. The doppel watched, obviously confused.

"Sorry, it's just that there's one tiny problem if you plan to pretend to be me. Actually, two or maybe three? First, you don't have all the information required to gain access to meetings with people all over this world that can and will place your underlings. Second, while a perfect mirror image of me you may be, you still aren't the real thing. And trust me, my contacts will spot you right off. If you cannot prove who you are, well, let's just say they'll have no trouble making sure you can become nothing. They protect themselves and their assets."

"And though I shouldn't have to mention it – if you try to eliminate me? My brother and father will be furious. Do you know what a free demon and a demon lord might be capable of doing to a doppelgänger?" Miranda didn't want to get them involved. She wanted to handle this on her own. She just needed Malcolm to be unsure and to keep herself safe until the end of this. The half-demon smiled brightly for the doppel, revealing her own double incisors to remind them she also was a free demon in this realm. She wouldn't go down without a fight.

"Well then, Ms. Garrett, I suggest you prepare." The shifter turned away from her. The facade faded away, leaving it in its true form once again.

When they backed off, Miranda took a deep breath.

"Are all the others placed?" Malcolm asked while they remolded their body into the nondescript human male they had been before the show of power. The demon was staring at him. Perhaps she didn't comprehend? "I need to know where we stand."

"Most have been or they're on their way to their next destinations. Those left are lounging around in my storage room in the basement. I have put my business on hold long enough. Since you and yours have come here, I have made no money and have broken law after law for you. I see no return to normalcy if you keep bringing more homeless, faceless doppels here."

"We have payment in plenty to compensate for your loss of business," Malcolm said matter-of-factly as if Miranda was absolutely going to agree.

"I said, no. I've risked enough." Her eyes glared at them. "My repayment of the favor I owed is done when the last of 28 is gone from here. Your others may not have permanent homes, but they have human faces and credentials. That's all I ever agreed to." She straightened her back and turned once again toward the door. She placed her fingers on the knob. Her voice was calm but determined as she spoke over her shoulder.

"I suggest you send your left-off companions someplace else to await a proper home. They will not stay here, especially while I'm gone. I don't like people staying in my business while I'm out." She made her way out of her office area. However, she found herself surrounded by three of the other doppelgängers. When she turned, Malcolm was right there within a few feet. He was holding up a smoky crystal ball in his hand. The smoke inside actually moved.

Miranda's eyes locked on the ball. She didn't look until he said another word.

"No leaving without your shadows to beckon. Bored doppelgängers explore, Miranda." With that, one moved with lightning speed to place the tip of a blade at Mira's throat while holding her tight. "Oh, and it seems you had a very particular set of slaying weapons tucked away out of sight. Look at how the power in the blade wants your soul...it must be a demon slayer, yes?"

"I told you, they'll never deal with you!"

"We shall see. It is a risk I will take. Whereas your continued freedom is not. So, you cannot communicate with the outside, you cannot shadow yourself from this place to another, and there is no emotional wavering so long as I use the sphere. And if you fight, we will cut you down and let the blades have at your soul."

"You'll pay for this!" They moved her body to the stairs as she growled. "I will see you pay. You ...have...my...vow!"

Malcolm smiled. "If you don't like people staying in your business while you are out, Ms. Garrett, I suppose you'll never be able to leave."

Chapter 27
The Sanctuary

Jean-Michel's sanctuary was only half of a mile from the pub. He lived in town, really. It made things easy, considering his alias was a professor of history and culture at the university. And tonight, he needed things to be easy. He felt Gabriel against him on the way and by the time they were in his drive, his shirt was unbuttoned and the man's hands were all over his chest.

He turned and put his arms to rest on Gabriel's shoulders so that they were close once again and he could taste the Councilor's mouth. When he pulled back, he was nearly breathless. They gawked at each other for a few seconds, as if trying to piece together what had just happened. It was just the stress, right? He needed to back out of this.

"Maybe we shouldn't..." Jean whispered, but his fingers on Gabriel's cheek and into his hair said something else. "We're breaking rules, Gabriel."

They were so very different – and bound by who they were physically, mentally, and professionally. These actions were flying in the face of all those things.

"Take the stick out of your ass. Live a little. How many times have I heard you say I think too much? And now *you're* doing it?" His words were confident, relaxed, and inviting, but Gabriel's breathing was nervous and his hands were shaking. Ignoring it for now, Jean took Gabriel's head in his hands and kissed that warm mouth again.

Before long, they were making their way into the house. The door leading from the carport was closed. Gabriel found himself pressed up against it; another kiss; another touch here; there.

Gabriel's stomach tightened just from the nearness of Jean's hands as they rested on his waist. Jean grabbed at the shirt and the buttons went flying. Gabriel gasped. Then, he was kissing the younger man again. Those rough hands slid over Gabriel's sides and up his back, enjoying the tight skin and muscle – so much tighter than his own.

Jean-Michel needed to feel Gabriel's hands upon him again, like before. He said nothing, and let his eyes speak for him. He could make Gabriel feel naked with his gaze and he knew it. That's what he did when he opened the door to the interior and walked by. Those blue-green eyes were staring into the man's soul.

Gabriel acted as if mesmerized, following Jean-Michel inside, his hands lifted to press onward across the expanse of bared chest and slid beneath the shirt to push it from Jean's shoulders. The Tasker was hairy, brawny to the build, and because he was so different, Gabriel seemed even more turned on.

Jean-Michel closed and locked the door before Gabe turned him around and he found himself embraced again. Pulling the Tasker closer, Gabriel raised up slightly to tease the lips that had taunted him so many times in the past. Capturing them for a hungry kiss, he intentionally pressed himself closer so that Jean could feel the hardening bulge at the front of his pants.

They turned, Jean-Michel leading with large hands that captured Gabriel's upper arms in a battle for dominance. He turned Gabriel once again and pressed the man's body against the other wall. One man began the kiss, and the other continued it. Soon, they were breathless again.

Jean-Michel gently teased the other man's lower lip. Then he let his shaggy face move across the smooth skin to find an ear. Once there, he pointed out something he'd almost forgotten.

"I'm the dominant; the top in most of my encounters. Will there be a problem with that?" They remained pressed close, the Tasker's fingers moving up and down beneath Gabriel's loosened shirt over his back and sides.

Eyes rolling back, his head thumped against the wall. Gabriel's breath caught when he heard the question. Yes, there was a question. Thoughts... He needed to answer a question. He could feel his heart pounding in his chest and just knew that if Jean kept prolonging this, eventually his poor heart would explode!

"No..." Gabriel licked his lips, "I... I want you any way I can get you." His back arched away from the wall and he rocked his hips against Jean. He knew he should give at least some thought to the repercussions of what they were about to do. But he didn't want to stop. The only thing on his mind was how the calloused fingers felt and how good it all would soon enough feel to them both.

Without another word or thought, Jean-Michel stepped back and pulled Gabriel with one arm to him. He dipped and the other man was quickly over the dragon's shoulder and being taken into the bedroom.

In all his life, Gabriel could honestly say no one had ever carried him in such a fashion. Once they were in the bedroom, Jean pulled him back over that shoulder. He fell backward onto the bed and a nervous laugh escaped once he was bouncing. He caught the sound of locks, but no one was at the door. Oh, right... the locking magic. He wondered what else the draconic man might be capable of with his magic.

Jean-Michel undid his pants and let them drop. Stepping on the sides of his shoes to remove them with each step, he paused, letting Gabriel finally catch up with him. He had nothing to be ashamed of. Unlike the younger man, he still had body hair that showed his age - salt, pepper, and cayenne mingled with dark auburn. He stalked, then crawled onto the bed and pushed the Councilor into another passionate kiss.

Gabriel's most private thoughts for years - were finally happening in reality. All those calls, those quick, mysterious encounters? Now that he had a chance at the real thing—everything stopped. Jean-Michel was catching his breath after the kiss and held himself above Gabriel.

"Wh.. what?" Gabriel asked breathlessly.

"I...I can't." The dragon growled as he settled back, straddling Gabriel's still-clothed legs.

"What the fuck do you mean, you can't?!" Gabriel's eyes were saucers.

"You're half drunk. You can't even walk a straight line. Your hands are still shaking, Gabriel. I won't have at you like this." Jean-Michel shook his head. "I shouldn't at all-"

"Don't do this. I'm not a child! I may be young to an ANCIENT... but dammit, I'm not! For my birthday this fall, I'll be 30 years old!" Why did he feel like he was a kid pleading to sit at the adult table? He felt like his mind was about to explode. "I have had nothing serious, because of—"

"You think this can be serious? Do you want more reasons we shouldn't be doing this besides the age gap and you being drunk? How about I'm a Tasker? You're a Councilor. I'm a dragon, you're a dragon mage who has sway over me." He started to move, but Gabriel reached up to stop him.

"If I have sway on you, then fine - don't stop! I want you, Senias!" Gabriel sat up enough to take the man's shoulders. He brought his would-be lover down over him again and let his arms move around and up Jean-Michel's back, touching the brand when he did.

Jean's eyes fluttered and his whole body shivered as the magic flowed between them. He groaned from the sensations but shaking his head to come out of the spell, pushed himself back up from Gabriel's embrace. Both men watched as sparkling lavender energy flowed from Gabriel's hands.

They were face to face, shocked, and within a split second, Gabriel realized his mistake. How had it been that easy? He could see it in Jean-Michel's eyes. He'd never seen such pained emotion on the man's face before. It tore him up inside that he'd caused it. "I'm sorry. I...I didn't mean it like that."

Jean-Michel got up and was pulling his pants back on as quickly as he could. He said nothing.

"Listen to me..." Gabriel began as he crawled down to the end of the bed.

"You gonna order me to do that, too?" The draconic eyes flared with power as the Tasker glared at him.

That's when both of them heard the sounds of the outer gate locks. The draconic man growled and turned to the door of the first-floor guest room.

"Fuck me," he grumbled as he stalked out of the room.

"That's what I was trying to do." Gabriel was now beet red as he punched the mattress. He got up and took some deep breaths before walking out of the bedroom and to the edge of the kitchen. "What's wrong? Who's out there?"

"Devon and Eva are the only two people allowed access to my sanctuary. They must be here," Jean-Michel groaned as he tried to button his shirt as much as possible.

"So…just… send them away! We need to talk." He didn't even try to straighten up his clothing. He didn't care that the two lycan who had known him since birth were about to walk in the door. It wasn't their business! The expanse of his tanned, bare chest was rising and falling. "We need to…"

"Do you remember any of the conversations we had earlier? I think we've talked enough." Jean-Michel pushed his fingers through his own hair.

Turning, Gabriel walked away, back into the bedroom, and sat up on the end of the bed. He placed his elbows on his knees and his face in his hands. He felt sick. God, he hoped not.

"Jean? Gabe?" Devon's voice wasn't close to the door, but they could still hear it.

Jean-Michel walked out to be met by Eva first.

"Where's Gabriel?" demanded the mate of Devon Weylyn. Her brown eyes were glaring at Jean-Michel accusingly. Her tawny-brown skin was still damp, and her reddish-toned, loose-textured curls were back from her face and in some places braided as if she had stopped her process without finishing. Though she was only five feet tall, her entire being was something that spoke of a force to be reckoned with.

Before Eva could snarl anything more at Jean-Michel, Gabriel pushed up from the side of the bed and called to her.

"I'm right here, Eva." Gabriel was disappointed, but he couldn't be upset with her for long. She had always been there to help him. Maybe she was supposed to be here – to stop them? Of course, she'd been a little too late for that. They'd stopped themselves.

"Gabe, you had me worried out of my mind." She came in and checked over him. "After the phone call with Jean-Michel, Devon called the Chamber. They attacked you?"

"Actually, they attacked Jean-Michel. He protected me." Even though he really just wanted to sit back down, Gabriel stayed standing there for her to look him over. His hand lifted to smooth through his hair, his shoulders drooping.

"Uh, you smell like you fell in the vat at a winery. Did you go bar hopping to celebrate getting ambushed?" She glared at the Tasker.

"We needed to relax and so we were relaxed and this is the safest place for him, Eva. For the love of…" He scratched the back of his head. The look the woman gave him only reminded him how much she intimidated him. So he made for the kitchen. "Forget it."

"So fought off a doppelgänger in the Chamber, hmm?" The big blonde scratched his whiskered jaw and looked his old friend over in that assessing way he had.

"Yeah, literally. Wanna smell my hands? Probably still stink of the creature," the dragon muttered.

Moving his amber eyes from the draconic male to the rumpled human male, Dev slowly lifted his brows in question.

"I can already smell enough, thank ya very much."

"Touché." Raudine made his way into the kitchen both to wash his hands and to make some coffee and gather the herbs for Gabriel before the younger man wound up with a hangover.

"Didn't we just talk about this shit? Are ya brain dead, on a death wish, or just plain stupid?"

"Maybe all three, ever think of that?" Jean-Michel muttered, knowing Devon would hear him even if the others didn't. He pulled out the coffee filters and saved one aside before putting the first into the coffee pot.

"Look, both of you need to calm down. I had a hell of a day between work and the attack. Jean didn't want me to go home and invited me out for a drink. I had one too many. I just need to sleep it off somewhere that very few have access to, so here I am."

"So long as you're not falling for anything that hussy has up his sleeve," Eva glared pointedly at Jean-Michel, who turned a humorless grin at her before going back to what he was doing.

She whispered, her hand on Gabe's arm. "I would've thought he'd bring ya home and not here. And especially not to seduce you."

"I wasn't the one doing the seducing!" Jean-Michel earned a glare from both of the people in the other room and he rolled his eyes.

"Oh yeah, you got a death wish," Devon concluded.

"I don't run into something wearing my face and acting like me every day and it was shocking." Taking a deep breath, Gabriel rubbed the bridge of his nose. "The lycan that were on duty at the Chamber fell for the deception quick enough that if not for Jean-Michel, I'd be dead. That thing would be enjoying my life, not me." Gabriel walked over to the bed and sat back down. His voice lowered and softened tremendously as he admitted, "I didn't want to be alone again…"

"You don't have to be alone at your house, Gabe." Eva sighed as she followed him. "You could've called us. That one is…"

"It's not the same, Eva." Gabriel snapped. His voice traveled, and he had everyone's attention. "I'm here because the one person who I've wanted for years finally wanted more than to just protect me. He's telling the truth, Eva. I came on to him and he's the one that stopped it; not me and not you. Stop acting like he's the villain."

The dragon had to pick his jaw up. He quickly busied himself scooping dried herbs and pinched a couple of fresh ones from the hanging herb garden in the back of the kitchen to put into the spare filter.

Eva's gaze dropped, and she nodded. "Don't go to sleep until you've had some elixir." Her hand touched Gabriel's shoulder before she made her way to the kitchen.

Jean could feel Devon and then Eva watching him, but he continued anyway.

"What do you have there?" Eva asked.

"I'm making the tea he needs before he goes to sleep. He has to be ready to finish his preparation when he wakes up and doesn't need the hangover." The dragon looked at the lycan incredulously. "You taught me how to do this, remember? I can do it."

"I taught you a lot of things. Don't mean any of it stuck." She crossed her arms over her chest. "Staying away from him fell right out the other side of your brain?"

"By all means, you do it." Jean took a step back and motioned for her to finish the chore. He growled low in his chest. Eva returned the sentiment as they passed.

Gabriel watched as Jean left the kitchen and went out the French doors onto the patio. He couldn't bring himself to go after his... What the hell was this man to him anymore?

CHAPTER 28

A NEEDED TALK

Devon watched with a slow shake of his head. He glanced over into the guest room, only a few yards away from the kitchen. Gabriel seemed lost and in a daze. Turning, he looked outside through the patio doors to see his old friend restlessly pacing in the cool mist of the dark, early morning.

"Can't believe what I'm about ta say," Dev whispered to himself. "Eva, love, he's not a swaddled babe with irresponsible parents anymore. He's a full-grown man with a mind full of stubborn thoughts, desires, and ideas all his own. Much as ya wanna protect him from all the world, ya just can't."

Her shoulders heaved up and then settled down as she took in her mate's words. She said nothing, but continued to tie the string around the makeshift tea bag and then placed it in the heated water.

Devon moved behind his mate to stroke his hands down from her shoulders to her elbows, and he pressed a kiss to the left side of her neck. He just nuzzled her there and held her for a bit.

"I know it's hard ta let go, but we did it for our born pups. I think it may be time ta let go of this one, too." Then, he added, "Want him living a lonely, bitter life of wishing and regret?"

"No." She turned to her mate while his face was still there and she took a deep breath and let it out. "I don't want him ta be lonely. But I don't want him hurt either, Devon. You know that dragon better than any. His history – especially with the Kennedys? What if Amelia was right to ask us to keep them apart? What if..." She sighed and shook her head.

"I know. It's difficult. But I also know you'll work it out. I'll be on the back patio with the old claw sharing a beer. Take yer time darlin'." He reached into the fridge to pull a few bottles out and made his way.

Eva heard Gabriel padding through the house, and she steeled herself. She had the teacup and grabbed the honey container before turning to face him.

"Here. This will keep the pains of the alcohol from visiting you." She felt her heart sink just a little. His hands were on his hips and he didn't look pleased at all. Oh, he looked so much like her eldest when he was finally tired of her trying to help. Devon was right. Was this happening again so soon?

"Eva, I…" Gabriel's mouth went dry and the normally eloquent Councilor found he couldn't finish the sentence as easily as he had thought. He took the cup, probably resigned not to finish, so she continued.

"This is about your dragon, isn't it?" She placed her small hands on the counter, her eyes searching Gabe's.

"No, this isn't about him. Well, it *is*, but it isn't." He looked at her with consternation in his expression. "You knew, and you said nothing." He shook his head and held his hand up to keep her from speaking. "Don't. Let me finish. Just…" He tried to laugh it off even while thinking of how to try again. He rubbed his forehead and sighed heavily. "You are very special to me. I hope you know that. But…"

"But?" she whispered.

"But being here is my choice. I know you want to pack me off to the house. But I want to be here with him, Eva. Do you understand what I'm telling you?" Gabriel hoped she did because he wasn't sure that he could explain things any better than that. He sat the cup down and added the honey.

"I always thought you'd find a nice handsome fella your age and, well, even if it were a lycan, at least you'd have a loyal, open beau. One not tangled up in intrigues and secrets. One without all those scars he carries with him."

Gabriel lifted the cup to his mouth and took a sip of the pungent brew.

"Dragons are trouble, all full of riddles and such. They're dangerous, especially for people in your family, Gabriel. You shouldn't be here and imagine what trouble you could find yourself in if the Crimson folks found out. You could lose your seat and who knows how they'd treat your Tasker."

When Eva mentioned the dangers, he nodded. He needed to know more! But only when he could handle understanding everything. At the moment, just listening was difficult.

"And you don't know half of the trouble that particular dragon happens ta be. He's already on Crimson's shortlist, what with his and that fang's crimes against humanity." Eva huffed. "How he wound up Jonathan's friend and Tasker after all that, I'll never understand."

Gabriel's fingers lifted again to rub at the bridge of his nose. He tried to let all that she said sink in. He took another drink of the tea and let it warm his belly.

"You're falling, aren't ya?"

"A long time ago," Gabriel admitted. "Come sit and talk to me until I pass out."

Eva glanced outside. Devon and Jean-Michel were out there talking. She wondered what they were saying to one another. Turning back to Gabriel, she nodded. Eva went around the counter and took his hand to lead him back to the cozy guest room.

"I got fifty that says not only is the lycan Councilor a grey-skin but so is that old crotchety thing ya call Skinner." Dev chuckled as he sipped the beer again, he'd had better, but how could anything compare to lycan moon ale?

"Skinner's Skinner. But Jonas? His men? I'm not so sure anymore. He's been putting up barriers left and right. Then tonight – for them to allow a doppelgänger through and not be overly cautious? They had seen Gabriel come in earlier." Jean rubbed the back of his head with the palm of his hand. "They must've thought I left. I'll err on the side of being paranoid rather than take Gabriel back there to be hunted. That's why I want one of you or a Weylyn guard with him. If I can't be there constantly, someone else needs to be."

Devon glanced back through the glass patio door to where his mate was staring at them. Once she disappeared further inside, the Alpha sighed big. Clearing his throat, he watched his best friend; his dragon brother.

"Seriously though, this goes sour and she'll have both our asses for it. Don't let ole windbag Skinner catch a whiff of this or there's no tellin' what he'd do to either of ya. As you so graciously pointed out, the last fella that took a fancy to ya ended up spending a long damn time in a deep hole – when they weren't beating him. I don't think that this young 'un would last so long."

"Sebastian turned himself in. That wasn't on me. He may blame me for it, but I'm tired of taking the flogging. I got him out as soon as I realized what had happened. It was all about crimes against humanity, not about me." Raudine's eyes stayed on the ground, and he hadn't taken even one drink of the beer. "I have a fault for pushing him away. I should have pushed him away sooner, but I ...I loved him. I denied things. I didn't save him soon enough. Those are my only failings." Facing Devon, he added, "That would never happen where Gabriel is concerned. I'd end myself before I let Skinner do anything to him."

"Would you really?" It was a statement of truth, but it was also very telling. Normally Senias had trysts. This no longer sounded like a drunken tryst. The wolf rocked back on his heels, his eyes showing his surprise. "If ya want ta protect him, wouldn't that best be done by stayin' away?"

"I've tried to stay away from him since Jonathan officially introduced us. It wasn't sexual then. It was his eyes and his heart. They differed from what I saw in all the others. But I'd been burnt by the hope that any human would be different from the generation before, especially Kennedys. I wouldn't let myself believe anything good about Gabriel. I did my best to stay away as much as possible." He put the beer bottle down and let off an exasperated sigh. "I don't know what I should do anymore."

Devon listened. It was all he could do - play devil's advocate and listen.

"So, I watched from afar. Started sparring with him over politics and stupid shit over the phone. Then... I had to talk to him. Hell, I'm his assigned Tasker. And then, this time? I couldn't run anymore." He chuckled at that thought. The memory from earlier in the night actually reddened his cheeks. "Imagine my surprise when he came on to me."

Finishing his beer, the lycan swiped his friend's untouched one because he didn't believe in wasting it. Also, he felt like he needed it. Devon took a drink and licked his lips before sitting in one of the large chairs. Leaning forward to rest his elbows on his knees, the lycan let the bottle dangle between his fingers.

"I've not found enjoyment with another man since..." Jean-Michel closed his eyes, recalling the fury on Sebastian's face when he had tried to help in the clinic. He pushed himself to continue. "If you were wondering, they assigned me to be Gabriel's Tasker. I had no choice. Not like it was with Jonathan."

"You didn't volunteer?"

"No!" Jean-Michel responded immediately, his blue-green eyes wide.

"And yer sure this ain't some game Skinner's playing with the both of ya?"

"He might've done it to put the screws to me, sure. Skinner knows I have a connection to the Kennedys. He knows what I am, but I've not confirmed a damn thing. But I admit, yes, that's a possibility." Jean-Michel's hands were at his sides, palms up in a near-surrendering stance. "Does that make any difference? Devon, you know I've not acted on any urges. You know that for a fact because you've been around me or Gabriel or both of us. Same as Eva."

"Yeah, but I can't read minds, and here we are, the kid with a crush on his mentor and that mentor actin' a fool for him." Devon tried a new angle. "That's not the making's of a healthy relationship."

"I've not taken advantage of our bond or knowing him or any of that. I'm not exactly his mentor, Devon. Even when his grandfather introduced us, I slacked on my mentorship so I could avoid him, just as everyone advised me to do."

Standing up, Devon finished the rest of the beer before tossing both bottles in the trash can nearby. He then made his way to stand before his friend with his arms crossed over his chest. Jean-Michel had no choice but to face him.

"Yer both Pack in my eyes." Devon held his hand out to his old friend and grinned, "If yer sure this is what ya want, I'll stop trying ta hold ya back. Yer giving up the chance at freedom if ya go down this road, though…"

"I understand that." Jean-Michel took a deep breath of the night air and made his way toward the doors to the house. "I know there's a lot to overcome. I'm not even sure where this will go. Not sure if there'll be anything. I just want to allow for the chance."

"And this investigation? Not to switch gears, but it's important and both of ya are involved."

"I may have drunk a few too many. If I get a couple of hours of sleep, we need to investigate where these things are staying. Pandora's Box."

"You think Mira's definitely in the middle of this?" Devon asked.

"Afraid, so." Jean-Michel turned to the door where Eva stood. "Is he asleep?" He left Devon to walk toward the short woman.

"Yes. But he took the elixir first. I made sure."

"Good. Good. You're welcome to treat this as your own home. That has never changed. Thank you for coming and apologies for my shortness… with you, especially. I should never try to get down to your level." The smirk as he passed told her he had definitely not lost his wit.

Eva swatted Jean's ass as hard as she could when they passed.

"Short means I'm the perfect size to cause the most damage. Don't ya forget that, now." She growled, but it was more for show than anything else.

Instead of watching him, she stepped outside to her mate.

Devon chuckled to himself at the tit-for-tat that was sorely missed between the two. He watched the dragon walk through the bottom floor of the house while Eva walked outside to him.

"What ya thinkin' bout all of this, lovely?" Her opinion mattered to him far more than any other. So, before they left the two to themselves, he wanted her insight on it all. Because the fact of the matter was – if Eva wasn't comfortable with this, Devon would march right inside, put Gabe over his shoulder, and take him home.

"We can't make a man's heart change without making that heart turn hard. The Goddess decides such things. Not us."

"Ah, but what about our word to the lady, Amelia?" Devon rumbled as he watched his friend's odd behavior. Through the glass they could see the Tasker, despite his weariness, stop at the guest room to watch Gabriel sleep. He'd never seen the dragon act like this before. Not even with the fang.

"He's smitten and has been for a while. As for the dragon, we're watching all those walls he'd built fall. Don't ya want yer old friend back?" As Devon stepped closer to her, she glanced up at her mate, then leaned against him. "This may be what makes it happen."

"It's happened." Devon slid his arms around his petite beauty.

"So your vow to Senias to keep him minding his P's and Q's so he can get his freedom from the Kennedy line – no longer means keeping them apart? And my vow to his grandmother that I'd be sure her angel stayed safe and happy – means letting them go to each other?"

"Crazy as it sounds darlin', yes... I think so."

Chapter 29
Waking Up

The first thing that Gabriel realized was that the arms that had been around him were not there. The second? His head wasn't killing him as he had thought it would. Whatever Jean-Michel and Eva gave him the night before had worked. Gabriel opened his eyes and groaned because of the light hitting his eyes. Damned window. Wait, where was he?

It hadn't been a dream. Had any of it been a dream?

Gabriel stood up, relieved to still have his clothes on. Well, most of them. His shirt would need to be replaced... the buttons were...somewhere.

He went to the bathroom, then he left the guest room. He walked around the lower floor to explore and just take everything in. The floors in this area were wood with a dark stain. The furniture sat on rugs beautifully woven and probably older than the immense trees providing shade outside.

The tables and chairs did not match the sofa. But they were of various eras as if someone had chosen one fashionable piece of furniture from each. One of the comfy living room chairs had more wear than the others. The side table near it showed markings from glasses being put on it without a coaster and also held an old pipe and tobacco pouch. There were no modern electronics in the room at all. There were papers on the middle table, Wall Street Journal, The New York Times, then several in different languages, and a magazine - The Economist. The light scent of vanilla and sweet tobacco hung in the air. There was also a hint of musk and something wild.

Gabriel took a deep breath. It helped him remember being close to Jean-Michel the night before. That was the scent...

Gabriel went to the kitchen. On the counter was a set of pills and a bottle of water. Next to that was a covered plate that contained wheat toast with a side of butter and marmalade. There was a note in Jean's handwriting.

In case you wake and I'm gone. For your headache. Eva should be around somewhere.

Folding the note carefully in half, Gabriel held it in one hand for a moment before finally putting it back down. It felt immature to keep it, and yet, he kind of wanted to.

He took up the glass of water and took the pills. Soon, he was chewing on the toast. Gabriel really couldn't imagine that all of this belonged to the smart-assed Tasker. He had expected a regular bachelor's pad.

Finished with breakfast, Gabriel climbed up the stairs before taking some time to walk around the upper floor. There were two guest rooms, an office with a small library, and then what had to be the master.

The door to the master called his curiosity. Gabriel opened it up slowly and once his eyes adjusted, he explored. He was grinning as he noted the bed. The person who made it made it for much more than just sleeping! They constructed the thing with natural wood logs. It was a tough four-poster with railings over the top for hanging netting or a canopy. It had nothing on it now. Literally, the posts began as oak tree trunks. They had carvings all the way up and someone kept them polished. Gabriel's free hand touched the smooth finish.

"You like it?" Eva asked before taking another drink of her tea. She was leaning on the door frame.

Gabriel jumped and stared, eyes wide. "What?" He flushed, but he answered honestly, "Yes, I do actually; like it, that is."

"Devon made it for him a long, long time ago. My mate loves to work with his hands and used to be quite the artisan. He made it from the type of tree that he saw was proper for his brother in blood... an oak. Full of strength, courage, energy, and a bit of wisdom."

"That's...a lot. He doesn't show a lot of that. I guess maybe the courage and energy?" Gabriel whispered. He smirked when Eva shrugged.

"Most people don't get to see the true Senias of Morias, do they? Just like most people don't get to see the true Gabriel Kennedy." She smiled. "Most people only know the very offensive, always on-guard Jean-Michel Raudine or when he's using his alias, Professeur Raudine." Eva motioned for Gabriel to leave the room. "The owner is not here. It's not proper to snoop."

"Morias? Is that...a surname or ..." Gabriel hated to admit that he hadn't been told any of this already by the Tasker.

"His clan name. Yes. It's used much like a surname among humans or a Pack name among lycan," Eva explained.

"Mmm.." Gabriel made his way down the stairs again.

"He wears a mask, much as you have for a very long time." Eva walked with him. "Even those like us friends rarely get to see the tender side of the creature anymore. For a very long time, I thought that tender part of him died of circumstance and cynicism. Then I saw a spark of it last night."

"I was just a little drunk. I...may have missed a lot." Gabriel let her step by and followed her down the stairs to the main floor again. "He was correct not to go too far. Hate admitting it, but it's true."

"Just a little, eh?"

"I remember being held by him." He tried to fidget, but his clothes were a mess and he kind of had nothing to fidget with. "We both wear masks because we have to, Eva, not because we really want to. The world doesn't accept us as we truly are."

"Oh, the world has changed, Gabriel. The world might not accept him, but it would accept you. I think it's more that you don't accept yourself."

Gabriel swallowed. All his life, the world, and his family had taught him to be tough. There was no room for a mousey, sick, effeminate kid in the Kennedy line. Gabriel didn't like his father. Never had. And he'd be lying if he ever said the man's death saddened him. It didn't help to be brought up when homophobia was acceptable.

"Maybe that's why you had to find each other. So you could take each other's masks off." Eva, ever the pragmatic one, shrugged at the theory and walked on to the kitchen. "And ta be clear, he argued with Devon about you. He watched you sleep. And later in the night, you had a nightmare or something. He came back to you and held you until about an hour before you woke up. The only reason he's gone is that I promised to keep you safe and get you to where you need to go so you can make this meeting happen and right this wrong."

"Wait, why did he argue with you over me?"

"Whether he was worthy. Whether he was ready." Eva raised her gaze back up to catch the expression.

Gabriel's mouth pulled up just a little at one corner. Jean-Michel had argued over him?

"Oh, now don't be giving me dat look there, Mr. Kennedy. Your taste in men hasn't led you to the proper place and his taste in ANYTHING hasn't led him anywhere good over the years. I don't want ta see you hurt; either of you. But... we had this discussion and I won't rehash it. Devon and I agreed to support whatever decisions your hearts lead you to. I hope the Goddess keeps ya both from being hurt by one another."

"That's not the goal, is it?" Gabriel walked across the room.

"Is it ever?" she asked, and Gabriel paused. "I'm just saying his history from the moment I met him til now is not but one adventure after another. Littered with tragedies."

"Tragedy?" Gabriel knew about Sebastian and knew that Jean had been with Mira in the past, but he knew nothing about any tragedies. He wasn't really sure where this was all going yet.

"It takes a lot to come back from tragedy, Gabe. He seems to trip and fall so much when he tries. And for a long time, Dev and I didn't think he'd even try anymore. Then came you."

"Eva," Gabriel paused to make the announcement. "I want this with him. But I don't want to force him. I don't want to be another mistake. I did something last night that...I need to make up for." Gabriel sighed. "I'll get the rest of my things. I need to go by the estate."

"We barely have time for the estate, but it can happen. If you hurry, you might change and get back out the door. With me driving, and you rushing, anything's possible, eh?" Eva sat the cup in the sink before heading to the door.

Chapter 30
SURPRISES

Devon pulled down a small alley while Derek continued to do his thing.

"Thank goodness the people around there believe in security systems. I've got several angles." Derek was busily busting into the systems he could so he could use the camera feeds.

As soon as the truck stopped, there was a bang on Devon's window. A scowling man, almost as big as a lycan, stood there. His eyes betrayed him, for the iris sparkled like rubies, reflecting the moonlight.

"It's been ages," Devon muttered before stepping out. "Dante, how about we talk out here?"

"Just keep in mind there are other doppelgängers around. Are you two all we get? The rescue my sister deserves?" Dante scoffed.

"Rescue?" Derek was suddenly concerned.

"Our mutual dragon friend wanted to know when we found out more about the doppelgänger business. I've tried to get him. Mira handles her own business. I didn't realize she might get in over her head until I got here, tried to go in, and..." He looked back over his shoulder. "Someone covered this place in some sort of shield. I'm a half-demon and I can't get inside. I can't feel my sister."

Devon could tell this was eating the incubus. Twins were almost always close. And these two twins had lived as partners in crime for centuries.

"I'm trying to learn what I can," Derek assured the big fellow. On his laptop, Derek was finally able to pull the proper camera angles. He got out of the truck and came around to put the laptop on the hood and his bag next to it.

There were five various cameras letting him know as much as possible about what was happening inside and around the place.

"Two people are in the store – the main floor – I'm assuming those are doppels. There's one walking around the outside. I bet that's one down the alleyway, here." he pointed it out on the screen. "Nobody has any business being down here, right? It's after hours?"

"That's where they get deliveries, but yeah…not now," Dante supplied.

"And I see two near the bank down the block. Why are they here? I thought they were going after Councilors."

"I imagine they had to go this route because of Gabriel and Vanishte and us. We were on 'em. They needed ta lie low." Devon's hands went to his hips, and he turned his head to ask Dante, "How the hell did Mira get into this up to her neck?"

"They took advantage of my sister. She's worked so hard for this, Weylyn. To have her own business without the shadow of the Underground over it? It took decades. And all those that claimed to give a damn about her were too busy with their own escapades to take notice she was in trouble. I don't know how the doppels forced her to risk it, but if they've harmed her at all…"

"A pissed-off demon ain't doing any of us any good." Devon put his hand on the man's upper arm but found nothing but air soon enough because Dante turned away. "Don't go out there. We've got a plan, Dante. We're not the only ones on this."

Dante turned back to the two lycan. "I'll go along with whatever gets my sister out of this safely."

Derek tried to keep his attention back on the video feeds. He explained the situation as quickly as he could.

"We need to know if there's an easier way into the building other than the front door or the delivery door. Both are being watched."

"I usually use the basement. But, I usually use my shadowing ability. I can't right now. The energy, it's keeping me out," Dante explained.

"So, she takes deliveries into the basement? There's a physical way in. Doors upstairs? I saw a balcony, but does it have fixed doorways or actual doors?" Derek changed the feeds around on the screen until he had chosen the best shots.

"There's the front door. Let me think." Closing his eyes, Dante visualized the layout of the store and a frown creased the corners of his mouth as he mentally worked himself through the place.

"The back door, but it's got the emergency alarm on it. There are balcony doors to Mira's private apartment and an office upstairs. They work. She usually takes deliveries on that main floor doorway onto the alley, but there's also an old basement entrance that isn't used anymore. It's covered by brambles and ivy on the backside. Miranda had it wired two years ago by a human outfit when there were a bunch of burglaries nearby." He tried to think of anything else that might be useful to them. "The balcony you see. If it's the one on the front, that's a facade. The real balcony is on the side."

"Thanks." Devon tucked his earpiece in place and turned to Derek. "You got Jean-Michel tagged?"

Derek touched the side of the screen and another window popped out to show his agent's vitals and a small GPS for current positioning. Devon's stats were now added. They could see Jean-Michel moving down an adjacent street on foot.

"Any changes to the plan?" Derek asked. "I can engage the Tasker whenever we need to."

"The plan is we get in that store and sort out what's going on. We help those who need helping and crack heads on those that don't. If we can keep a witness, we do it. But most of 'em so far prefer to kill themselves."

"What do you need from me?" Dante's gaze shifted back and forth between the two lycan.

"As difficult as this may be, you stay put with Derek. They obviously know what ya are and are prepared ta use that against ya. So don't make things worse for yer sister by trying anything."

Dante scoffed, but licking his lips, nodded to the old Alpha.

"Keep him in the know but outta trouble. Be ready." Devon backed away from both of them.

"You got it, Pops." Derek finished his calibrations and realized there was another rumble coming from his Alpha. He turned back to Devon. "What?"

"Don't call me that in the field." Devon took off around the corner but stopped immediately. "Shit. There's about ta be trouble." His amber eyes took in the newly arrived trucks and cars and the one at the lead of this caravan was none other than Jonas Airsight himself. "Derek, get outta there. They've got Crimson with 'em."

"What is this? Turf wars between packs? Or..." Dante watched on the screen as Derek pulled up the scene. "He's in on it?"

"We think...maybe. Yeah. He told us not to investigate anymore. He's our Councilor and we're supposed to do as he says, but I...I just don't think that's Jonas Airsight. I hate ta believe it, but..." Derek was in contact with Jean-Michel while this was happening.

"Fuck this."

"Dante, no!" Derek didn't grab the demon quick enough.

"I thought I warned you?" Jonas walked away from his car and put his hands on his hips. He faced down Devon Weylyn in the street.

"Well, you know how hard-headed us Weylyn are, Jonas. Especially when people ain't doing their jobs."

Devon growled as both Derek and Dante got dragged around the building. One guard with them was carrying Derek's bag and the laptop.

"Where's the Tasker?" Jonas moved directly in front of Devon.

"You may have rights ta take us in, but you got no rights ta Dante there. And ya got no rights to anybody else..." Devon stood his ground.

"I'm a Councilor. Don't matter that I'm lycan and represent you and all Packs in the Americas. If I suspect supernatural wrongdoin' I report it and Crimson handles the business. And I ain't got nothing but suspicion where all three of y'all are concerned."

"You? Suspicious of us?" Devon let his body shift into the larger, wolf-hybrid version of himself. He growled and pushed forward to Jonas.

The Councilor shifted and grabbed Devon's muzzle before those sharp teeth could do any damage. Then he shifted as well. He threw the other lycan over his shoulder. The two, who looked very much like classic werewolves, squared off.

Dante took the moment and turned quickly to headbutt the Crimson agent behind him, and he fought the one that had Derek's hands behind his back. Derek was momentarily free. Or so he thought.

Just as he grabbed for his bag, the cuffs he wore glowed with an electrical light. Crackling energy moved from the cuffs through their bodies. It had them down in an instant. The two were convulsing and screaming in pain.

"Stop this or it'll continue," Jonas threatened as the two lycan were face to face, moving in a circle, growling.

"Pops!" Derek roared as the energy threw him into his hybrid form and then back into his human so quickly that the pain was intense.

"Stop it!" Devon shifted back to his human form and held his hands out in surrender. As soon as he did, the torture of the other two stopped. One of the Crimson guards moved forward to shackle Devon.

"Where's the Tasker?" Jonas asked again, also returning to his human form.

"I don't know. A Tasker does his own thing. You know that. Especially this Tasker." Devon growled as Jonas reached into Devon's ear to grab the piece of technology that was still there.

"Load 'em up. Two of 'em for disobeying direct orders from their Councilor and all of 'em for showcasing powers in a public place." Jonas turned from them and walked over to his own vehicle.

Placing the earpiece in his ear, he cleared his throat. "I know you won't talk, so listen. We've got your allies. Crimson agents watched it all go down, so we'll charge them, and rightfully so. You can either turn yourself in or be ready to pay the consequences." He then took the piece from his own ear, dropped it on the ground, and stepped on it.

Chapter 31
CONFRONTATION

Sebastian Evansworth had returned to his lair to sleep before waking to plait his hair for the Council meeting. He passed through security and made his way to the Chamber. The vampire was trying to focus on business instead of the pretty blonde doctor that had garnered his attention and his dreams.

Seeing Kennedy present did not surprise him in the least; the man lived and breathed work either in this room or in an office. Eva Weylyn was quietly knitting in a chair near the tables in front of the Council seats and the podium and witness stands.

"The meeting isn't until 11 pm, Councilor Evansworth. What brings you so early?" Gabriel actually paused in his work.

"Your Tasker sent word to me that a discussion amongst a few of us was necessary prior to the meeting. I assumed you told him this?" Something seemed off with the human, but he wasn't sure just yet what it was.

"It's possible that I said something about it, but I didn't tell him to get you here sooner. Sorry. I saw your report here, along with Dr. Keene's additions and the autopsy report. You worked with her to make sure we could test blood samples to see who's a doppelgänger and who's not. That's amazing work, Sebastian. Thank you for promoting the meeting and also for that."

"I didn't do it for you."

"You did it for him?" Gabriel asked out of nowhere.

"No," Sebastian scoffed as he walked closer. "I did it because I'm a selfish bastard that wants to see whoever tried to take me out – go down." The vampire was at the other side of the table from the human Councilor.

"I see." Gabriel went back to review the information. That unnerving sensation of being watched had him looking back up. He locked glares with Evansworth. "Something else?"

"I don't know." Sebastian was observing this man like he would observe something in nature as a scientist. It was just part of who he was. And because Gabriel was human, he didn't see an issue with it. "Why do you seem different?"

Eva paused and looked up from her work.

"I beg your pardon?" Gabriel arched a brow at him. "Different?" Gabriel took a deep breath out of annoyance. "What are you on about, Evansworth?"

"You're focused, but..."

"I appreciate you taking the time to help me get this meeting set up. What else do you need?"

"One got a damn good swipe in at me." Sebastian's eyes wandered from the boxes and paperwork back to the other Councilor. "Because we're dealing with doppelgängers, when I see someone acting odd, like you being so relaxed compared to the normal way you go about things, well, it makes me have a second look."

"I'm definitely not a doppelgänger. And that you were so brutally attacked should help you understand my urgency to make sure I have these documents in order," Gabriel went back to picking up papers and considering their use, then moving them to a different pile. "Anyway..."

Stepping closer to the table where Gabriel was studying paperwork, the vampire caught the faintest familiar scent and actually took a step backward as if someone had slapped him.

Eva stiffened when she saw the vampire back up so quickly.

"I had a good night of sleep after being attacked myself. Obviously, it wasn't as deadly an attack, but—"

"He'll grow tired of you, you know?"

Gabriel's attention immediately flashed up to the vampire.

"When the excitement of you fades away, he will, too. He will never give himself to you. You are a Kennedy. Your family bound him." Sebastian nearly spat the word. "I'd remember that every time you're with him." He couldn't help being spiteful. Not after everything he had been through for that fucking dragon.

With as much composure as he could manage, Gabriel Kennedy stood to his full height and gazed directly into the eyes of the vampire across the table from him.

"No matter your past, it doesn't make you an expert on him. Nor are you by any means an expert on a Kennedy – much less this Kennedy. Besides, there's nothing between us. And I'm not asking anything of my Tasker."

Glancing over his right shoulder straight at the lycan female, Sebastian gave a somewhat harsh grin.

"Nothing between them then, Eva Weylyn? If that's the truth, then you should teach him what it means to lie with our kind and not bathe well enough before coming into a room full of them."

Eva gave Sebastian a rather bored expression.

"I've been around Raudine for several days now – working on this matter – so why wouldn't I smell of him?"

With a low chuckle, Sebastian had to give the younger man credit for trying. "Right..." He crossed his arms over his chest.

"He smells like Raudine because he stayed in his home. Had you been listening, instead of sniffing and getting your knickers in a wad, you'd realize you weren't the only one dat got attacked by doppels." Eva went back to her knitting. "They attacked Gabe, too. He was in danger, so his Tasker insisted we all stay at his warded home. I probably smell a little like the man, too. I was there. And I used his shower, his towels..."

"He won't believe you." Gabriel took his seat and went back to the paperwork before him.

"He'll believe me because he knows nothing would give me so much pleasure as rubbing that pale face in something that pisses him off. It'd be fun to tell him his ex moved on while he was still so pissy, ain't dat right, fang?" Eva's eyes turned golden when she let her lycan senses pop through.

"Fuck off, Eva. Go back to your knitting." He wanted to say that he had moved on. Or...maybe he had moved on. It wasn't entirely up to him, was it?

"Hey, that was uncalled for, Evansworth. I thought you were the charming, lordly sort. What happened?" Gabriel didn't like disrespectful behavior. Especially from a fellow Councilor.

"You asked, fang." Eva didn't get upset. On the contrary, she seemed to be entertained.

Approaching the table again, Sebastian leaned over to scan the images and information. "For what it's worth, I'm glad the attack wasn't successful." Before either could say anything, the vampire added, "I'd hate to see what new spoiled human ass they'd fill the seat with."

"Funny, I thought you were rather fond of watching human asses..." Eva mumbled. She continued knitting.

"Oh, I am. Just not when they sit atop shoulders and talk." He smirked, doing his best to play off his earlier loss of control. His focus went back to Kennedy, but the other Councilor ignored him.

The door opened and the human form of Vanishte entered the chamber escorted by a Crimson guard, wearing a sash that designated him in this building.

"Russell Weylyn, what are you doing here?" Eva scowled at her son.

"Don't say it..." the dark-haired lycan passed his mama to deliver the defendant to their seat. Unlike Devon and Derek, Russell was small and his brilliant blue eyes were a contrast to his mother's and father's more amber-colored eyes.

"You should be with your Alpha," she growled.

"I'm doing what my Alpha told me ta do. He wanted me with Lady Vanishte and you. Besides, the Director shifted out Weylyn guards with the ones that were here before." Russell made a huff. "I gotta do as I'm told if I want ta be a Tasker someday. You know that, mama."

"Really?" Eva put away her knitting.

"Vanishte, welcome," Gabriel walked around the table to greet Russell and the doppelgänger leader.

"It's quiet." Vanishte pointed out. Their eyes take in the chamber, their hands wringing in front of them. A doppelgänger's nature was to hide and not speak up. That was far from what Vanishte was doing.

"That's why I wanted you to come in early," Gabriel explained. "So you can get over your nervousness. Oh, and one of the other Councilors is here." He cleared his throat. "This is Councilor Sebastian Evansworth."

"So you are the reason for this meeting." Sebastian performed appropriately, smiling while tucking his pride and annoyance back into his chest.

"I am afraid so, Councilor Evansworth," Vanishte said quietly. "I am eternally grateful to you for helping us find legitimacy."

"Vanishte, the Elven Councilor will also arrive soon and after her, the rest will present themselves. They will question you while I make sure that I prove your case and do my best to filter anything inappropriate. I can only caution you to keep your emotions under control and answer only what we ask. I would hate to see you dismissed before being fully heard."

"Should I remain in this form?" they asked.

"You can, or if you want to show them your truth, that's fine," Gabriel assured.

Vanishte allowed their form to shift before their eyes. They were now the gray-skinned being but wore their human clothing.

"Let's practice, shall we?" Sebastian went to his seat behind the table and focused on Vanishte. "How did you get to this world?" He wanted to give the doppel an example of how it would feel to be center stage.

"We applied for and were granted temporary credentials so that we could make our case through the European portal."

Gabriel felt his phone vibrate. Taking it from his pocket, he nodded to Sebastian and walked away. This wasn't a blocked number, but he didn't recognize it.

"This is Gabriel Kennedy."

"You're fucking difficult to get hold of."

The voice was unmistakable. Gabriel felt a shiver as he remembered that night at the Inferno and the way the half-demon's power had made him feel. "Why are you calling me?"

"Because your friend, Miranda? My sister? She's in trouble, Gabriel. And I have my hands tied." There was a bit of a snarl on the other end of the phone. "Literally."

Gabriel looked at the phone again and realized the number. "You're at..."

"Yeah, we got one call. You're mine. Jonas and a bunch of Crimson agents were at Pandora's Box. They had the right weaponry and technique. I hate to admit it, but they caught me off-guard. So was Devon."

"What? Devon?" Gabriel's heart lurched. "Anyone else?"

"Derek – everybody that was supposed to be helping my sister. We think she's being held inside her shop. There's an anti-magic barrier of some kind. I can't feel her or get to her. I don't see your Tasker, though. So he may still be out there. We'll need help later. You worry about my sister. She knows all about this. I don't know why she's in it, but she knows. And, Councilor?"

"Yes?" Gabriel tried to sound confident. How could he? Everything was falling apart.

"I'm sure she'll testify. You just have to get her there." The call ended, and Gabriel was still standing there in shock. Everyone had gone quiet.

Sebastian left their witness and walked over to Gabriel, who was calling someone else by now. Eva was also walking toward the human Councilor.

"Dante called with information. It seems our theory about Miranda Garret was correct. She's being used. I'm not sure about the details, but Dante just called to tell me she's being kept at her store. This is turning into a hostage situation and what's worse is... Jonas had Devon, Derek, and Dante arrested. He's definitely in on this. We need to out him."

"Devon can't stay in a cell. Not again..." Eva was already looking at the door.

"Don't. There's nothing you can do for him." Sebastian whispered to the woman.

"He was a prisoner in the wars. He's claustrophobic, you ass. This is gonna be hell for him. You can't leave him in there..."

"We'll get them out." Sebastian's voice was more strained as he spoke. "If you leave and everybody's rattled, they get their way... whoever we're talking about here."

"If we questioned whether Jonas was in on it...I think we know now. Jean-Michel is still out there. I have no idea where." Gabriel paced. If the damned group wanted him off his game, they got it.

"He may need help," Sebastian ventured.

"Ya think?" Eva growled and tried to make her way around Sebastian, but he took a step to block her again. Her eyes turned dangerous.

Gabriel had just been finding out about that kind of trouble. He'd even experienced it once during this investigation. It pained him to admit it, but maybe Sebastian was right.

"That shop is filled with magic. And according to you, there may be doppelgängers." The vampire's eyes shifted between the two.

"And you're immune? They attacked you before, Sebastian," Gabriel pointed out.

"I don't just rely on magic or magical trinkets. My mind can handle things and by the way, I survived that attack because I know how to fight them. I assume because you never got Skinner in your corner that Crimson isn't helping? And you're using the Weylyn guards here, so there probably aren't any spares to help."

Gabriel and Eva both wore skeptical looks.

"I've been an ass, I admit it."

This had both Gabriel's and Eva's attention. They side-eyed one another and then both faced the vampire.

"Let me make up for it? We have a bit of time. Let me help."

"But Sebastian, you must be here to support this meeting. You and Minlial are the only other sponsors." Gabriel paused while other Councilors were coming into the Chamber along with their people.

"It doesn't matter who voted to get the meeting going, what matters is corroboration, Kennedy. You need a majority vote to get them to act on anything in here – including blood tests. And you can't force these Councilors to give you that without some sort of proof." Sebastian pointed out. "All you have is the word of a disenfranchised doppelgänger who has remained here illegally after her papers expired. How far do you wager that gets you?"

"I'll still need you here, along with whatever proof or witnesses you can manage. How do you plan to be in both places? Pandora's Box is clear across town. And I have to keep everyone busy while you handle this..." Gabriel's fingertip went to the bridge of his nose to ease the headache that threatened.

"Kennedy, you're full of hot air. You can stall if need be." Sebastian moved away from them. "I don't travel by normal means. I know where I'm going. Keep watch here. I'll help him and bring them back."

Chapter 32

Opening Pandora's Box

Derek's message to him had been correct. There was a sphere of power around the northeastern corner of the block, the core of which seemed to emanate from Pandora's Box. The Tasker could see a very light shifting of color, where the energy coalesced. Thank goodness for a flask of the good stuff.

The Tasker walked down one of the side streets to an alleyway a few blocks from Mira's shop. He didn't want to risk portaling too close, though the situation tempted him to do so. He was going in blind at this point.

Jean-Michel made sure it was dark enough, and no one was around before climbing the sign close to the building. He boosted himself off a window frame, grabbed the lip of the rooftop, and yanked himself up. He didn't stay still long once he was off the street. Jean-Michel nearly flew between buildings, slid down A-frame rooftops, and sprang over air conditioning units.

Again, without breaking stride, he dove off the rooftop to grab hold of a fire escape ladder that immediately lowered to the ground. The loud clatter of that landing didn't go unnoticed, but he was out of easy sight. As soon as he could, the Tasker slipped further away, leaving the Crimson agents that were now patrolling the area to find nothing. He double-timed it around the back building to the next alley and around.

The upper floor of Pandora's Box had a balcony. That was his way in. But he had to be careful of any locks and alarms. Jean-Michel stepped back until he was up against the wall opposite the target building. He could already feel the drain of the energy here. Parkour was the order of the moment. Running across the small space, the old warrior jumped, kicked off the wall of Pandora's Box, bounced to crouch up to the opposite wall, kicked again, and landed on the outside of the balcony floor, hanging onto the railing.

He froze, waiting for movement. There was none. Pulling himself up from here was a pain in the ass, but he managed it. He'd feel this in a day, that was for sure. Slipping up and over the iron railing, he went low to be sure no one had seen him or was in the room next to him.

"I could have made that easier, but it's so much more amusing to watch you work through your human body's physical constraints," Sebastian whispered from the side of the balcony.

"How did you get up here without magic? I hope you didn't just give us away."

"I used my claws and my abilities. Did you forget we vampires have more animalistic gifts than you have? You used to like my claws."

Jean-Michel scoffed before he went to the double doors. "Do you know what's happened, then?" Locked. Sighing, he crouched and pulled out a thin, black leather case and chose the correct picks.

"How could I not? I was there when Kennedy got the news. So... I'm here. And by the way, if I got us caught, we could handle it. We've handled dregs of humanity before. What're a few doppelgängers?"

"I don't know. They almost killed you. And that was just one of them. It looks like they took Jonas and I always pegged him as powerful as Devon, at least. You tell me?"

"Hmmm." Since the vampire couldn't argue that point, he turned his gaze to the door, and the click of the lock tumblers gave way. "I can't use magic here, but I can use my mental prowess." He held up a finger, ~ I believe our mind speak may work. It might give us a headache, but it could be helpful. ~

~ What are you even doing here? That the same Sebastian who had been so angry with him at the clinic was offering to help him and using their connection to mind speak blew his mind. ~ Don't you have a meeting to attend and a fellow Councilor to support? ~ Jean-Michel asked.

~ Yes I do in fact, but seeing as how the Chamber is getting infested with doppelgängers, and you lost your backup, and your Councilor's task is rather impossible without additional proof to help corroborate... ~

Jean-Michel opened the door slowly before putting away his picks. But his eyes regarded Sebastian.

~ You left Kennedy there, possibly surrounded by enemy doppelgängers? ~

~ Of course, I didn't. Your friends from pack Weylyn are taking care of your precious Councilor. I doubt any of them are doppelgängers...yet. ~ Sebastian rolled his eyes.

The Tasker and the vampire stepped through the doorway and immediately felt a more intense mental fog wash over them. Ten seconds later...they were both able to function. Closing the doors quietly, Jean-Michel drew one of his guns. His eyes focused on Sebastian.

~ Are you trying to speak or take a shit? ~ The vampire asked. Using telepathic speech in this kind of energy, regardless of it being mentally formed and not magical, definitely didn't feel good. A headache began immediately.

~ It hurts like hell. ~ Jean-Michel tapped his head with his free hand. ~ I can. Just fuckin' gives me a headache. ~ He started moving slowly across the room, gun canted down. ~ I know there's a limited amount, maybe 28 if Mira was estimating properly. We scrubbed their next bunch coming through yesterday. ~

~ The explosion south of downtown? That was you? ~ Sebastian asked.

~ Yeah, ~ he replied, still moving through the room toward the other side. Where were the stairs?

Sebastian adjusted to place his back to Jean's back, letting his preternatural eyes try to take in as much of the room as possible before moving.

~ You know, you should be happy I'm here. Having a Councilor present to be a witness while your lycan are going against their own Councilor's orders could be useful. ~ Sebastian followed while saying nothing out loud.

~ Funny you should justify being here. Especially after yelling, screaming, and spitting at me for daring to check on you at the clinic, Bastian. ~ His eyes squinted to see the other side of the room.

~ Don't call me that. ~

Jean-Michel swore he heard a quiet growl from his partner in crime.

~ Derek had two doppels in his sights on the ground floor. So be aware. I can't see from this angle, ~ Jean-Michel ignored the vampire's ridiculousness. ~ Someone taught them how to ward against magic or use a damned powerful magical item. Otherwise, I would have already gotten Miranda and been done with this mess. ~

Sebastian followed his own instincts, leaving Jean-Michel to follow. The glare the Tasker gave thin air was scathing. Did Sebastian forget that they were in modern-day times? He wanted to remind the vampire that their quarry might be armed, but he realized that he could no longer even force himself to speak mentally – an innate telepathic ability he had because he was a dragon. It made his head hurt too much. Whoever wove this magical ward was damn good. Or, it was using a magical item, and the closer they got, the more powerful it was. Jean-Michel made his way slowly down the stairs.

By the time he almost reached the bottom, he heard a scuffle from further in the back of the room. Pottery crashing, glass breaking, wood splintering, and the sound of a vampire snarling.

The doppelgänger that was closer to the window, and the staircase was definitely not wearing human skin yet, and they hadn't noticed the Tasker. They were so focused on helping their fellow doppel that the Tasker could reach out from between the staircase railings to grab them. Pulling them by the material they were wearing for a shirt, Jean-Michel slammed the doppelgänger's head into the side of the staircase. The doppel wobbled and went tumbling backward. Jean-Michel was over the rail and had his gun aimed at their head as they got their wits back.

"Don't move!" Things had gone quiet back where Sebastian and the other doppelgänger had been fighting. "Sebastian?" Jean-Michel called, his eyes never leaving the doppelgänger before him.

"Sorry, I was busy trying to find something to tie that one up with." Sebastian walked forward, wiping some blood from his lip. "They do actually hit hard."

"Yeah, try ten or more at a time—" The Tasker's senses told him something was off. "Don't you dare!" The doppelgänger he had subdued had foam coming from their mouth and was convulsing on the floor. He felt the neck and could already feel the loss of a heartbeat.

"What about yours? Did you knock it out?" Maybe if they kept one knocked out, they wouldn't be able to poison themselves. They could use a witness. He turned toward the door but then realized something. Sebastian did not smell like Sebastian. Jean-Michel's eyes narrowed. A growl emanated from his chest that seemed almost inhuman.

"Why do these things like becoming me?" With a cough, a second Sebastian appeared from behind the shelving unit. Leaning on it, one hand lifted to cover the right side of his chest.

"It's your pretty face," Jean-Michel quipped before the fake Sebastian shoved him backward. With a snarl, Jean-Michel turned to see the impostor rushing through the store to get away. He was soon chasing after the doppelgänger.

Finding themselves trapped, the doppel turned to face their opponents and grinned, showing fangs of their own. Their nails lengthened, and they prepared to fight.

"Oh, that's just bestial. I may have better animalistic gifts than you, but that's just nasty. I don't look like that," Sebastian whined. "Handle business. I'll keep going." The vampire made his way down the stairs, limping as he went.

Jean-Michel tried to raise the gun and fire, but the doppel dodged and managed a powerful blow. Jean-Michel was grabbing the thing under the arms and hoisting it over his head. It landed on the other side of the office, near some boxes. The doppelgänger snarled and rolled away as Jean-Michel fired.

"How fast are you fuckers?!" The doppelgänger sprinted with preternatural quickness back toward the front of the building for another try at a getaway. Knocking it out was no longer on the agenda. He fired the gun and the thing's brains splattered all over the front window. "Not faster than a bullet."

"Senias! Get down here!" Sebastian yelled.

Hearing his dragon name, the Tasker ran down the stairs and hopped over the railing when he could to get down the stairs as quickly as possible. The scene he faced when he got to the basement had him staggered.

Spider webs clung to the corners and drifted down like sheer silk from the ceiling in various places. Since almost no fresh air drifted down here, it was musty and held the odor of wood and old paper and cloth. From what he could see, the other side was actually more closed off, and a portion of it had a humidity and temperature control center.

"Where?" Jean-Michel spoke right before he saw a trail of dark liquid. It was blood. It led from the stairs around to the other side of the space. He swallowed and turned to make his way around the stairs so he could actually see what was on the other side. "Oh, gods…Mira…"

He couldn't take his eyes off of Miranda Garrett, chained between two large support beams, blood dripping to form the pool beneath her.

Chapter 33
The Council

Eva Weylyn remained in her seat in the audience area in front of the presenting Councilor's place at the podium. Russell Weylyn had remained at the door. They had their suspicions, but without testing, how could they be sure? How could they prove anything? Gabriel had to stall and also introduce the case while hoping they could find a witness – hoping Miranda was still alive.

Without Sebastian here, Gabriel would have no immediate support. He hadn't been able to talk with the Elven Councilor, Minlial Nedian since their first meeting on this subject.

"I speak for several of the other Councilors and myself when I say that this meeting needs to begin." The speaker was, of course, Jonas Airsight.

"We are still waiting on Sebastian Evansworth…" Gabriel began but got cut off by another Councilor, who apparently didn't want to be there either.

"I believe we can safely assume that Sebastian Evansworth will be late for the meeting, Councilor Kennedy. Since he's late, that he sponsored this meeting can speak for his decision later on or you can always put off the decision until he is available per the standards." Leave it to Iscariot, the magus, to hurry things along. Gabriel tried to keep his scowl to a minimum. "If anyone wishes to keep the judgment from being completed until he returns, that is fine. But you may go forward for us to save on time."

Gabriel's gaze went to Eva. He had no argument, so he made his way to the central space and placed his palm on the large red ball at the top of the podium.

"I, Gabriel Kennedy, Councilor for the Human Species, call this meeting of the Crimson Council." The sphere glowed, and then a burst of magical energy rippled outward over the entire chamber.

He removed his hand. "Let us begin." He sought the gaze of each Councilor before clearing his throat.

"I see that several of you have brought your own security to this meeting. At this time, I'd like them all to step out and take a seat in the lobby of this chamber. Once we are in this Chamber Room, we should be safe. We've tightened security." He motioned with his hands so that Russ along with the other Weylyn and pre-tested guardians were available to handle the crowd.

"Why is this necessary?" Jonas balked first.

"Don't be such an insecure creature, Jonas," Nelash Fulgal, the Demonic Councilor, challenged. "I thought lycan were the best at fighting their own battles." Nelash motioned for his guards to go outside as Councilor Kennedy had requested. For his trouble, the demon got the lycan's glare. The lycan Councilor did finally motion for his guards to leave. After all, everyone else seemed to be slowly following the lead of Nelash.

"This meeting was called due to recent activities of doppelgängers on this side of the portals. Where this world may have had a rare experience with such a species before now, the population and industry of these beings are on the rise. My reports show that recent doppelgänger activity is not harmless at all." Lifting a folder, Gabriel continued. "Each of you has a folder just like this before you. Within it, you will find copies of every murder, abduction, and attack that has occurred within the last three months. We have tied all of them to doppelgängers of a specific sect." He could feel the sudden tension in the air.

"I'll give you some time to read over the information while we wait for the last Councilors to arrive." Gabriel cast Eva a glance. The lady Alpha nodded and went to the doorway. When she returned, she was walking in front of a very pale grey, androgynous form wearing a long pencil skirt, blouse, and over-jacket. As they had in practice, Vanishte made their way to the witness stand in the center of the room between Gabriel and facing the others seated in the half-circle.

"My fellow Councilors may I introduce you to Vanishte," Gabriel spoke after noting every reaction in the room. "They have come before us today to represent their race. Doppelgängers have their own story to tell, and Vanishte is going to shed some light on recent actions."

THE COUNCIL

The demon Councilor, Nelash Fulgaul, regarded the doppelgänger as if he were appraising her worth with his eyes before commenting.

"Madam, as interesting as this all may be, doppelgängers are not approved to be here in this world without specific control bands and magical identification. The European Council decided this and therefore other Councils uphold it." His hands were steepled in front of him, but he didn't move closer. He also did not engage in the normal banter he would have given Kennedy. He seemed genuinely curious. Gabriel hoped that was a good sign.

"First, I understand that this world has given to processing masculine and feminine differently, but I assure you that clothes are simply a necessity. We doppelgängers have no actual male or female, and therefore you should speak to me accordingly, with no gender indicators."

Several of the Councilors nodded while either watching the witness or reading over the information Gabriel had provided.

"Very well. But if you know you are here illegally and Crimson can arrest you, why do this?" The demon asked.

"We came to this side of the portal, legally, with all said credentials, and were in the process of making our place on that Council, when they suddenly dismissed us from our goal. This was inappropriate, placed my people in danger, and left me with no choice but to seek support elsewhere to do exactly what you just spoke of. I challenge the European Council's decision. The Crimson Guards of this North American Sector have arrested me and I have been under house arrest ever since. I know what fate will befall me should I fail. I accept that. Councilor Kennedy is defending my right to be here. I hope to overturn this ridiculous ruling." Seeing that they now had the Council's full attention, Vanishte gained confidence and pushed onward.

"I am here to petition for Crimson to recognize doppelgängers as a legalized race in this realm. We will abide by specialized rules for our presence, just as every other race and species has had to do. Compromise is fine. I also ask for Councilorship for my people, so that we would have a voice among you. If we have a place and legal recourse when criminals come to call, they can no longer force my people into servitude; into villainy."

"What do you mean by 'forced'?" the Elven Councilor asked.

"Our people are being hunted and recruited by either an organization or private persons who wish to cause direct violations to Crimson, the Council, and everything that these institutions represent. Many renegade doppelgängers have already made their way here through illegal portals or through smuggling. Me and mine? We do not want judgment to fall upon those of us who will abide by the laws of Crimson on both sides of the portals."

There were mumbles between some Councilors and their staff. To think that any organization held power over Crimson and its Council was quite a leap for many of them. Not to mention, people rarely took it well when people broke laws to prove a point.

"And yet, you have broken the law to be here?" Councilor Nedian asked.

"Not originally. We, I and my comrades, had legal visas for the time that we took to present our case to the European Council. I submit that they unfairly denied us the time we had so diligently fought to earn before the Council. We handled everything legally and with due diligence. They guaranteed us our time to speak and bring our case to the Council. Then, because of an investigation into local misdeeds that some of the Councilors blamed on doppelgängers, they dismissed us and our entire species is being held responsible for these murders."

"For the record, European Crimson agents detained a suspect in the murders Vanishte speaks of. He was not a doppelgänger. He is still being held. Vanishte's group did not get a second chance." Gabriel needed to interject where it was appropriate.

"The agents forcefully took us to the portal in Nice to be returned to our own world. Our visas had not expired. We were told that until investigators could unravel the case, our entire species could not legally come to this world of Gaia. This is not fair."

"It's actually an overreach by that Council, per directive 74," Gabriel pointed out.

"There has only been one precedent of such a decision. The European Council made that judgment against dragon kind. I've researched the background and even in that case, I question the logic. Can you truly hold the actions of a few against an entire species? We would normally look down upon this."

"Did they have to get the approval of other Councils for that precedent?" Joseph Iscariot asked.

"Yes. There was only one other, but they reached out for judgment from both Councils before making this harsh of a decision," Gabriel replied.

"And yet, our own Crimson agents are investigating recent doppelgänger activity here in Whitley – investigations encouraged by Councilor Kennedy himself." Jonas pointed out the thing that might make Gabriel look like a hypocrite. The other Councilors looked at him. Joseph returned his attention to Gabriel.

"You did contact me to warn me, Gabriel. So which is it?" Joseph Iscariot asked. "It takes a lot to confuse me, but you've accomplished that! Are we making a judgment against doppelgängers, or are we listening to the reasons we should allow them to make their case for legal rights here in our world?"

"Allow me to explain," Gabriel swallowed. "Unfortunately, there are the rogue doppelgängers who are being exploited by someone. With no proper leadership in Crimson, they have nothing to lose. That is why..." Gabriel didn't get to finish before Jonas interrupted.

"And you want these creatures to be protected?"

"We believe that whoever is contracting with the renegade doppelgängers is replacing as many Councilors and high-ranking politicians as they can. That is why this is an emergency. Let me just point out that Director Skinner appointed your Pack guardianship of the Chamber here in Whitley this month, Jonas. Those guards allowed me to be attacked by a doppelgänger in this very room. I believe you are compromised."

That definitely caused a ruckus. Gabriel sighed as the Councilors began arguing amongst themselves. He looked over to where Sebastian should have been. Had he made a mistake? Would they lose sight of the point, because he had provided too much information? Should he have waited for Sebastian to be there?

Gabriel and Eva watched as Dr. Samantha Keene walked in quietly. The other Councilors were still discussing the situation at hand.

Sam made her way to the first row to sit with Eva. Gabriel took a moment to walk from the podium to meet her.

"Dr. Keene, why are you here?" Eva asked quietly as Gabriel joined them.

"Councilor Evansworth called me. He said to be here with the new blood testing supplies we came up with. He also said to bring antihistamines for lycan and vampires that we helped make at the clinic, along with some emergency medical supplies. But, I don't see anyone hurt..." she was watching the Councilors arguing with passion, "... yet."

Eva turned a worried gaze to Gabriel. His hands were white-knuckled before he returned to the podium.

If there were fake Councilors, they didn't want to admit anything. The real Councilors didn't want to believe anyone could infiltrate their untouchable organization. The only one not calling him an idiot was the Demonic Councilor. Gabriel watched the demon, who was sitting directly across the large table from his podium. Eyes that shimmered like finely cut rubies in the chamber's light were the only things that revealed he wasn't just a very large, well-dressed human.

And apparently, Gabriel's frustration had been all the catalyst Councilor Fulgaul needed. The demon stood up and his voice was thunder.

"ENOUGH!" He slammed his fist onto the table, cracking the wood and leaving scorch marks all around the impact point. He cleared his throat and waited for silence. Once everyone was quiet, he looked at Gabriel. "The floor is yours again." The demon sat back down.

"Thank you, Councilor Fulgaul." Gabriel cleared his throat before he continued. "This meeting is not about our pride." He studied the Councilors, and then his gaze moved to the lycan Councilor, "It's not about your wounded ego, Jonas. Let us focus on the proven fact that doppelgängers have been filtering into this and possibly our other sponsored world without hindrance. Some have been killing people along their path. The European Council accidentally created this problem. The doppelgängers seek life in our worlds and the only way to have it is through illegal means. They kill out of necessity because people and organizations are coercing them. That would mean that those using the doppelgängers are also responsible for murder and conspiracy, possibly treason."

Gabriel opened the packet of paperwork on his podium. "I suggest you read everything I've provided to you and digest it before you make rash decisions. Rash decisions got us here. Let's do better."

There were glares darting all over that chamber. However, everyone was quiet and collected. They were scanning over the paperwork in the files before them. The Elven Councilor was the first to speak.

"You say you and your kind are being forced to come into this world. But there is one incident in this file that speaks of a doppelgänger acting on its own against a Crimson Agent – an agent who had identified himself." Councilor Minlial Nedian lifted the paper from her folder. She stood up to place it on the table in front of her. The purple fae gaze moved from the paper to Vanishte. "Can you explain this to me? If the doppel had simply complied with Crimson law, the agent would have arrested them. They would be processed back to their own homeworld. Instead, they attacked and tried to take on the form of the officer."

"What if the doppel were acting in self-defense?" Joseph Iscariot was always one who studied a situation before deciding his opinion. The magi were the closest to humans of all that were in this world. They simply had a natural ability with magical energy and longer life spans than the humans they lived among. Gabriel had watched him read everything before speaking further on the subject. "You know as well as I that appearances can deceive Councilor Nedian. We must often cast spells of truth to be sure a Crimson Agent's recounting of the evidence is correct. I see nothing in this report that mentions this protocol being followed." He turned his attention to Gabriel. "I take it Crimson got a pass on the death of this doppelgänger?"

"Without a place on the Council, there was no one to speak on behalf of the deceased doppelgänger. Until we investigate, there is no push to know if the doppels are perpetrators or victims in each case. That's one reason to get this race of beings a Councilor. For example, had Vanishte turned themselves in before seeking me out and explaining their conundrum to me, they would still be in prison to be processed into their own world. There would be no hearing, no judgment – because there is no one to defend doppelgänger rights."

"Right, so these cases are here, not investigated – to prove the numbers?" Joseph surmised it himself, but he made the question clear to everyone.

"Yes," Gabriel replied.

"Are you questioning the honor of a Crimson Agent?" Councilor Nedian asked.

"Absolutely," Iscariot replied without hesitation. "You should never believe that a person placed in a position of power over another is beyond reproach. Crimson should have a constant cycle of retraining, reassigning, and retesting. Our lycan and demonic friends have provided this system to our Crimson law enforcement. However, that does not mean some problematic sorts won't slip through the cracks. Nobody is perfect and being an agent can be stressful. I do not automatically believe an agent over an alleged perpetrator. Nor should you."

"Crimson and the Council should investigate all supernatural deaths by the hands of any Crimson Agent or Tasker. They should be taken case by case," Ishtar Sacryl, the Djinn Councilor, commented quietly. The blue-haired, porcelain-skinned human had almond eyes and no normal blush or change of skin tone on any feature. Their voice was a brush of wind as they spoke. "That is why Councils meet. We do not simply decide on law. We decide on guilt, innocence, and proper future courses of action, including punishment and change."

"The alleged perpetrator attacked a Crimson Archivist. The Crimson Agent came to her aid." Ezekiel Skinner called this out from the doorway. "As angry as that makes me, I agree with Joseph, that you should take these case by case and that you should always make sure of the validity of the reporting officer's testimony."

"Welcome Director Skinner. Happy you could make it in time to impart some clarity." Gabriel took his paperwork and lifted it to straighten the papers by tapping them together on the podium. He watched as the suited director made his way down to him.

Skinner handed Gabriel a file and then placed the rest in a pile. The Director picked up the picture resting before the elf, then held it up in front of the doppelgänger on the witness stand.

"She was an archivist for Crimson. She is one of five important Crimson agents that have disappeared in the last two months. Her name was Molly. She had a family that had to be told. She was only 27." He let that sink in.

"It is a difficult loss, I am sure," Vanishte responded the only way they could.

THE COUNCIL

"I did not invite you, Director Skinner," Gabriel pointed out.

"Mmm.." he nodded, "I know, but when I saw the listing you had prepared, I thought it best you and your fellow Councilors get the entire picture."

Skinner turned back to the Chamber full of Councilors to continue. Gabriel squeezed the bridge of his nose.

"We have an idea that people are being hunted and replaced by doppelgängers and those doppelgängers who are all working together to exploit their newly garnered positions. I and my agents had been investigating for some time before Councilor Kennedy made it his business. We believe it has everything to do with a movement orchestrated by your people to get control, Vanishte." Ezekiel put the photo back on the desk and began passing out the files to the left and right. "Let me guess. Now you're here to get legitimacy so that doppelgängers can receive forgiveness for their crimes?"

"We do not want wrongdoing forgiven, Director. We want wrongdoing to be prosecuted properly and investigations to be handled properly. You are holding doppelgängers responsible and killing them every time, justifying the kill. But, with no one to fight for further investigation, we will not know the full truth. Why would I and those like me come forward to report this, if we wanted to infiltrate your organization and world?" Vanishte replied with their quiet logic.

"Because Crimson was secretly investigating you and yours." Skinner shrugged. "And when things get hot, CYA. Cover. Your. Ass."

Skinner was drawing doubts with his newly added information. CYA? Gabriel swore that was exactly what Skinner was doing for his own ass right this very second. The man had every right to be here, true, but the timing couldn't have been worse.

Gabriel regarded his watch and then glanced over at Eva and Sam. Eva shrugged.

"People and organizations using doppelgängers can compromise Crimson, Director Skinner. The three Councils in Gaia and the one forming now in Ordia? Are they compromised? Are you also compromised? Would that not make it in your best interest to interrupt this meeting to assert the same?" Gabriel challenged. He had no choice. He was running out of options.

The Director of Crimson in North America looked perturbed by the assertion. His glare landed on Councilor Kennedy. Most of the other Councilors were discussing the new files and the allegations made by both men. The Demonic Councilor aimed his vicious grin, normally something reserved for those he viewed as lesser, directly at Skinner.

Chapter 34
Handling Business

"There, on the floor." Sebastian pointed out the crystal with the moving smoke inside of it. It sat in some of Mira's blood.

With a growl, the dragon had the thing in his hand and stepped back just in time to be missed by a swipe from Mira's clawed fingernails. She screamed and cried all in one long wail.

Jean-Michel took the crystal over to the side workbench and grabbed a crowbar. Hefting the crowbar, he smashed the cursed object, shattering the anti-magic field all around them. Immediately, his headache was gone! Tossing the tool aside, he moved back to where Sebastian was studying their half-demon victim.

"She's the star of the show. So...we have to take her in." Sebastian said it out loud, though he didn't actually make a move.

Senias took a deep breath. Then he made his way forward.

"What are you doing?"

"You said it yourself. She's the star of the show. These doppelgängers all have their way out prepared. They want to die if they get caught. Mira's the only one that knows what's happening and can tell the Council. We have to take her in. And...she's drained. So, someone has to help her. Might as well be me." The Tasker started his way to her again, only for Sebastian to jerk him back.

"She'll drain you to where you may not return. And then what? If she takes energy from me, I..." He looked down and swallowed. "I'll take blood from you. It'll be done and we can all get back. Right?"

Jean-Michel's eyes were as large as saucers. He took in Sebastian's words. Nodding, he stepped back.

Miranda felt their emotions; their souls' energy called to her. The ruby-red pupils took in the two stronger people.

"Mira," Sebastian whispered before moving toward her again.

"No.... get back." She whispered, her voice weak.

"But we need to get you out, my dear. I know it's been a long time—"

"Don't touch me!" This time the words were a snarl, and before their eyes, the vision of human beauty shifted. Her skin was paler than even that of the vampire. Her veins were more pronounced; black beneath the skin. A pair of bat-like wings were on her back and she used them to fight the chains.

Her double fangs were now buried in her lower lip to ward off a different pain. She jerked on the chains again and screamed, a frustrated sound from deep inside of her. Chest heaving, her hungry eyes found the vampire moving closer.

"I don't want to hurt you." She was crying as she spoke. "Don't make me hurt you."

"I know, but remember what I taught you a long, long time ago, my dear? I know my limit. Remember?" Sebastian coaxed as he stepped to the chain. With his preternatural strength, he ripped it from the column. Staggering, she wound up hugging the other column. The other chain bound her to it.

"I owed him, same as you owed him, Frenchie...when you got Bastian out," the half-demon said, her voice shaking. She knew she couldn't guarantee anything. The emotions flying around were making this so much more difficult. "I kept all our secrets. I promise."

"What?" Sebastian looked back at the dragon, eyes large.

"You owed, who?" Jean-Michel asked. He needed to know.

"I had to help them, to keep Dante safe. I had no choice. Please, it wasn't just about me." She coughed, falling, only her wrist keeping her up where it was being held by the shackle.

"Mira?" Sebastian moved forward and ripped the last shackle out.

"No, Mira..." Jean-Michel had the half-demon on one side and Sebastian had her on the other. They held her and moved her to the back wall, where the Tasker gently patted her cheek to wake her up.

"She's a succubus, you idiot!" Sebastian leaned in and took the woman's face between the palms of his hands and kissed her. The dragon watched as the succubus grabbed hold of the vampire and lifted them both.

"Right..." That's when he heard the sounds coming from upstairs. "Shit...they're telepathic. These two called in back-up." He scrambled up and took off running to the staircase. He reached for the gun and realized he'd left it upstairs, where the doppel had knocked it out of his hand. Looking around the area of shipping containers and stored antiques, the dragon found an old fireplace set. "Well, okay," he grabbed the poker and began taking the stairs two at a time. Rounding the corner toward the front entrance of the store itself, he realized there were at least two if not three!

The dragon roared like he once did in the old days of being a Celtic warrior and put everything he had behind the weapon. He had at least caught them before they had come very far. He knocked the first one backward, running it through with the poker. Setting his foot to the thing's body, he jerked the metal rod back out and slung it at the next one's head.

Jean-Michel got hit from the side by one he hadn't even seen and was on the floor watching the first doppel struggle, its body already reshaping. He wound up shoving himself upward, his attacker stumbling back. He turned to the side and slammed the doppelgänger into the metal stair column before staggering back to find himself in a good corner, so he could keep them from surrounding him.

And then, there was a high-pitched scream that came seemingly from every direction. He grasped his ears as he watched Miranda, in her demonic form, shoot up the stairs. The demoness lifted the first doppelgänger off the ground. She held him up, her ruby eyes glittering in the bit of light filtering in from the streetlamps.

"Make sure Malcolm knows... I will come for him." She smiled viciously before she seemed to take a deep breath. Her eyes glowed with red power while taking this doppelgänger's energy. The magical energy pulsed like a heartbeat, an aura around the captured shifter before Miranda took another deep breath and that aura left the doppel to be absorbed into her own. She tossed the gray-skinned being to the ground, a shriveled, dry husk of its former self.

"Jean-Michel, Bastian needs you," Mira got out of the way so the Tasker could go to the vampire. "I'll handle the rest of the doppelgängers. I owe them."

"Of course..." The Tasker wasted no time in running back down the stairs and leaving the very pissed-off half-demon to her chores.

"Sebastian?" Jean-Michel moved quickly toward the vampire.

Sebastian chuckled where he sat against the back wall of the basement. "At least...it's not as small as ...as that damned cell Crimson had me in."

"Bastian, you need to take blood." Jean-Michel repositioned himself.

"Just... let me... go... what do I have, Sen?" When he spoke, his words slurred, his eyes closed as pain reverberated through his chest and he coughed again.

"We can stop this. You know that. That was part of the plan, remember?" The dragon held his wrist over Sebastian's mouth. "Nick the artery. Blood's the only magic in this body. You can have it."

"Did you really make a deal? For me?" Sebastian seemed to marvel at the dragon. "That's why...you've been working for Skinner?"

Jean-Michel's eyes remained on the vampire's face. "As soon as I knew." He pressed his wrist against Sebastian's mouth. "Now, don't make it all be in vain. You've got more to live for."

"Mmm..no..." Sebastian turned, trying to refuse. "I tried to hate you for so very long."

"I know. I wanted you to hate me. Thought hate was better than something I couldn't give you. Something I always ruined. You deserve better. There is someone better out there for you." He cupped Sebastian's face, tears welling in his eyes. "Don't give up on life. Not when I just got my faith back in it. "

"What are you waiting for, Bastian? You know we can't have this party without you," Miranda's voice was happy and hyper as she appeared out of a shadow right by the vampire's side.

Jean-Michel held his wrist up to the pretty demon. "The artery, Mira. Please."

Miranda used her sharp nails to rend the flesh down to his artery and she did so without hesitation. Jean-Michel shoved his wrist into Sebastian's mouth. "Take from me. Do it now!" His growl was one of command. He'd no longer beg the damned vampire.

Even if he'd wanted to fight it, Sebastian couldn't. Instinct and habit took over. His fangs sank in and the coppery taste flooded his mouth. There was a sharp intake of air through his nose as the dragon's magic tickled across his senses.

HANDLING BUSINESS

Jean-Michel's eyes closed, and he groaned in pain. Sebastian drank down several mouthfuls before releasing the Tasker's wrist. The magical blood worked faster and was much more effective than human blood. The Councilor cried out as the magic rushed through his system. His eyes glittered and went wide. The vampire rolled over to a kneeling position with his forehead on the floor. He was soon gasping for air.

"You... bastard..." Sebastian groaned.

"Yeah, well, I've been called worse. You'll thank me later, you dramatic shit." He dried his eyes with a swipe of his arm. Not new to being wounded, the Tasker grabbed up a piece of material that was on one of the antique chairs to the side and wrapped his wrist tightly.

"That piece was priceless." Miranda scolded before tsking him and helping wrap the wound. The half-demon shifted with a flash of light back into the lovely olive-skinned, dark-headed human form she had been born to. "I don't care what they do to me or my business anymore. I can testify. Those bitches are going to pay."

Chapter 35

THE JUDGMENT

"What of the Councilors?" Gabriel asked Skinner.

"I've not found any evidence of a conspiracy to replace Councilors. Other important people that are less conspicuous yet very useful? Yes." Skinner answered as he finished making his way down to the pulpit area, to stand before the Councilors seated at the crescent table. Vanishte sat on the witness stand to the side, but the debate was not just about them and their experiences.

"Really? Because I would wager my money that there's a doppelgänger in this very room, pretending to be a Councilor." Gabriel had lost his control at this point. He knew it, so he went all in, despite knowing he'd need others to help him out in the proving.

"Are you that paranoid?" Skinner challenged.

At the Council Chamber door, Russell Weylyn and another of the guards held the door wide to allow Tasker Jean-Michel Raudine inside. His shirt was covered in blood and filth, as was Councilor Evansworth's clothing, who was right behind him. Following them was Miranda Garrett, who was likewise a bloody mess. The spectacle caused another small uproar.

"I ask that the Council allow Vanishte to step down from the witness seat, to be recalled when it is appropriate. I call Miranda Garrett to be my next witness." Gabriel waited patiently for the other Councilors to come back to order.

"Why would you need to call her as a witness?" The Demonic Councilor asked. "As she is a demon in this world, she is my responsibility. Should I speak with her before this continues?"

"It's okay. I'm not the one in trouble, Nelash...this time." Mira smirked at Councilor Fulgaul before passing the doppelgänger to make her way to the stand. Vanishte left the witness stand and

Jean-Michel motioned for her to take a seat in an area nearby, just in case she needed to be recalled.

Ezekiel touched Mira's elbow before she passed and whispered something to her. He then bowed his head to her and handed her his kerchief for her face before backing off.

"Let me explain. Miranda Garret's testimony, coupled with what Crimson clean-up crews will find at Pandora's Box, should be all you need to have this situation done and over with," Gabriel announced. He noted his Tasker remained between Mira and the podium he stood at.

Sebastian went to Samantha and leaned in to whisper to her. He followed her gaze to the mess that was his blood-soaked clothing. He mouthed the words, "I'm fine, but…" Samantha made her way out of the chamber quickly while the vampire Councilor walked to his own seat at the crescent table.

The Tasker's eyes watched Skinner. The man betrayed nothing. Both of their tails might be on the line here. Though the dragon would have liked nothing more than to see Ezekiel Skinner squirm, he worried that in doing so, his own part in so many underhanded plots would be open to the world. He couldn't help letting his concerned gaze fall on Gabriel. At least the human Councilor was doing everything for the right reasons.

Mira turned to the Councilors. She wore ripped, bloody clothing, just like the others that had come in with her, but she carried herself as if she were a queen.

"Miranda." Gabriel had his fingers steepled before him at the podium as he considered his line of questioning. Before he could even begin, his witness had decided upon a course of action.

"Someone forced me to help a group of doppelgängers led by one called Malcolm. He said he needed 30 host bodies for his group with more to come. Then he said he only needed 28, then 25. I believe he no longer needed those bodies because they took their actual targets." She paused before continuing, "He may have had them replacing Councilors."

"How do you know they took Councilors?" Ishtar of the Djinn asked.

"Malcolm was pleased. He was proud. He felt accomplished when he spoke of not needing as many hosts, and I do not know how many already had bodies before he came to me." Mira pointed to herself, "I'm a succubus. My specialty is emotion. I know what I felt."

The Councilors were silent.

"Who was the sponsor of the doppelgängers?" Gabriel continued where Mira had left off. Why not keep going?

"I assume portals. I don't know how they actually got here," Mira replied. "Who? He never said. An Ancient. That's what he told me. I needed proof. See, I and my brother were once indebted to others when we first went into business. A deal got called in. At first, I had no choice because of my nature and then I had no choice because of threats. Finally, they trapped me in my own shop. Nearly killed me." Everyone could see the emotion in her eyes.

"I see. But do you know who they were working for?" Gabe couldn't help that his eyes skimmed over to where Skinner stood, stoic, but eyes locked on the witness.

"They never tell you exactly who. It was for an Ancient in Tal'Secus. In my world, that could be anyone over the age of millennia. So, that's the only clue I had. Ancients are very secretive. That's how they've lived so long, Gabriel. Often, we didn't know who our benefactors were. Intermediaries usually made the bargains. This time, Malcolm presented me with an envelope with a specific seal on it. I knew that seal and that I owed a favor, and you know how seriously we demons take our deals, favors, and vows."

"So you cannot tell us who the sponsor is?" Gabriel deflated.

"Sorry," Mira turned her gaze to the Tasker. "I recognized the seal of Tal'Secus...a warped version of St. George and the Dragon. If I didn't do what this Ancient wanted, I'd lose everything. I don't know if you've ever lost everything, Councilor Kennedy, but it's an experience I prefer not to repeat." Her eyes bored into Jean-Michel's soul.

"When did Malcolm get in touch with you?" Gabriel shifted gears.

"The night after you had contacted me, actually." When she heard mumbling from the other Councilors, she turned to them and scolded, "Oh, come on. Other than the Djinn, I and my brother have helped every one of you. And what Gabriel asked for was not illegal. He was investigating the doppelgängers and wanted to know if I had heard anything about them, thanks to my business." She smirked before turning to look at Gabriel. "I don't think Councilor Kennedy knew about who I was in any other capacity than a collector and seller of antiquities and magical artworks and items. I dealt with his parents and grandparents before him."

Gabriel cleared his throat and nodded curtly. Jean-Michel could tell that his Councilor wasn't sure if he should be relieved by the vindication he had received or embarrassed that he'd not known her other pastime.

"What did you do for the doppelgängers who approached you?"

"I found lives for them to take over. I thought I was doing well. I found the bodies of people that were dying already and had made plain that they wanted an end with dignity or those who were brain dead. It's part of my line of research that can be difficult, something I hadn't done in a very long time. But when you're threatened..." She took a deep breath and swallowed before continuing, "I tried to keep things as legal and ethical as I could in such a situation. I did. But that's not all they wanted." Miranda took a moment and then continued. "I found out too late that they were eagerly taking on the lives of others who weren't ready. Remember what I said about the change in numbers? He would talk to someone on his phone. He would meet with people. I hate to say it, but he used my shop as a base of sorts. I was afraid that my connections and customers would soon become victims. That's when I tried to put a stop to it. Malcolm used an anti-magic area of effect. Then they chained me up. When Malcolm was done with me, he bled me. Left me for dead."

"What else did they request from you? I'm talking about when my Tasker and I first questioned you?" Gabriel asked.

"My scenting crystals and other convenient magical items. Doppels don't have a scent and if they can't use things belonging to the person they're using, the crystals can at least give them a human or lycan odor. The magical items were mostly weapons. Some were slaying weapons, I'm afraid. I collect those to be destroyed and there was a set wrapped up, but they demanded those."

"Convenient," Councilor Jonas closed the file in front of him.

"No one asked you," the Demonic Councilor glared at the lycan.

"They don't have to." The lycan growled loudly and stood up, his hand hitting the table as he did. But the demon stood as well.

THE JUDGMENT

"No one speaks until we know everything. You know full well that no decisions made in this chamber can be proper unless we have the true Councilors present. Councilor Kennedy and Lady Garrett should continue. Then we need to know who they've replaced." Councilor Fulgaul's demonic red eyes were full of mirth and challenge. "I haven't been part of a good hunt in quite some time."

"How can we be sure this is not some witch hunt – as the humans like to call it?" Councilor Nedian, asked with concern. "She admits to aiding and abetting them while she knew they would kill innocent people to replace?"

"As I stated, I had no choice."

"You were trying to deliver on an oath to an Ancient. Yes, we've heard. An oath is so much more important than living beings?" The magus Iscariot raised a brow.

Ezekiel kept himself properly apathetic, but he hadn't left the room.

"For demons, yes. If we break our deals, we pay with a piece of our soul." Mira waited.

"I apologize Gabriel. I was willing to give this situation a serious going over. But I cannot in good conscience approve of a legitimate place on the Council or lifting the ban because I do not believe all the claims." The Elven Councilor was moving her hand as if she would touch the reddish sphere at the front of her desk.

"Councilor Nedian, I would assume that you would at the very least want to investigate her claims fully," Sebastian interjected before the elf touched the sphere. "If you don't, I damn sure do. I'm covered in blood because I went to check on Madame Garrett – whose business is in my coven's territory. I found myself attacked for the second time by a doppelgänger!" Sebastian was having none of it. His stern countenance found Gabriel. "Get on with it. Let her name them and we'll draw blood if we have to."

"Draw blood? They tested our blood when we became part of the Council." Councilor Jonas Airsight visibly shuddered. "I hate needles."

"Yes, our blood samples are on file, along with the reactionary properties. Luckily, three of the doppelgänger bodies remained around long enough to gather samples. Thanks to Dr. Keene's sanctioned research, she now has a method of not only comparing our blood to our previous samples, but she has a litmus of sorts that can let us know who's got the proper blood and who is actually a doppelgänger trying to pass as another species." Councilor Gabriel Kennedy explained.

"Now, if you'll allow me to continue." Gabriel cleared his throat and asked Miranda, "What do you know about the doppelgänger's plans to replace Councilors?"

"They had plans for everybody, but there were whispers about lycan. And when they trapped me, I noticed they were looking specifically for Fae slayers. For elves."

"Is this because I doubt your word?" Minlial stood up, her shocked face glaring angrily at the succubus. The implications were obvious. "Gabriel, surely you cannot be serious? You know that taking of blood is a sacred act to an elf."

"Can we risk not testing, Minlial?" Gabriel pointed out.

"It only takes the majority. With that, Director Skinner can make himself useful and call in the Council Doctor and Medical Guardian to bring the blood drawing kits. We can end the doubts once and for all." Sebastian shrugged, then smirked, his fangs showing. "You know a little blood play never hurt anyone."

Ezekiel Skinner's piercing eyes shifted from Miranda to Sebastian. He nodded slowly in agreement. He pulled out his phone to make the order.

"My vote is – yea." Sebastian's glare was bright.

"The testimonies of Lady Vanishte and Miranda Garrett are further evidence that gives probable cause to the blood testing." Councilor Ishtar Sacryl pointed out. "We, as a Council of Crimson, make decisions that affect not only individual people's lives, but the fate of whole nations and species. I want to be part of a Council that is above reproach. I second the yea."

"I third it," Gabriel added.

"I don't like needles, either, but why not?" Joseph Iscariot nodded. "I believe that's a majority, yes?"

Gabriel quietly excused Mira from the stand, and she made her way to the seat in front of Jean-Michel and near Vanishte.

"I see no point in this.." Councilor Jonas rumbled low.

"In case I need to repeat myself, your Pack was on guard duty the night I got attacked." Gabriel's voice became lower and more threatening. "So I insist." His gaze was hard and his jaw tightened.

"If you'd rather, I can always bite you and tell them if you're a doppelgänger, Jonas. I've had the pleasure of becoming an expert on them recently." Sebastian grinned, showing his fangs.

The Chamber door opened and a man in dark blue scrubs stepped in carrying a basket of sterile blood testing equipment.

"I approved the shift from Jonas' pack guards to Weylyn's pack guards. I vetted them when they showed up and had Dr. Keene retest their blood after the attack. We used the tests Dr. Keene developed, and those will be the same tests we use here. Dr. Keene, if you'll administer and explain." Skinner crossed his arms over his chest. "I've not been able to vet any of you, because this is the first time you've met since the doppelgänger situation became an issue." Ezekiel rolled up his sleeve and sat in a chair nearest to a side table where the doctor was prepping a station.

"You first?" Vanishte seemed impressed.

"Well, I don't want people to question me. I may be a thorn in most of these people's sides, but I am definitely just me." Skinner watched as the doctor set the tourniquet in place.

"And done. I've got yours," Sam had already drawn from Skinner and placed the pad over the skin so he could hold it. "I'll draw from Vanishte. That way, all of you can see the differences."

The doppelgänger made their way to the chair Skinner had vacated.

"To explain," Dr. Keene began. "The only thing in these vials is the anticoagulant and the added element we used to ascertain magical resonance for any supernaturals. That's enough." The blood from Ezekiel slowly changed from dark red to bright red with a slightly yellow sparkle to it. "Director Skinner's file states he is a human blooded by Magi. His blood turns brighter because of that." Setting it aside in a vial rack, Sam held up Vanishte's sample. This time the blood within darkened to almost a black substance and then continued to change colors and thickness. "Vanishte is a doppelgänger, and because of the shifting nature of their make-up, their blood does something oddly similar when it meets the element."

"Is there any other way to test?" Jonas asked while he watched what was happening.

"Doppelgängers have a higher temperature, but that's not really a clear indicator, not as clear as the blood test," Samantha pointed out.

"Just to clarify, you have it on record that a demon's blood may turn green when mixed, correct?" Nelash asked as he nonchalantly turned up his sleeve.

"Yes," Sam smiled as she motioned to the next two chairs. "I've also seen an ifrit's blood turn purple. It's all about the enzymes. Lycan and Elven blood are very similar in makeup to human blood. Vampire blood is like human blood, with the addition of whatever blood they've recently imbibed. So it should have the same reaction."

"The girl knows her stuff. Good to see," the Demonic Councilor chuckled.

"The doctor, who is a woman, knows her stuff," Samantha corrected, before looking at the Demonic Councilor, chin up.

"Oh, apologies, doctor." Councilor Fulgaul got up from his chair, and the rest of the Councilors followed suit. When Jonas got near him, the demon made an overly-polite flourish to Jonas, "Accused of treason first."

Gabriel had to keep himself from smirking at the way Councilor Fulgaul was enjoying this. It was as if the demon had already decided. Or maybe Nelash just enjoyed seeing others suffer?

Jonas stalked past, a lycan rumbling in his chest. All the Councilors began making their way to the table to have blood drawn.

The Elven Councilor paused halfway there. She tapped the chair she had stopped behind and then turned to look at the door. Russell Weylyn's crystalline blue scowl met her gaze. She turned to Councilor Kennedy, who was also watching her.

"No..." Gabriel whispered under his breath. He placed his hand on the table for support as he realized that such a long-lived soul may be no more. How? How had they accomplished so much so quickly? He had only met with her the day before. So much knowledge and experience – gone? Same with Jonas. Lycan could live for centuries, millennia even. This wasn't just murder, it was so much more. Gabriel swallowed and paused for a moment to digest the possibilities.

"I'm sorry. I had no other choice," the elf apologized to Gabriel. She was shaking. She made her way to Vanishte. "Know that I didn't take her life, Vanishte. But I didn't believe you. I didn't believe they would ever hear us. Your teachings kept me from taking a life. But...Malcolm forced me to play this role."

"Guards!" Director Skinner called.

Russ opened the door, and speaking in grumbles and growls, he told the other guards who to handle. They made their way around the room to take the imposter of Minlial Nedian by the shoulders. As they did, the beautiful Elven features melted away to reveal a gray-skinned doppelgänger with fewer wrinkles and worn areas than Vanishte had on their skin. She sounded like she was sobbing. There were several wide-eyed reactions to the shifting of form.

"Didn't kill her? Then where is she?" Gabriel asked as the guards took the doppelgänger into custody. "Where is Minlial? There are people who care about her that will be waiting. She has a family!"

"I don't know. Malcolm would know. He was the one that came through first. He set everything up for us. I just...I don't know where he is. I didn't see him after he placed me. He goes by a male facade almost always. If you are giving us a chance in your world, I will testify to everything I can." The doppelgänger focused on Gabriel. "I did not murder her, I swear."

"Do you know who Malcolm was working with? The Ancient?" Gabriel asked, moving closer even as the guards were placing magical manacles on the doppelgänger.

"No. It was all very secretive. Malcolm is much more powerful than we are. They helped us with this...at first. It was the only way we had. I came over because of my family. They need help. Vanishte sent us word we could no longer flee our horrible home. I needed help. Malcolm said the people they worked with could provide help. Please, Vanishte, help my family!" The young doppelgänger begged as they were being led away.

"This situation is why they will need to be approved and they need their own Councilor. They need someone to present their case before a judgment gets passed. Then, they wouldn't need to be desperate and fall victim to villains." Gabriel removed his cufflink and rolled up his sleeve.

"I'm handling Councilor Evansworth and your Tasker next. I believe Director Skinner wanted that since they came in covered in blood after wrestling doppelgängers in the field?" Samantha grabbed a tourniquet.

"I rather like blood play, so don't worry about hurting me. You won't need the elastic band either. I bleed easily and I've recently fed well." Sebastian chuckled as he sat back in the chair, his sleeve already rolled up.

"Keep an eye on him. He's blood-drunk," Jean-Michel whispered to Dr. Keene.

"What?" Gabriel had heard the comment. So many questions swam through his head right then. But his primary concern was whether there was some special color a dragon's blood might turn. His Tasker, on the other hand, didn't seem concerned in the least.

Jean-Michel's eyes met Gabriel's as he sat in the chair Sebastian had just vacated.

The Tasker's blood resembled that of the Director's sample, maybe brighter. Sebastian's was a proper color, then shimmered brighter, like the Tasker's blood color before muting once again. Gabriel's blood was also a bit of a brighter color; definitely not doppelgänger dark.

Jonas watched as his blood sample was mixed with the chemical. It didn't change at first, but then slowly it darkened to black.

"Afraid of needles?" Gabriel scoffed.

Jonas may not have been a lycan, but he had every weapon that an experienced Alpha lycan had. And he brought them to bear. He shifted and grew three times the size he normally would be. He slung the chair across to knock the human Councilor off his feet while lifting the table to take out as many of the others as he could.

When the Weylyn bitch thought about attacking, he grabbed her by the neck and threw her aside into her own pup before rushing forward. Gabriel was just getting up, trying to get his senses back and his breath.

Jean-Michel had little time to think and yet so many thoughts crossed his mind. He thought about having lost himself, that little girl on the train...her eyes – full of faith in magic and in him. They reminded him of Gabriel's eyes. He wasn't like the others. Gabriel wasn't empty. Of all the humans in the world, he had to get stuck with the very one that made him give a damn...

The Tasker leapt between Gabriel and the hybrid form of Jonas. He took the bite to his forearm and lifted a leg to kick away. The false Jonas Airsight let go, the inertia bringing his enemy to him. The false lycan lunged forward, aiming for the jugular.

The other lycan guards shifted and pulled the Jonas doppelgänger off their center. He fell away from Jean-Michel, sending the Tasker stumbling backward at the same time. The guards surrounded them. One guard tossed a net that pulsed with energy over the thing, and the doppelgänger finally lost their stolen form.

"Jonas had a family and led a Pack!" Eva shouted.

"All the better! They don't deserve the life they had...none of you deserve it! You take it for granted!" The doppel struggled, even though the battle was clearly over.

"Take him away, now," Skinner ordered as he brushed himself off. He turned his attention to where Gabriel Kennedy was staring gape-jawed at his Tasker, who was lying on the floor in a pool of blood.

"Senias," Gabriel whispered. He watched as his Tasker literally held the side of his neck. Gabriel moved forward to pull him into his embrace. He placed his hand over the wound and kept pressure there. Realization dawned on him. "You could've been free..."

"If I let you die...I'd no longer... have a reason." The dragon smiled at Gabriel. "You're not like the others. Don't ever... be like the others."

Gabriel wouldn't let go. There were words being said around them, people were trying to pull them apart, and he just kept looking into his Tasker's eyes. His Ancient's eyes. His dragon's eyes... His *love's* eyes? He watched those beautiful eyes close.

Gabriel pulled Jean-Michel close against his chest and cried. His hand felt the brand where he held the dragon's back. He'd done everything right. How could things still go so wrong? The hands tugging him, the people yelling at him, it all faded into nothing. He had faith. He'd found what he'd been searching for all his life. And now it would be taken from him?

"No!"

The electricity all around them flickered and a burst of pale purple energy crackled through Gabriel, down his hands where one palm remained over the brand and the other on the torn neck. And then, there was a pulse of energy from that release that flung everyone off of their feet and into the darkness.

Chapter 36
WHAT HAS HAPPENED

After the clean-up and tying up loose ends, Ezekiel Skinner had been responsible for breaking the news to the families of those who were gone. There was very little solace for them in knowing that there would be further investigations and trials to hold people accountable. He figured it was the least he could do, considering he'd been responsible for most of it.

The elves had to be told that Minlial Nedian was missing. They would need to appoint a new Councilor. No one was talking, and he did not know where that bastard Malcolm had gotten off to.

"Tricky, tricky, tricky." The feminine voice spoke from the shadows ahead of him just before the faint glimmer of sharp yellow topaz shined in her eyes. "Hello Zeke, it's been a while." There was a quick flare from her lighter as she lit her cigarette and she waited for him to come to her.

"E...mmm...Amanda. It's lovely to finally see you. Come out. No one's around. Not that it'd matter much."

The brunette stepped more into the light so that he could see her better and she thumped ash off to the side. She hadn't really changed much since last they'd met, but then again she rarely did except in hair style and clothing. She lifted one perfectly arched brow at him before dropping the rest of the cigarette and crushing it beneath her heel.

"That was a waste." Ezekiel chuckled as he watched the dragoness. "I hope the rest of your visit is not."

Slipping one hand into a pocket of her slacks, she turned the other palm upwards to create a spark of energy in the center of it that crackled then disappeared. "You told him another portal was imperative and yet you lacked the means. You are now presented with the means to see that accomplished."

"I'm afraid there will not be as many willing to work for us. The temperament of the Council has changed. Everyone is paranoid and that will not be helpful. Malcolm is not willing to come forward, and I can't blame him. We need to weigh the need versus the possible consequences. You and I can do that and come to a decision, I'm sure."

"No more doppels, then?"

"We can try, but my suggestion would be to know our targets beforehand and have someone from Tal'Secus ready to take them in this time. I was told to deal with the plan to implicate the twins using this scheme...and you see how well that went."

"By who?" Amanda asked.

"Morfesa of Falias. Not that I minded. My past concerning those two made me eager to be rid of them." The expression of interest on her face at the mention of the Ancient did not pass his notice. It was fleeting before she smiled and took his arm.

"Well, this visit doesn't have to be all about Tal'secus business, does it?" The dragoness Emriess, or as the human world knew her, Amanda Proctor had been a good ally over the centuries. They'd enjoyed one another's company many times off and on. Neither of them sought to cling to the other, but it did ease the boredom from time to time.

"Honestly, I'd prefer that it not be just business, my dear."

Samantha stretched and sighed. Where was she? Oh... Oh right...

She remembered telling him he needed to stop showing up in places covered in blood. The vampire lord already had her attention, the dramatically wounded bit could stop. He had been anything but wounded in the back of her car in the earliest hours of the morning.

Now they were in her home. The light-blocking shades remained drawn over wooden blinds to keep the unwanted sunlight out. Luckily, it wasn't daylight just yet. She let her arm and hand gently reach across to the other side of her queen bed so she could be sure he hadn't left. Fingers moved to rub over a strong calf.

What exactly had they been doing last that landed them on opposite ends of the bed?

Oh... right...Sam smiled wickedly. There was a low rumbly chuckle from the opposite end of the bed.

"Good to know that I didn't completely wear you out." Sebastian reached over to draw her leg to him. He rubbed his strong fingers against the bottoms of her feet, working his fingertips against the tense muscles.

"Oh, God... you do foot massages, too? You just keep upping the ante here, Bastian." Sam closed her eyes and luxuriated in the kneading on her tired feet.

"Mmmm, I do a lot of things."

"I would reciprocate, but I'd just hurt you. Believe me, this isn't... mmmmm—" The doctor felt like purring as he hit a really needy spot, "This isn't me being lazy, it's me being kind." His nails brushed along the arch of her foot. Sam squealed and pulled her feet back up toward her body. She laughed before criss crossing her legs beneath her so she could sit up closer to his face in the bed. As she did so, her blonde hair fell over her shoulder and the covers fell off around her. "You hit a ticklish spot. Guess I forgot to mention I'm ticklish." Blushing, she wondered if he could tell in this light.

"Ahh," Sebastian pushed up on an elbow and watched the way she positioned herself and how the covers pooled at her waist. He reached out to stroke the back of his knuckles over the swell of her nearest breast.

She loved the way he touched her. She'd never had a man do that before, and it excited her.

He laid back, drawing Samantha with him.

"Will they expect you at the clinic later?" His hands meandered over her naked body. "If not, there are still a few hours before sunup. We can do a lot in a few hours."

"I'm sure they won't mind picking up the shift," she replied breathlessly. Oh, he just knew how to touch her. But she knew things, too. Her right hand reached down beneath his arm and soon she found his hardening cock. "If you don't mind keeping me happy." She stroked him twice, slowly; fingers playing over his foreskin. "Because I don't mind keeping you happy."

"Ohhhh..." Sebastian chuckled and he let his fangs slide over the soft skin of her neck. "Mmm, I believe we can keep one another *very* happy, Sunshine."

"Thank you all for coming back to meet after such a brief recess. The last two days have brought to light all doppelgänger infiltrations. We have found those who were missing, and the search continues. Others, well, we have shared condolences with their families." Gabriel spoke to the gathering of Councilors he had called back to session three days after everything had gone down.

"Now that we know those within the Chamber have passed the test, we need to approve an investigation into Malcolm, set up an investigation into any case that may involve doppelgängers, and hold judgment on all other doppelgängers who were found. More importantly, I believe you all can see now that the doppelgängers need a Councilor. Vanishte was to be their Councilor before the European Council made their decision to revoke documentation."

Gabriel continued speaking as everyone else took their seats once again. There were people missing, but life moved on. He would show his respects to them when this was done.

"Those doppelgängers and any others out there in this world? They have no reason to come forward because they know they are illegal. But if you give them a means for legal and acceptable integration to Gaia, just as we've done for all other supernaturals, they have a vested interest in upholding our laws and reporting infractions. I ask that the North American Council of Crimson open the case to provide legalization of doppelgängers and begin proceedings to vet Vanishte for Councilorship."

"Not a problem," Joseph seconded the next motion, seeming quite happy to do so after all the drama.

"Official documentation of this situation needs to be delivered to the other Councils. New Councilors will need to be appointed.

And these investigations continued." Gabriel pointed out, before letting his gaze wander over those still in attendance.

"They nearly infiltrated us on our own sacred grounds. I doubt this will be easy to rectify. My suggestion is that we who witnessed everything agree to weekly meetings and added security measures until this situation has a more complete resolution." Councilor Fulgaul suggested.

"After being nearly killed twice, I couldn't agree more." Sebastian seconded before anyone else.

"Very well, weekly meetings here and added security. I want to make sure meetings in this chamber stay as secure as possible." Gabriel Kennedy didn't care to be attacked in such a fashion again.

"Please tell me what you need of us, Councilors," Vanishte couldn't hide the joy on their odd gray face, the eyes showing it most.

The Councilors dispersed from the Council Building near midnight, some making their way to the park next door, where they could travel magically with no one the wiser.

Gabriel stepped out onto the lighted front sidewalk where there was a black SUV waiting for him. Eva opened the passenger door, and seeing him pause, she closed the door and came over to him.

"What is it, ma boy?"

"I had to change my designation tonight. I...I don't know what to think about it."

"We all thought the magic had skipped your generation. Not your fault. It was just as much a surprise to you as it was to us. But it was a delightful surprise, don't ya think?" Eva turned when she heard another vehicle approach. This time, it was a bright red classic truck. She smiled when she saw it pull into the parking lot not far away. Devon was waving out the window.

"So, what is it, then?"

"Human of Magus blood. I'll keep my position because it still stands that I'm foremost human and many of my ancestors had the same designation and remained human Councilors." Gabriel looked up as Devon joined them.

"And just where have you been, sir?" Eva asked as she put her arms around her mate.

"Just dropped Derek off to get his motorcycle where he left it last. It was at Dante's, Eva. I think we may need to have a talk with that pup about being around that demon gal."

"Oh, my mate...that one's not a pup anymore either, remember?"

Gabriel's attention was somewhere else. The man getting out of the driver's side of the truck had his heartbeat fluttering. Jean-Michel leaned back against his truck and waited, watching him.

"I believe I have another ride, Eva. Thank you for being here. Good night Devon." The Councilor walked and then almost jogged to the truck. He kept control of himself here, in public, like always. This was his Tasker, after all. As far as anyone else was concerned, they had shared a momentary but thrilling connection of energy between them. That energy saved the Tasker's life right after Jean-Michel had done his duty to protect Gabriel.

Jean-Michel walked with Gabriel to the other side of the truck, where the older man opened the passenger door for him. This time, he didn't hesitate to get into the front seat. Jean closed the door behind him, turned to wave at the lycan couple, and then made his way back to the driver's side.

"There goes trouble," Eva giggled and shook her head.

From the park nearer the building, Councilor Fulgaul watched the interaction with curiosity. He turned once he knew he was alone and walked to the very back of the patch of land, closer to the forest that separated this place from the main campus of Whitley. No one could see him from this position and he knew there were no cameras.

As he walked, his form melted. That body reformed into a nondescript human man in jogging pants and a tank. He had a very forgettable face. It was perfect. Putting a toothpick in between his teeth, he began jogging away from this block to go find something to get into.

Chapter 37
Coming Together

Jean-Michel Raudine was Gabriel's Tasker. Therefore, it didn't seem unusual at all for them to leave together, especially after everything that had happened a few nights before.

"Where are we going?"

"My Sanctuary," Jean-Michel spoke softly, for his mind was a whirl. They were both quiet for a few of the turns and so he finally asked, "Have any more questions off the top of your head, Gabriel?"

"I have hundreds of questions, Jean-Michel." Gabriel made a low chuckle. "What's your favorite place to visit?"

His brow rose as he looked aside at his passenger. "Ireland. When the fields are fully green and colorful with flowers." He let his eyes enjoy Gabriel, and he asked, "What is your favorite place to visit?" Jean-Michel's mind was awhirl with thoughts about laws and rules and promises. So many things stood against this. Yet, he didn't offer to take Gabriel to his estate.

"I don't have one. I travel for business, so I haven't really had a reason to sightsee in any of them." Gabriel cleared his throat.

"We'll need to rectify that," the dragon whispered. A quick glance told him he'd made Gabriel blush. "Since we're alone, I would prefer you call me Senias. Or Sen." He took a quick deep breath and his hands gripped and released the steering wheel.

"Thank you, Senias." Gabriel couldn't help the grin on his face as they pulled up to the next traffic light. "Next question is why did yours and Evansworth's blood look like Joseph's when Sam tested it in the Chamber? He's a magus, but you two aren't…"

"I had you worried there for a bit, huh?" Senias grinned. "Truth is, though I am sporting a ruggedly handsome human body, some of my draconic magic flows through my veins and gives it that look. Sebastian had to drink some of my blood back there at Pandora's Box. The doppelgänger had at him. The blood on me was mostly Mira's blood and his blood. But, as you could see by the way he was so hyper, the blood did him good."

"Oh." Gabriel was quiet as they turned into the circle where the Tasker lived.

"You don't like the idea of me feeding him?"

"It shouldn't bother me." Gabriel kept his eyes on the road.

"That doesn't mean anything. What matters is how you feel. Talk to me." Senias wanted to encourage honesty and openness. Unlike most of his previous entanglements, this one... he had decided would be different.

"I'm just trying not to imagine Sebastian at your neck. I can't help it. You had a past. Apparently a very meaningful past." He shook his head just slightly. "Guess it's a good thing you were there then."

"It was a good thing he was there. He helped. And you don't have to worry about him taking blood from my neck. That's not something we do anymore." Once he had parked, the Tasker sighed. He left his hand on the gearshift momentarily while his mind continued to spin off, warning after warning.

Gabriel turned sideways in his seat to face the dragon. His fingers touched the top of Senias' hand. The touch prompted Senias to turn his hand. He placed Gabriel's fingers on the softer skin of his inner wrist. There was a still-healing scar.

"Mira had to rip me there. I placed the wrist over his mouth so he'd drink. It's a less dangerous and less intimate way to help a vampire in need. What he and I had is long gone, Gabriel."

The man's fingers moved over the scarred wrist and his brown eyes found those of his dragon once again. His hand moved onward to entwine their fingers.

"Do you realize the risk?" The dragon asked rather than getting out. "What risk you put yourself in if you... and I...finish what we started?" They had been at this point before.

"My entire life has revolved around the rules of being a Councilor and regulations of the Chamber along with the strategies of the business. I was often in the spotlight. So yes, I realize. But someone once told me that the world wasn't worth saving if one couldn't enjoy it." Gabriel sighed. "You make me enjoy it. You make me want to enjoy it... more and more."

"This is insane," the dragon whispered, as he turned to look into Gabriel's beautiful brown eyes. "But somehow it's perfect."

Senias used his entangled hand to pull Gabriel closer. He wanted to taste the Councilor once again. Their lips met, and he decided then and there to enjoy what he had denied himself the night after the pub; something he'd denied himself for over two centuries.

When the kiss ended, they were both breathless. Gabriel couldn't stop himself from licking his lips. "Never broken these particular rules before, have you?"

"No. I've not had any reason to." He let go of the other man and they both got out of the vehicle. Senias paused and held his hand up, closing his eyes. A soft glow of blue passed outward like a ripple from the man's body on a horizontal plane.

"I've never known you to be a stickler for rules, Senias," Gabriel whispered as he watched.

The dragon motioned for Gabriel to follow him in. His smirk was one that told his conspirator that he was considering the questions, even if he was slow to answer.

"I don't give a fuck about the rules unless the rules catch up to me. And in this case, I don't want that to happen, because there would be dire consequences on both sides." He unlocked the back door and held it open for Gabriel. "Crimson can be a jealous creature, Gabriel. And Magic? Sometimes more so." Once the Councilor had passed, he locked the door.

As soon as they were beyond the threshold, Senias pulled Gabriel by the front of his perfectly pressed shirt. He wanted a deep and delicious kiss. His hands moved over the material of Gabriel's shirt to feel the muscles below, and he groaned.

Tossing his jacket aside, the heat that Senias gave off quickly overtook Gabriel. He'd try to gain some leverage but then lost ground when Senias kissed him again.

He shuffled backward several steps while Sen's lips moved over his, stealing his very breath away. The press of a wall against his back helped support him against the ferocity of the draconic male. Gabriel swore his lover was determined to taste as much of him as possible. He loved it!

Gabriel's fingers were curling in the Tasker's shirt, tugging it free of the pants. Long, masculine fingers crept beneath to smooth over the solid flesh that tensed at his touch.

Unlike him, Senias was a man who didn't bother with keeping his body smooth and perfect. Beneath the shirt was coarse hair that led a trail down to his hard cock. He had a few scars as well. As his fingers moved through the wiry hair, Gabriel found he rather enjoyed the sensation. It seemed they were indeed opposites, and that turned him on even more.

It shocked Gabriel to hear himself groan. His back was against the wall. The feel of the man pressing fully against him made his whole body tingle with excitement and pleasure. The kiss ended and Senias moved his mouth from bruised lips to Gabriel's shadowed chin and then to his neck. All the while, his hands moved downward.

There was a sharp intake of breath as he listened once again to the buttons bounce and click, click, click against the tile floor. That bit of a gasp was also a response to touching the veritable rod his lover had ready for him. Gabriel felt the air rush over his heated skin. He'd need to get more shirts if they continued this.

Senias slowed; asking, "Have you ever been with one of us? With a supernatural?"

"Once. It happened several years ago." Gabriel was nearly panting. It was the rush of excitement mixed with a nervous feeling that was spreading through him. "Wasn't a terrible experience, but could have been better. I don't think he cared about what I thought." Gabriel's hands moved along the dragon's waistband, opening the material so he could truly feel the uncut length of his soon-to-be lover. "Are you different from other men?"

The Tasker's palm rested on the sidewall to steady himself as Gabriel touched him. "No, I have a human body. It's just...I'm trying to keep myself under control. We supernaturals can be a bit more wild and untamed than humans."

The sound of the dragon's husky chuckle made Gabriel grin.

"Don't worry, Sen... the last thing I want in a lover is control..."

"Oh, I'm fairly certain you'll thank me for it later." Senias kissed Gabriel's neck, letting his teeth sink into the soft flesh below the man's ear just enough to elicit a quiet whimper when he took the next breath. He wouldn't break the skin, but he'd definitely leave a mark.

"Fuck..." Gabriel swallowed all other thoughts after that word.

"Yes, that's what we're about to do." While Gabe stroked the sensitive flesh he had in his hand, Senias made a purring sound somewhat similar to a lycan rumble. It came deep from the chest and was something that many dragons who took human form kept from their other bodies. Senias stopped the pull of flesh to teeth before whispering into Gabriel's ear. "Let's get rid of these barriers."

"But...we're not in the bedroom." Gabriel seemed mystified as Senias backed up and undid his pants. He pulled the material of both the pants and the underwear down, releasing Gabriel's cock to bounce against his body at attention.

"We don't need a bedroom for this." Senias put a hand over Gabriel's shoulder and the other moved between his legs to find the proper hold. He heard his lover cry out in surprise when he hefted him up and over the back of the huge couch. The dragon took off his own clothes as he walked around the overstuffed piece of furniture, drinking in the sight of the startled man. By the time he was kneeling on the edge of the cushion, he was completely nude, just like his lover.

Gabriel kept his body waxed and tanned. His cock was cut like most Americans. That was fine. He was a work of art that the dragon wanted to devour. With that thought in mind, he kissed his lover once more before slowly making his way down that perfect body, tasting and teasing. Getting to the end of the couch, he leaned down and took Gabriel's hard cock in his mouth and began sucking, his tongue moving along the veined bottom to thrill. He hadn't enjoyed the taste of a man in a very long time. Senias was showing Gabriel how much he missed this.

For his part, the normally uptight Councilor was finally letting go and showing Senias how good this felt. He groaned loudly and his hips were already moving in time with the fellatio he was receiving. Senias felt Gabriel's fingers in his hair. With every taking, he growled against the tip that hit his throat and then sucked as he released.

"Holy...fuuuuck..." Gabriel had to pause, his fingers curling into the cushion while his other fingers tightened on his lover's wavy copper-brown hair. "Won't... last... long..." He was inhaling without letting out a breath. Senias moved his middle finger on his free hand into the slobber that had run down Gabriel's girth. Soon enough, that finger was exploring the darker recesses of Gabriel's body, pushing up and in and then curling before being pulled out again.

"Sen! Oh...Sen!" Gabriel sounded like he was about to lose his breath!

Feeling the tightening of Gabriel's body and hearing his name cried out, the dragon intensified his actions. He nearly swallowed Gabriel's cock and groaned around the head. His finger worked quicker and deeper with each cry. Soon enough, Gabriel's body rewarded him with a warm, salty release that drifted down his throat.

As Gabriel tried to catch his breath. He was vaguely aware that his body was being moved. Senias could tell the man was in a daze of ecstasy, and so he took full advantage of it. He spat on his cock and moved forward to press the head of his cock against that wanting ass. He pressed in and heard Gabriel gasp in response. The dragon only waited a moment to let the man readjust himself before he was pushing the rest of the way inside. He held himself above Gabriel, their gazes meeting. They spoke more in that silent, vulnerable moment than ever before.

It was after at least an hour or more of intense pleasure that the two finally collapsed on the huge couch they had used. No one had ever moved Gabriel through so many positions...ever. Blissful despite his lover getting every nerve in his body to fire off, Gabriel rested there on top of Senias. He was slowly catching his breath. Covered in sweat as he was, Gabriel rolled so that they were chest to chest and he was partially on Senias and partially on the huge couch. That was the best he could accomplish.

He lay on the hairy chest and closed his eyes, just listening to the heartbeat of the other man. Normally, he would get up, shower, dress, and go home at this point. It was Gabriel's rule until now. Right then, all Gabriel wanted to do was close his eyes, let his guard down, and just sleep.

Senias was quiet. His breathing and heartbeat were steady. Gabriel felt the Tasker relax beneath him and marveled at how different this was. Eva had been correct. Neither of them ever let their guard down. They both wore masks, however, at this moment? They were both open and trusting. Gabriel allowed himself to enjoy the gratifying moment. Finally, he lifted his head so he could see Senias.

"Well, that was definitely a first for me." His body ached and felt sore, but there were absolutely no complaints.

"What is a first for you?" Now it was the dragon's turn to be curious.

"Turning over control to another. I rarely bottom."

"You... did a good job?" Senias chuckled as he gave the compliment. "Wasn't sure if you wanted the compliment or what?"

"I'll take it." Senias couldn't see his smile, but it was there. And then he had second thoughts. "Should I go, Sen?" Gabriel asked, not so much because he wanted to, but because he wasn't sure what Sen's arrangements were. It would be rude to assume he was welcome to stay. It would be presumptuous to think this was what he had fantasized about with the Tasker.

"Only if that's what you desire, Gabriel." Sen stroked the backs of his fingers against Gabriel's skin as he spoke. "If you're not comfortable here, once we can stand, my bedroom suite is at the top of the stairs."

"Here is fine. I can't really stay all night even if I wanted to. Wouldn't look right, would it, me leaving here in the morning? We don't want to push things too far, do we? We get a few hours at most." Senias had been the one to caution him they were playing a dangerous game here. So what they had would have to stay as private as possible. A research meeting between Councilor and Tasker was easy enough to explain. But a meeting that would last all night long, not so much.

Gabriel took a deep breath and confessed, "I've never shared my bed with a lover. So.. not sure if I kick or snuggle. I do know I don't snore." The feel of the warm, solid body beneath him was actually pretty soothing. Gabriel knew better, though. It was a mistake to get attached. Lovers never lasted long and Senias had a history that said he didn't like attachments.

"In some ways, it's a wise decision."

"You mean not sharing my bed with a lover?"

"Yeah," Senias whispered. "There's nothing in this world so precious as those few seconds of your life when it blesses you with love and attachment. However, when you lose it, the pain is like nothing else. So it is definitely a double-edged sword." His fingers moved absently over Gabriel's skin. Clearing his throat, the dragon whispered, "Sorry. I've been reading too much Keats."

"Keats was a romantic, careful there or I'll start thinking you are too." Gabriel was in that lull between awake and asleep when he replied. "I like Keats though. There isn't much from that era of authors that I don't like, to be honest. Guess I'm a lush for the older things. Explains why I spend so much time in the Chamber." Senias had spoken as if Gabriel was the family type of man when they both knew he was the exact opposite. He was a businessman. He lived and breathed it. So why did that feel so inappropriate while lying here in the man's arms?

"You're the bearer of an old soul, Gabriel." Senias moved his head to cuddle into the soft pillowed arm of the couch and Gabriel could feel the man's muscles relax. His eyes closed. ~ I saw it in you long ago. ~ Sen spoke using his mental voice while drifting in the afterglow.

What should have felt like an intrusion was actually quite soothing as Gabriel listened to Senias' voice in his head.

~ Byron, Keats, Shelley, Eyre… ~ there was a bit of a chuckle as he added, ~ Wilde. Can't forget Oscar. There are plenty in the library that were written in a similar style. I'm sure. ~

Gabriel gave over to sleep before he could answer. It was the most relaxed he'd ever been with another person, especially a lover.

Four hours later, Gabriel woke, still half lying on his lover. His dragon lover. It amazed him they'd been so comfortable as to not need to change positions. The feel of the warm, solid body beneath him was actually pretty soothing. Was it too much to hope that this would continue?

After glancing at his watch, Gabriel sighed. It was time to get moving. His whole body ached, and certain parts of him were definitely protesting. Alas, Gabriel begrudgingly slid his clothes back on.

The larger man groaned and couldn't help going into a stretch when the sounds of movement in the room woke him.

"Where are you going?" Senias asked.

"I need to get home for a shower and change. I'm expected at the office for a meeting in three hours. It's okay. One of my drivers is on the way. They're all Pack Weylyn, so they'll be discreet." Gabriel didn't even try to close his shirt. Leaning down, he kissed Senias lightly on the lips.

With a wicked grin, the draconic man reached out to caress fingers along that perfect chest above him. But Gabriel pulled away.

"If you must. I have this thing called keeping up appearances to do as well. Professeur Jean-Michel Raudine has classes to teach. But it only takes me a few minutes to get from here to there." He turned onto his side to watch his new lover.

"Call me later. We'll make plans." They could at least enjoy being around one another without suspicion. Gabriel couldn't resist one more kiss. Only this one was a long, thorough kiss so that the dragon wouldn't soon forget.

The dragon didn't get up, he just laid back on the couch and sighed. The sound of a text notification followed the click of the door latch. Jean-Michel padded into the kitchen to find his phone. The message was from Derek.

– *We need to talk about File 32. Skinner knows everything.* –

https://racheldadams.com/

The side stories of Senias and his friends in **The Life & Loves of a Dragon** are available in Rachel's Ko-fi shop! Or, if you ever want to try out KindleVella, they are all there!
Remember, you can get the prequel series along with the main urban fantasy series **The Dragon Tasker Series,** and later, the companion books on eBook, paperback, and hardback through your retailer of choice and directly through Rachel's website.
We have so many stories to share with you!
Follow the link below to find out more!
https://racheldadams.com/

Made in the USA
Columbia, SC
28 January 2024